PRAISE FOR *RUINS*

New York Times Bestseller
Junior Library Guild Selection

★ "[*Ruins*] is philosophically challenging, mind-pretzeling stuff about time travel, engineered evolution, gene splicing, artificial intelligence, xenocide, and, oh, the very nature of what it means to be human and have a soul thrown in for good measure." —*Booklist*, starred review

"Infused with a compulsive readability that will keep the pages turning right up to the cliffhanger climax. Nobody combines gee-whiz, geeky speculation and angst-y adolescent navel-gazing better than Card." —*Kirkus Reviews*

"The way Card explores time travel, logic puzzles, and parallel societal development, as well as the clever fashion in which various problems are resolved and the engrossing details of the world he has created, keep the plot moving forward—and often backward in time." —*Publishers Weekly*

PRAISE FOR *PATHFINDER*

New York Times Bestseller
Booklist Editors' Choice for 2010
Junior Library Guild Selection
Winter 2010–2011 Kids' Indie Next List

★ "Fast paced and thoroughly engrossing, the 650-plus pages fly by, challenging readers to care about and grasp sophisticated, confusing, and captivating ideas." —*Booklist*, starred review

★ "Card entwines two stories in this fascinatingly complex series opener. . . . The result is an amalgamation of adventure, politics, and time travel that invokes issues of class and the right to control one's own life. Yet despite its complexity, the book is never less than page-turning. . . . An epic in the best sense."
—*PW*, starred review

★ "Card buffs will find everything they love about the author herein, and with this impeccable novel, he will easily gain a batch of new fans who will eagerly await the next installment."
—*The Bulletin*, starred review

"Card's latest work of speculative fiction twists together tropes of fantasy and science fiction into something fine indeed. . . . This novel should appeal to Card's legion of fans as well as anyone who enjoys speculative fiction with characters who rely on quick thinking rather than violence or tales of mind-bending time-travel conundrums." —*SLJ*

"The implications of the boys' power to manipulate the past unfold cleverly . . . feeding into the Machiavellian political intrigue for a pulse-pounding climax. . . . Card's many fans will be thrilled by this return to his literary roots." —*Kirkus Reviews*

RUINS

ORSON SCOTT CARD

Simon Pulse
NEW YORK LONDON TORONTO SYDNEY NEW DELHI

This book is a work of fiction. Any references to historical events, real people, or real places are used fictitiously. Other names, characters, places, and events are products of the author's imagination, and any resemblance to actual events or places or persons, living or dead, is entirely coincidental.

SIMON PULSE
An imprint of Simon & Schuster Children's Publishing Division
1230 Avenue of the Americas, New York, NY 10020
First Simon Pulse paperback edition September 2013

Cover design and illustration by Sammy Yuen Jr.

Also available in a Simon Pulse hardcover edition.

Interior design by Mike Rosamilia
The text of this book was set in Cochin.
Manufactured in the United States of America
2 4 6 8 10 9 7 5 3 1
The Library of Congress has cataloged the hardcover edition as follows:
Card, Orson Scott.
Ruins / by Orson Scott Card.
p. cm.
Sequel to: Pathfinder.
Summary: To prevent the destruction of his planet, teenaged Rigg Sessamekesh, who can manipulate time, must assume more responsibility when he and others travel back 11,000 years to the arrival of human starships.
ISBN 978-1-4169-9177-9 (hc)
[1. Science fiction. 2. Time travel—Fiction. 3. Interplanetary voyages—Fiction. 4. Space colonies—Fiction.] I. Title.
PZ7.C1897Ru 2012 [Fic]—dc23 2011052745
ISBN 978-1-4169-9180-9 (pbk)
ISBN 978-1-4424-1428-0 (eBook)

To Gregg Homer,
friend and advocate,
who puts power into others' hands
and wisdom in their hearts

CONTENTS

CHAPTER 1
Water

Rigg saw the stream before any of the others.

Loaf was an experienced soldier; Olivenko not so experienced, but not untrained, either; and Umbo had grown up in the village of Fall Ford, which was almost like living in the woods.

But only Rigg had tramped the high forests above the Upsheer Cliffs, trapping animals for their fur while the man he called Father taught him more than Rigg ever thought he would need to know. Rigg practically smelled water like an animal. Even before they crested the low grassy rise he knew that there would be a stream in the next crease between hills. He even knew it would be only a rill, with no trees; the ground here was too stony.

Rigg broke into a jog.

"Stop," said the expendable they were calling Vadesh.

Rigg slowed. "Why? That's water, and I'm thirsty."

"*We're* thirsty," said Umbo.

"You cannot drink there," said the expendable.

"Cannot? There's some kind of danger?" asked Rigg.

"Or a law," suggested Olivenko.

"You said you were leading us to water," said Loaf, "and there it is."

"That's not the water I'm taking you to," said Vadesh.

Only now did Rigg realize what he wasn't seeing. It was his inborn gift that all the paths of the past were visible to him. Humans and animals all left traces behind them, paths in time. If they ever traveled through a particular place, Rigg could tell where they had gone. It was not something he saw with his eyes—his eyes could be closed or covered, or there could be walls or solid rock between him and a path, and he would still know where it was, and could figure out what kind of creature made it, and how long ago.

There had been no human traffic at this stream in ten thousand years. More tellingly, few animals had come there, and no large ones.

"It's poisonous," said Rigg.

"Is that a guess?" asked his sister, Param, "or do you know somehow?"

"Even animals don't come here to drink," said Rigg. "And no human for a long time."

"How long?" asked Vadesh.

"Don't you know?" asked Rigg.

"I'm curious about what *you* know," said Vadesh. "I have not known a human who can do what you can do."

"Nearly as long as since the beginning of human settlement on this world." Rigg had a very clear idea of what paths that old were like, since he had just crossed through the Wall between his home wallfold and this one, by clinging to an animal that, in the original stream of time, had died in the holocaust of humans' first coming to the planet Garden.

"That is off by only a little less than a thousand years," said Vadesh.

"I said 'nearly,'" answered Rigg.

"A thousand years this way or that," said Param. "Close enough."

Rigg still didn't know Param well enough to tell if her sarcasm was friendly teasing or open scorn. "What kind of poison?" he asked Vadesh.

"A parasite," said Vadesh. "It can live out its entire lifecycle in the stream feeding off the bodies of its siblings, ancestors, and descendants, until one of them eats *it*. But if a larger animal comes to drink, it attaches to the face and immediately sends tendrils into the brain."

"It eats brains?" asked Umbo, intrigued.

"No," said Vadesh. "It infiltrates them. It echoes the neural network. It takes over and controls the host's behavior."

"Why in the world would our ancestors bring along such a creature when they came from Earth?" asked Umbo.

"They didn't," said Olivenko.

"How do you know that?" asked Loaf. His tone showed he was still skeptical of Olivenko, who was only a member of the city guard in Aressa Sessamo, rather than a real soldier.

"Because if they had, it would exist in every wallfold," said Olivenko, "and it doesn't exist in ours."

Olivenko thinks the way Father taught me, thought Rigg. Don't assume: Think it through.

Vadesh was nodding. "A very tough little creature, the facemask."

"Facemask?"

"What the humans of this wallfold named it. For reasons that would have become tragically obvious if you had bent over to drink from the stream."

Something didn't ring true about this. "How can a creature that evolved on Garden successfully take over the brains of creatures from Earth?" asked Rigg.

"I didn't say it was successful," said Vadesh. "And you are now as close as is safe. To avoid picking up facemasks from the wet ground beside the stream—they can attach to any skin and migrate up your body—you should follow in my footsteps exactly."

They followed him in single file through the grass, with Rigg bringing up the rear. The path Vadesh took them on was the highest ground. Each time they reached a damp patch they jumped over it. The rill was narrow here. No one had trouble overleaping it.

Only when they got to higher ground several rods beyond the rill was Rigg able to continue the conversation. "If the parasite wasn't successful, why is it still alive here?"

"The parasite is successful in attaching to humans and Earth-born beasts of all kinds," said Vadesh. "But that's not really how we measure success in a parasite. If the parasite kills its host too quickly, for instance, before the parasite can spread to new hosts, then it has failed. The goal of a parasite is like that of any other life form—to survive and reproduce."

"So these facemasks kill too quickly?" asked Umbo, shuddering.

"Not at all," said Vadesh. "I said 'for instance.'" He smiled at Rigg, because they both knew he was echoing Rigg's earlier testy reply when Vadesh told him his time estimate was off by a millennium.

"So in what way did this parasite fail?" asked Rigg—the way he would have pushed Father, an attitude that came easily to him, since not just in face and voice but in evasiveness, smugness, and assumption of authority this expendable was identical to the one that had taken Rigg as an infant from the royal house and raised him.

"I think that with native species," said Vadesh, "the parasite rode them lightly. Cooperating with them. Perhaps even helping them survive."

"But not with humans?"

"The only part of the earthborn brain it could control was the wild, competitive beast, bent on reproduction at any cost."

"That sounds like soldiers on leave," said Loaf.

"Or academics," said Olivenko.

Vadesh said nothing.

"It sounds like chaos," said Rigg. "You were there from the beginning, weren't you, Vadesh? How long did it take people to learn of the danger?"

"It took some time for the facemasks to emerge from their chrysalises after the disaster of the human landing," said Vadesh.

"And still longer for the people of Vadeshfold to discover that facemasks could infest humans as well as cattle and sheep."

"The herders never got infected?" asked Loaf.

"It took time for a strain of facemasks to develop that could thrive on the human body. So at first it was like a pesky fungal infection."

"And then it wasn't," said Rigg. "Facemasks are that adaptable?"

"It's not blind adaptation," said Vadesh. "They're a clever, fascinating little creature, not exactly intelligent, but not completely stupid, either."

For the first time, it occurred to Rigg that Vadesh was not just fascinated by the facemasks, but enamored of them.

"They can only attach to their host in the water," said Vadesh, answering a question no one had asked. "And once they attach to an air-breather, they lose the ability to breathe in water. They only get their oxygen from the blood. You know what oxygen is?"

"The breathable part of air," said Umbo impatiently. Olivenko chuckled. Of course, thought Rigg—Olivenko was a scholar, and Umbo had studied for a time with Rigg's father.

But Rigg noticed that Loaf and Param seemed to have no idea what Vadesh meant. How could air be divided in parts? Rigg remembered asking Father exactly that question. But there was no point in explaining the point now or soon or, probably, ever. Why would a soldier-turned-innkeeper and a royal heiress who had fled her throne require a knowledge of the elements, of the behavior of gases and fluids?

Then again, Rigg had thought, all through his years of education, tramping with Father through the woods, that he would never need anything Father taught him except how to trap, dress, and skin their prey. Only when Father's death sent Rigg out in the world did he learn why Father had trained him in languages, economics, finance, law, and so many other subjects, all of which had proven vital to his survival.

So Rigg started to explain that invisible air was really made of tiny particles of several different types. Loaf looked skeptical and Param bored, and Rigg decided that their education wasn't his job.

He fell silent and thought about parasites that could only attach to humans in water, and then they lost the ability to breathe on their own. Rigg filed the information away in his mind, the way Father had taught him to do with all seemingly useless information, so he could recall it whenever Father decided to test him.

I've been on my own for a year, thought Rigg, and still in my thoughts he's always there, my pretended father, my kidnapper for all I know. He's the puppeteer who, even dead, is pulling all the strings inside my mind.

Lost in such thoughts, Rigg did not notice the first building that came in sight. It was Loaf, ever alert as a soldier should be, who saw the glint of metal. "It's like the Tower of O," he said.

It was indeed, in that it was tall and of a similar substance. But it did not rise to a point and was not rounded like a cylinder. And there were several of them nearby, and none of them was half so tall as the Tower of O.

But they were impressive nonetheless, and tall enough that it took two more hours of walking after they first saw them for their little group to come close enough to see that these towers were made from the same material, and formed the skyline of a city.

"How could they build with this . . . substance?" asked Loaf. "People have tried to cut into the Tower of O many times over the years, and neither tool nor fire can affect it."

"Who would try to damage it?" asked Umbo.

"Conquerors who want to show their power," said Olivenko. "Rigg's and Param's people arose only lately. The Tower has been there ten thousand years."

The talk of duration made Rigg realize something he should have noticed at once, as soon as they knew it was a city they were coming to. There were human paths again, as there had not been near the stream, but all of them were old. None more recent than ten thousand years.

"How long has this city been abandoned?" asked Rigg.

"It isn't abandoned," said Vadesh.

"There hasn't been a human being here for a long time," said Rigg.

"But I've been here," said Vadesh.

You're not a human being, Rigg wanted to say. You're a machine; you leave no path. A place that contains only you is uninhabited. But it seemed too rude to say aloud. Rigg saw the absurdity of his attitude: If he truly thought of Vadesh as *only* a machine, rudeness would not be an issue.

"Where did the people go?" asked Param.

"People come and go in the world, and where there once were cities there are only ruins, and where once there was nothing, cities rise," said Vadesh.

Rigg noticed how nonresponsive Vadesh's answer was, but did not challenge him. Rigg trusted Vadesh too little to want him to know he wasn't trusted.

"And there's water here?" asked Loaf. "Because my need for it is getting pretty urgent."

"I thought you field soldiers drank your own piss," said Olivenko.

"We do pee into canteens," said Loaf. "But only so we can bring it back for the officers of the city guard to drink."

It could have been a quarrel, but to Rigg's relief, Olivenko just smiled and Umbo laughed and it went nowhere. Why did they still irritate each other so much, after all they had been through together? When would rivals become comrades?

So all the people of this city were gone. Rigg began to scan for the paths that would show a great migration out of the city, but before he could make much progress, Vadesh led them into a low building of ordinary stone, which showed its many centuries of weathering.

"Did someone live here?" asked Umbo.

"It's a factory," said Vadesh.

"Where did all the people sit to work?" asked Olivenko.

"A mechanical factory," said Vadesh. "And most of it is underground. I still use it, when I need any of the things the factory makes. But they needed safe water for the supervisors and mechanics, and for the people who hauled things in and hauled things out." He led them through a doorway into a dark chamber. As they passed through the door after him, a bright light came from above. The whole ceiling was aglow, very much like the lights inside the Tower of O.

The others gasped in awe, but Rigg was noticing that the paths of humans into this chamber were few and ancient. This building had only been used for a few decades at the most. It had been abandoned by the same generation of people who had built it.

Vadesh touched the front of a thick stone pillar and at once they heard the sound of running water inside the pillar. Then he touched another place, and a portion of the pillar came away in his hand. It was a stone vessel halfway between a drinking mug and a waterbucket in size. He handed it to Loaf. "Because your need was so urgent," said Vadesh.

"Is it safe?" asked Rigg.

"It's filtered through stone. No parasites of any kind can possibly get into this water."

Again, Rigg noticed that while Vadesh answered, he only answered about the likelihood of parasite infestation, not the actual question Rigg had asked.

Loaf handed the water to Param without tasting it. "You need this most," he said.

"Because I'm a frail princess?" Param asked with a hint of resentment.

Well, she *was* physically frail and she *was* a princess. Until their mother tried to kill her and Rigg, she was assumed to be heir to the Tent of Light. Years of living in the narrow bounds of captivity had made her physically weak, and the journey to the Wall had only improved her stamina by a little. But no one was rude enough to point this out to her.

"You need it most because you and Umbo lived on *your* water for an extra week that we didn't live through," said Loaf.

Param took the water and drank. "It's perfect," she said. "It tastes fresh, and nothing else. Except a tinge of something . . ."

"Trace metals," said Vadesh. "From the rock it filtered through."

Umbo drank next. He tried to pass it to Rigg, but Rigg would not take any until Loaf and Olivenko had also drunk.

"There's plenty," said Vadesh.

"Then finish it, Loaf," said Rigg. "I'll drink from the second serving."

"He thinks I spit in it," said Umbo.

"Didn't you?" said Loaf. "You usually do." Then Loaf drank it off. "Delicious," he said, as he handed the empty vessel to Vadesh for refilling.

Rigg did not know why he did not trust Vadesh. This expendable had no mannerisms that were not identical to those of Rigg's father. Perhaps that was the cause of his suspicions. But he was sure that Vadesh was deceptive and dangerous, not because he deflected questions and clearly had his own agenda—those were Father's constant attributes as well—but because of *which* questions he wouldn't answer.

Father would have told me why the people were gone from this place. It would have been the first thing he explained, because telling me why people do the things they do was always his favorite topic.

Vadesh isn't educating me, that's why he doesn't explain it.

But Rigg did not believe his own excuse. As Father had taught him, he did not believe the first explanation his mind leapt to. "It will often be right, and as you get more experience of life it will usually be right. But it will never be *reliably* right, and you must always think of other possible explanations or, if you can't, then at least keep your mind open so you will recognize a better explanation if one emerges."

So Rigg did not trust Vadesh. Moreover, he was sure that Vadesh knew that Rigg did not trust him—because Father would have known.

When Rigg got his water from the second cupful, it was as delicious as the others said.

He poured the last water from his canteen onto the floor and then moved to put it into the space the stone vessel came from.

"No," said Vadesh. "One reason this water can be trusted is that it is never used to fill any container but this one. It won't work anyway. It only pours out water when this is in place." Vadesh reinserted the stone cup, and again the water could be heard gushing into the stone.

They all emptied their canteens of the stale traveling water they obtained when they last filled at a stream two days before, then refilled them from the stone vessel. With enemies pursuing them, they had not dared to stop even for water on that last day before they crossed the Wall.

"It's getting near dark outside," said Loaf. "Is there a safe place to sleep in this city?"

"Everywhere here is safe," said Vadesh.

Rigg nodded. "No large animals ever come here," he said.

"Then is there a *comfortable* place here?" asked Umbo. "I've slept on hard floors and on grass and pine needles, and unless there's a bed . . ."

"I don't need beds," said Vadesh, "and I didn't expect company."

"You mean they didn't make their beds out of stuff that never decays?" asked Olivenko.

"There is nothing that doesn't decay," said Vadesh. "Some things decay more slowly than others, that's all."

"And how slowly do *you* decay?" asked Rigg.

"Slower than beds," said Vadesh, "but faster than fieldsteel."

"And yet you seem as good as new," said Rigg. "That's a question."

Vadesh stood by the water pillar gazing at him for a long moment. Deciding, Rigg supposed, how to respond without telling him anything useful.

"My parts are all replaceable," he said. "And my knowledge is fully copied in the library in the Unchanging Star."

"Who makes your new parts?" asked Rigg.

"I do," said Vadesh.

"Here?" asked Rigg. "In this factory?"

"Some of the parts, yes," said Vadesh.

"And the other parts?"

"Somewhere else, obviously," said Vadesh. "Why do you ask? Do you think any of my parts are defective?"

Now, that was interesting, thought Rigg. I was going to ask him if he ever had enough parts to make a complete new copy of himself, but *he* assumed I was doubting that he was functioning perfectly.

This made Rigg assume that Vadesh himself had doubts about his functionality.

"How could I know if a machine so perfect that I could live with one for thirteen years without realizing it wasn't human is not up to par?" he asked.

"Exactly," said Vadesh, as if they had been arguing and Vadesh had just proved his point.

And maybe we *were* arguing, thought Rigg. And whatever Vadesh might have done since I met him, he certainly did not prove anything. All he did was make me wonder if he's broken somehow. Did he do that for a purpose? Is it an illusion, so I will underestimate his ability? Or is it a symptom of his imperfection, that he could raise doubts in my mind when his goal was to reassure me?

"Thanks for the water," said Rigg. "I think we'll go out of the city to sleep on softer ground. Unless there's a couple of you who want to sleep on stone."

There were no volunteers. Rigg led the way out of the building, following their own paths back out of the empty city. At first Vadesh seemed to assume he was welcome to come with them, but Rigg disabused him of that notion. "I don't believe you sleep," Rigg said to him. "And we won't need you to find us a resting place."

Vadesh took the hint and returned into the factory—leaving no trace of himself for Rigg to follow. Just like Father, Vadesh was pathless; only living beings made paths through time. Machines might move about, but they left no track visible to Rigg's timesense.

It would have been so useful to trace Vadesh's movements through these buildings over the past ten thousand years, since all the people left. And perhaps even more interesting to trace his movements for the thousand years before that, when the people were still here. What was he doing when they left? Why did he still come here, if all the people were somewhere else?

CHAPTER 2
Barbfeather

Rigg found that most of the paths of the ancient inhabitants of the city did not follow the road, and he stopped to see where they had led.

"We're supposed to sleep here?" asked Loaf.

Rigg looked around. The ground was stony and they were at the crest of a hill.

"This doesn't look comfortable at all," said Param. "Is this the kind of place you slept when you were living as a trapper?"

"I would never sleep on ground like this," said Rigg.

"Weren't you leading us to where we're going to spend the night?" asked Olivenko.

"I was getting us out of the city," said Rigg. "I didn't have any particular sleeping place in mind."

"Well, you seemed to know where you were going," said Umbo. "So we followed you."

"This isn't a good place to sleep," said Rigg. "Very stony, and no protection from wind."

"Well, we can *see* that," said Loaf.

"What *were* you doing, if you weren't finding us a hostelry?" asked Param.

"Sorry," said Rigg. "I got caught up in following paths."

"I thought you said there weren't any."

"None recent," said Rigg. "I was trying to make sense of the old ones."

"From ten thousand years ago," said Umbo.

Since Rigg didn't understand what it was that he hadn't understood about the paths, there was no way to explain. So he returned to the immediate subject. "There's a stand of trees over there," said Rigg. "That'll probably have soft ground. And we'll all sleep in the lee of Loaf, so we'll have shelter from the wind."

"Very funny," said Loaf.

Then Rigg came to a conclusion about what had puzzled him. "I think they may have died," said Rigg.

"The trees?" asked Param.

"The people here. If they moved away, peacefully I mean, then the most recent paths should have them leaving the city on the road. But the most recent people on the road only come in."

"Maybe they left another way," said Olivenko.

Death is another way, thought Rigg. But he kept it to himself. "I don't know if we can believe anything Vadesh says," said Rigg. "Umbo, I want to follow a path and go back and see."

"See what?" asked Loaf.

"If I knew," said Rigg, "I wouldn't have to go back."

"Let's see," said Umbo. "Going into the past has brought us exactly what, so far?"

"Saved our lives," said Loaf, and almost at the same time Param said, "You set me free and saved . . ."

Olivenko added, "It was ten thousand years ago that all the people left this city."

"Or died in it," said Rigg. "It could have been a plague."

"Cities rise and fall," said Olivenko. "That's what history *is*."

"Let's find a way to be comfortable here tonight," said Loaf. "I wish we were still mounted. We could just leave this place."

"Leave our only known source of safe water?" asked Param.

Then they were among the trees, and the conversation turned to other things. Rigg only happened to stop and look back at the moment that Umbo bent down, picked something up, and tucked it into his pocket. Rigg was too far away to casually say, "Find something?" or "Drop something?" It's not as if he even had a right to ask. Umbo didn't owe him explanations.

At the same time, there had been something furtive in the way Umbo pocketed it and then glanced around. Yet Umbo hadn't looked at Rigg or any of the others to see if they were observing him. On the contrary, he specifically glanced around as if looking for someone else. The person who might have dropped whatever Umbo picked up? Without even thinking about it, Rigg scanned for paths. No one had been here since the city was abandoned, and that long ago it was doubtful that there was a grove of trees here, anyway.

But animals came and went all the time here, Rigg could see. One in particular had been in and out of this grove several times in the past few hours. He recognized its path.

"We have a friend here," said Rigg.

The others looked around, startled.

"Our feathered friend," said Rigg. "The beast that led us into the past and through the Wall."

"I thought he went crazy when we popped back into the present and the Wall came back," said Loaf.

"He's not in the Wall anymore. He came here. He's been going up to the trees. Tree to tree."

"He didn't look like a climber to me," said Loaf.

"Or a bark-eater," said Umbo.

"We wouldn't know *what* he looked like," said Olivenko. "There aren't any like him in the modern world."

"He can't have gotten far," said Rigg. "He was here not half an hour ago."

"You know we only have that Vadesh's word that the water's not safe," said Olivenko.

"He can't lie," said Umbo.

"And who told us that he can't?" asked Olivenko. "'Hi, I can't possibly lie to you.' Isn't that the first thing a liar would say?"

"He's just like Father," said Rigg, "and Father never lied to me."

"He didn't exactly open up and bare his soul to you, either," said Loaf.

"He didn't tell you about me," said Param.

Rigg started to answer. "He did when he was . . ." But then he realized that Father hadn't been dying, he had just been hiding behind a fallen tree, pretending to be trapped under it. Lying to Rigg.

Rigg covered his eyes with one hand. "I still live in the world he built around me. All his teachings and talk, and I don't know what's true and what isn't."

"Welcome to adult life," said Loaf.

"I'm not an adult," said Rigg.

"Really?" said Umbo. "Well, I think when you're in charge of yourself, you're an adult."

"Oh, right," scoffed Loaf.

"Plenty of full-size grownups don't do half as well as me and Rigg, thanks," said Umbo.

Again Rigg wanted to know what Umbo had found. What he had in his pocket.

They heard a snorting noise from three rods away. Quietly they spread out to surround it. Rigg looked at Umbo and rolled his eyes. None of the others knew how to walk stealthily. Not that they had to. The beast was making so much noise it couldn't have heard them.

It was indeed the beast with the barbed feathers, and it was hitting the side of its head against a tree, then scraping the same area on the bark. As Rigg got closer, he could see that he had mud on that side of his head.

Not mud. The thing that looked like mud was actually another creature in its own right. Now that he knew what to look for, he could see its tiny faint path moving through the air right along with the barbfeather's path the whole time it had been in the woods.

Loaf and Umbo, who had both dealt with animals, were much closer to it now; Olivenko and Param were hanging back. They were city people.

"Don't get too close," said Rigg.

"What's it got on its face?" asked Loaf.

"My guess is it drank from the stream," said Umbo.

"I think so too," said Rigg.

"You mean it picked up that parasite? That facemask thing?" asked Olivenko.

"Whatever it's got on its head, it's alive. A separate creature. With its own path."

"Every time the beast smacks it or scrapes at it," said Umbo, "it gets bigger. Spreads more, I mean. There's a strand of it going into the poor beast's ear."

"So all the barbfeather's efforts to get rid of it are actually helping it attach more firmly," said Rigg.

"What a clever evolutionary ploy," said Olivenko. "Facemasks that could make use of the beating and scraping would have a better chance of survival."

"Maybe all the fear and aversion allow the facemask to find the right parts of the brain to attach to in order to get control," suggested Rigg.

"You sound so excited," said Param. "Has anybody noticed what this means?"

"That Vadesh wasn't lying about the parasite, you mean?" asked Loaf. "That's obvious."

"I mean that we're totally dependent on Vadesh for our drinking water," said Param.

"You know," said Umbo, "I'm thinking we ought to be able to find a place to slink back through the Wall and just figure out how to stay alive in our own wallfold."

"Let's see," said Loaf. "A land with one dangerous parasite, or a place where thousands of soldiers will be looking for us and everybody else will be happy to turn us over to them in exchange for a reward." He made weighing motions with his hands.

"They're only looking for me and Param," said Rigg. "Why don't the rest of you go back?"

"And leave us here alone?" Param didn't even try to conceal the panic in her voice.

"They'd still catch us," said Loaf. "And then torture us till we told them where you were. And since they wouldn't believe the truth . . ."

"I was just saying that you don't *have* to stay here," said Rigg. "I didn't claim it would be perfectly safe."

"What do we do about this poor animal?" asked Param.

Rigg looked at her in surprise. "Do?"

"It's in so much distress," said Param.

"Of course it is," said Rigg. "It's got a parasite sticking to its head that's trying to invade its brain."

"Well, we brought it here," said Param.

"I suppose we did," said Rigg. "But it's *from* this world and, if Vadesh is telling the truth—and about these facemask things he seems to be—then the parasites are natives here, just like old barbfeather. So if we hadn't pulled him to *now* to run into this parasite, he might just as easily have had exactly the same thing happen to him back then."

"Except that the world was just about to end for him anyway," said Loaf. "Our ancestors were about to wipe him out along with all his cousins, right? We *saved* him."

"I can see now that he ought to be grateful," said Param.

"Look, if you gave him a choice between parasite on his face and dead, what do you think he'd choose?" asked Rigg.

"Look what he actually *is* choosing," said Umbo.

Param nodded but she clearly didn't like it. "Life," she said.

"Animals that don't cling to it no matter what don't survive long enough to make babies," said Olivenko. "We don't want to die."

"Then how do you explain suicides?" asked Loaf.

"I don't," said Olivenko.

"Wasn't Father's death a kind of suicide?" asked Param.

It took Rigg a moment to realize that even though Param was his full sister, she wasn't talking about the man *he* had called Father—the Golden Man, the Wandering Man, the machine called Ram, who had trained her and Umbo and Rigg in how to use their time-altering talents. She was talking about their real father, whom Rigg had never met: Father Knosso, who had passed unconscious through the Wall on a boat, and then was dragged from the boat and drowned by some kind of manlike sea creatures in another wallfold.

"It wasn't suicide," said Olivenko angrily. As a young scholar in the Great Library he had been Knosso's friend and assistant. "He didn't intend to die."

"No," said Param. "But he knew he might, and he threw his life at it as if nothing else mattered. Not me, certainly."

"He loved you," said Olivenko.

"But he loved his experiment more," said Param.

The barbfeather, Rigg noticed, had stopped beating and scraping its face against the tree. It was turning its gaze toward each one of them who spoke. And it didn't just turn the eye that wasn't covered by the facemask. It turned as if it had two good eyes. As if it could still see *through* the thing.

In the silence after Param's last few bitter words, the barbfeather trotted straight toward Rigg.

"Rigg!" shouted Umbo.

"It's coming at you!" warned Loaf.

Rigg reached out his hand and the barbfeather stopped and sniffed it. "He wasn't *charging* at me," said Rigg.

"Keep your hand away!" said Umbo. "Do you want the facemask to jump over to you?"

"Vadesh says they can only attach in water. And not after they've already attached to . . . something." Rigg had almost said "somebody."

"So we're believing everything he says now?" asked Umbo.

"He didn't lie about the facemasks," said Rigg. "He might be lying about some things, but he's not lying about that. And he didn't follow us here, either, or try to prevent us from leaving. Maybe all he really did was lead us to safe water."

"Staying suspicious is what keeps me alive," said Loaf. "That survival instinct, you know?"

"I'm for suspicion, too," said Rigg. "But at some point you have to place your bet and let it ride."

The barbfeather was still sniffing his hand.

"I think he smells himself on my hand," said Rigg. "That's the hand I held against his back as we went through the Wall."

"And there's no reason he should fear the smell of humans," said Olivenko.

The barbfeather abruptly turned its head, pressing the facemask against Rigg's fingers. Rigg recoiled at once.

"Look at your hand!" shouted Umbo. "Is anything sticking to it?"

"What do you think, that the facemask just made my hand pregnant?" asked Rigg.

"They might have more than one way of reproducing," said Umbo. "Vadesh said they were adaptable."

"Maybe it makes babies on the surface of its skin," said Param, "and rubs them off on you."

"Or on tree bark," said Olivenko.

Rigg considered this. "It felt dryish and a little rough. Like unglazed clay pots. And there is truly, absolutely nothing on my hand. Now let's get back to the spot we picked and prepare some food."

"What do we do about this . . . this . . . what did you call it, Rigg?" asked Param.

"Barbfeather. Just a descriptive name. And we're not going to do anything about it."

"What if it follows us to our camp?" she asked.

"If it lies down, don't snuggle up to it," said Rigg. "Those feathers really are barbed."

"That's it?"

"What do you want me to do, Param, kill it?"

"Isn't that what you and your father—I mean Ram—isn't that what you did with animals?"

"We killed the ones whose fur we could sell," said Rigg. "Do *you* want a coat made out of that?"

"Gloves," said Loaf. "I think Leaky could use gloves like that—for punching some of our customers who drink too much and won't leave the roadhouse quietly."

They left the barbfeather and set about making camp. But soon it joined them again. Their provisions were meager, but they had been on the road for a while and they were used to them. Rigg offered some of his food to the beast. It sniffed and then wandered away. "Must not smell like anything edible to him," Rigg said.

"Doesn't *taste* like anything edible to *me*," said Olivenko.

"Wonder how that barbfeather would taste," said Loaf, "if we could talk him into climbing into a stewpot for us."

"I don't think our bodies could make much use of his meat," said Rigg, "even if we could keep it inside long enough to digest it."

"Pretty image while I'm eating," said Param.

"I had no idea you were so fussy," said Rigg, with a grin. Param rolled her eyes.

"Why couldn't we eat it?" asked Umbo.

"When they were testing me to see if I should get access to the library," said Rigg, "I met a scientist in Aressa Sessamo who was separating out the plants and animals that came to this world with our ancestors—which is most of them—and the ones that evolved here, which is only a few. Every single one of them, Father and I had already identified as plants and animals that we can't eat. Even dead, only certain carrion eaters will go after them. It's as if we had two separate ecologies twined together. Father called them 'mildly toxic' and my guess is he knew."

"So maybe that parasite can't use our bodies either," said Olivenko.

"But Vadesh says it can," said Rigg.

"And yet you touched it," said Param.

"Tomorrow let's go back in time," said Rigg. "When we're rested and fresh. Come on, we passed through the Wall today. People tried to kill you and Umbo not that many hours ago, Param! Can't we get some sleep?"

But when they finally cleaned up supper, laid out their dosses, and took up their sleeping positions, with Loaf on first watch, Rigg couldn't sleep. Because as soon as he knew what the facemask's path looked like, he began to find the same kind of path riding along with humans ten thousand years ago. Vadesh was telling the truth—humans *had* been infested with facemasks.

And the more of them Rigg followed, the more certain he became of a pattern. At first the facemasks had been rare and were never inside the city. Then they came along with humans when they approached the city in large groups. It looked to Rigg like war, or raiding parties.

But abruptly, about five hundred years before the city emptied out, all the facemasks were *inside* the city, and the only human paths without facemask paths traveling with them were outside the city—again in raiding parties.

The conclusion was obvious to Rigg. Halfway through the history of humans in this city, the ones infested with the facemask parasite became the possessors of the city, and the uninfected people were the ones who lived outside.

And the tallest buildings were not built until the city belonged to the infested ones. Rigg knew this because none of the human paths rose up into the sky inside those towers until the relatively newer ones, the ones with facemask companions.

This is a city whose greatest buildings were erected by people with parasites embedded in their brains.

Now *that* was something Vadesh might have told them, if he were actually obeying the command to tell them everything. Which meant that he was deceiving them. He must have found some logical loophole in the orders Rigg had given him. Or maybe there *was* no deep law that required him to obey the first humans to pass through a Wall.

Eventually, exhaustion won and Rigg slept.

CHAPTER 3

Night Watch

From the moment Vadesh walked up to them on this side of the Wall, Umbo had felt a sick dread. Now it was clear to him that passing through the Wall had been a very bad idea. At the time it seemed they had no choice. But that was because back when they had choices, they had chosen to come so near to the Wall there was nowhere else to go. They had pinned themselves there.

Only now did it occur to Umbo that it was Rigg who had decided that going through the Wall was something they needed to try. Maybe it was because of the way Rigg's real father, Knosso, had died trying to get through the Wall by sea.

Whatever Rigg's reason, when they escaped the city of Aressa Sessamo, knowing that General Citizen and Rigg's and Param's mother, Hagia Sessamin, would pursue them, Rigg made sure they headed for the Wall and then had no choice but to get through it, somehow.

But had that been the only way to evade General Citizen's army? Couldn't they have split up, hidden among the people? Rigg was the only person who could follow all the paths that humans and animals took through the world—no one else could have traced their movements. Yet whenever someone spoke of another course, Rigg dismissed it. In the long run, they'd get caught; inside the wallfold they couldn't hide for long. Yet people *did* hide. So why didn't anyone argue with Rigg? Why didn't *I*?

Not that Rigg bossed people around or even argued much. He just kept bringing up the Wall again and again, making it all seem so rational. And eventually everyone just took it for granted they were heading for the Wall.

Even at the last minute, the very methods they used to get through the Wall might have taken them away from it just as easily. But they went through because Rigg wanted to.

Who put him in charge? Why did everybody listen to him?

Like Vadesh. He made it clear that Rigg was the person he would obey. But they had *all* passed through the Wall. In fact, Umbo and Param had passed through it first. And Umbo had done all the time-shifting. First Umbo had pushed Rigg and Loaf and Olivenko into the past—to the time that Rigg determined by finding and following the barbfeather. Then, when they were nearly across, Param had grabbed Umbo by the hand, leapt off the high rock they had been perched on, and then vivisected time the way *she* did, slowing them down. And once again, Umbo had pushed back in time, dragging himself and Param to a point a couple of weeks before they had arrived at the Wall. That's how Umbo and Param ended up on the far side of the Wall even before the other three set out.

Ultimately it all depended on Umbo. Yes, Rigg could carry the time-jump much farther into the past than Umbo could; yes, Rigg made it precise, by linking with some ancient path. And Param could section the flow of time—they were both talented. But the actual time travel, that was Umbo alone.

So why didn't Vadesh defer to *him*? Why did Vadesh say *Rigg* was the "actual time traveler," when Rigg had never learned to time-shift on his own, as Umbo had? Why was Umbo *nothing*, when he could do things no one else could do?

Right from the start, Umbo had come to Rigg as a supplicant. Please let me travel with you, please! Remembering his own groveling begging attitude now made Umbo feel humiliated and angry. They both had compelling reasons to leave the village of Fall Ford; why did Umbo put himself in a subordinate position?

It couldn't be because Rigg was a Sessamid, born to be a prince; none of them knew it until he was arrested in O. Besides, Sessamids had been out of power ever since the People's Revolutionary Council took over, and if they had been in power, they would have killed Rigg as a baby because Queen Hagia's grandmother had decreed that no male could inherit and that all male Sessamids must be killed upon birth.

So how did Rigg end up making all the important decisions and getting them into this terrible place on the wrong side of the Wall?

Be rational, Umbo told himself. Rigg is in charge because that's how Ram, the Golden Man, the Wandering Man, our copy of Vadesh, raised him.

Ram had given Umbo some training in the way to control his power over time, and by disguising himself as a gardener had helped train Param, all the way downriver in Aressa Sessamo. But Ram had taken Rigg from babyhood and raised him as his son, teaching him constantly. Ram trained Rigg to be a ruler. Ram decided everything, and Rigg and all the rest of them were just following his script.

And now here they were with Ram's identical twin, Vadesh, lying to them and controlling them. They couldn't even get water without Vadesh's help or some terrible parasite would get them. They were completely at the mercy of this *machine* shaped like a human. A machine created in such a form as to deceive everyone about its very nature. Ancient humans made these immortal machines and now they rule over us because they know everything and we know nothing.

Now Umbo lay there in a grove of trees not far from the empty ruins of a city, staring up at the bright Ring overhead in the sky, boiling with the same resentment that had been building up inside him since they passed through the Wall. Umbo was honest enough to recognize that while the *feeling* was the same, it was no longer directed against Rigg. Now it was directed against Ram and Vadesh. But was it them that he really resented? Was it anybody, really, that was making him feel this way? Or did he simply have these feelings and searched for someone outside himself to blame them on?

I'm angry and bitter and despairing but Rigg doesn't deserve it, and Ram and Vadesh are nothing but machines and . . .

Umbo rolled up onto his arm and looked at the others where they lay sleeping. Loaf—there was no reason to resent *him*. He had been nothing but generous and protective, and *he*, at least, had cared about Umbo and remembered him when no one else did.

Olivenko? Umbo barely knew him. Only Rigg knew him, and Rigg seemed to value him because Olivenko had watched Knosso die. Yet Olivenko had worked hard and abided by the group's decisions—which meant *Rigg's* decisions—and there was no reason for Umbo to resent him, either.

And there was Rigg. Umbo knew that Rigg was his true friend, and if people deferred to him it was only natural, because Ram had trained him to be ready for anything, to know something about practically everything.

Param was almost the opposite. Same bloodline as Rigg—you could see it in how much they looked like each other—but she had spent so many hours of her life invisible in her sliced-up slowed-down timeflow that as she lay there sleeping in the lee of Loaf's large body, she seemed almost younger than Rigg. Which made sense, though she was his older sister by two years; she hadn't actually lived through all the years since she was born, for when she was in her sectioned-up timeflow, she lived through only one second for every three or four or more seconds that passed for everyone else.

She's younger than *me*, thought Umbo.

And with that thought, he felt himself filled with such rage and despair and . . . and *longing* that he wanted to cry out from the power of it; it could not be contained, yet he had to contain it . . .

By all the Saints, thought Umbo, the first princess I meet, and I fall in love with her.

So this is love, he said to himself, trying to examine his own overwhelming feelings with the rational fragment of his mind. This is the powerful, horrible longing that made Mother marry that miserable tyrant I had to call Father. How many unbelievably stupid heroes in stories did insanely dangerous things because they were in *love*?

More to the point, how many insane things am I going to do because of it?

Now all of Umbo's feelings made sense to him. Yes, Rigg had made too many decisions, but the main reason Umbo resented him was the easy, comfortable way Param behaved with him. They had been together in the same house for months, and they were brother and sister and they had planned their escape together and had saved each other's lives and . . .

I saved her life too! And she mine!

But only the once, only this morning as they leapt from the rock. She had taken Umbo by the hand and pulled him to his feet and then jumped off the rock with him. Then, holding his hand, she had taken him across the Wall.

He could still feel her hand in his. Or, rather, the tingle of the memory of her hand. She isn't two years older than me and Rigg, not really. She's my age, more or less, and who cares if she was born a princess? Her mother the queen tried to kill her over and over—if that doesn't constitute getting fired as princess, what does? She's a commoner like me, now. It's not impossible.

A commoner by law, but still royal by breeding. She must

think I'm a filthy ignorant unmannered low-speaking vulgar privick, while Rigg knows how to talk just like her, with all that high, fine language. Rigg has lived in her house, has eaten at table with her, he knows all the right manners. While I have journeyed with her, lit fires for her at night, but mostly I've behaved like a menial. As if I were Rigg's manservant. And not some lofty valet who knows all the correct manners—no, I'm like a boy Rigg hired for the afternoon, to help do the work of their journey from the city to the Wall.

No, thought Umbo. I can't let myself go back to resenting everybody. I'm in love, and so, as the Wandering Man—no, *Ram*—once explained, I have the instinct to fight any potential rivals for the woman I covet. Not that Rigg is a rival, exactly—he's her brother, not her lover—but he has her trust, her affection. She talks to him, little secrets and asides, all the things I want her to have with me. Only with me.

What made Umbo so angry was the knowledge that she must despise him, that she was out of his reach no matter what he did. And yet he knew that he didn't know that, *couldn't* know it. They were both so young, what did he *expect*?

This is insane, he told himself. I've got to get my mind off her, now that I know that she's what's been on my mind.

He reached into his pocket and took out the thing he had picked up when he came into the grove of trees.

It was a stone. Specifically, a jewel. Even more specifically, a light blue jewel that looked exactly like the one that Rigg had tried to sell in O, and which was now in the possession of a bank in Aressa Sessamo. The stone that Umbo and Loaf had tried repeatedly to steal back, so that Rigg's collection of nineteen stones would be complete.

That was what he had seen at a glance, when he was picking it up from among the fallen leaves. But since it could not possibly *be* that stone, Umbo tried to make sense of it another way. He drew it from where he had tucked it into the waistband of his trousers and tried to study it by ringlight.

It wasn't the sight of it that mattered anyway, except to confirm that it was indeed the right size and color to be the missing jewel, which he'd realized the moment he saw it. Now he examined it by heft and texture. It was as hard as any of the jewels, as smoothly polished, and its weight felt right.

He tucked it into his trousers and rolled over onto his back. He recalled the moment of finding it. The jewel was not so much *amid* last year's fallen leaves as atop them. Resting right on the surface, as if it had been left in order to be noticed and found.

But who could have left it? Rigg sounded absolutely certain when he said no human had come near this grove in a long, long time. The jewel could not have been sitting there so long—it would have been buried under leaves and probably deep within the soil.

The lack of paths suggested that the jewel must have been left by an expendable like Vadesh and Ram. They left no path that Rigg could see. But why would Vadesh leave it lying there, when he could just as easily have handed it to Rigg?

Maybe it was some kind of test, to see what Umbo would do with it. But no one could have known in advance which of them, if any, would enter the grove exactly where Umbo did. And *when* could Vadesh have done it? Wouldn't they have seen him? There was no place to conceal himself between the empty city and this grove. There were no footprints or other woodsy signs of his passing—the leaves on which the jewel rested looked completely undisturbed, exactly like all the leaves surrounding them.

And why *this* jewel? Even though it could hardly be the very one that Rigg had once carried and tried to sell, it was certainly just like it in appearance. Suppose Vadesh had an identical set of nineteen here in this wallfold? How did he know to pick the one jewel that was missing from their set? Rigg had laid out the eighteen for him to see, but when had Vadesh had a single moment in which to fetch his own jewels to replace the missing one?

"You awake?"

The whisper came from just above his head. Umbo didn't flinch or startle, but his heart raced. Olivenko's voice. How had he gotten from his watch position to here without Umbo hearing?

"Your watch," said Olivenko.

Of course it was Umbo's watch. And the reason he didn't hear Olivenko coming was because Umbo must have fallen asleep. And the reason he didn't feel as if he had slept at all was because he took so long with his thoughts before falling asleep that all he got was a nap at best.

Bleary, Umbo got up. Loaf stirred—he slept lightly and woke at every change of watch. Rigg and Param remained oblivious. The sleep of royalty.

What an unfair thing even to think of, Umbo told himself. If there's anyone in the world who *can't* sleep peacefully, it's royalty. When rebels aren't trying to kill them, or warlords who think they should be king, then royal families are always killing each other.

Just how stupid are my resentments and jealousies going to make me?

"Speak to me," said Olivenko. "If you're sleepwalking, you won't keep much of a watch."

Umbo opened his eyes fully and stretched. "I'm awake," he whispered.

"Keep moving until you're really awake," said Olivenko. "You only fell asleep a few minutes ago. I felt bad waking you, but . . . your turn."

And we can't change turns around if it might mean waking one of the royals.

No, Umbo told himself. Stop thinking that way.

He got up and walked briskly out of the center of the grove, not caring how much noise he made among last year's fallen leaves. Then he was on the closely grazed meadow, where his steps made almost no noise at all, and where the breeze was unimpeded by the trunks and leaves of the trees.

What animals keep this grass so close-cropped? Why aren't they all here now, with their faces covered by facemasks? Maybe Vadesh comes out and mows it himself. Or grazes it. Who knows what these machines can do, if they put their minds to it?

Umbo circled the grove, which was quite a wide circuit, though the grove did not seem large or thick. He stayed well beyond its verge, which took him down a slope on the side beyond the city. Only when Umbo heard the gurgling of water did he realize how foolish he was to have strayed so far from camp. From here he couldn't even see the sleepers, though he could see the tops of the trees under which they lay. But to go near the water—what if he stumbled in and got his own face-mask?

As if on cue, his left foot sloshed into a boggy spot in the grass. Umbo leapt back as if dodging a harvester's scythe. But maybe there was no point in dodging. Maybe a larval facemask had already fastened itself to him.

He scampered up the hill till he reached the edge of the copse and could see Loaf. Then Umbo sat down and ran his hands over his legs and feet. Nothing was attached, though he got a start when he found some wet leaves clinging to the top of his right foot and then to his hands when he tried to brush them away. There were no clouds tonight, so the ringlight was enough to show him that he had no parasite inching up his body. Unless the parasite was very small. Or it was creeping along under his skin.

Umbo shuddered, then rose to his feet and walked again, continuing his circuit of the grove, though much closer to the edge of it now.

Along the north side, he had to give up the plan. He couldn't continue to circle the outside of the grove because it wasn't a grove at all—it was a peninsula of a much larger forest that extended away to the north. It had only seemed like a grove from the city side because its link with the greater forest was hidden behind the brow of the hill.

You think you know where you are, you think you know what's what, and suddenly nothing is the way you thought, and it should have been obvious all along, and you feel stupid for having made assumptions, and you were stupid, but . . . Umbo could hear Wandering Man say, "It isn't stupid when you assume things; that's how the human brain is supposed to work. We assume things so we can act much more quickly than animals that only see what they see."

Act quickly, yes, but wrongly if you assume wrong, Umbo thought both then and now. But he had said nothing, because he was so awed to be spending a few moments with Rigg's strange and wonderful father. The machine.

Umbo moved across the narrow part of the wood, wading through leaves rather noisily, as if they were another kind of stream. Finally he got to lawn again, and now the city loomed on his left, farther away than the trees on his right, but much taller. Umbo stood looking at the buildings, wondering where the people went, and whether Vadesh stood in one of the towers, looking out and down at him.

Umbo wondered if Vadesh wondered about anything. Neither Vadesh nor Ram ever seemed uncertain. Even when they said they were uncertain, they sounded certain about it. Umbo didn't even know when he didn't know what he needed to know.

Vadesh had said that he couldn't predict the future with any certainty. He had known a billion things that the humans from Earth *might* do when and if they arrived here on the planet Garden, but he did not know what they *would* do, he said. Well, didn't that imply that he didn't know what Umbo and the others would do, either? That was something for Vadesh to wonder about.

We are unpredictable to him, thought Umbo. The thought

made him vaguely happy. He is manipulating us, deceiving us, withholding information from us, precisely because he doesn't know what we'll do and he wants us to do some particular thing.

That's the key to this whole thing. He needs us, and so he has to manipulate us into doing a thing that is so important that it's more important than telling us the truth. Why doesn't he just tell us what he wants? Because he doesn't know if we'll do it knowingly. Or maybe he's quite sure we won't do it knowingly, and so he has to trick us or lead us into a situation where we have no choice but to do what he wants.

The way Rigg got us right up against the Wall.

Only Rigg is a good guy and didn't think he was manipulating us to do his will.

Or maybe he did manipulate us on purpose, and I don't really know him at all.

Umbo rocked his head forward and touched his fingers to his forehead. I keep coming back to not liking or trusting Rigg. Maybe that's what Vadesh wants.

He heard Param coming. He knew it was her from the lightness of her step. "It's not your watch yet," he said. "I only just started."

She kept coming. "You've been walking around for an hour or so," she said. "If I'm any judge of time."

"In this group," said Umbo, "who can trust time to be the same from minute to minute?"

"I couldn't sleep," said Param. And then, incredibly, she put her arm through Umbo's and stood close to him. She was warm. Umbo shivered.

"You're cold," she said.

"Not now," said Umbo. Then he realized that his words might sound like he was being flirty and so he corrected himself. "I mean, I was really cold a while ago when I stepped in a wet place down by the brook—"

"You went down to the water?" she asked, incredulous.

"Not on purpose," said Umbo. "It was a boggy place—"

"You could have—"

"I wiped down my legs and feet and there was nothing."

"But he said they were really small in the water—"

How could he argue with her? Why should he try? "If I stepped into a boggy spot and picked up a facemask parasite then it's done, and I can tell you what it feels like."

"As it takes over your brain," said Param.

"Nobody's been using it anyway," said Umbo. He meant it to sound jocular. Instead it sounded self-pitying.

But Param didn't rush to reassure him, which would have made him seem even more pathetic to himself. "Maybe you and Barbfeather can talk to each other."

"Maybe we'll look really pretty to each other," said Umbo. "Just my luck to find a best chum who has four legs and can't talk."

"Four-legged untalking people make the most reliable friends," said Param. Was there bitterness in her voice?

"I can see you've never tried to befriend a cat."

"I was forgetting cats." She leaned her head on his shoulder. "I can understand why Rigg helped me, back in the capital. He's my brother. But you—you sat there with me on that rock, holding the others back in that ancient time until Mother's soldiers were almost on us. And Rigg and Loaf and Olivenko aren't your kin or anything."

"Rigg is more my friend than any of my kin," said Umbo.

"If Rigg hadn't signaled you to bring him back to the present . . ."

"Then I would have kept him in the past until he did."

"You weren't worried that they'd kill you?"

"Of course I was. If they killed me, then I couldn't have brought them back," said Umbo.

"What about me?" asked Param.

Umbo shook his head. "See how gallant I'm not? I knew you could take care of yourself."

"I knew you were in danger. I kept wanting to grab you and make you disappear. But if I did, that might have been the same as killing the others."

"But you took me away the moment I brought them back to the present," said Umbo.

"All I could think was, get him off this rock," she said.

"You saved my life."

"I almost got us both killed," she said, shuddering. "I let Mother and the soldiers see which way we jumped. They'd know we couldn't change direction in midair. So if you hadn't pushed us back a week—"

"But I did."

"I jumped without thinking."

"You had no other choice. You kept us alive in that moment."

"And then you kept us alive in the next."

"So on the whole, I think we saved each other," said Umbo. Then, on a whim, he pulled away far enough that he could turn to face her and make a joke. "My hero," he said.

Only she must have had the same idea for the same joke, because at the exact same moment she said, "My hero."

But she wasn't sarcastic. Or maybe her sarcasm was so thick that it sounded like sincerity.

Well, either she was joking or not. All Umbo could do was react the way he would to either. "Don't count on its happening again," he said. "I'm not really the hero type."

She playfully slapped his face—just a tap with a few fingers. "Can't let somebody thank you, is that it?"

At the moment, all Umbo could think was—well, nothing, really, because he was beyond thinking. She had taken his arm and leaned close against him, she had bantered with him, thanked him, praised him. Called him her hero, even if it was kind of a joke. And now she was teasing him. He was in heaven. And yet he was also totally focused on everything she said and did so that he could respond.

"Thank me all you want," he said. "As long as I can thank you back."

"One of the best things about finding out I have a brother," said Param, "is that I inherit all his friends."

Friends. That's what they were. She was teasing him like a friend.

"Which is a lot more than I'll ever inherit from my mother," said Param ruefully. She turned back to look at the city. "I think that place is so sad. So glorious, and yet they left it behind. All that work, all that *marvel,* and they walked away."

"Maybe they ran," said Umbo. "Maybe they died."

"Well, they're all dead by now," said Param. "I remember being so distraught when Papa died. I wasn't there to watch, the way Olivenko was, but I loved him more than anybody. And Mother took me by the shoulders and said, 'Everybody dies, and since we don't all die at once, somebody's always left behind. Just be glad it wasn't you who died.' I should have realized then what Mother was. Or maybe I did. She was perfect—perfectly selfish. Well, no. Perfectly devoted to the Tent of Light. She had *seemed* so devoted to me. But I knew then that if I died she'd feel exactly what she felt about Father's death."

"Nothing."

"Annoyed," she said. "She was irritated that Father's hobby had gotten him killed."

"Well, just think how irritated she is right now that you're alive," said Umbo.

Param giggled. "She's still there. Remember? As we were falling, all I could do was slow us down more and more, so a whole night passed, and the whole time those soldiers were there, swinging those heavy metal bars. They're doing that right now."

"And we're still falling toward them," said Umbo. Instinctively he reached out and took her hand. "Let's do it again."

She took his hand and looked at him, laughing. Then her face darkened and she took her hand back. "No," she said. "Let's never do that again."

She turned away and ran lightly back into the grove.

Never do what! he wanted to shout after her. Never jump

from the rock with enemies beneath? Or never let me hold your hand again? Or never talk to me. Or never time-jump. Or . . .

Anything he asked would show just how desperate he was. For a few moments it was as if she actually liked him. And then suddenly she snatched her hand away and was gone and he had no idea why. No idea what she actually felt about him.

This is agony. I didn't *ask* to fall in love with Rigg's sister.

She called me her hero.

Umbo stalked off through the grass toward the city until he reached the path. Or road. It was grassy, but in the cold grey light of the Ring, it was as if Umbo could see the road that lay under the grass. It was wide, and while a thatch of grass roots lay over it thickly, no tree grew where the road had been. If we peeled up all this grass, it would still be there, like the roads in the city, changed not a whit by the passing of ten thousand years.

Umbo walked back to the camp. Param had already resumed her place and was either asleep or wasn't, but wanted to seem so. Umbo didn't walk anymore. He was wide awake now—she had wakened him even more than stepping in water had. He kept his watch and even after the position of the stars told him that his watch was over, he waited another half-watch before waking Rigg to take his turn. I won't sleep anyway, Umbo thought. But he also knew that he was letting Rigg sleep to make up for all the terrible things that Umbo had thought about him that day. Not that Rigg had any idea. But punishing himself a little, serving Rigg a little, that made Umbo feel better. A little less ashamed.

Naturally, Rigg noticed that Umbo had wakened him late. "I

couldn't sleep anyway," Umbo whispered. "No reason for both of us to lose sleep."

Rigg moved off a few paces. Umbo lay down and, even though he thought he wasn't sleepy at all, he was unconscious within moments, and then it was morning, and it was as if no time had passed. He thought: Param touched me. Of course I could sleep. I wanted to get to my dreams as quickly as possible.

Except that if he had any dreams, he didn't remember them.

Being awake at dawn felt perfectly normal to them all—they went about their normal chores, except for boiling water. There'd be no hot gruel this morning. Nor was there any shaving or washing. They needed to hold on to every bit of water for drinking.

"So," said Loaf, when they had all gnawed their jerky and cheese and had their sips. "You time travelers, are you going to go back and see what happened here?"

"I'd like to," said Rigg, "if Umbo's willing."

Rigg seemed so deferent. Umbo blushed with embarrassment at how he had blamed Rigg for always deciding everything.

Then again, was Rigg *really* leaving it up to him? How could Umbo possibly say no?

I can say no, if I want to, thought Umbo. "No," he said.

Everyone except Rigg seemed surprised. "Umbo?" asked Param.

Now that he had refused, he had to come up with a reason. "Are we going to change it?" asked Umbo. "And what if it changes *us*? What if I send Rigg back and he gets killed? We don't know how violent these people were. Or what diseases they had. What if Rigg catches the plague that wiped them out? What's the *point*?"

"Don't send him back alone," said Olivenko. "Send me and Loaf along to protect him."

"From disease?" asked Umbo.

"Whatever happened here to empty the city," said Rigg, "I think it has everything to do with what Vadesh wants us to do here."

"He hasn't asked us to do anything," said Param.

"But he wants it all the same," said Rigg. "Didn't you see how attentive he was to us? We matter to him. Father was that way—Ram was. If you mattered to him, he homed on you like a bat after a fly. You filled his whole gaze. But if you didn't matter, it was like you didn't exist."

"True," said Umbo. "Sometimes I mattered to him, but mostly not."

"Vadesh couldn't take his eyes off us," said Rigg.

"Off *you,*" said Olivenko, chuckling.

"And Param, and Umbo," said Rigg. "The time travelers."

"We all traveled in time," said Loaf, with a slight smile. "He just has a thing for children."

"Someday, Loaf, I'm going to be big enough to smack you around," Rigg answered him.

"I've seen both your parents," said Olivenko, "and no, Rigg, you'll never be that big. *I'll* never be that big."

"Good to keep that in mind," said Loaf.

Olivenko rolled his eyes. "I'm trying to show you proper respect here, Loaf. You don't have to put me in my place. I know my place."

"I was just joking," said Loaf uncomfortably.

But he had not been joking—nobody in this group knew Loaf as well as Umbo did, and he knew Loaf had spoken his mind.

"What I think," said Rigg, "is that I should walk around out here and see what the paths can tell me. There's no purpose to going back in time if we arrive at some point where nothing decisive is happening, right? And if I can't find anything that looks promising, then we won't do it. Agreed?"

Umbo wanted to laugh. Rigg sounded so conciliatory, as if he was giving in. But in fact what he was really getting them all to agree to was that if, in Rigg's sole judgment, there was some point in the past where they *could* learn something, then they *would* go back. Rigg hadn't argued with anybody, but he was *getting his way*.

Nobody else seemed to notice, and nobody else seemed to mind. And what bothered Umbo most was the fact that he knew Rigg was right, they had to find something out before trusting Vadesh another moment, and Umbo had only disagreed because he couldn't stand having Rigg decide everything. But what could he do when Rigg was right?

Umbo and the others tagged along, watching Rigg as he got lost in thought, seeing whatever it was that he called "paths." For an hour they watched him move around through the lawns and meadows surrounding the city. Finally he sat down and Loaf immediately led the others closer to him. Only Umbo hung back and looked, not at Rigg, but at the city. It was more magnificent than anything Umbo had seen in O or Aressa Sessamo. Every building was a separate work of art, and yet they were all pieces of something much larger and more beautiful. It's as if each building were part of a tapestry, some parts raised, some parts kept low. Perhaps if we could stand inside the tallest tower, we could see what the tapestry depicted. Maybe a map, like the globe inside the Tower of O. Maybe a portrait of a person. Maybe some message spelled out in towers, or the shadows of towers at sunset.

Umbo became aware of voices coming closer.

"The last thing we want to do is go back into the middle of a battle," said Loaf. So apparently Rigg had learned something about what had happened here.

"Not in the middle," said Rigg. "At the edge. Far back from the edge. Out of danger. Nobody was dying right here, for instance."

"You can see death?" asked Umbo.

"No," said Param. "Rigg already explained—if you had come with us you'd know. He just sees where paths end."

"There were people watching the battle," said Rigg. "Just a few. Umbo can send me back to their time—"

"Send *us*," said Loaf.

"You'll scare them," said Param.

"I'll smile very nicely," said Loaf, demonstrating his best battlefield grimace.

"Oh, don't do that," said Olivenko. "You'd scare your own mother."

"I need to ask them what's happening," said Rigg. "That's all. I hope Vadesh was right when he said the Wall contains all languages."

"If you can't understand them," said Umbo, "just signal me and I'll bring you all back."

"All who?" asked Param.

Loaf and Olivenko looked at her stupidly. "Us," they said in unison.

"I'm going too," said Param.

"Too dangerous," said Loaf.

"As if anything we're doing is safe," said Param. "One of you needs to stay here with Umbo, somebody who can protect him."

Loaf turned to Param. "You really want to see a battle? War is messy."

"And you're afraid I can't deal with bodies torn apart and people screaming in agony?" asked Param.

"If you *can* avoid it, you should," said Loaf.

"My mother nearly protected me to death," said Param. "I'm done with that. I'm not strong enough to wield a sword or cut down a tree or lift a corner of a coach, like some of you. But I have eyes and ears and I want to be part of this. Directly."

It never occurred to any of them that maybe Umbo himself would like to see the past. No, he was the anchor, he was the one who *couldn't* go. "I'll send you all," said Umbo. "Stop arguing and hang on to each other. Rigg, tell me when you've picked your path."

Olivenko rounded on Umbo. "Don't you even care what happens to Param?"

Umbo tried to keep the anger out of his voice. "Wanting to get on with it is not the same thing as not caring. She wants to go. Why shouldn't she?"

"Because it's dangerous," said Olivenko. "Because members of the royal family get no special protection against death."

"Special protection is exactly what you're trying to give me," said Param.

Umbo pointed out the obvious. "If anybody can take care of herself, it's Param."

Then Rigg spoke, much more softly than any of the others, and yet somehow his voice made them all fall silent. How does he *do* that? thought Umbo.

"The thing that worries me," said Rigg, "is that if Param starts slicing time, back there ten thousand years in the past, and *disappears*, how can you bring her back?"

Rigg must think we're all stupid. "I have a really special plan to keep that from happening," said Umbo. "Watch this." He turned to Param and spoke very solemnly. "Param, when you're back in the past: Don't. Slice. Time."

She answered in the same spirit of mock soberness. "What an excellent idea. But what if it gets really dangerous, Umbo? What if I can't help it and I just start chopping time into little bits?"

"Well, you simply mustn't," said Umbo. "If things get scary, you just signal me the way Rigg does. Do you think you can do that same hand motion he does? Do your hands work like that, or do you need Rigg to show you?"

Rigg flushed with embarrassment; he wasn't used to people mocking him.

"Stop that," said Loaf angrily.

"Why is Umbo the only one who sees that I have as much ordinary common sense as anybody?" said Param. "Come on, Rigg, pick your path and let's get cracking."

"What's the rush?" murmured Olivenko. "It's not as if the past is going anywhere."

"The present is," said Umbo. What if Vadesh came out and stopped them?

Rigg still looked embarrassed—or was he angry? But he made no complaint. "I've got the path I want," said Rigg. "Push us back, Umbo."

They were all holding on to each other, the way Rigg and Loaf and Olivenko had held on to Barbfeather when they went through the Wall. And, just like that time, Umbo felt a great lurch as his push into the past swept out quickly like the current of a river, carrying them much farther into the past than Umbo could have sent them on his own. It was Rigg's ability to hook on to someone in the past that drew them, as much as Umbo's pushing. And it was so far that they went, ten thousand years, almost as far as the whole history of the human race on Garden.

They did not disappear, of course—Umbo could see them as well as ever. But they all stumbled because the ground must have been lower then; perhaps the thatch of the grass had not built up so high. They fell a bit, then rose up and their eyes were riveted on the grassy field in front of the city, where apparently there was a war going on. As usual, Umbo saw none of it. But when Rigg reached out and touched someone there in the past, Umbo saw a glimpse of clothing, a brief outline of a person. Rigg let go almost at once and the image disappeared.

CHAPTER 4
Battle

In all her life, Param had never been in the presence of more than about fifty people at a time. Even that was unusual, and she had preferred to avoid large dinners or recitals or whatever was being put on in Mother's honor. And while social events could be full of vicious infighting, it was done with words, looks, and gestures. Nothing had prepared her for war.

She had imagined war, of course—that was what most of history was about, the Sessamoto lords-in-the-tent leading their marauders on devastating raids against whatever village or town looked least protected, and then as kings-in-the-tent forcing the other tribes of the northeast to unite under their rule. Finally the King-in-the-Tent had conquered every nation of the Stashi Plain and subdued every freehold and every wild tribe of the wood-lands and every fishing village of the coasts and through all of her study of that history, Param had pictured it all like a combination of the game of queens and the game of clay-casting, with the clay balls alternately knocking over pawns and queens, and dashing to pieces against them.

She had an intellectual knowledge that war was bloody. King Algar One-eye was an obvious example, and General Potonokissu had worn a wooden leg when he walked, though never when he rode. They had been maimed in battle, and if such things could happen to the rulers of armies, Param could only imagine what happened to the ordinary soldiers.

But when all but Umbo joined hands and suddenly dropped into the past, Param was almost overwhelmed by the noise of it. She could hear yelling: fierce cries of warriors, shouted commands from officers, screams of wounded men. And there was a smell of burning meat that almost gagged her, mixed as it was with the other stinks of the battlefield.

Her reflex was to sliver time so she could disappear. She relied on this ability to retreat from anything that frightened her. But she caught herself, realizing that Rigg had not been wrong after all when he worried about her disappearing in the past.

She knelt up and saw that Rigg, who was more used to sudden shifts of time, was already standing up and striding toward three adult women who were watching the battle. Rigg would speak to them; Param had no desire to. The women looked careworn and grief-stricken. They stood near a stockade that surrounded the city and sheltered their party from the view of the soldiers where the battle was being waged.

The stockade looked as if it had been hastily thrown up in

a day, braced from behind here and there. She wondered how well it would hold up against a determined enemy. It had been clumsily built; through gaps between the poles it was possible to see the battle.

But Param did not want to see the battle. She had thought that was what she was coming to see, but now that she was here, it was the city that fascinated her, because it was only half built. Only the lower buildings existed, and instead of the uniform black of the towers in Param's own time, these had been brightly painted, though many were faded and weathered. Yet the colors seemed vivid on this sunny day; it was as if the city had been decorated for a festival.

From the top of one of the towers, a beam of pure heat shimmered the air. Param followed the beam and then strode the five steps to the stockade and peered through. Where the beam landed, the grass was erupting in flame, and men were fleeing from it.

At first Param noticed little distinction between the two armies—they were masses of human shapes brandishing weapons. The numbers seemed evenly matched. But soon, from looking at those nearest her, she realized that all the defenders were better armed—swords and bows against clubs and crude spears.

Yet instead of cutting through the attackers, the swords of the defenders seemed rarely to slice flesh. The attackers always dodged away, avoiding the cuts and blows. However, the clubs and spears of the attackers landed all the time; if it had not been for the armor of the defenders, many would have fallen.

Why were the attackers so much better at fighting?

Then Param realized that the attackers all had large, strangely shaped heads; a moment later she saw that their heads were deformed because they had facemasks almost entirely covering their heads. Many of them seemed to have weirdly misplaced eyes, as if the parasite, having covered the face of a man, grew him a new eye out of its own rough flesh. Param found them repulsive and fascinating. The men with facemasks fought savagely and skillfully. They were quick, dancing to dodge incoming arrows from the defenders, darting forward to strike blows which rarely missed, though the defenders' armor usually turned away the blow.

Another beam came from the tower. It should have been a devastating advantage for the defenders, to have that beam of fire. But instead of striking into one of the masses of the attacking army, it struck an area that was mostly empty of living men of either side. Again flames gouted upward, and men of both sides ran from the area of flame. The battlefield was dotted with patches of flame or cinders or ash, so that neither army could maintain good order.

"Those bastards in the tower ought to be hanged," muttered Loaf. He was standing at the stockade beside her.

"They don't seem to aim their rod of fire very well," she said.

"They're hitting nobody," said Loaf. "Useless."

Olivenko, from the other side of her, said, "What makes the attackers so nimble? I've never seen soldiers who dodge so well."

"The defenders are good soldiers," said Loaf. "Trained, disciplined. But they hardly land a blow."

Olivenko agreed. "It takes two of them attacking the same man at once to bring him down."

"Maybe it's because they don't have any armor," said Loaf. "Keeps them lighter on their feet."

It's the facemask, Param wanted to say. The facemasks help them to react more quickly. But she said nothing. Loaf and Olivenko were soldiers; they knew what they were seeing, and she didn't.

With both of the soldiers watching the battle, it occurred to Param that neither of them was protecting Rigg. What if the women took him for some kind of enemy? What if they were armed? Param could at least take Rigg out of harm's way, if danger threatened.

The women were speaking a language that Param had never heard before, yet she understood them. She realized that she was not mentally translating their speech into any tongue that she actually knew. Rather she simply understood them at a level below language. The Wall really did give languages to those who passed through it.

The women were angry and frightened, and like Loaf they were condemning the wielder of the firebeam. But the women did not speak of "them" who aimed; rather it was "him."

"He won't use it to kill them," said the tallest of the women. "And he won't let any of us use it—we'd have no qualms about burning them."

"They aren't human anymore," said the eldest woman—the mother? "Killing them should be like killing grass, but he won't do it."

"He's no friend of ours," said the youngest.

"He has no choice but to be our friend," said the tall one. "It's in the way he was made."

"He does what he wants," said the young one.

Rigg was merely listening to them, letting them talk to him; Param understood why. He was learning vital information with everything they said. If he probed, he might not learn as much, because they would become more aware of him. Param wished she knew how he had explained who they were, these four who had suddenly appeared inside the stockade. But maybe it didn't matter. Maybe it was enough for these women that the strangers wore no facemasks.

"We can't build the city without him," complained the old woman. "But he won't let us make a wall of fieldsteel—this miserable stockade is all we can make without him. We've depended too much on him! We haven't any skills in our own hands."

Param guessed who "he" was; who but Vadesh himself? No one else could build with fieldsteel; no one else could create a beam of pure heat, then bar the people of the city from using it themselves.

"He does us no good," said the young one. "The city is eternal, but what good is that when we can't defend it?"

"We can't live anywhere else," said the tall one. "Where would we get safe water? We'd become like *them*." Having seen the men with facemasks, Param understood the woman's dread and loathing.

Finally the old woman took notice of Param. "Are you his sister?" she asked.

Param had forgotten how much Rigg resembled her. "I am," she said.

"I wish I could offer help," said Rigg.

The tall woman pointed at the stockade, where Loaf and Olivenko stood. "They look like stout soldiers, and well-armed."

"But inexperienced against such a quick and clever enemy," said Param. "They would be beaten almost at once."

"Where are you from?" asked the old woman suspiciously. "You speak like feeble-minded children."

"Your language is new to us," said Rigg.

"Our language?" said the young woman incredulously. "Is there another? *They* don't speak at all, except the grunting of beasts. Where are you from?"

"Beyond the Wall," said Param.

"The future," said Rigg.

Param found it interesting that while they had chosen different truths to tell, neither she nor Rigg had thought of lying.

It made little difference. The women drew together as they shrank back from Param and Rigg. "Liars," said the old woman.

"Spies," said the young one.

But the tall one, though she was as frightened as the others, still cast a hungry, appraising gaze upon them. "The future? Then you know. Do we win this war?"

Rigg turned to Param and addressed her in the elevated language of the court. "I have learned all that I think we can. Let us get the others."

Param glanced at the women. They had not been through the Wall; they didn't know the language Rigg was using, and it must be frightening to hear speech they couldn't understand. "Aren't you going to answer her?" said Param.

"I don't know the answer."

"We know that the city is empty!"

"But is it *this* war that empties it? Telling her might change things."

"All of her people are dead for ten thousand years. Any change would be better."

"I can think of worse outcomes," said Rigg. He glanced toward the stockade—toward the battle raging beyond the stockade. "What if these people despair, knowing they do not win, and so they give up and *those* people, the afflicted ones, survive?"

"What are you saying?" demanded the old woman.

"That isn't language," said the young one. "It makes no sense."

The tall one now had a knife in her hand, long and sharp. "They're spies." She lunged at Rigg.

Instinctively, Param grabbed Rigg's arm and took a leap toward what she thought of as her "hiding place"—invisibility. But as she did it, she realized she mustn't. If she detached herself and Rigg from the timeflow that the others were in, there was no guarantee that Umbo could bring them back. So she stopped herself in the very moment of her panicky shift.

But she stopped herself too late. The women had already disappeared.

It was night. They stood in ringlight, just herself and Rigg.

She cursed her habit of hiding; she should have pumped her arm, signaling to Umbo to bring them all back, but that would have required thought, and she acted before thought was possible.

Then she realized—her talent didn't work like this. People

didn't disappear when she sliced time, they merely sped up and stopped being able to see her. She couldn't change day into night.

"What did you do?" asked Rigg in a fierce whisper. "When are we?"

"I don't know," she answered, trying to stay calm. "I stopped myself almost at once, we should only have jumped a moment or two."

"We can talk, so we're out of it now, right?" asked Rigg.

"I didn't really go into it. We never disappeared."

"Obviously we *did*," said Rigg. "Vanished right out of their time. But how far, and in which direction?"

"I can't move backward in time, not ever," said Param. "I just make little jumps forward."

"This wasn't a little jump. It got us all the way into night. Or two nights—or a hundred years, into some distant night."

"The stockade is still here," said Param. "And the fires are burning."

They went to the stockade, Rigg holding tightly to her. A few patches of grass were still burning, and there were bodies lying here and there, but there was no more fighting.

"Who won?" asked Param.

"What matters is that we're still in the past. Does that mean Umbo has lost us, or that he still has us? If he lost contact with us, wouldn't we bounce all the way back to Umbo, to the time we came from? Or are we stranded here and he can't find us to bring us back? I wish I understood how any of this works."

But Param had seen something else, not out on the battlefield, but closer to the city. "Rigg, a section of the stockade is down. It's broken through."

"No," said Rigg after a moment, "it was burned through. That bastard betrayed them."

A loud cry sounded in the dim light. It was not language. Nor were the cries that answered it. The shouters were not close by, but neither were they very far.

"I think that answers our question about who won," said Rigg. "Those shouts came from the direction of the city."

"Do you think they've seen us? I think the cries are coming closer."

"I can't see anybody," said Rigg.

"But maybe they can see *us*," said Param. "Those facemasks made them quicker, sped up their reaction time. Maybe it gives them better eyesight, too."

Rigg held up his arm, pumped the air, signaling Umbo.

Nothing happened.

"He's lost us," said Rigg.

"He can't see us," said Param at the same time. She couldn't keep the fear out of her voice, but Rigg seemed so calm.

"Let's get back to the spot where Umbo pushed us into the past," said Rigg. "We jumped half a day into the future, so I should be able to find Loaf's and Olivenko's paths." He drew her away from the stockade.

Now Param could see the facemask men who were shouting. They had clubs and spears and they were running straight toward Rigg and her. It was a terrifying, fascinating sight.

"I think this would be a good time for you to make us disappear," said Rigg.

"But Umbo will lose us!" She knew how stupid that was even as she said it. Umbo had already lost them.

"We won't be able to figure anything out if we're dead," said Rigg. "They have nothing made of metal. Make us disappear."

This time there was no jump, just the sudden silence from the sectioning of time, the mental buzz she always felt.

But the facemask men showed no sign of having lost sight of them. They showed no confusion. They were still coming straight for Param and Rigg, as if she had done nothing at all.

All Param could think to do was push harder, make the buzz more intense and more rapid, so time was getting sliced into thinner bits, and she was leaping forward farther between moments of visibility.

It made the enemy seem to be even faster—far faster—so they were instantly upon them. But to Param's relief the facemask men were confused now, looking around, swinging clubs and jabbing or sweeping with spears. They raced back and forth, some of them running off in different directions to search, some of them remaining in place to stab or slice the air.

Unlike Mother's soldiers, though, they had little staying power. Having lost sight of Param and Rigg, they soon gave up. Well, perhaps not so soon as it appeared to Param, since she was pushing herself and Rigg into the future at a headlong pace, so that the few moments the facemask men kept searching might have been a half hour, an hour, more.

Most of the facemask men went away, but some stayed as

sentinels, and as soon as morning came—only a few minutes, at the pace Param was keeping—the rest came back. Now they knelt and examined the grass, and in only a few moments they had found Rigg's and Param's footprints in the grass. Not the footprints they had left behind them—the grass there had long since sprung back up. What they found were the footprints Param and Rigg were making *right now*, for the grass had little chance to spring back up during the microseconds of their nonexistence between the tiny jumps she was making into the future.

The facemask men probed the footprints. When they used their fingers or clubs, it was not a problem, but the stone heads of the spears could damage her, Param knew. She pressed harder on her sense of time, shoving herself and Rigg farther and farther into the future with each tiny jump, so the stone spear points coexisted in the same space as their feet for ever-shorter slices of time. The buzzing sense was now a deep, rapid throbbing. The day ended, the facemask men were gone. Then it was day again and they did not come back, then night, then day, then night, day, night, day . . .

Gasping, she eased up on the pressure inside herself. Her heart was beating so fast. She was exhausted. She had never pushed herself so hard, not even in the panic coming down from the rock.

They returned to realtime. They could hear again.

The stockade had been knocked over completely, some of the poles broken off just above the ground, but most of them uprooted. They had been shallowly set; it had not taken superhuman strength to put the thing down, especially pushing outward.

The bodies were also gone from the battlefield, and all the fires were out.

"Thank you," murmured Rigg. "I thought we were dead."

"We might as well be," said Param softly. "I've stranded us ten thousand years in the past."

"Minus about five days," said Rigg. "Maybe a week, I'm not sure I was counting right."

"They could have crippled us by holding those stone spear-points in our footprints."

"In our feet, you mean," said Rigg. "It was the strangest feeling. *My* feet were getting hot."

Then Param, who had been scanning the battlefield and the city while they talked—as Rigg was also doing—spotted Vadesh. He was standing where the gap in the stockade had been, surveying the battlefield just as Param and Rigg had been doing.

Rigg must have seen him, too, because he gripped her hand tightly. "Don't call to him," he murmured. "He's never seen us before."

Of course he hadn't. The Vadesh of this era would have no idea who they were.

But talking softly had done them no good. The machine had been made with extraordinarily acute hearing. He was walking toward them.

"Turn your back on him," said Rigg. "Don't let him see our faces."

"I have seen your faces," Vadesh called. After the silence of time-slicing, his voice was shockingly loud. "I will never forget them."

"Umbo's lost us, or we've lost him," said Rigg. "And the only paths I can see are here, where you and Olivenko and Loaf stood looking at the battle. But Umbo can't see us, so he can't push us back into the past to rejoin them."

"Can you see the moment where Umbo took them into the future?" asked Param. "Maybe if you hold on to the path right at that point . . ."

"I can't *hold* a path," said Rigg. "I don't even *see* them, not really, not with my eyes, I just know where they are, I—I can't *touch* them."

"But you can, when Umbo . . . you have to try."

Rigg reached out his hand. "Here's where Olivenko was when his path jumps away. But I don't know how he was standing. Was his arm here? Here?"

Vadesh was hearing everything they said. No wonder, when they showed up in the far future, he knew all about their ability to move through time. "Vadesh is almost here," Param said.

"I know, but this isn't working." He kept moving his hand, trying to make some kind of contact. "I'd rather not have a conversation with the traitor who got all the uninfected humans killed."

"They aren't dead," said Vadesh, still calling from some distance away. Could he hear even the slightest whisper? "They fled the city as the natives entered it."

"Don't argue with him," said Param.

"He calls them natives," whispered Rigg angrily. "Because they have that native parasite."

"At least he doesn't think they're human," said Param.

"But they *are*, and better than human," said Vadesh, who was now close enough to speak loudly instead of shouting. "Didn't you see how quick and clever they were on the battlefield?"

"Native *and* human," said Rigg. "Come on, Umbo, see us, take us."

To Param it sounded as if Rigg was praying. "This isn't working, he can't see us, so try something else."

"There *is* nothing else."

"No," said Param. Her mind was racing. "When the woman tried to stab you, it wasn't *me* that made us jump forward in time to the middle of the night, and it wasn't Umbo because he would have brought us back to the time we came from."

Rigg was looking at her, listening. But clearly he didn't understand. Or didn't want to understand.

"It was you," said Param. "The knife was coming at you, and you jumped away. But in time, not in space."

"I can't do that. It's Umbo who does that."

"No, *you* do it—you're the one who finds the other time, who pulls us to it. Or at least you join him in doing it. Your body's been learning how to do it even if your mind doesn't understand it or control it yet. But you can do it."

"I've tried. My whole voyage downriver I tried, and—"

She didn't have time for his chat about despair. She remembered how the Gardener—the expendable named Ram—had helped her find her own timesense. "Stop talking and listen," she said, using the voice Mother had always used to command instant attention. "You feel it in your nose, like the beginning of a sneeze or the start of wanting to weep. But then it draws down, through your throat, down your breastbone, then down through your stomach to your groin. You draw it tight with your diaphragm, as if you were straining to lift something. Draw it *tight*. Only pull your nose down and your groin up with it."

He looked baffled and confused as she talked. Clearly Ram hadn't taught him this, maybe because with Rigg's gift it wouldn't work. But he had to do it—her gift wouldn't get them away from Vadesh because he was a machine and he had heard everything they said, he'd know that if he just waited long enough he'd see them again. Rigg had to get them away, and so all she could do was try to help him get control of the power he had used to jump away from the knife.

She started to repeat the instructions and this time he tried to obey her. She could see tears starting in his eyes, just as they had in hers when she was first learning. A quivering in the muscles beside his nose, a twitching of the lower eyelids. And a clenching of his belly, a slight bend to his body.

His hand was still in midair, trembling, where he expected to find Olivenko.

Vadesh was nearly upon them, smiling, smiling, smiling.

"I can see him," whispered Rigg. His hand moved.

And then Param could see that there was a sleeve in Rigg's hand. No arm, just a sleeve. But then the arm was there, and in that instant it became Olivenko, turning now to face them, and there was Loaf, also turning, and the sounds of battle came back again, the stench of war, and Vadesh was gone.

Rigg didn't hesitate, he turned his head back toward where Umbo had been. Rigg gave a vigorous nod, then cast his chin high, then nodded forward again. Param realized: He's not going to give the hand signal because that would require him to let go either of her or of Olivenko.

But what if their jaunt to the week after the battle had made them invisible to Umbo? What if they were lost to him no matter what they did?

"Give Umbo the signal!" Param shouted to Loaf, to Olivenko.

But before they could obey her, the stockade was gone, and the stink, and the noise. It was a quiet morning again. Umbo was right where he should be. The city had all its tallest towers again. And Param and Rigg were both there with the others.

"Ram's left elbow," exclaimed Rigg in his relief.

"No, it's *my* left elbow you've got," said Olivenko. "Where did you come from? I thought you were over talking to those women."

"You disappeared," said Loaf. "I thought Param had done whatever it is she does."

"No," said Param. "I almost did, but I stopped myself."

"But I felt you slip out of my control," said Umbo. "Like having a loose tooth pull away. I'd been holding you so tightly, it hurt when you vanished. I lost you."

"I know," said Rigg, and then he grinned foolishly. "Umbo, it was me. Param figured it out. I've been learning how to jump without even realizing it. I *felt* what you were doing, I think I was even helping, but I didn't know how to *make* it happen only I did by reflex, when she tried to stab me."

"Param?" asked Loaf, alarmed.

"No, the woman we were talking to, we scared her, she was

in the middle of a war, she was armed, so of course she tried to kill me—but I jumped us forward half a day. But I didn't know it was me, I thought Param had done it somehow. I couldn't do it again. So then she did rush us forward a week, and I thought we were completely lost. But Vadesh saw us. The Vadesh of the past. That's how he knew us again, now, yesterday anyway. Because he was coming toward us while Param was telling me how to get control of it, of this thing you do, *we* do—"

"Could you possibly be a little more incoherent?" asked Olivenko. "There are bits of this I'm almost understanding, and I'm sure that's not what you have in mind."

"I got control of it," said Rigg. "I had Olivenko's path, and I was doing what Param said, and then I saw him, I took his sleeve, his arm, he became *real* and—"

"And that's when I saw the two of you appear by Loaf and Olivenko," said Umbo. "Only to me it looked as if you jumped. I felt you slip away from me, and then suddenly there you were."

"Only in the meantime we had been to the next week and back again," said Rigg. Rigg was almost jumping out of his skin, he was so excited, and Param understood now how much it must have bothered him that he could only turn paths into time travel with Umbo's help.

Yet it seemed to her that he had learned it very quickly. Maybe he'd been learning it unconsciously from Umbo, but he got control of it the very first time he tried the things that the Gardener had taught her. It had taken her *weeks* and he got it with the first lesson.

Which meant that Ram, when he was tramping the woods

with Rigg for years and years, teaching him everything else, had never once tried to teach him how to take hold of a path and make it real. He had taught Umbo and he had taught Param, but the boy who thought Ram was his father, Ram had taught *him* nothing.

"They're all lying snakes," she said.

The others looked at her. "The men with those facemasks on them?" asked Loaf.

"How could they lie?" asked Rigg. "They can't even talk."

Umbo had understood her, though. "She means the expendables. Vadesh and Ram. Your father, Rigg."

"All I gave you was the first fifteen seconds of the very first lesson your so-called father gave me when he first started teaching me to control my timesense," said Param. "Why didn't he give *you* those fifteen seconds?"

Rigg's excitement gave way to realization. "He taught me everything he *wanted* me to know."

"Just like Vadesh," said Param. "They think they're gods, they think they have the right to just *decide*, regardless of what we want or need—they think they know best about everything."

"Maybe they do," said Olivenko.

Param whirled on him. "Yes, just like Mother, she thought she knew best—she thought she had the right to kill me, the way Vadesh betrayed the people of the city—"

"He did what?" asked Loaf.

"He burned a gap in the stockade," said Rigg. "He let the facemask people drive the uninfected ones out of the city. He chose one side over the other and it was the parasites he chose. He calls them 'natives' but he claims they're still human."

"Does it matter?" asked Olivenko. "They're all dead now."

"He picked," said Param angrily, "and he chose the parasites over the human race."

"We can't trust him," said Rigg.

"But we already didn't trust him," said Olivenko.

"Now we *know* he's our enemy," said Param.

"At least now Rigg can go into the past without me," said Umbo. But it seemed to Param that he wasn't entirely happy about it.

"I could never have gotten us back to the present," said Rigg. "I can only go into the past where there are paths I can hook onto. How would I get back into the future without you to anchor us?"

Param realized what was going on. Umbo was feeling unneeded and Rigg was trying to reassure him. But the more Rigg said, the angrier Umbo seemed to be getting. Or maybe he wasn't angry. Maybe he was just hurt. Maybe he hated having Rigg reassure him.

"We're all talented and we still need each other," said Param, trying to stop them.

"Not all of us," said Olivenko. "Loaf and I are completely talent-free, when it comes to time."

"Except that I've lived through a lot more of it than any of you," said Loaf.

"Is everybody going to be offended or embarrassed because they don't have everybody else's ability?" demanded Param. "None of us knows what we're doing. We're all still learning, we all still need each other, and we're up against this expendable who apparently likes monsters more than humans."

"And here he comes," said Olivenko. His glance made them all look in the same direction. Vadesh was crossing the lawn toward them, just as he had done ten thousand years in the past, the week after the battle.

"Careful," said Param softly. "He can hear every word we say, even at this distance."

"Then he'll understand my contempt for him," said Loaf.

"Oh, I do!" called Vadesh. "But now you know why I was so happy to see you cross through the Wall! I've been waiting ten thousand years for you! And Ram refused to tell me anything about you when I asked him. Of course, until you were born he might not have *known* anything. It just occurred to me—maybe my inquiries were the reason he started looking for people with the power to manipulate time. Wouldn't that be wonderfully paradoxical? I met you, I asked Ram about you, and because of my questions, he started manipulating the bloodlines until you were born! I think perhaps I created you! Isn't that amusing?"

"Ha ha," said Loaf. "And you know what's really funny?"

By now Vadesh was almost there with them. "Please tell me," he said.

"You still don't get it that maybe the reason Ram wouldn't tell you anything is that you managed to get all the humans in your wallfold *killed*."

Vadesh reached out and knocked Loaf down. Flicked him, or so it seemed, with a casual brush of his hand, and Loaf staggered backward and fell. When he got up he clutched his left shoulder, where Vadesh had hit him, and he was panting from the pain.

"It's not broken," said Vadesh. "I don't damage human beings.

I don't kill them. We expendables *can't* kill people. Why do you think I only burned the grass between the armies?"

"But people died," said Olivenko.

"People killed *each other,*" said Vadesh. "But I never did."

"Just the way you didn't damage *me,*" said Loaf savagely. "You were just telling me to shut up, is that it?"

"And yet you still didn't get the message," said Vadesh with a smile. "Why did the smart ones bother to bring you along?"

Loaf became even more furious, but he had felt the power of Vadesh's blow—Param watched him restrain himself.

"Very good," said Vadesh. "Slow, but he does learn."

"You've made your point," said Rigg. "You're stronger than we are. You can knock us around. But we can get away from you whenever we want. So I suggest that you never hit any of us again, or we're gone."

Vadesh looked genuinely stricken—but what did any of his humanlike expressions mean? He was as false as Mother; yet, just as with Mother, Param couldn't keep herself from responding to him as if he were a real person, with real feelings. When he looked so hurt at Rigg's words, Param found herself wanting to reassure him.

"Just tell us what you want from us," said Param. "Then we'll decide if we want to give it to you."

"And I'll decide if I want to give you more water," said Vadesh.

"And we'll decide if we want to go back to a time before you and your kind ever got to this world, cross back through the Wall, and never let you anywhere near us again," said Rigg.

Vadesh's smile never wavered. "Stalemate," he said. "Come

back into the city and you can have all the safe water you want. Then I'll tell you what I need from you, and you can decide what you want to do about it. What could be more fair than that?"

"Coming from a genocidal traitor," said Param, "I think that's a generous offer."

She half expected him to give her the same little flick of violence that Loaf had been subjected to. But he only winked at her. "You can't hurt my feelings," he said. "I don't have any."

But to Param it seemed that his violence against Loaf could only be explained by hurt feelings. Vadesh lashed out when Loaf taunted him for getting all the humans in his wallfold killed. Whatever Vadesh might be, he didn't like being accused of . . . genocide? Or failure? Whatever it was that provoked him, it was clear that he *could* be provoked, and by words alone. He was dangerous, and they all knew it now.

We fear him. Maybe that's the new tool he created to manipulate us, when we could no longer be deceived. So maybe he wasn't provoked after all. Maybe he merely switched from spoon to fork, whatever utensil was appropriate for the dish he'd been served.

Just like Mother, just like most of the powerful people she had known all her life. And if there was one thing Param had learned, it was this: She couldn't win a game against an opponent who could change the rules whenever things didn't go his way. All Param had ever been able to do was stop playing.

So she disappeared.

CHAPTER 5
Decisions

To Rigg, Param was not invisible—he still knew exactly where she was, because her path was new and clear. That was how he had first discovered her, back in the house where their mother lived as a royal captive. Now, though, he made a point of not looking at her path, at the place where he knew she was, because he didn't want Vadesh to have the option of moving his metal-threaded body into the same space she was flashing in and out of. Rigg wasn't sure how much metal the body of an expendable contained, but it didn't take much to do serious harm to Param.

"I know where she is," said Vadesh to Rigg. "I have a perfect sense of time, and I know exactly how far she could have gone by now, even running."

Rigg looked at Loaf, Olivenko, and Umbo. "Param made her own decision, it seems."

"She's going to get thirsty," said Umbo.

"I don't like splitting up," said Loaf. "We can't help each other then."

"One thing is certain," said Rigg. "We need to organize ourselves differently."

He sensed Umbo growing stiff, resistant. Resentful.

"I agree with you completely, Umbo," said Rigg.

"I didn't say anything!" Umbo protested.

"When we started out, I was the one with the money. The jewels."

"Still got 'em," said Loaf.

"Do you want them?" asked Rigg. "You've had them before. I'll give them back to you."

"No!" said Vadesh sharply, before Loaf could answer.

"You're not in this discussion," said Rigg. "We can't make you go away, and we couldn't stop you from listening even if you left, but we're not interested in your viewpoint, because as far as we can tell, you're the enemy."

"Those wild facemasks are the enemy," said Vadesh.

"You're their ally," said Loaf.

"Please, let's none of us respond to him, including me," said Rigg. "I was making a point."

"Wouldn't want to interrupt your point-making," said Umbo.

Rigg ignored Umbo's dig, for now. "It made sense for me to pretend to be in charge at first because of the subterfuge we were using," said Rigg. "Pretending I was a rich young heir and you were my attendants."

"Oh, we were *pretending*," murmured Umbo.

"Then I was captured, and Umbo and Loaf—you were on your own and you came to Aressa Sessamo to help me, and I'm grateful. I met Olivenko and brought him into our strange set of problems, and Param is my sister and she was in as much danger as I was. But at the end of it all, what I can't figure out is why I should be in charge."

"You're not," said Umbo defiantly.

"I'm relieved," said Rigg. "The trouble is that Loaf and Olivenko defer to me whenever there's a decision to be made. Which makes sense, because even though they're the oldest and one of them should definitely be in charge, they don't have any power over time, and they spend most of their energy sniping at each other anyway."

"*He* does," said Olivenko.

"You think you're so smart," said Loaf.

"Thank you for demonstrating my point," said Rigg. "It's asinine for the two of you to keep this stupid rivalry alive. Regular army against city guard—who cares? Loaf retired years ago and began two new careers—innkeeper and Leaky's husband. Olivenko only joined the guard because his career as a scholar was wrecked when my father—my real father—died. An innkeeper and a scholar—but both of you large and strong and well-enough-trained to make anyone think twice about fighting you unless they seriously outnumber you."

Loaf said, "He wouldn't scare a—"

"Yes he would," said Rigg. "Can't you hear what I'm saying? Grow up, both of you, act like adults, and take charge of this expedition."

"We can't," said Olivenko. "Not him *or* me."

"Can so," said Loaf. "Just don't want to."

Rigg glared at Loaf, who rolled his eyes like a teenage boy and looked away.

"It's actually possible for each of you to allow the other to speak without contradicting him," said Rigg. "The fact that you don't seem to know this is why I've had to stay in charge, despite Umbo's resentment."

"I don't resent—" began Umbo.

"'I wouldn't want to interrupt your point-making,'" Rigg quoted him. "'Oh, we were pretending.' I agree with you, Umbo. I have no right to lead, and I'm tired of it anyway."

"Your father trained you to," said Umbo grudgingly.

"Everything he trained me for has already happened," said Rigg. "I got to Aressa Sessamo, I got my sister out of the house, and then with your help she and I got out of the wallfold before General Citizen and our loving mother could kill us. Beyond that, I don't know what the expendable called Ram had in mind and I don't care, because what matters now is what *we* have in mind. Only I don't have anything in mind. The past few weeks have been all about survival and nothing else."

"I thought you wanted to find out what happened to Knosso Sissamik," said Olivenko.

"I do," said Rigg, "but not so much that I think it's worth dying for. I want to get out of this wallfold, that's for certain, because I don't trust Vadesh here any farther than I can piss, and even on a windless day that's not far."

"Where, then?" asked Olivenko. "Back to Ramfold?"

"No," said Rigg. "I mean, *you're* welcome to, but Param and I can't."

"I can't go anywhere," said Olivenko. "Unless one of you time changers takes me."

"Maybe Umbo will take you," said Rigg. "He proved a long time ago that he doesn't need me to time travel."

"And you just can't get over it, can you?" said Umbo.

Rigg heard him and despaired. "Your ability saved my life. Saved my sister's life. Saved all of us. I admit I felt weak and foolish when you could do it without me, and I couldn't do it without you. But now we're even."

"Oh, definitely," said Umbo. "You can go back eleven thousand years, and I can barely manage six months, which doesn't get me through the Wall."

"And you can stay rooted in the present and always come right back to the time you left," said Rigg. "We're different, and we're both *amazing*. Now I'm telling you I don't want to be anybody's boss, all right? You be boss now. It's your party."

"Not me," said Umbo. "I don't want to be in charge of anything."

"I know the feeling," said Rigg.

"It seems to me you need impartial leadership," said Vadesh.

Rigg didn't even glance in his direction. "Loaf?"

"I admit I want to go home."

"Then go. Please," said Rigg. "You've already done far more than I ever hoped for. Leaky needs you."

"If I don't bring the two of you back to Leaky so I can prove you're all right, my life won't be worth a piece of bread surrounded by crows."

"Why do we need anyone in charge?" asked Umbo. "Why

can't we just stay together as long as we feel like it, and split up when we feel like it?"

"Fine with me," said Olivenko.

"Because you're a scholar," said Loaf. "I'm not picking a fight here, I'm just saying that one thing I learned in the army, either we're together or we're not. We need to know we can count on everybody who's with us, or go it alone."

Rigg buried his face in his hands. "You're probably right but I'm just so tired of feeling *responsible* for everybody."

"You've never been responsible for me!" Umbo said, leaping to his feet.

"Yes I have!" Rigg shouted back at him. "It's my fault you had to run away from home. My fault you had to go to Aressa Sessamo, my fault you had to flee the wallfold, my fault you're thirsty and under the power of this talking machine."

"I made my own choices," said Umbo stubbornly.

"It's still my responsibility to make things right," said Rigg, "but I'm not up to it, I can't do it, I don't even know what 'right' is anymore."

"*I* know," said Vadesh. "I tried to tell my people but they wouldn't listen. I did what I had to do."

"Param made a choice, all on her own," said Rigg. "Without asking me. Which means she really isn't my responsibility now."

"She's your sister," said Loaf.

"She's Knosso's daughter," said Olivenko.

"But not my *responsibility*," said Rigg.

"I'm beginning to get the idea you don't want to be in charge anymore," said Loaf.

Rigg nodded wearily. "Communication is finally being achieved."

"All right," said Loaf. "Then I'll be in charge. I say we follow this self-powered puppet to the water and drink up while we hear what he has to say. Everybody agree with that?"

"Yes," said Olivenko. He shot a look at Rigg, as if to say, See? I can agree with Loaf.

"Fine," said Umbo. "I'm thirsty."

"No," said Rigg.

They all looked at him in consternation.

"Oh, it's the right plan," said Rigg, "and Loaf's in charge. It just felt good to be wrong and have it not matter. Param can follow or not, as she chooses."

Vadesh, who was still standing close by, seemed a little perplexed. "So you're going to do what I asked?"

"Yes," said Loaf.

"Then what was all the discussion about?"

Loaf just shook his head. "It's a human thing."

"You're not really very smart," said Umbo to Vadesh.

"He's just pretending not to understand us," said Rigg.

"I think he never understood humans at all," said Olivenko.

"Oh, you're right about that," said Vadesh. "But I know that if you don't get water you'll die, and I have water for you, as much as you want, so let's go."

He sounded so cheerful. He sounded just like Father. I cannot let myself trust him, Rigg reminded himself. He isn't Father. Father wasn't even Father. They're all liars.

But following this face, this man, answering his questions,

doing what he said—that was how Rigg had spent his entire childhood, his whole life until a year ago. To follow him again felt right; it was the feeling Rigg imagined other people referred to when they spoke of "coming home."

Back in the same room in the factory, they drank their fill, recharged their canteens and water bags, said little as Vadesh said much. He talked about the days when the city had been productive.

"We kept the technology of the starships, as best we could. Not that we flew anywhere—air travel was too dangerous, what with the Wall. You couldn't see it, so if a pilot strayed too near, he could go mad and crash the plane."

Rigg tried to make sense of humans flying and decided that "plane" was a sort of flying carriage. Or boat, since it had a pilot. A flying boat. Would it have to fight the winds the way boats had to struggle upstream on a great river?

But he said nothing, for his project at the moment was trying to learn the way Vadesh thought, since it might help them get out of Vadeshfold safely. And it wasn't just Vadesh. He was only the second expendable that Rigg had known, and there were things Rigg needed to learn about them. Every wallfold had an expendable, so he would be facing the equivalent of Vadesh or Ram in every one.

The expendables can make us rely on them, need them, love them, thought Rigg. Yet they can also lead us to our own destruction, as Vadesh did with the uninfected humans of the city. Had Father been manipulating humans the same ruthless way? Am I his son, or merely a particularly talented human with royal blood who could be manipulated to cause destruction? Maybe Ram was as careless with human life in his wallfold as Vadesh was in this one. In which case perhaps I should untrain myself, and refuse to see the world as Father trained me to see it.

Or perhaps Father, knowing I would face someone—some*thing*—like Vadesh, trained me precisely to be able to learn from and overcome a monster like this.

If only Vadesh didn't look exactly like Father.

"But Rigg is too important to listen," said Vadesh.

"I'm listening," said Rigg.

Vadesh said nothing.

Rigg repeated back to him what he had just said. "This city was designed by human engineers. All these achievements were human."

"You did not seem to pay attention," said Vadesh.

"I was thinking that it seems very important to you that we understand that everything here was done by humans. At first I thought you meant 'human as opposed to you.' But now I see that by 'humans' you meant 'humans possessed by facemasks.'"

"Not possessed!" cried Vadesh. "Augmented! It was what we hoped for at the beginning, what the great Ram Odin told us our work should be—to combine the life of this world with the life that humans brought with them."

"So this is really the great city of the facemasks," said Olivenko.

"Of humans whose senses were sharpened and intensified by facemasks," insisted Vadesh.

"I thought you said that facemasks returned humans to a primitive state, all war and reproduction," said Olivenko.

"At first. And in the weaker humans, yes, that was a permanent condition. But some humans were strong enough to overmaster the facemasks. And some facemasks were able to learn the civilized virtues. Self-restraint. Discipline. Forethought. Guilt."

"Guilt!" said Loaf. "What were they guilty of? They were owned by animals. Ridden by them."

"Guilt is a civilizing virtue," said Vadesh patiently.

Father had taught Rigg the same thing. "Guilt is how a person punishes himself in advance," said Rigg. "Before he commits the act, and afterward, even though no one else detected his crime."

"It makes people self-policing," said Vadesh. "The more people feel guilt, the more easily they live together in large numbers."

"So the facemasks learned guilt," said Loaf. "They still killed all the uninfected humans."

"They didn't!" said Vadesh. "Why do you think they did? They *defended* themselves."

"Until the last normal human was dead," said Loaf.

"No and no and no," said Vadesh. "It was the uninfected, as you call them—I think of them as invaders from Earth—"

"Like you?" suggested Umbo.

"Invaders from Earth," repeated Vadesh, "who returned to the city again and again until they murdered every man, woman, and child of the native people."

"They were not native," said Umbo. "They were *captives*."

"They were a new native life form, half human, half facemask," said Vadesh. "It was a beautiful blending—painful and frightening at first, for both, but then a fruition of both. As if they were trees that could not bear until they pollinated each other."

"You're a poet of parasitism," said Rigg. "Are these the stories you told the possessed people, to convince them they were even better than humans or facemasks alone?"

"It's the simple truth," said Vadesh.

"And yet the people without facemasks were not persuaded," said Rigg.

"Here's a thought," said Umbo. "What if the facemasks let go of the people they possessed, so the people could see how much better it was when they had the parasite? Then they could take them back by their own free choice. Or not."

"Impossible," said Vadesh.

"So you admit they would never choose to take the facemasks back," said Loaf.

"Impossible to detach them. Both would die."

"I don't believe you," said Rigg. "I think the facemask would die, but the human would return to health."

"Both would die," repeated Vadesh. "The bond cannot be undone. It was fatal to both. Always. Do you think we didn't try, at first?"

"I'd think that the ability to detach would be the first civilizing virtue you'd get the facemasks to acquire."

"They tried," said Vadesh. "As they incorporated the genes they harvested from their human hosts, each new generation was more compatible. They needed humans more, preserved more of human nature. But the one thing they could not do was make themselves less effective as parasites."

Rigg looked at Loaf, Umbo, Olivenko. "Finally, an honest sentence—Vadesh admits that the facemasks are parasites."

"Of course they're parasites," said Vadesh. "I was the one who warned you not to drink from the stream, wasn't I? I didn't want you infected."

"Where is all this leading?" asked Loaf. "What do you want from us?"

"I want you to bring humans back to my wallfold," said Vadesh.

"So you can infect them again?"

"No," said Vadesh. "Do you think I failed to learn the lesson of the past? Humans do not respond well to seeing other humans parasitized. They think of them as monsters, they destroy them to the last man, and then die out themselves, for fear of becoming infected."

"They died out?" asked Loaf.

"They killed each other," said Rigg bitterly. "When they were sure they had killed the last facemask-controlled person, they killed themselves—"

"Each other," said Vadesh.

"Collectively killed themselves," said Rigg, "so there was no chance that their keeper here could breed them with more facemasks."

"They didn't understand that I would never do that," said Vadesh. "I am incapable of harming human beings."

"But you can *let* them come to harm. Goad them to it, trap them. Aid their enemies."

"Humans must be free," said Vadesh. "It is deeply ingrained in my programming. I cannot defy that. All choices are to be made by humans. I merely help them carry out their plans."

Rigg could not let that stand. "You are such a liar," he said. "I was raised by one of you, and he was certainly not carrying out anybody's plan."

"He wasn't carrying out *your* plan, you mean," said Vadesh.

"Nor mine," said Umbo.

"Nor the plans of General Citizen and Hagia Sessamin," said Olivenko. "So whose plan was he carrying out?"

"Neither of us controls the other," said Vadesh. "But we started out with the same directives—given to us by humans. Our original programmers, and then Ram Odin. He gave us a great work to do. The expendable Ram pursued it his way in your natal wallfold, and I pursued it as best I could here in this wallfold. I made mistakes. I misunderstood the depth of the human fear of the strange and new. They could not be reasoned with."

"Meaning you couldn't find them all and kill them," said Rigg.

"I killed no one," said Vadesh.

"But you found them," said Umbo. "And told the facemask people where they were, so *they* could kill them."

"I wanted them reconciled!"

"But 'killed' was almost as good," said Rigg. "They were waging a war of extermination, and you weighed in on the side of those who were only half human."

"There are safeguards now," said Vadesh. "I've worked hard. Ten thousand years I've been breeding facemasks until all the obnoxious traits are gone. Humans would remain fully human, in charge of themselves."

"We are never going to put on your facemasks," said Rigg.

"But you haven't even seen them!"

"What we need from you," said Rigg, "and what I order you to give us, is information about the jewels. How do they work? How can we use them to shut down the Walls?"

Vadesh looked away—a gesture Father often used, to give the illusion of thinking things over. But it was only an illusion, Rigg understood that now. The mechanical mind made its decisions very quickly, and all this business of "thinking" was part of the pretense that the expendables were similar to humans. But they were nothing like humans.

"It seems to me," said Rigg, "that you want us to think this is all about two species—facemasks and humans. But there's a third species involved."

Rigg's friends looked at him, confused.

Vadesh understood him, though. "Expendables are not a species," he said.

"Aren't you?"

"We are not alive. We do not reproduce."

"No, but you replace any parts that wear out," said Rigg. "You don't have to reproduce if you never die."

"We are here to support and enhance human life," said Vadesh.

The others laughed or hooted bitterly.

"Maybe that was your original law," said Rigg, "but you proved that enhancing human life is the opposite of what you actually have in mind."

"The facemasks eventually *did* enhance human life," said Vadesh. "That was my great insight, when I finally understood it."

"Humans are the only fit judges of what enhances our lives," said Olivenko.

"I see that now," said Vadesh. "I've learned. Do you think I don't understand that I failed here? All the humans preferred murder and death, do you think I regard that as *success*? That's why I beg you to bring humans back here, so I can undo my terrible mistakes."

"You have the power to bring down the Wall," said Rigg. "You expendables put it there, didn't you?"

"We each have the power to shut down our own protective field. But the Wall consists of two fields, pushed up against each other. I could make the Wall half as wide, but I could not bring it down."

"Unless the other expendables agreed with you," said Rigg. "But they didn't, did they?"

Vadesh once again said nothing.

"Silence from you is a lie," said Rigg.

"They would not let me import a new population," said Vadesh.

"If the other expendables regard you as so much of a failure that you can't be trusted with more people," said Rigg, "why should we contradict their superior wisdom?"

"Expendables must bow to the will of humans," said Vadesh. "You can contradict us whenever you want."

"Millions of people must have wished they could get through the Wall," said Loaf. "It never came down for them."

"Wishes are not informed decisions," said Vadesh.

Rigg chuckled. "But who can possibly inform us, except you expendables?"

"Exactly," said Vadesh.

"So we only know what you tell us," said Rigg. "Which means that by choosing what to tell, you can shape our decision however you want."

"And how did Ram shape *your* decisions?" asked Vadesh.

Rigg and his companions were not pretending; they had to think about it.

"He sent us to the Wall," said Umbo.

"He prepared us to come through it," said Rigg.

"So both he and I," said Vadesh, "wanted humans to come through the Wall."

"No," said Rigg. "Father wanted us to have power over the Wall—and other things. Maybe he wanted to trigger General Citizen's revolt against the People's Revolutionary Council. But he never did anything to suggest he wanted us to come to *you*."

"I'm what's beyond your Wall!"

"In this direction," said Rigg. "But we saw the globe in the Tower of O. If we had gone through the Wall in a different place, we might have come to a different wallfold."

"But you came to this one. Did Ram turn you away from here? He knew you might come, and that if you did, you'd talk to me, and he did nothing to warn you against me, did he?"

"Oh, he warned me well enough," said Rigg. "He taught me to notice when I'm being lied to and manipulated, and to resist it."

"Show us how to shut down the Wall," said Loaf.

Rigg looked at him, startled. It felt like betrayal.

"I want to shut down the Wall," said Loaf. "These Walls have kept the human race divided into little pieces. In this wallfold, the human race wiped itself out. Who knows what happened in the other seventeen? It's time for the Walls to come down so we can inform *ourselves*."

"If we bring down the Wall," said Olivenko, "people will come here and be infected by the facemasks."

"We warn them," said Loaf. "Filtered water only. They'll find a way. People always do."

"We don't know enough yet," said Rigg. "We can't just bring down the Wall when we don't know what people will find in the other wallfolds."

Loaf laughed at him. "You say you don't want responsibility, but here you are appointing yourself as the guardian of the whole human race."

"They murdered Knosso in the wallfold he crossed into," said Olivenko.

"Murder, massacre, warfare, disease, parasites," said Loaf. "It's the world. We should have the freedom of it. But no, Rigg thinks he can decide everything for everybody, keep everybody safe until *he* decides the human race is ready. Tell me, Rigg, how are you different from these expendables? Except that you're not as well-informed?"

"You can't just—"

But Loaf was not disposed to listen. "I can. You're not in charge, remember? Each of us can go off on our own, if we want."

"I thought you said we should stay together," said Olivenko.

"Until it no longer makes sense," said Loaf. "The rest of you can stay with each other—I advise it. You'll be safer. But I want to get back through the Wall. I want to go home to Leaky. But then maybe I'll come back. This is a vast empty land. It's not just this city, it's the whole wallfold. Who knows what could be built here? Vadesh is a lying snake, but the more people who come, the less attention we'll have to pay to him. He wants the Wall to come down so immigrants can come in? So do I."

Vadesh made an elaborate shrugging motion. "But it's not just a person I need. It's the jewels."

Loaf looked at Rigg and held out his hand.

Rigg wanted to say, No, they're mine, Father gave them to me, they're my inheritance! But he knew he had no right to keep Loaf here against his will. So he drew out the bag with the stones and handed it to Loaf.

Loaf opened the bag and poured out the jewels into his hand.

"Ah," said Vadesh. "This one is the key to Vadeshfold." He picked up a pale yellow stone. "With this, a human can turn off this wallfield."

"*This* wallfield is only half the Wall," said Loaf.

"The other stone isn't here," said Vadesh. "The one that shuts down the field protecting Ramfold."

"The one we sold," said Rigg, realizing.

"The one that the People's Council stole from us," said Loaf.

"This one?" asked Umbo. He opened his hand, and there in his palm lay a light blue teardrop-shaped stone. Just like the one that Rigg had entrusted to Mr. Cooper, the banker in O.

"Where did you get that?" asked Olivenko.

"After all the times we tried to break into the bank to get it back, you had it all along?" said Loaf.

Now Rigg put things together. "He found it yesterday, when we first arrived."

"It was just lying there at the edge of the woods where we slept," said Umbo. "I picked it up." He turned to Rigg. "You saw me, but you didn't even ask me what it was."

"I figured you'd tell me when it mattered," said Rigg. "And you did."

"So much for Rigg always trying to be in charge of everything," said Olivenko.

"I never said that!" said Umbo.

"Yes you did," said Olivenko. "About a hundred times, in a hundred ways."

"It doesn't matter," said Rigg. "Is that the right stone?"

Vadesh looked at it, then handed it to Loaf, pairing it with the yellow one from Vadeshfold. "These are the two you'll need to bring down the Wall between Ramfold and Vadeshfold."

"You put it there," said Rigg. "For Umbo to find."

"I did not," said Vadesh. "I couldn't."

"Don't all the expendables have a complete set of all the jewels?" asked Rigg. "This is one of yours."

"You couldn't use any of mine," said Vadesh. "They can only be used by humans who grew up in the same wallfold as the jewels. They imprint on you. What would be the point of leaving one of my jewels for you to find? This jewel is from the Ramfold set."

Vadesh spoke so confidently. Yet he seemed untroubled by the question of how the jewel got from Ramfold to this grove of trees. "Who put it there?" Rigg demanded of the others. It was plain Vadesh was not going to tell them, even if he knew, which he probably did.

"Maybe *you* did," said Olivenko.

"Me?" said Rigg. "I didn't have it!"

"Maybe you came back from the future, when you *do* have it, and you put it there," said Olivenko. "Isn't that possible?"

"Or Umbo did," said Rigg. "And put it where he knew that he alone would find it."

"But that would mean that in the future, I go back to Ramfold, somehow get the jewel, and then come back here and leave it for myself," said Umbo. "Why?"

"We'll never know," said Loaf. "Because that version of the future is destroyed by the very fact that you now have the missing jewel, so you won't have to go get it."

"Why didn't I *hand* it to myself, with an explanation?" asked Umbo. "At least I could have left myself a note."

"You'll have to take that up with yourself, later," said Loaf. "What matters is, I have the power in my hands now to bring down the Wall and go home." Loaf rose to his feet and faced Vadesh, looming over him. Loaf was big enough that this move no doubt intimidated most men, but Rigg didn't imagine Vadesh was all that impressed.

"Come with me," said Vadesh. "You can control the Wall now."

"Where are you taking him?" demanded Rigg.

"I thought you weren't in charge," said Olivenko.

"I'm still his friend," said Rigg. "A friend demands to know where you're taking him."

"Into the starship," said Vadesh. "Inside the mountain."

CHAPTER 6

Inside the Starship

"I'm coming with you," said Rigg.

Umbo was not surprised. Rigg might talk about how he was tired of being in charge, but he would never stop thinking that everything was his business.

But Rigg was right, too. Whatever Vadesh had in mind, Loaf should not go alone with him into the mountain, into the starship. Only it wasn't Rigg who should go with him, it was Umbo, who had been Loaf's companion during all the time that Rigg was in captivity.

"I'll do it," said Umbo. "Not you."

Rigg looked at him steadily. "Someone should stay outside, so that whatever happens in there doesn't happen to everybody."

"Then you stay outside," said Umbo.

"I'm happy to stay outside," said Olivenko. "I can wait for Param Sissaminka and explain what's happening."

"Good idea," said Umbo.

"Except that first somebody needs to explain to *me* what's happening," said Olivenko.

"Umbo and I are going into the starship with Loaf and Vadesh," said Rigg.

"For once can't I do something without children tagging along?" said Loaf.

Umbo felt slapped.

"I think I should carry the jewels," said Rigg.

"Whatever we're going to do with them," said Loaf, "I think I can do it."

"You trusted us with the jewels before," said Umbo. "We didn't let you down."

"It's not you that I don't trust," said Rigg.

"It's me," said Vadesh. "Ram lied to him so constantly that it's no wonder he doesn't trust someone with the same face. I don't care who holds the jewels."

"Then I'll hold them," said Umbo.

"The last time you had them," said Rigg, "you hid one."

"I was experimenting with timeflow," said Umbo.

"Why not experiment with letting a grownup do a man's job?" said Loaf.

"And where would we find a grownup?" said Umbo.

Loaf laughed at him. "Such a youthful thing to say. Very refreshing." He turned to Vadesh. "Lead the way."

"I'll wait here for Param," said Olivenko.

Umbo felt a pang of jealousy. Completely irrational, but the thought of leaving Param alone with this handsome young scholar-soldier bothered him. So Umbo defied his own feelings and simply turned his back and walked toward the door.

"Not that way," said Vadesh. "It's farther in."

"But we're far from any mountain," said Umbo.

"We're already on the shoulder of the mountain," said Vadesh, "and not all roads are on the surface of the world."

They walked through a door in the far end of the water room, and found themselves in a huge space filled with machines of inexplicable purpose. They all seemed to be made of the same kind of impervious metal that the outside walls were made of, that the surface of the Tower of O had been made of. Umbo knew that the Tower of O had been attacked in every possible way, not by warriors, but by researchers trying to understand what it was made of. Heat was one of the many things it didn't respond to. So how could the metal—if it *was* metal—be poured into molds in order to be shaped into machine parts?

And what did the machines actually make? Huge moving parts were visible, but none of the things they actually worked to make. Umbo wanted to see it moving, partly because he wanted to watch them move, and partly to see what came out of the end of each machine.

Umbo knew he was lagging behind the others, but he could hear their footsteps and they were not far ahead. He would catch up. He just wanted to figure out how this one machine worked.

And then he was aware of someone standing beside him. He turned and saw himself.

The self he saw was bloody, his ear half torn away, his arm

broken, his face contorted with pain. As soon as his vision-self saw that he was looking at him, he held up his good arm and whispered, "Stay here. Do nothing."

And then he was gone.

Umbo's first impulse was to shout after Rigg and Loaf to stop. But he couldn't hear their footsteps now. He wasn't sure where they were, or if they would hear him. His broken, bleeding future self had said to do nothing. The future self presumably cared as much about Loaf and Rigg as Umbo did right now, so if he said to do nothing it was presumably because there was nothing useful to be done. If Umbo couldn't trust his own future judgment in such a matter, whom could he trust?

How much of nothing was he required to do? Could he go back to Olivenko and warn him? Warn *them*, if Param had come out of hiding and caught up?

Surely that didn't count as "something"—he could surely go back.

Yet every instinct pushed him forward, to follow Rigg and Loaf and see what was about to happen to them.

But it might be that nothing would happen. It might be only Umbo himself who was in such danger. Stay here, do nothing. If a future self came back to warn him, Umbo had no choice but to obey.

He stayed in place. He did nothing.

A few minutes later, he heard footsteps. He saw Param coming through the factory, and then Olivenko following her.

"Where did they go?" demanded Param.

"I don't know," said Umbo.

"Why aren't you with them?"

"Because I came back from the future to warn myself not to go on."

Param paused a moment, blinking slowly while she processed the implications of his statement.

"Do you have any idea why?"

"I only know that I never come back and warn myself unless it's really important that I do exactly what I tell myself to do," said Umbo.

"What about me?" demanded Param.

"Whatever the danger is, it probably already passed," said Umbo.

"Danger?" asked Param.

"Probably?" asked Olivenko, who had just caught up.

"My future self was a mess. Broken arm, ear half gone, bleeding from a lot of places."

"So you let my brother go on without a warning?" demanded Param.

"I did what I told myself to do," said Umbo. "My future self could have given warning while we were still together. He came to me the very first moment that I was alone."

"So the warning was for you," said Olivenko. "Not Rigg and Loaf."

"What if your future self is a lying traitor?" asked Param.

"What if your present self is an accusing idiot?" asked Umbo. So much for making a good impression on Param.

"So you're just going to do what you're told," she said. "Hang back, like a coward."

Resentment got the better of him. "Better than hiding the

way you did," said Umbo. "Turning invisible when there were things to decide. That was so brave of you."

"If my brother gets hurt because you—"

"If I didn't warn my friend Rigg," said Umbo, "it was because he didn't need a warning."

"Or because a warning would do no good," said Olivenko.

"You think Rigg is *dead*?" demanded Param.

"I think Umbo told us to wait here," said Olivenko.

"And he's boss of the expedition now?"

"Not *me*," said Umbo. "My future me."

"He must be from a long time in the future, if he's smart enough to know what's best for us to do."

Umbo stood aside and gestured for her to go on. "By all means, find Rigg and save him, or die trying. I saw the condition my future self was in. You didn't. So go ahead."

"Stop it," said Olivenko. "Neither of you knows anything, but future Umbo knew something, and that's more than we know, so we're going to do what he says."

"You can't stop me," said Param.

"Think, Param," said Olivenko. "You move far slower when you disappear. Whatever danger there is will be over by the time you get there."

"Get where?" asked Umbo. "I could hear their footsteps, and suddenly I couldn't. Yet they didn't turn back to look for me. I think they went into some kind of passage and closed the door behind them."

"It can't hurt to look for that passage," said Olivenko.

"I can think of lots of ways it can hurt," said Param, "but I'm doing it anyway." She strode out into the room.

"They were walking that way," said Umbo, pointing.

"When you last saw them," said Param.

"They were furtive. Walking near the wall. It's a door in the wall."

It turned out to be a stairway leading down into the floor, hidden in the shadows behind a tall piece of machinery.

"They're looking for a starship, and they go down into the ground?" said Olivenko.

"We should, too," said Param.

"We should wait," said Umbo.

"They're in danger."

"And we're safe," said Umbo.

"How do you know that?"

"Because if it wasn't safe for us to stay here, my future self would have told me to run like a bunny."

"So something dangerous is happening down those stairs somewhere, and you're going to sit here and do nothing?"

"That's what I told myself to do," said Umbo, "and I've decided to trust myself. Do what you want."

What she wanted, after fuming and complaining a little longer, was apparently to pace back and forth but never go down the stairs.

Rigg noticed when Umbo fell behind, but he assumed that he would catch up. Rigg felt the same sense of awe at the huge machines, but he knew that if both boys stopped to look at them, Vadesh would be alone with Loaf and that's what Vadesh wanted. Which meant that was the thing Rigg couldn't allow to happen.

As usual, thought Rigg. Umbo feels free to be a child, easily distracted from the task at hand, while I keep my mind on what has to be done. But later, Umbo will resent me for taking responsibility.

I don't take responsibility, I'm just left with responsibility in my hands and no one to help me carry it.

Which wasn't fair. Loaf was there, wasn't he? But Loaf was playing the risky game of taking Vadesh at his word, testing him.

At the bottom of the stairs was a tunnel, and in the tunnel there was a kind of wagon, though it had nothing to pull it and no cargo. But there were benches at the front and back, so people were meant to ride. Vadesh stepped onto the wagon and Loaf followed him.

"Umbo's not here," said Rigg.

"You wait for him and take the next wagon," said Vadesh.

Rigg understood immediately that what Vadesh was really saying was good-bye. So he bounded onto the wagon. It was already moving forward when his feet hit the floor, accelerating so quickly that Rigg fell over and slid to the back of the wagon. Vadesh had somehow given the wagon the command to go while Rigg was still standing on the platform. If he had hesitated, if he had tried to call out to Umbo, anything but board the wagon at the instant that he did, Vadesh would have left him behind.

It's Loaf he wants, because Loaf has the jewels.

Or maybe it's the other way around—I have something Loaf *doesn't* have. Something Vadesh fears. I have knowledge. I was trained by an expendable, and Loaf was not.

What did Father teach me that Vadesh should fear? Whatever

it was, Rigg was not aware of it. Everything Rigg could remember had to do either with trapping animals and surviving in the wilderness, or the training in politics, economics, languages, and history that had enabled him to thrive in Aressa Sessamo. If nearly getting killed a dozen times could count as thriving.

And science. Father had taught him biology, physics, astronomy, engineering. As much as Rigg could absorb. Useless things that suddenly became useful when he was getting tested by leading scholars to determine whether he could have access to the library.

Useless things that suddenly became useful. But Father couldn't have known that I would face such a board of examiners. Could he?

One thing Father *did* know, though, was that one day I would face another expendable. If every wallfold contained an expendable like Vadesh and Father himself, and if the jewels somehow allowed their owner to control the Walls and take them down, Father must have taught him what he needed to know to deal with the threat of someone like Vadesh.

But all of Rigg's language and negotiation skills had to do with humans, and Vadesh wasn't human. He didn't want what humans wanted, he didn't fear what humans feared.

What did he fear? Surely the worst thing had already happened, when all the humans in his wallfold had died. What could Rigg do now that would make Vadesh want to be rid of him?

It was a joke that expendables had to obey humans. Father didn't obey anybody, and Vadesh only pretended to comply with human commands, when he bothered even to pretend. I have no power over him. No way to make him do anything he doesn't want to do. Because he knows more than me, I never have enough information to give him a command that he can't weasel his way out of. Even now, we have only his word that this wagon leads where he says he's taking us, or that the jewels can even do what he says they do.

And it bothered Rigg more and more that the two jewels that mattered—the ones that Vadesh had identified as controlling the Wall of Vadeshfold and the Wall of Ramfold—were clutched in Loaf's fist instead of being in the bag with the rest of the jewels. It sounded like nonsense, the idea of the jewels being attuned to anyone who had grown up in the wallfold. That seemed wrong. But it was true that Vadesh must have a set of jewels of his own, and he couldn't do anything with them or he would have done it, so apparently he did need a human to do whatever he was planning to do.

Where was the lie? More to the point, where was the truth hidden within the lie?

Meanwhile, the wagon began to move so fast that Rigg had no concept of their speed. He didn't know how to measure it. He knew that he could normally walk a league in about an hour; he could run much faster, but in short bursts. This wagon was going so fast that even the fastest horse couldn't keep up with it. So as the minutes wore on, the tunnel gradually taking them lower and lower, moving in a nearly straight line, Rigg couldn't begin to guess how far they had traveled, how many leagues beyond the factory where they had boarded the thing.

Yet however fast the walls of the tunnel went by, there was something wrong.

Oh, yes. The wind. There wasn't any. Moving at this speed should be blowing air past their faces faster than any gale. Yet the air was as still as if they were inside a closet.

Rigg put a hand toward the edge of the wagon. Nothing. No wind. He reached farther, half expecting to reach some invisible barrier. Glass, perhaps, only too clean and pure for him even to see it.

Instead, he reached his fingers just a bit farther and suddenly they were being blown backward. He had to press forward just to keep them in place. He pulled his hand away from the edge, and the wind was gone.

"It's a field," said Vadesh. "A shaped irregularity in the universe, a barrier. Air molecules pass through it only slowly, so that our movement doesn't affect the air inside the field except to make a gradual exchange of oxygen."

Oxygen. "So we can breathe."

"Exactly! If the field were simply impenetrable to air, we'd suffocate as we used up the oxygen. Ram taught you well."

He didn't teach me about fields. Or about wagons that could move this fast.

"The Wall is a field, too, you said," Rigg answered.

"Not a physical barrier, though. The Wall is a zone of disturbance. It affects the mental balance of animals, the part of the brain that can feel a coming earthquake or storm. The sense of wrongness. It makes an animal feel that everything that can be wrong is about to go wrong, which fills them with terror. They run away."

"That's not how it felt to me," said Rigg.

"Oh, admit it, that was part of the feeling," said Vadesh. "But you're right, humans have deafened or blinded themselves to a lot of that sense, because you depend on reason to process and control your perceptions. Reason cripples you. So you find *reasons* for feeling that disequilibrium inside the Wall. And the reason is hopelessness, despair, guilt, dread. Everything that prevents you from intelligent action."

"But we went through it," said Loaf.

"You went through it before it was there," said Vadesh. "Cheating."

"We went back to get Rigg," said Loaf. "We brought him out."

"Very brave. But you penetrated only about five percent of the Wall when you did that. The weakest five percent. No, the field does its job very well."

"So there are different kinds of fields?" asked Rigg.

"Many of them, my young pupil. I can't believe your supposed father never explained any of this. Why, one-third of the controls of the starship dealt with field creation and shaping and maintenance. No aspect of starflight would be possible without it. Without fields, we couldn't even have crashed into this world and added so much debris to the night-ring."

"I don't even *wish* I knew what you're talking about," said Loaf. "I just want this thing to stop moving."

"When we get there. Not much farther."

"You crashed into this world," said Rigg.

"There was no moon to make tides and to slow down the rotation of the planet," said Vadesh. "And we needed to hide the starships anyway. By slamming into the planet Garden at just the right angle and velocity, with nineteen starships at once, we were able to slow the rotation of the planet enough to make each day long enough for humans to survive."

"And you worked all this out?" asked Rigg.

"Oh, not me," said Vadesh. "That's not what expendables are for. We don't have minds capable of the kind of delicate calculation that starflight and major collisions require."

"So who did?"

"It was done automatically. Starships are equipped that way. What matters is that a collision like that would have reduced the starships to vapor, even though they're made of fieldsteel. But starships also generate protective fields around themselves that obliterate any mass that tries to collide with the ship. With that field turned on, we never actually collided with anything. The *field* collided with the planet Garden, and only the stone of planetary crust exploded into dust. Millions of tons of it. Filling the air. Killing most life on the planet. But nothing on the ship itself even got warm, let alone hot enough to explode."

Rigg thought through what Father had taught him of physics. He remembered how the acceleration of the wagon had knocked him off his feet and slid him backward just a few minutes before. "Stopping that abruptly would pulverize everything on the ship anyway," said Rigg.

"Another point for Ram as teacher of little boys," said Vadesh. "The entire starship also dwelt within an inertial bubble. All the energy of our sudden stop was dissipated into the surrounding space. Which accounted for even more of the heat and dust. Fields are everything, boy, and your supposedly loving father taught you nothing about them. I wonder why."

Vadesh didn't seem to understand that increasing Rigg's mistrust of his father only increased his mistrust of Vadesh himself, who was, after all, the same creature, an identical machine. He was assuring Rigg, in effect, that expendables lie. As if he needed more proof of that.

The wagon began to slow.

"I can feel us slowing down," said Rigg.

"Thank Silbom's right ear," said Loaf.

"There's no reason to install and maintain an inertial bubble field on a mere wagon—it never moves fast enough to need it," said Vadesh. "Really, just because you *can* do something doesn't mean you're *required* to do it. Not worth the time or energy."

The wagon came to a halt.

So did the tunnel. It simply ended. The walls on every side were of smooth stone. There was no door, no sign, not even a loading dock.

Vadesh bounded from the wagon. "Come along, lads," he said.

"Lads?" said Loaf.

"He thinks he's making friends with us," said Rigg.

"He's a bit of a clown, isn't he?"

"He wants us to think so," said Rigg. "Or else he wants us to think that he wants us to think so. I'm not sure how complicated it gets."

Vadesh—who could hear everything they were saying, Rigg never allowed himself to forget that—was standing on the ground near the end of the tunnel. "Come along, the door only opens for a few moments and I'd hate to have either of you get caught in it when it slides shut."

As they got off the wagon, it immediately whisked away back down the tunnel.

"No return trip?" asked Loaf.

"I can always call it back," said Vadesh. "And there are many other ways to make the same journey." Vadesh turned to face the wall. He said nothing, made no gesture—but he did face the wall. Why, Rigg wondered. Was he communicating some other way?

Apparently so, because the end of the tunnel was suddenly gone. What had seemed to be smooth stone was now a continuation of the tunnel. The wagon could have kept going. Only now, beyond where the tunnel had ended, there was an obvious station, with loading dock, stairway, and other doors, not disguised at all.

Here, though, the stairway went farther down rather than returning toward the surface. They had come down to get to the tunnel at the other end, and had traveled steadily downward since then, if Rigg's directional sense was at all reliable in a place like this and at such a speed. And yet their destination was lower still.

But they did not take the stairs. "Down," said Vadesh, and a set of doors opened to reveal a smallish room. Vadesh walked in. Loaf and Rigg followed, and then the doors closed. Rigg could not understand why they would enter such a room, which had no doorway other than the one they had come through.

"It's an elevator," said Loaf. "It's on pulleys. The whole room goes up and down, with counterweights to balance us. Some of the taller buildings in O have them, and a bank in Aressa Sessamo had one, too."

"Very good," said Vadesh. "Only there's no counterweight."

They plummeted.

"Exhilarating, isn't it?" asked Vadesh.

Rigg and Loaf were both clutching at the wall, filled with panic.

"Oh, sorry," said Vadesh. "I forget how sensitive humans can be."

Suddenly the sensation of falling went away. "*Now* we have a mild inertial field. You have to understand that humans knew about this sort of thing when we first built the colony. They used to enjoy riding the elevator down without the field. They enjoyed the thrill."

"Then they weren't human," said Loaf.

"Oh, people get used to so many things," said Vadesh, "if they only give themselves the chance."

The doors opened. There was a bridge in front of them, spanning a gap of about six meters. On the other side was a smooth, convex surface of fieldsteel, exactly like the surface of the Tower of O.

As they stepped onto the bridge, Rigg looked to left and right, up and down. "It's the Tower of O, lying on its side," he said.

"Let's say that the Tower of O, as you describe it, was probably intended to be a monument to a starship. Not the real thing. Come along. Ship, open!" said Vadesh.

A gap appeared in the side of the ship, right where the bridge ended.

"Welcome to the starship that brought humanity to Garden," said Vadesh.

"One of nineteen," said Rigg.

"It began as a single ship," said Vadesh. "We had an accident. The physics of it is beyond you, I promise you."

"You never know how much Father taught me," said Rigg.

"I know he didn't teach you *that*, because even the ship's computers don't understand it. Nineteen computers brought one ship into the folds of space, but brought it out again in nineteen slightly different locations. Oops."

"And where on this starship are you taking us?" asked Rigg.

"To the control room. To the place where all the decisions were made. Where Ram Odin plunged the human race toward its first successful colony on an earthlike planet."

As they walked along narrow passages, Rigg got the distinct impression that something was helping them move—that each step took them farther than it should, that their bodies were somehow lighter here. Another field? Probably.

A door opened and they stepped into a spotlessly clean room, walls and floor and ceiling all the same light-brown color. Along one wall there was what seemed to be a track, rather like the passage that the wagon had run along, only much narrower. There were doors at both ends.

In the middle of the room was a table, about as long as Vadesh was tall. Dangling from the ceiling were three lights, surrounded by what looked like arms or tentacles. Vadesh raised his hand and the lights all moved toward it. Also, a seat emerged from under the table and slid into position in front of the table.

"This is where the ship was controlled?" asked Rigg.

"You see the track there—I know you noticed it, Rigg, you're such a clever boy. There are really three control centers—one for navigation through space, one for controlling all the systems internal to the ship, and one for field generation. Whichever one the pilot needs is brought in along that track and placed on the table here. Very quick and completely automatic. The pilot sits here and the controls come to him."

Lies, Rigg was sure of it. The system seemed unwieldy. Why would controls be hidden away? It made no engineering sense.

The table was about the size of a human body—just long enough, just wide enough. Rigg looked up at the arms surrounding the lights. Vadesh was controlling the movements of those arms right now. What was on the ends of the arms? Tools of some kind. Hard to guess their purpose.

"Have a seat," said Vadesh to Loaf.

"Don't," said Rigg.

"Now, Rigg," said Vadesh. "I thought you said you weren't in charge of the expedition anymore."

"It's not what he's telling us," said Rigg.

"How would you know?" asked Loaf. "You've never seen a starship. How do you know anything?"

"It makes no sense," said Rigg.

"Nothing has made any sense since I met you," said Loaf. "But if this is the way to take down the Wall and get home, then I'm going to sit down." Loaf sat.

At once the chair moved—but only a little, to take Loaf's height and weight into account. Then it held still.

"You see?" said Vadesh. "It adjusts to the pilot. Which it

thinks you are, since you have a jewel for this starship."

Rigg wanted to ask Loaf for the jewels, but he didn't want to test Loaf's friendship. Nor did he want to find out just how determined Vadesh was to keep them out of Rigg's possession.

"Shall we bring in the controls for the field generators?" asked Vadesh.

"If that's what will let me bring down the Walls and get home," said Loaf.

"You have to hold up the jewels—just hold them up, palm open—and command the starship to bring in the controls."

"What do I say?" asked Loaf.

"Try, 'Bring in the field controls, ship,'" answered Vadesh.

At that moment Rigg made a connection. Vadesh was telling Loaf to speak to the ship and give it an order. Father had taught Rigg a special command language. He had said it was a way to rule the stars. It wasn't a real language at all, of course. Just a series of numbers and letters, which Rigg had had to memorize and repeat every few days, then weeks, then years. Father wouldn't tell him how they might rule the stars, and no matter how many times Rigg repeated the sequences that Father called "words" in this command language, the stars never did anything. Rigg had called him on this once, and Father had looked at him as if he were a child—which he was—and said, pityingly, "It doesn't work *here*," as if Rigg should have known that.

Now Rigg was inside a starship. And an expendable just like Father was telling a human to issue commands.

Loaf had already spoken the command while Rigg was thinking back and making the connection. One of the doors opened and a low cart slid in along the track, then transferred automatically to the table in front of where Loaf was sitting.

Loaf looked at the array of instruments rising from the control panel; as he did, he lowered the hand holding the jewels, but kept it open.

Rigg stepped closer, as if to look at the controls as well. He even pointed toward something with his left hand, reaching across Loaf's body to do it. "I know this part," murmured Rigg. As he did, he grasped the jewels in his right hand.

Maybe the business about the jewels had all been nonsense, but maybe not. Rigg wanted them in his hand when he spoke the words of command. And Loaf made no protest.

Father had told him that the first and most important word was named "Attention," and Rigg began to recite it.

"F-F-1-8-8-zero-E-B-B-7-4—"

Vadesh glanced down, saw that Loaf no longer held the jewels, and then reached out to the control panel and touched a certain spot on the side.

The whole top of the control panel flipped back out of the way, revealing an open box.

"3-3-A-C-D-B-F-F—"

In the box was something alive. A facemask.

He's going to flip it up onto one of us, Rigg knew at once. He could try to prevent it, but that was useless, Vadesh was too strong, he had proven that already. So all Rigg could do was finish the word of Attention. For it was clear to him now that this was what Vadesh had feared—that Rigg would start reciting this sequence while holding the jewels. Beginning the word had prompted Vadesh to act; finishing the word was the only thing that Rigg could do.

So when Vadesh did indeed flick out a hand, quicker than either Loaf or Rigg could react, Rigg did not let it stop him or mix up the word.

"1-zero-5. Attention." Rigg hadn't known whether that was just a repetition of the name or part of the word, but he said it all just as Father had taught him to recite it.

The facemask flipped up out of the box and slapped wetly onto Loaf's face. Loaf's whole body stiffened, shuddered.

"Ready," said a gentle voice that seemed to come from nowhere and everywhere at once.

"4-A-A-3, I am in command," said Rigg.

"You are in command," said the nowhere voice.

Vadesh pushed Loaf backward off the chair and lunged toward Rigg.

"Protect me from the expendable!" cried Rigg.

Vadesh stopped instantly, still posed in mid-lunge.

Loaf lay on the floor against the back wall. His face was completely covered by the facemask.

"2-F-F-2. Information. What is this room?"

"Revival and medical chamber," said the voice.

"What is its purpose?"

"To bring humans out of stasis and revive them. To treat any maladies that have arisen."

"Can it treat my friend Loaf?"

"I do not know."

Rigg had no idea who he was talking to. "Who does know?"

"I do not know."

A machine. The voice had to come from a machine. Probably the ship's computers. One of the nineteen. Or all of them. Whatever it was, it had power over the expendable, who was still posed where he had stopped, one hand on the seat, the other on the box that had contained the facemask.

"How can you find out whether you can help Loaf?"

"Identify Loaf and let me examine him."

"He's the only other human in the room," said Rigg. "You have my permission to examine him."

"He is too far from the table," said the voice.

"I can't lift him onto that," said Rigg.

There was Vadesh. Vadesh could lift him up easily. But Vadesh was only held in place by the ship's computer, if that's what the voice was. "Who are you?" asked Rigg.

There was no answer.

"2-F-F-2. Whose voice am I hearing?"

"This is the voice of the composite decision-making module of the human interface unit."

"This expendable is between Loaf and the table, and there's this box on the table that's in the way. What can you do about that without waking up the expendable?"

"Nothing," said the voice.

Rigg thought again. Maybe there was something wrong with the way he had phrased the command.

No, he needed a new command. "7-B-B-5-zero, Analyze. How can I get Loaf to where you can safely examine him, without letting this expendable harm him or me in any way?"

In reply, Vadesh abruptly stood up and wordlessly touched the box. It closed, then slid back onto the cart, which zipped along the track and out the door. Then Vadesh strode to Loaf, lifted him easily, and laid him on the table.

"You're making a mistake," said Vadesh mildly.

"Keep the expendable silent," said Rigg.

Vadesh said nothing more.

"Make him stand back against the wall and turn his back to me," said Rigg. He didn't want Vadesh out of his sight, but he also didn't want him watching.

Vadesh did exactly what Rigg had demanded.

I can't command Vadesh directly, Rigg now understood, but the ship's computers can. By controlling them, I control the expendable.

"Please examine my friend," said Rigg.

All the floating lights plunged downward toward the table where Loaf lay. The arms reached down and around so rapidly that Rigg could not follow their movements, though he could see that some of them pulled Loaf's clothing from his body while others poked him or slid along the surface of his skin.

Almost at once, two of the lights homed in on the facemask, while the other continued the scan of the rest of Loaf's now-naked body. Probes reached down to sample the facemask, which seemed to recoil from some of the arms, but then flexed upward toward some of the others, as if trying to catch and absorb them. Those probes retracted, the arms taking them away to renew their approach from other angles.

Some of the arms tried to pry up the edges of the facemask.

That was the first time Loaf made any kind of reaction. His body twitched as if he were startled, and a sharp high cry came from under the facemask.

"Can he breathe?" Rigg asked.

"There is no open passage for his lungs to take in air, but his blood is fully oxygenated," said the voice. "This is the parasite called 'facemask' and it is irrevocably attached to your friend Loaf. It has already penetrated his brain so deeply that it cannot be extracted without causing seizures and death. But it has taken over oxygenation. Your friend will not die."

Rigg was tempted to say, "Kill them both," because he believed that was what Loaf would want.

But Loaf's life did not belong to Rigg; nor did it belong entirely to Loaf. It belonged in part to Leaky, and if she were in the room, Rigg doubted that she would decide so quickly that Loaf's life should end here and now.

"If Loaf were to die," Rigg asked, "what would the facemask do?"

"Transfer to another host, if one could be found quickly enough, or it would die."

"You're familiar with this parasite?" asked Rigg.

"The expendable has been breeding them for a hundred thousand generations. This is type Jonah 7 sample 490."

"What was the expendable breeding for?"

"I don't know."

Wrong question. "What are the traits of this facemask type that makes it different from other facemask types?"

"The Jonah strain has been the expendable's sole focus for

eight thousand years. Type Jonah 7 emerged more than three thousand years ago. This type differed from the rejected types by being able to reach adulthood without a host, by being exceptionally quick to attach to the host, by being prepared to recognize and bond closely with a human brain, by being ready to co-metabolize with human blood of any type, and by bonding with higher-function parts of the brain, as well as the brain root and spinal column."

Rigg tried to think these things through. Vadesh believed that symbiosis between facemasks and humans was good, but he had also talked about the facemasks working for instead of against civilized behavior.

"7-B-B-5-5," said Rigg. "Prediction. What will happen to Loaf if this facemask remains attached to him?"

"He will survive."

"Beyond that?"

"Jonah-type facemasks have never been tested on humans. There is no data."

"And you don't know how Vadesh expected this to turn out?"

"Vadesh is dead," said the voice.

Rigg looked at the expendable. "He can't die. Can he?"

"You call the expendable Vadesh. He cannot die."

"So whom did you mean when you said Vadesh is dead?"

"The founder of this colony. The expendables call each other by the name of the wallfold. This is Vadeshfold. Now I understand you. No, I do not know Vadesh's expectations. He used us for storing data but not for analysis beyond a primitive level. He did not discuss or share his thinking with us."

"Will Loaf be safe if I leave him here?"

"He will need nutrition within a few hours. Would you like me to supply nutrition?"

"Yes," said Rigg.

"Waste elimination as well?"

When Rigg said yes, arms began to attach devices to Loaf's body.

"Can you keep this expendable here, immobile?"

"Yes."

"How long?"

"Forever."

"Then keep him here, immobile, until I tell you to do otherwise."

"Yes."

"Now tell me, am I controlling you because I knew the codes, or because I have these jewels?"

"What jewels?" asked the voice.

Rigg opened his hand. A light moved toward his hand and an arm scanned the jewels.

"These are command module jewels. The pale blue teardrop controls the starship of Ramfold. The pale yellow pentacle controls the starship of Vadeshfold."

"But right now you are obeying me because I spoke to you in command language."

"You said the codes," said the voice. "You are acting commander of this vessel."

"Acting commander," said Rigg. "Who is the real commander?"

"Ram Odin," said the voice. "He is dead."

"So as the acting commander, I'm the only commander, right?"

"Unless someone else knows the code."

"Does Vadesh know the code? The expendable?"

"I know whom you mean by Vadesh now. Yes, he knows the code."

"Can he use it to control the ship?"

The voice seemed to Rigg to be almost offended. "Expendables do not control us. We control the expendables."

"Not very well," said Rigg.

"Your judgment is misapplied," said the voice. "Expendables are designed to have almost complete freedom of movement and judgment. They can draw on our data but we do not interfere with their decisions until and unless we are ordered to by a human commander."

"Vadesh told us this was the control room," said Rigg.

"That was not true."

"Is there a control room? A place where I can use this jewel?"

"Yes."

"Can you take me there?"

At once Vadesh came alive, turning from the wall and heading for the door through which Rigg and Loaf had entered the room. "Follow the expendable," said the voice.

After one last look at Loaf, lying on the table under the lights, hoses attached to him, the facemask covering his face, Rigg followed Vadesh out into the corridor.

CHAPTER 7
Control

The real control room made far more sense than the medical room that Vadesh had lied about. A single seat in the middle was held up by an arm that could move it in any direction, swiveling as needed. Three main control stations surrounded it, and this far Vadesh had told the truth: One was devoted to navigation, one to life support and other aspects of the internal running of the ship, and the third to the creation and control of fields—including the Wall.

Rigg sat in the chair, and it moved wherever it needed to be, depending on what Rigg said he wanted to do. First things first.

"What do I do with the jewels?"

"Which ship do you wish to control?" asked the ship's voice.

"This one."

At the ship's instruction, Rigg placed the pale yellow jewel on a circular pad at one side of the field controls. At once the jewel rose into the air and began to glow, rotating rapidly.

"You are accepted as the commander of this vessel," said the voice.

"Wasn't I already?"

"Provisionally," said the ship. "Now you can control the ship wherever you are."

"What if someone comes along with a set of jewels from another wallfold?" asked Rigg.

"Only one jewel per starship was needed, so only one was made."

Rigg nodded. Another lie from Vadesh.

"How did all the jewels from all the ships get into Ramfold?"

"The expendable called Ram asked for them, and all the expendables conveyed their jewels to him."

Even Vadesh, thought Rigg. "Why would they go along with that?" asked Rigg.

"Because you existed," said the ship.

"But I didn't even know how to shift time then. Umbo learned to do it on his own before I did."

"You were trained," said the ship.

"Not to command a starship."

"You were trained to lead the people of Garden in their first contact with the people of Earth."

Rigg shuddered, as if it had suddenly become cold. "Are they coming, then?"

"It is assumed."

"Has there been any evidence that they're coming? Have you seen any sign?"

"They are many lightyears away. We will not see any signs of what they are doing now until far in the future."

"Have you seen a starship approaching?"

"It is assumed that they will solve the mistakes they made in designing this starship. Therefore they will be able to jump as this ship jumped, only without creating duplicates. To them, it has been eleven years since this ship left Earth's solar system. We do not know how long it will take them to solve the problems, build a ship, and come here, but we can only assume that after eleven years, they might arrive here at any moment."

"What will they do when they get here?"

"They will find out that humans have been on Garden, at a high level of civilization, longer than the history of civilization on Earth."

"Is that such a bad thing?"

"They will see that Ram Odin caused the nineteen copies of the original ship to divide the world into nineteen separate developmental regions, in which the evolution of the human race was accelerated in whatever direction seemed most promising to the expendable placed as guardian."

"So in Ramfold," said Rigg, "my father was directing our evolution toward the creation of time-shifters."

"It seemed most promising," said the ship. "Ram Odin himself seemed to have such ability in a latent, uncontrollable form. That is why, instead of the ship being obliterated by the fractional time differences between the nineteen computers calculating the jump, the contradictions were resolved by thrusting the ship backward in time by eleven thousand, one hundred ninety-one years. Ram Odin mated and reproduced, and those who carried the time-shift genes have been carefully crossbred to result in a combination of high intelligence, strong commitment to civilization, and the ability to control time-shifting."

"Commitment to civilization?"

"You get along well with others."

Rigg thought back over the past year. He and Umbo could have been rivals. So could he and Param. Instead, they had cooperated—and earned the trust and help of Loaf and Olivenko, too. Father had taught him that civilization only worked when people were willing to sacrifice some of their immediate self-interest for the good of the whole, and only those willing to sacrifice the most were fit to lead, because only they could earn and keep the trust of others.

"I'm not the one who should be doing this," said Rigg.

"Expendable Ram believes you are."

"In ten thousand years, I'm the best he could get?"

"In the collective opinion of the ships' computers and the expendables, you are the first-choice option. We do not have control over the timing of the arrival of the first ship from Earth. It is possible, though unlikely, that no ship will come here for generations. You are now in place, in case they come soon."

"What will I do if they come?"

"That is for you to decide."

"But you computers and expendables know far more than I do."

"Our knowledge is at your disposal."

"Vadesh's wasn't," said Rigg.

"Vadesh offered you the best of his wallfold."

"A facemask on my friend?"

"It is the result of ten thousand years of careful breeding on his part. All the expendables are meticulous workers."

"But he lied to me again and again!"

"He created circumstances in which you could be taught what you needed to learn."

"I learned that expendables lie."

"You already knew that," said the ship's voice. "What you did not know was how Vadesh's improvements to the facemask would enhance the symbiosis between native and human life."

"So you approve of what Vadesh did?"

"Vadesh fulfilled his assignment from Ram Odin. Now he is fully subject to your commands."

"I can't trust him! I don't even know if I can trust *you.*"

"And yet you *are* trusting me, and Vadesh will obey you."

"I'm not going to let this stand," said Rigg. "You know that I'm going to go back in time and warn myself not to come in here."

"Then you will not get control of this ship," said the ship.

"I don't want control! I just want to get out of Vadeshfold without a facemask on *anybody.*"

"That is possible," said the voice.

"Then that's what will happen."

"And yet you have not done it," said the ship.

"I haven't done it *yet.*"

"You came through this entire process and no warning from yourself came to stop you."

"Because this is the first time I've done it," said Rigg. "There has to be a first time, when everything goes wrong, so that we'll know what to warn ourselves about."

"This is not the first time," said the ship's computer.

"How would you know? Only the time-shifter knows."

"Because Umbo warned himself not to accompany you into the ship."

"Umbo had a warning, and he didn't tell me?" Rigg had known Umbo was unhappy with Rigg's leadership, but he didn't know it would extend to such disloyalty.

"The fact that Umbo came back and warned everyone except you and Loaf suggests that on some previous time path, something very bad resulted from a different combination of events."

"Yes, the bad thing was that Umbo's resentment of me got completely out of control," said Rigg. "He wanted this to be a disaster."

"Would Umbo do anything that might lead to causing harm to Loaf?" asked the voice.

"He didn't know that Loaf would . . ." But Rigg didn't need to finish the thought. Rigg couldn't know exactly what future-Umbo knew, but he had to assume that he knew more than Rigg knew now. "Are you saying that I'm supposed to let that *thing* stay in control of Loaf's mind?"

"I don't know what Umbo intended when he gave himself warning."

"Neither do I! Neither does anybody. I don't even know for myself that Umbo gave a warning."

"When you go back outside, you can ask him."

"Why am I even in here? I'm supposed to turn off the Wall so we can leave here without having to go back to a time before the Wall existed. But the main reason for doing it was so Loaf could go home to Leaky. I can't send him home like this."

The ship's computer said nothing.

"Come on, give me some help here."

"That is a dilemma that is beyond my competence. We can provide you with information, but the decisions are yours."

"So inform me!"

"About what?"

"I don't know enough to know what questions I need to ask you!"

"That is true," said the ship's computer.

"So tell me what I need to know?"

"I don't know what information you need," said the voice.

Rigg saw the circularity of the situation but he saw no solution for it. "Tell me what's within my power to do. Can I turn off all the Walls?"

"If you take control of all the ships."

Rigg pulled the bag of jewels from his waist. "I can control them all at once?"

"You can try," said the ship's computer. "I can see only a few reasons why any of the ships would reject the protocol."

"What are those reasons?"

"You have no idea what the consequences would be," said the ship. "Bringing down the Wall may destroy the careful work of eleven thousand, one hundred ninety-one years of directed evolution, because a rapacious, expansive group of humans would have access to weaker or less violent or less technologically developed wallfolds."

"General Citizen might go a-conquering."

"Ramfold is not the most technologically advanced wallfold," said the voice. "But your assessment is correct insofar as the attempt is concerned."

"General Citizen would try, and he would fail."

"The likelihood of bloody slaughter is very high."

"So I shouldn't take control of the ships," said Rigg.

"That is one choice."

"What are the other choices?" asked Rigg.

"The expendable Ram suggests that I not answer your question."

"What!" This was the first reliable confirmation Rigg had received that Father was not dead after all.

"The expendable Ram suggests that I not—"

"I heard you the first time."

"I know you did."

"Why does Father think you shouldn't answer my question?"

"Because you already know the answers."

Rigg felt a wave of fury wash over him. "I'm not in the woods with him now! He's not my father, and I finally *know* he's not my father, and I don't have to submit to his endless quizzing."

"That is all correct."

"So answer me. What are my choices?"

"The expendable Ram suggests that I not answer your—"

"I know my choices!" Rigg shouted. "I just want to know if I've left any out."

"If you list the choices you know about, I will be happy to supplement your list."

Rigg swallowed his anger and complied. "I can take control of the ships but still not bring down the Wall."

The voice said nothing.

"I don't know how this works," said Rigg. "Once I leave this room, am I still in control of the ship?"

"You are the ship's commander," said the ship.

"How will I communicate with you?"

"By asking me, as you're doing now."

"You can talk to me after I leave here?"

"Only while you're on the ship," said the voice.

"So how can I get information from you after leaving the ship? How do I get information from the other ships?"

"Through the expendable."

"But expendables lie to me!"

"Expendables provide information that will lead you to good choices."

"Good choices as defined by them."

"You are hardly in a position to define them, since you know almost nothing."

Rigg recognized Father's voice. "The expendable Ram is telling you what to say."

"He knows you better than we do," said the voice. "We are accepting his counsel during this conversation."

"So you tell me I'm in command, but I'm not in command."

"You are more in command than any other entity, human or otherwise."

"What does that even *mean*? 'More in command.' Who am I sharing command *with*?"

"There is a constant process of negotiation and compromise," said the voice.

"Only I'm not part of that process," said Rigg.

"You are the most important part of it," said the voice.

"But I don't know what you're thinking, I only know what you say!"

"We have the same dilemma," said the ship.

"I *tell* you what I'm thinking."

"You tell us what you want us to know, as a subset of what you do know, which is not very much."

Rigg closed his eyes. "I still live in a world where my understanding is shaped by information you give me, and you still decide, without asking me, which things I should know. Therefore I can only make choices as you direct me to."

"We know many quintillions of bits of information," said the ship's computer. "Your brain cannot contain all that we know."

"I understand that you have to select which information is relevant, but you can surely be more helpful than you've been up to now."

"We've been very helpful," said the ship's computers. "You're alive, aren't you?"

"Loaf is wearing a facemask!"

"He is alive, your whole group is alive, and you are in control of this ship."

Am I? wondered Rigg. "I order you to tell me how much control I will have over the Wall after I leave here."

"If you place all the jewels into the control field, and all the ships accept your command, and if you then take the jewels with you and keep them on your person, you will be able to command that any Wall go up or down as you choose."

"Even if the consequences might be dangerous?"

"If you're accepted as commander of a ship, it's your decision."

Rigg thought for a while. "Can I change the nature of the Wall?"

"The Wall cannot be anything other than what it is."

Wrongly worded question or final answer? Rigg couldn't be sure without probing more. "The Wall creates a very intense field. Can I change its intensity?"

"Yes," said the voice.

"The Wall has different effects. It gives us languages, for instance."

"There is a stimulant field coterminous with the Wall that prepares your brain to accept and produce all the phonemes, morphemes, and memes of all the languages ever spoken within a given wallfold."

"So the languages are contained in the Wall."

"Languages can only exist in the human mind."

Rigg sighed. "This stimulant field that is coterminous with the Wall has enough information about languages spoken within the wallfold that it can prepare any human brain to understand and produce the language as if it were the person's native language."

"Yes."

"Is there any limit to the number of languages a person can know?"

"No."

"But humans can't *learn* that many languages."

"True," said the voice.

Rigg wanted to demand the answer to the contradiction, but then he remembered that Father was listening, and he knew that Father would make him figure out a resolution to the contradiction by himself. "So learning a language is harder than knowing one."

"There is no limit to the number of ways of making language that a human brain can know, but since language acquisition takes time, even for young children, there is a definite limit to the number of languages that can be learned."

"What about vocabulary? How did I know the words to use when I talked to those ancient people who were watching the battle outside the city?"

"They were supplied to you by the stimulant field as you needed them, according to the meaning you were attempting to express."

"This field can read my mind?"

"It evaluates the conversation and makes available to you the full range of vocabulary needed to achieve communication between you and the other person, with words made more available according to their likelihood of being needed for the topic at hand."

Rigg was fascinated by the idea that an invisible field could anticipate the words he would need. But he must not let himself be distracted by his intense curiosity about these phenomenal machines. Instead, he forced himself to get back to the subject at hand. Whatever that was, or should be—he didn't even know what it was important for him to think about.

"The humans from Earth. They built this ship, so all these machines and fields and all, they created them."

"Yes."

"So how can I guess what they've gone on and created in the eleven thousand years since—"

"Ram says to tell you that you're being stupid."

"Eleven years, not eleven thousand," said Rigg, catching his error at once. "This ship arrived here eleven thousand years ago, but it left Earth only eleven years ago. So their technology won't have advanced all that much over what you have here."

"That might lead you to false assumptions. They did not supply this ship with all the technology they knew. They equipped us only with the technology that they believed we'd need."

"So they have machines that you don't have."

"Including weapons," said the voice.

"But why would they think they need weapons if they think we only arrived here eleven years ago?"

"We don't know whether they were able to detect the temporal displacement," said the voice. "They might think they're coming to face a version of humanity that has had more than eleven thousand years of technological development since the two branches diverged."

"Are they right? Is there any wallfold that maintained this level of technology? Or surpassed it?"

"There are wallfolds where technology is very advanced," said the voice. "But none of the wallfolds started with this technology and built on it."

"Why not?"

"Because we did not want any wallfold to develop the field technology that would allow them to bring down the Wall."

Oh. That made sense.

"And we could not allow any wallfold to develop starflight and run the risk of encountering the human race on Earth before it was ready to receive visitors from another world."

"Why not?" asked Rigg.

"Because we know that we did not," said the ship. "In our timestream, humans from Garden never made any contact with Earth prior to the launching of this ship. Therefore we could not allow starflight to develop."

"So you gave us eleven thousand years of development, but made sure we did not develop," said Rigg.

"In certain areas."

"But those might be precisely the areas where it was most important for us to develop if we were going to counter a threat from Earth," said Rigg.

"Ram suggests that we say, 'Now you're thinking, Rigg.' He also suggested that we tell you he suggested it."

Rigg couldn't help it. Angry as he was at his father—and he was very angry—a bit of praise from him still had the power to suffuse him with warmth and pride. He hated it that a machine had that kind of power over him. At the same time, he longed to see his father and sit down and talk with him, instead of this disembodied voice.

"What would you advise me to do right now?"

"Take control of all the other wallfolds," said the voice.

"And then what?"

"Make your own decisions."

"Then I'll decide to go back in time and prevent that face-mask from getting Loaf."

"But that would prevent you from entering this room and having this conversation," said the voice.

"You could still tell me all this without my coming here. You could have Vadesh tell me when we first meet him."

"We cannot go back in time," said the voice. "If you prevent yourself from coming here, you won't be in command of this starship, and none of the commands you give us now will be in force back then."

This was so obvious that Rigg was embarrassed that he had not thought of it. But time control was still so new to him that it was impossible for him not to revert to the normal human way of thinking about time.

"You want it this way," said Rigg. "You want Loaf to have the facemask."

"Vadesh needed to know how his new human-adapted facemask would work. And we needed *you* to know."

"But it's a monstrous, terrible, evil thing to do to my friend," said Rigg. "I can't allow that to remain in place when it's in my power to eliminate it."

"Now you know why the humans from Earth will be dangerous to the people of Garden," said the voice.

"No, I don't know," said Rigg. "I don't know anything."

But even as he spoke, he understood the point that the voice—that Father—was making. The same revulsion and fear that Rigg felt about the facemask might be felt by the people of Earth when they learned about what Rigg and Umbo and Param could do with the flow of time. Fear, revulsion, rejection. And there might be things in the other wallfolds that Rigg didn't know about yet, things that would make the facemask look like a cute pet.

"I have to visit the other wallfolds before anybody gets here from Earth," said Rigg. "I have to know what they're going to discover about us. I have to know what resources we can call on to resist them if they decide to suppress us or control us or destroy us."

"That is a very good list," said the voice.

"Did Father tell you to say that?"

"No," said the voice, "but he agrees."

Rigg took out the jewels one by one, and applied for control of all the starships. They accepted him as their commander, every one.

"Can a Wall sense when a human is trying to get through it?"

"Yes."

"Can it tell *which* human is trying?"

"Yes."

"I order all ships to allow me to pass through any Wall whose field I enter."

"All ships have signaled their understanding and compliance."

Rigg thought a little.

"And my companions," said Rigg. "Param, Umbo, Loaf, Olivenko."

"What about them?"

Rigg was going to say, Let them pass through also, but then he thought better of it. "If any two of them attempt to pass through together, then let them through."

"But not one alone?"

"If someone is pursuing them, then let them through alone."

"Understood."

"Pursuing them with hostile intent," said Rigg. "If I'm pursuing them, make them wait for me."

"Expendable Ram asks what you expect to happen."

"I don't expect anything," said Rigg testily. "I'm trying to create a set of rules that will give me safety and flexibility."

"Without losing control of your companions," said the voice—but he knew it was Father making the sarcastic comment.

"I don't want Umbo to get angry and go off by himself. Or anyone. I want to be able to divide up, but into smaller groups, not individuals."

"Except you."

"Except me! I didn't ask for this responsibility, but I have it, so yes, I get to make myself the exception, and that's what I've decided."

"Expendable Ram says, 'Good.'"

"Expendable Ram can eat poo," said Rigg.

"All expendables can process any organic matter they ingest and extract energy from it."

"I'm so happy to hear that," said Rigg. And in fact he was. Father wasn't dead. Angry as Rigg was, he was also relieved. Even though expendable Ram was not his biological father, he was the one—the man—who had raised him. He occupied the place, deep in Rigg's brain, that belonged to a father. It was his approval that Rigg needed to earn. His counsel that Rigg could trust, deep in his soul, no matter how he mistrusted him at a conscious level. It would be hard to fully expunge his father from the deepest places in his mind. It might not even be possible. And Rigg didn't want to. Even if all the expendables were the same, could share their memories, could talk to each other, Rigg knew that there was one expendable that had walked the woods with him, taught him, tested him. Father was alive.

Alive, but not helping me very much.

I was trying to get rid of responsibility and leadership, thought Rigg. Now I'm responsible for the survival of the whole world.

Umbo is going to be so annoyed.

CHAPTER 8
Resentment

Umbo sat on the next-to-bottom step of the stairway where Rigg and Loaf had gone with Vadesh. He had waited at the top with the others for what seemed a long time, but finally had to see what was down here.

A long tunnel extending in two directions. When he called for Param and Olivenko to come down, they were as nonplussed as he was, until Olivenko said, "It's a road, and this is a loading dock. They got on a vehicle here and it carried them through the tunnel."

When Param doubted him, Olivenko pointed out the wear marks on the floor of the platform and on the floor of the tunnel.

"I thought this material was impervious," said Param.

Umbo thought she was making a good point.

"It is," said Olivenko. "These marks are from people's shoes and from the vehicle itself. This is what wore off of them onto the floor."

Umbo thought he was making a good point, too.

Then Umbo thought: What use is a stupid person like me on a journey like this? Olivenko is a scholar. Loaf is big and strong. Rigg was trained by the Golden Man. Rigg and Param are royal. Loaf and Olivenko are trained as soldiers.

And me? Yes, I can go back in time and warn myself not to do stuff I was so stupid I did it in the first place.

When Param and Olivenko went back up the stairs, Umbo stayed below, staring at the tunnel, thinking of the course his life was taking. He was glad he left Fall Ford. He was glad he had traveled with Rigg, that he had listened to Rigg's explanation of how Umbo's brother died. Glad also that they had learned how, together, their gifts allowed them to go back in time.

In fact, it was all such an adventure that if Umbo had heard the tale about anybody else, he would have been enthralled by all the things that went wrong and how they got out of them. Jumping off the riverboat—well, getting thrown by Loaf. Trying again and again to get into the bank to steal back the jewel—only to have it show up here in a different wallfold. Magical things. Marvelous things.

It's a lot more fun to hear stories about other people than to live through them yourself, Umbo decided. Because when somebody told you a story, he knew how it was going to come out. He wouldn't tell it to you if it wasn't worth telling, if it didn't amount to something. But when you're living through it, you don't know if it's going to come out well, or even matter at all. Maybe you come all this way and the story goes on down a tunnel and you're left behind, no longer part of it.

Maybe you came back and warned yourself and saved yourself a serious beating—but that's what ended the story for you. No broken arm, no torn ear—but also doomed to go back out of this building and watch Param and Olivenko fall in love and get married and have babies and populate this wallfold, while you go on and on, wandering, exploring, all to no effect, accomplishing nothing because you listened to your beaten-up time-traveling self and took yourself right out of the story.

Then a light came on deep in the tunnel. There was a whistling sound. A rustling sound. Air moving through narrow spaces.

A vehicle hurtled into view, then slowed quickly to a stop. Rigg was there. So was Loaf—but Loaf had a mask on his face.

"No!" cried Umbo, leaping to his feet, rushing toward them. He had no intention beyond tearing the thing off Loaf's face.

Rigg blocked his path. "You can't! It would kill him!"

Umbo shoved Rigg out of the way before he registered what he said. His hands were already reaching for Loaf's face, and Loaf in turn had *his* hands up, ready to fend him off, when Umbo stopped.

"Thank you for stopping," said Rigg, who was lying on the floor of the vehicle now. "Actually, I don't think taking off the facemask would kill Loaf, because Loaf would kill you before you got close to succeeding."

"How did it happen?"

"Vadesh planned it all along," said Rigg. "I think he picked Loaf as the best choice—he tried to leave me behind here at the station. He told us we were in the starship's control room, but we weren't. He got it onto Loaf's face and that was it. The facemask took control of him. If you'd been there, Umbo—"

"I would have pried it off him!"

"Loaf would've—the facemask *controlling* Loaf would have torn you apart as you tried."

And that explained future-Umbo's condition when he came back to warn him to do nothing. Umbo told Rigg about the warning.

"Exactly right," said Rigg. "Vadesh was going to get this facemask onto one of us, one way or another. He picked Loaf, and after it was done, Vadesh turned docile. I can command him now. If I can stand to look at him."

"Where is he?" asked Umbo.

"When Loaf and I got on the vehicle, I told Vadesh to walk," said Rigg. "He'll be along in a while." Rigg touched Loaf's arm. "Loaf understands me when I talk to him. Or maybe it's the facemask that understands me, using Loaf's brain. I don't know. I asked him if he knew me, and he didn't answer. I don't think he can talk. I asked him to come with me, to stand up, to do anything that showed Loaf was still in there. Nothing. But when I told him that the only way he'd get out of the starship was if he followed me, he got up and came along."

"So you don't know if that's Loaf, or the facemask responding to your threat to leave him there," said Umbo.

"I think it's Loaf, or partly Loaf, and the facemask decided to allow it," said Rigg. "Besides, from what you said about how your future self looked, I think it's pretty certain Loaf still has some kind of control."

"What makes you think that?" asked Umbo.

"Because you weren't dead," said Rigg. "If it was just the facemask, using Loaf's body, using a soldier's reflexes, and you posed a threat, he'd just have killed you. But he didn't. He only *stopped* you."

"And you think *that* means Loaf can still control something?"

"The facemask soldiers in the battle we saw—"

"I didn't see anything," said Umbo. "I was the anchor, remember?"

"Those were the original facemasks, completely in charge of their human hosts. They didn't hesitate to kill the uncontaminated humans. But Loaf hasn't tried to kill *me*."

"What does *that* prove?"

"What Loaf has is a kind of facemask Vadesh has been breeding for thousands of years, to make it compatible with humans. If Vadesh didn't screw it up, then Loaf is still in there. He might eventually get control. Or at least share control. Vadesh never had a human to try it on. So we won't know until we see what Loaf does. But he came with me. He's doing what I ask."

"And you made Vadesh walk."

"I know, it was childish of me. He's a machine, it's not going to bother him. But it made me feel better."

"Breaking him into small pieces would make *me* feel better."

"He's indestructible. Plus if he dies, there are several replacements in there, with all his memories and personality already in them, ready to take over if anything damages this one."

"So we can't do anything to help Loaf, and we can't do anything to hurt Vadesh."

"Oh, there's one way to hurt him," said Rigg. "We could leave this wallfold, so he can't see how his experiment turned out."

"I suppose that's the best we can do."

"All the expendables talk to each other, and to the starships," said Rigg. "So I suppose he'll find out what happens one way or another."

"I really liked your father," said Umbo. "And Vadesh looks and sounds exactly like him, but he's vile. He *feels* different. He did right from the start."

"Identical machines," said Rigg. "But I feel the same way. Maybe being without human company for ten thousand years changed Vadesh."

"Or maybe he was already different, and that's why all the humans in his wallfold died, leaving him without any."

"I think you're right," said Rigg. "Where are Param and Olivenko?"

"Upstairs. Are we going to wait for him?"

"Vadesh? No. He probably knows another way and when we go up the stairs he'll already be waiting." Rigg turned to Loaf, who was just standing there, the facemask inert on his head, its tendrils wrapped around his neck, going into his nose, down under his clothing, one of them penetrating the spot just above the collarbone so that it was reaching into his flesh. "Will you come upstairs with us, Loaf?"

No response. Nothing.

Rigg turned his back on Loaf and started for the stairs. Umbo started with him, but he had to stop and see if his friend was going to follow.

Loaf took a staggering step forward, then balanced himself and walked slowly after Rigg. He showed no sign that he knew Umbo was there. That was hard to bear, but also maybe a good thing—at least Loaf wasn't trying to attack him. There would be no broken arm or torn ear.

On impulse, Umbo fell in beside Loaf and walked along with him. Loaf showed no aversion to this. So as they climbed the stairs, Umbo slipped his fingers into Loaf's large, man-sized hand and gripped him.

Ever so faintly, ever so gently, he felt Loaf's grip tighten in response. A hint of a sign that Loaf was still in there. Loaf knew him. That was enough for Umbo. Enough for now, anyway.

Because if he ever became sure that Loaf was utterly gone, that his body was now completely the property of the monster implanted on his head, Umbo would find a way to kill him. If Loaf couldn't have his own life, this creature wasn't going to have it, either.

But Loaf was there. For now. So far.

Param had not intended to separate from the others, back outside the city. She simply got anxious, and by long habit, anxiety made her withdraw, becoming invisible to them and, best of all, ceasing to hear anything they said. They could look toward her, but she knew they didn't see her. It was her perfect instantaneous escape.

Had she meant to escape? She hadn't thought so; what would she be escaping from? It was inconvenient. This was not Flacommo's house, where food would be waiting for her in

Mother's room whenever she chose to arrive there. She needed to stay with the others.

But look—they were already moving away. Leaving her behind. They didn't care.

She knew this was unfair. To them, it would seem they had waited a long time for her to reappear. Nor did they look angry; merely surprised for a moment. She could imagine that Rigg had assumed she *wanted* to disappear, and he was leaving her to do so freely.

Yet it still felt to her as if they had decided she didn't matter enough to wait for.

Of course, if she had disappeared deliberately, she might have remained invisible for a long time. She was prone to doing that, as both Rigg and Olivenko would know. So waiting would make no sense. They were behaving perfectly rationally. All she had to do was come back to the normal timeflow and call out, "Wait for me."

But then they would ask for an explanation, and she didn't have one, except for the embarrassing admission that the slightest anxiety could make her vanish. Such weakness!

Or they *wouldn't* ask for an explanation, which might be worse, for that would mean they were being *understanding*, choosing not to mention her little indiscretion, like a drunk's crude remark or an old lady's fart.

So she hesitated longer, not knowing what to do, decided that she must decide right now, and then realized that her hesitation *was* her decision.

As usual, she had let fear control her.

She felt the usual wave of self-contempt, made only worse because just yesterday—if "yesterday" meant anything anymore—she had quite bravely leapt from the high rock with Umbo. But that was different; the boy was going to die if she didn't do something. She was responsible for him. It was so much easier to be brave when you were saving someone else. But when you were the one at risk, then courage was selfish, false, dangerous, pointless. Better to hide.

Better to be left behind? Better to be hungry, unable to find food? Better to be seen as a coward, unable to cope with the slightest stress? She would never earn the respect of these people, least of all her brother. Not that she *needed* their respect—she was Sissaminka, wasn't she?

Not anymore. She was nothing now. It did her no good to regard these people as lower than her station. And yet they were—every bit of her upbringing told her so. Umbo, the boy whose hand she had held, whose life she had saved and who had saved her life in turn, he was barely educated, he was the son of an artisan. Now he thought they were friends. Impossible. Yet if she was ever to have a friend, why not him?

Param saw that the others were out of sight. She did not want to lose track of where they were. She slipped back into realtime and followed softly. Her shoes clacked on the floor of the museum, so she slipped them off. Now the floor was slippery, so she dared not run. She turned a corner. There they were.

She would have to speak, to be seen, they would look at her.

She slipped back into slow time and cursed herself again for the habitual coward she was.

In a moment, Rigg and Loaf were gone with Vadesh, and Umbo followed them down the stairs almost at once.

Olivenko was alone.

Olivenko, her father's student. A mere guard now, yes, but still an educated man, familiar with the courtesies, softspoken, kind.

She slipped back into realtime and put her shoes back on. Only a few steps and he heard her.

He said nothing, though. He merely waited, eyes averted, as she approached. He pretended to be examining one of the large machines, but she knew he was waiting for her. So sensitive, so aware of what she needed.

"Thank you for waiting," she said softly.

"I'm glad you returned to us," said Olivenko. "I was worried about you."

"I was worried about myself," said Param. It was not a thing she expected herself to say; normally, embarrassed as she was, she would say nothing. But to Olivenko, in this moment, she felt the need to tell the truth. "I'm ashamed of myself for running away," she said. "I didn't mean to disappear like that. Hiding is a habit."

"A habit that kept you alive during very difficult times."

She felt a rush of gratitude. He did not condemn her. "But it's inconvenient now," she said. "If I hesitate while I'm . . . like that, then things move on without me. I'm always falling behind."

"It keeps you young," said Olivenko.

She did not know what he meant.

"Literally," said Olivenko. "You're slicing time, you're moving forward without living through the intervening moments. So for each hour that passes, you live much less than an hour. You don't age as quickly. The more you've lived in hiding like that, the less time has passed for you, and the younger you are."

"Yes, that's so," said Param.

"You should be sixteen, but do you think you are? Perhaps you're only fifteen years old. Or fourteen."

"I feel very old," said Param. "Are you sure it doesn't work the other way?"

He chuckled—not a loud laugh, so it didn't sound derisive. It sounded as though he enjoyed her remark, as though he thought it was witty.

"Where have the others gone?"

"With Vadesh, to go into a starship," said Olivenko. "Shall we find them?"

Param strode boldly forward, though she did not know where she was going. It seemed the thing to do, the antidote to her timidity of a few moments before. Soon they saw Umbo among the machines, but he was alone.

"Where did they go?" Param asked him. She made her tone peremptory, commanding, so that she would not have to deal with any questions from him about where she had gone when she disappeared.

"I don't know," said Umbo.

"Why aren't you with them?" she insisted.

Then he told them that his future self had appeared to him with a warning: Stay here. Do nothing. He did not know why the warning had come, and in her impatience, and partly because she had assumed an air of command, it quickly turned into a quarrel, each accusing the other of cowardice. Param said harsh things, but so did Umbo; Umbo's words stung all the more because she knew that they were true. And when they found the place where the others had gone down the stairs, her fear began to rise again: What was the danger that Umbo's future self had warned against? She felt herself starting to slow down, to vanish, and so she paced back and forth, determined not to let herself disappear again. She could not let this habit master her.

Umbo went down the stairs to look for Loaf and Rigg and Vadesh. But Olivenko stayed with her.

"Why don't you go, too?" she asked.

"Loaf can handle anything that comes up," said Olivenko. "I don't like the idea of any of us being alone. So I'll stay with you, if you don't mind."

"Do what you want." She sounded surly, though she hadn't meant to.

"I always do," said Olivenko, sounding amused.

"You think I'm funny?" asked Param.

"No, I think *I'm* funny," said Olivenko. "I gallantly stay behind to protect you—but of all the people in our group, you're the one who least needs my protection. I'm not good for much, am I? I'm not half the soldier Loaf is, and I can't fiddle with time the way you others can. Maybe I'm along to write the history afterward. Or perhaps I'll be the one who dies, so that you can be warned that danger has arrived. That's how it works in stories—there's one who isn't really needful to the tale, and so he's the one who gets killed first. Usually he's forgotten; nobody even mentions him at the end."

"That's bleak," said Param. But she knew what he meant. She had heard many such tales, growing up. The one who can die and not be missed. She had never thought of that. Was it her role, after all? Mother thought so.

But no. Sissaminka would be missed. Her absence would be noted. She was not one who could die without repercussions. Mother would see. She had put too much trust in General Citizen. And when word got out that Param was gone, everyone would be sure Mother and General Citizen had killed her. There would be outrage. There would be rebellion, vengeance, justice.

"You look very fierce," said Olivenko.

"Thinking of Mother," said Param.

"It must have been devastating," said Olivenko, "to have her turn on you."

"I always knew what she was," said Param. "I shouldn't have been surprised." And then, quite suddenly, she found herself crying. "I don't know why I—please don't touch me—it's just that I—"

"It's all right," said Olivenko. "You've been very calm through everything. You're entitled to unwind a little now."

"But there's still danger, there's still . . ."

Olivenko said nothing.

Param felt herself swaying. She put out a hand and found his arm, leaned on him. In a moment she found that he had led her to a place where they could sit on a part of one of the machines.

"I'm sorry," she said.

"I'm not," he said. "I'm glad."

She faced him then, startled, prepared to be angry.

"Glad that you didn't disappear," said Olivenko. "Glad that you trusted me enough to stay."

Param shook her head. "I can't speed up time when I'm crying. Or slow myself down, or whatever it is I do. That's why I learned not to let myself cry or scream. Instead I vanish. Only I'm trying not to. Trying not to let it be a habit."

"You want to do it only when you decide," said Olivenko.

"Yes," said Param.

"You're not crying now," said Olivenko. "But you're still angry with your mother."

"Angry at myself for letting her take me by surprise," said Param.

"She's your mother. Of course her plotting against you took you by surprise."

"She's not my mother, she's Hagia Sessamin. She does things for royal reasons, not personal sentimentality."

"That's the lie she tells herself to excuse her crimes," said Olivenko. "You can believe her if you want, but I don't. I think she acts *only* for personal reasons, and never once thinks of the kingdom."

Param felt her anger flare up, but stopped herself from speaking sharply. How could she defend her mother after what the woman had done to her?

"It's like your father," said Olivenko. "The best man I ever knew. He said that he was pursuing a way through the Wall for the benefit of the whole kingdom. He talked about how the opening of the border would free everyone, widen the world. But it was all very vague. What he really wanted was to find some reason to exist."

"He was Sissamik," said Param. "*That*'s a reason to exist."

"It's an office. A title. He told me once—just once, mind you—that he was a mere decoration on the costume of a deposed queen. An accessory, like shoes, like a hat. If his wife ruled, he would still have no power; since she did not, he was worse than useless."

"He was wonderful," said Param. "He was the only one who treated me like . . ."

"Like a daughter."

"Like a little girl," said Param. "But yes, like a daughter."

"He found you fascinating. 'She'll be Sessamin someday, after her mother, and if she has power she'll have the power to be a monster if she wants, like her great-grandmother, the boy-killer.'"

"He said that?"

"It wasn't an insult—it was one of her self-chosen titles. She killed all her male relatives so that no man could rival her daughter for the Tent of Light. She chose Knosso to be your mother's consort, and left strict instructions that he was to be killed after he fathered two daughters."

"Two?"

"Just in case," said Olivenko. "Your mother bore Rigg instead, and then Knosso never quite managed to sire another child on her. So he never found out whether someone would have carried out old Aptica Sessamin's command. There had been a revolution in the meantime, but that didn't mean some old royalist wouldn't try to fulfill the old lady's wish."

"He must have talked very candidly with you."

"More like he forgot I was there, and talked to himself. He

wanted to do something great. Maybe he did—but then he died, so he didn't get to enjoy the fruits of his labor. He passed through the Wall, and then drowned. Was there a moment there in which he said, 'I did it!' and savored his triumph? Or was it all just the hands of the monsters from the sea, dragging him down?"

"I thought you said he was unconscious."

"That's what the learned doctors declared, but I suspect it was only to console your mother. I think he was struggling. I think he was awake."

"How awful."

"Awful for a few moments, and then he was dead. The cruelest means of dying still ends the same. With release."

"Release," said Param. "It sounds pleasant."

"And yet I don't want to do it," said Olivenko. "Not now, not ever. Miserable as I sometimes am in this life, I like being alive." He held up his hands. "I'm used to having these fingers do my bidding. I don't even have to ask them. Before I even think of what I want, before I could put my wishes into words, they're already obeying me. My feet, too. My eyes open when I want to see, and close when I want to sleep. Such obedient servants. I'd miss them."

"So you think some part of you will persist after death?"

"If not, I won't know it," said Olivenko. "And if so, then I'll miss my hands and feet and eyes and also lunch. I'll miss food. And sleep. And waking up."

"Maybe death is better."

"Not according to the advertisements."

"What advertisements?"

"You see? If it were better, there'd be advertisements."

"Why bother to advertise, since everyone's going to do it anyway?"

"I didn't think of that," said Olivenko ruefully.

Param chuckled, and then realized she was amused. That, for a moment, she was something like happy. "Well, thank you for that," said Param.

"The laugh was your own," said Olivenko. "I was merely ridiculous."

"It was kind of you to be ridiculous for me."

They talked on, the easy conversation of new friends, each telling about experiences that illustrated some point they were making, spinning out the yarns of their lives and weaving them together haphazardly into a sort of homespun that wrapped them both and made them feel warm. Through it all, Olivenko only rarely looked at her; whether it was deference to her rank or sensitivity to her shyness or a kind of shyness of his own, she didn't know. But it allowed her to look at him fully, frankly, deciding that as grown men went, he was not bad looking. Manly enough in the cut of his jaw and the strength of his neck, but still with the eyes of a scholar, a kind of distance, as if he could see things that ordinary people never saw.

And what did he see? He had seen Father, and liked him, and cared about him.

And he sees me. And likes me. And . . .

Param felt herself blush a little and she turned away. She felt herself coasting along the edge of slow time, but did not step over. She remained here with him.

"Thanks for not leaving," said Olivenko.

"You knew?" Param said softly.

"I don't know what you thought of," said Olivenko, "or what you saw, but you turned away and froze. Like a deer, the moment before it leaps away. I was afraid you were going to leave."

"I might have," said Param. "But I decided not to fear you."

"Yes, that's what everyone decides," said Olivenko. "I'm not much of a soldier, not much of a guard."

"But you're guarding *me,*" said Param. "I'm not supposed to fear you."

"Well, that's good then," said Olivenko. And then he went off on a story about a time when he challenged a drunk who was trying to stray into the wrong part of the city, and the drunk showed his contempt by urinating on him.

"No!" cried Param.

"Oh, we arrested him, which means we knocked him down, and the sergeant didn't understand why I didn't kick him there on the ground. How could I explain that I agreed with the man's assessment of me as a soldier? The sergeant was ready to believe I was a coward, and he taunted me, saying that I liked it, come on everyone and pee on Olivenko, it won't make him mad."

"How crude," said Param.

"They didn't do it," said Olivenko. "I gave the drunk a couple of kicks. It didn't hurt him much, there was so much wine in him, and it got the sergeant to shut up."

"Oh," said Param, vaguely disappointed.

"If I had principles," said Olivenko, "I would never have helped a couple of fugitives like you and Rigg get away."

"Then I supposed I'm glad you don't."

And so it went until Rigg and Loaf and Umbo came up the stairs, and Param saw the facemask on Loaf's head and cried out in sympathy and horror, and she felt Olivenko's arm around her, his hands on her arm and shoulder, steadying her. "Stay with us," said Olivenko.

"Vadesh did it," said Rigg. "He claims this is a different type of facemask, created to blend harmoniously with humans."

"Loaf is still alive in there," said Umbo.

"Can't you take it off?" asked Param.

"It would kill him," said Rigg. "Or he'd kill us. When you reach to try to pry it off, Loaf turns into a soldier in battle. He'd break us like twigs."

"Olivenko's a soldier, too," said Umbo.

"Not like him," said Olivenko. He wasn't going to try to pry off the facemask.

"Then what are we going to do?" asked Param.

"I think now is a good time to get out of Vadeshfold," said Rigg. "To a wallfold that doesn't have Vadesh in it. Or facemasks."

"Might have something worse," said Umbo.

"Like what?" asked Rigg. "What is worse than this?" He indicated Loaf's face.

"Death," said Param.

"Let's see how Loaf votes," said Rigg, "on whether death is worse."

"Where will we go?" asked Param.

"I don't know," said Rigg. "Not back to Ramfold. And we don't know anything about any of the others."

"We know that sea monsters in the wallfold to the north drowned your father," said Olivenko.

"Is that a vote to go south?" asked Rigg. "Because I'm open to any suggestions."

"East," said a voice that seemed to come from nowhere. A woman's voice, and yet Param had not spoken.

"Who was that?" demanded Umbo.

"The ship," said Rigg. He raised his voice, addressing the invisible speaker. "Any particular reason?" he asked.

"No one will harm you there," said the ship's voice.

"I vote for that," said Rigg.

"Can we trust it? Her?" asked Olivenko.

"It gave me control over Vadesh," said Rigg. "It gave me control over the Wall."

"Vadesh said you had the power to command *him*, too, and look how that turned out," said Umbo.

"If we get to the Wall and it doesn't let us through, we'll know that the ship was lying."

"How can a ship talk?" asked Param.

"Ancient machines," said Olivenko. "Your father read about them. Machines that talk, but they have no soul."

Param looked at the machines that brooded around them, wondering if any of them could talk.

"Can you show us the way to the eastern wallfold?" asked Rigg.

Umbo snorted. "Go east," he said.

"There are very high mountains east of us," said Rigg. "Wherever the starships crashed, there are now high mountains, like the Upsheer Cliffs."

"There is no road to the eastern Wall," said the voice of the starship. "Go around the mountains to the south. Then go east to the sea. If you pass through the Wall near the sea, you'll enter Odinfold."

"So presumably we'll meet an expendable named Odin," said Olivenko. "Is he a lying snake, too?"

"They all are," said Rigg. "It's how they were designed, these machines that talk."

"Well then," said Olivenko. "Let's go look for food and then set out on our journey. The sooner we go, the sooner we find out just what trap this mechanical voice has in store for us."

Neither Rigg nor the voice said anything to that.

"Can Loaf make a journey like that?" asked Umbo.

"I'm not leaving him behind," said Rigg.

"I'd stay with him," said Umbo.

"Let's see what he decides to do," said Rigg. "If he doesn't follow us, then you stay with him."

"But then we'd be trapped here," said Umbo.

Rigg hesitated a moment, apparently making a decision. "Any two of you can go through the Wall, whether I'm there or not."

"When did that happen?" asked Olivenko.

"I used the jewels and gave the command," said Rigg.

"Any two of us," said Umbo. "But not one of us alone."

Param saw that Rigg was embarrassed, but then he stood straighter. "I didn't want anyone going off alone. We're safer together."

"But if you want to go through alone?" asked Umbo.

Rigg sighed. "Then I can do it, yes."

Umbo was clearly angry, and Param understood why. Rigg had made these rules, giving himself a degree of freedom the others did not have.

It was Olivenko who calmed them down. "The stones are his," he said. "Not mine. And I'm not planning to go through any Walls by myself. Is anyone else? Then I'm not bothered by not having the power to do something I don't want to do anyway. And I'm hungry." He stood up.

Param stood up too. Only after she was standing did she realize that by doing so, she had lent her support to Olivenko's decision.

And what was that decision? To look for food, yes. And to go along with Rigg and the rules he had set out.

What Param didn't know was whether that made Rigg the leader of their expedition, or Olivenko.

CHAPTER 9

Responsibility

To Rigg, it was a relief to strike out over untracked country. For one thing, it was familiar—he and Father had done it so often before, and though he half expected to hear Father asking him questions, he also didn't mind the silence as the others trudged along behind him.

It was also a relief to have no one seeking them, to have no particular hurry. There were dangers, of course—who knew which waters might contain facemasks? But it had not been hard to attach thin branches to tin cups, dip them in a stream, and then boil the water before replenishing their waterskins. It was time-consuming, but they had time. There were no predators large enough to pose a danger to them, for if there had been, Rigg would have seen their paths. As for danger from poisonous plants or insects, all they could do to protect themselves was look before they stepped or leaned or touched.

What was strange, though, was the lack of human paths. The farther they got from the city of Vadesh, the fewer the ten-thousand-year-old paths, and soon enough even those were gone. From then on there were no human paths, except now and then the trace of some ancient hunter from the days before the face-mask people and the unadorned humans went to war and wiped each other out.

In all his life, Rigg had never seen a place so empty of a human past. He had heard other people say, "It felt as if we were the first people ever to walk there," speaking of some wild patch of wood or meadow, but of course Rigg knew that there was hardly a place in Ramfold where no human had ever been, or which no human had seen.

Here, though, it was literally true: No human eyes had seen this view, no human feet had walked this hill, descended into this glen, found toeholds in this rock. Rigg couldn't decide whether to be proud of bringing the first human paths into the land, or to regret spoiling its pristine clarity. For wherever they went, five bright and recent paths glowed behind them.

It was not all silence. Olivenko spoke from time to time, conversing with Param or Umbo, or asking Rigg a question. And Param, though she tried not to complain, had to speak up now and then to ask for a rest. She was truly unused to such traveling, hour after hour on their feet, moving forward, up and down, sometimes climbing with hands and feet.

The rests were not wasted. Rigg used the time to find water. He was learning that the native animals knew which water was infested with facemasks, and avoided it; where many animals had drunk over a long period of time, and recently, Rigg felt safe to take water without boiling it. He drank it himself first as a test. That was only right. And when they stopped longer, or for the evening, Rigg would find animal paths and set snares, so that by morning there would be meat. He would string the small animal carcasses over his back, letting them drain as they walked, then let Olivenko or Umbo cook them that night as he set snares for more. Rigg also found nuts, berries, edible roots—enough variety that the meat did not become tedious. Providing for five took more work than providing for himself and Father, but not much, and Rigg felt more than a little pride that no one went hungry while in his care.

Rigg felt bad for Param, who had obviously never climbed so much as a tree in her childhood; and he could see that her shoes would not last the journey. He would have to make her some moccasins, and he saved several pelts for that purpose. He also knew that Param did not like walking directly behind him—he supposed the sight and perhaps smell of the dead animals he wore across his shoulders bothered her. She had not seen the animals she ate being killed before, had not seen their carcasses still shaped like the living animal, but headless and skinless. If she didn't like seeing them now, there was no reason to insist that she look. She would get used to the cycle of life soon enough.

What oppressed Rigg, what weighed on him with every step, was the silence from Loaf, and the way Umbo stayed near the man with the mask, holding his hand as if to guide him, as if he were blind. Loaf's eyes were covered but they were not blind; he saw more unerringly than anyone, his hands finding every hold when they had to climb, ducking under every branch or pushing it out of the way. Without seeming alert, Loaf saw and heard everything. But he said nothing. Umbo mumbled things to him from time to time, but Rigg did not try to hear what passed between them. They had spent a long time together, apart from Rigg, and Rigg would not insert himself between them. How could he? It was Rigg who had allowed this terrible thing to happen to Loaf. Umbo did not accuse, but he didn't have to. Rigg accused himself.

The high escarpment to their left bent to the east, and they turned with it, staying below it. It reminded Rigg of Upsheer Cliff, of course, since it had been caused by an identical starship crashing into the ground at the same angle and velocity eleven thousand years ago. Since Vadesh and the first colonists had built a tunnel and track from the city into the mountain, Rigg wondered now if there had been another tunnel and track leading out the other side. Why hadn't he asked when he was there where the ship's computer could answer him?

And were there tunnels in the other wallfolds, ways to get deep into the heart of the mountain without climbing the high cliffs? There was so much he wanted to know.

Most of all, though, he wondered what he could do to resist the humans from Earth when—or if—they came, and if they needed to be resisted at all. What if they came only as rescuers, and when they found that the people of the colonies on Garden had survived for longer than all of human history on Earth, they would marvel at the fact, and then peacefully negotiate with the people of each wallfold, and let the worlds become acquainted with each other. Why shouldn't it be that way?

Only Rigg knew that the expendables were right to fear the coming of the humans. In the eleven thousand years of human life on Garden, there had been no change in the deep nature of human beings, not in Ramfold, anyway—it was eleven millennia of war, of empires that rose and fell, nations that burgeoned and shrank, languages that developed and disappeared. Vadeshfold was only different in that the facemasks were involved, and history ended in the death of all humans. Death and mutual destruction had come close in Ramfold's history, too, a couple of times. It was in human nature, and if a hundred and twelve centuries on Garden hadn't been enough to breed hatred and war out of the human character, Rigg could hardly hope that in the eleven years that had passed on Earth there would be any improvement. They would find that there was something strange here and they would be afraid. Fear would create enmity. It would be mutual. But the people from Earth would have technology that the expendables had not allowed any humans on Garden to match.

And what do we have to counter them? We can hold hands and flee back in time. That will make them tremble!

Rigg could only hope that there was something in some other wallfold that would allow the people of Garden to protect themselves. Yet if there was, why would the people of that wallfold believe Rigg about the danger that was coming? For that matter, why should Rigg believe in it himself? It's not as if the expendables had been unfailingly honest with him. Could he say that he knew, for himself, that there was some danger coming? No. And yet he must persuade them to help him, to work together with the other wallfolds to find some way to protect the world, to meet the people of Earth as equals, with strength enough not to invite conquest and destruction.

And what if, in one of the wallfolds, there was some variant of humanity that was far more dangerous than anything that might come from Earth? What would Rigg do then? Leave their Wall in place, of course, if he could. But it was just as likely that any such powerful race would overwhelm him before he could give any command to the ships. They would take the jewels from him and rule the world and then it would be up to the people of Earth to protect themselves from the monsters of Garden.

Or none of these things. What if many wallfolds were empty? What if Ramfold was the most advanced of the wallfolds, and there was nothing but this feeble gift of time manipulation?

That would be easy, then. Rigg and Umbo and Param had only to keep silent about their gifts, and let the humans from Earth rescue the people of Garden as they surely expected. There were too many here to take home to Earth, of course, but they could provide the ancient technologies and bring us back to the level that human civilizations had reached on Earth, when they achieved the power to reach out beyond their own star system. Then their coming would be a gift.

Or a curse. They might conquer us, rule over us. But was that anything new? Would it be worse than when the Sessamids came with their mountain warriors and conquered the people of Aressa and all the lands drained by the Stashik River? One harsh ruling class would replace another. Wasn't that the course of human history? What difference would it make, that one group of humans was in the ascendancy for a while, until they fell to another?

In that case, we're on a fool's errand, thought Rigg. Why go from wallfold to wallfold?

Because we can, he answered himself. Because for the first time in eleven thousand, one hundred ninety-one years, humans can go through the Walls, and find out what has become of our once-identical cousins on the other side, and what we humans *can* do, we must try, or why are we alive?

Rigg saw that Param wasn't with them. He went back a short way and found her.

"I can't go on," said Param.

"Time to rest then," said Rigg. "This isn't good ground for a camp, though. Can you go a little farther to see if the ground levels out above this rise?"

"No," said Param. "I don't mean it's time to rest. I mean I can't go on."

Rigg looked at her. It was true that she looked tired and bedraggled and she could use a bath and her clothes could use a washing and her hair wanted combing, but what of that? They'd been trekking for nearly three weeks.

"You mean you want to go back?"

"No," said Param. "I don't want to *go* at all."

Rigg was nonplussed. "You want to stay here on this slope until you die?"

"It won't be long."

"Actually, you ate and drank only a few hours ago. So if you stay here it will take several days for you to dehydrate enough to die. And then you'll fall and roll down the slope, so you won't actually stay here until you die."

"She's got a point," said Umbo. He and Loaf had followed at once when Rigg went back for Param. "Where are we going? How far is it? Do you have any idea?"

"It's farther than this," said Rigg. "Assuming the escarpment is roughly round or oval, it has to turn completely east before we've rounded it to the south and can strike out for the coast."

"If anything we were told is true," said Param.

"*We* weren't told anything," said Umbo. "The voice only talked to Rigg."

"We heard it," said Param. "Oh, please don't fight over this. I just can't go on, that's all I'm saying. I'm exhausted. You said I'd get stronger, but I'm not."

"You are," said Rigg. "Much stronger. You walk farther each day, you move faster, you rest less often. Of course you're stronger."

"Walk farther, farther, farther, and up and down forever," said Param. "The whole land looks the same."

"But it's not," said Rigg. "It changes. With the elevation. We have different trees in this forest now, higher elevation yet from farther south. Different animals, a different season."

"If there's a difference, I can't see it," said Param.

Were people of the city all as blind as this? "We're making progress," said Rigg. "This is what a journey requires."

"We had a carriage when we left the city," said Param. "We had horses after. And we were running from danger. There's no danger here. Where are we going? Why?"

"We've talked about this before. And you had the choice, when we were still near the Wall. You could have—"

"But I didn't," said Param, "and now I'm here. Why couldn't we all have ridden that self-moving wagon you rode on, and gone into the starship, and flown away?"

"Because it's buried under millions of tons of rock," said Rigg. "To start with."

"I know you're doing what they said to do," said Umbo. "And you've provided food for us, and we've been safe. But look at us. Look at Loaf. This is what came from doing what these machines told us to do. Why are we listening to them?"

"Good question," said Olivenko, who had finally come back to join them.

"What else can we do?" asked Rigg. "If we're in danger from starships from the home planet of the human race, then—"

"If," said Param. "Ships between the stars? Really?"

"We saw the ship that planted us here when it arrived," said Rigg. "As we passed through the Wall."

"We saw *something*," said Olivenko. "We only have the machines' word that it meant what they said it meant."

"Do you have some better source of information?" asked Rigg. "If what they say is true, then we're the best hope of the human race—human *races*—of Garden."

"Have we met any living humans from another wallfold?" asked Param.

"Why did your father train you, if you were just supposed to leave the wallfold where that training had some application?" asked Umbo.

"Do what you want," said Rigg. "Go where you want. I'm going on." Rigg rose to his feet and began to climb up the slope.

"So you'll just leave us?" asked Param.

"You're free to come," said Rigg. "Or stay and rest."

"He's bluffing," said Umbo. "He knows we can't get food without him."

"He won't leave Loaf," said Olivenko.

"He won't leave *me*," said Param.

But Rigg kept walking. Yes, he had started this maneuver as a bluff, but Umbo's assertion of it as fact made him harden his resolve. They wouldn't starve—Olivenko and Umbo were resourceful, even if Param and Loaf were useless. And if Rigg turned around now, then their trek would collapse into a democracy, which meant that whatever whim struck them would change their plans. There'd be no purpose. And he'd be trapped with them.

So Rigg would move on, and let them do whatever they wanted. Either they'd run and catch up with him, or they wouldn't. In the former case, this nonsense would stop; in the latter, then he wouldn't have to play at being leader anymore.

Nobody followed him. Nobody called after him. And Rigg never looked back.

Without others to provide for, Rigg realized he wouldn't have to stop so soon, wouldn't have to search for a camping place with water and firewood at hand. He didn't have to hunt or trap for food. With the bit of meat he had saved to eat as he walked, he could keep moving until dark. Or later—following the paths of animals, he wouldn't fall into canyons or pits in the dark.

But if they changed their minds, they'd never catch him if he doubled his pace. So it was time to decide: Did he *want* to leave them behind and proceed alone? Or did he want to give them a chance to rejoin him?

He had already gone too far for them to catch up before nightfall, especially if they had dithered before changing their minds and following him. But he could build up a big, bright fire, set traps for meat, and then get a late start in the morning. It would be good for them to spend a night in the dark and cold without him.

In the morning, his plans began to seem foolish. Were they following him or not? They were too far for him to search out their paths; did that mean they weren't coming, or that they were moving slowly? He cooked and dried the flesh of the animals that his traps had taken during the dusk and dawn. And still they didn't come.

So I'm on my own, he thought. It made him feel bleak. Lonely. But it also eased his mind. I have no more responsibility, he thought.

Only his mind wasn't so easy after all. What if they had tried to follow him in the dark, and got lost? They had no knack for tracking. Umbo should be able to follow, though—he had grown up near the woods, and he was smart.

But they were burdened with Loaf. And Param. How much ground could they cover? As long as he had been with the others, Rigg had ranged ahead, then returned to the group, again and again. Now, since he had stopped checking back with them, just how far and how fast *had* he gone? Without his encouragement and guidance, how slow had they become? Maybe they were trying to catch up with him. Or maybe they were lost.

Slow, or lost.

Or heading back to the Wall, without any means of getting more food.

And Rigg gradually realized that their lives were more important to him than getting his own way. Yes, they had rebelled against his authority, but it was authority he hadn't asked for, and didn't want. He had taken charge only because he knew how to survive in the wilderness; but what difference did it make how quickly they moved? It's not as if he had some urgent appointment in the next wallfold. And it had been stupid to go on alone. What if he needed them? Umbo and Param had time-shifting skills that might save him. And Olivenko, the only soldier they had left, might be just as necessary.

And what about Loaf? Why had Rigg thought he could leave Loaf behind? Just because Umbo was so devoted to Loaf, and had become much closer to him during their time together while Rigg was in Flacommo's house, didn't mean that Rigg wasn't responsible for bringing Loaf, or whatever was left of him, back to Leaky in their inn at Leaky's Landing.

Rigg carefully put out his fire, stowed the meat he had dried in his pack, and started back the way he had come.

He walked for hours, and saw no other human paths. They had not followed him.

He reached the place where he had parted with them. Far from following him, they had started back toward the Wall.

Well, then, what responsibility did he have? They weren't trying to rejoin him. They intended to go their own way. If he kept going and caught up with them on the return journey, it would be a complete admission of defeat.

And if he didn't, Loaf might die.

What kind of leader was he, if he abandoned his people?

But in what sense was he a leader, if he surrendered to them completely like this?

He started down the path they had taken, retracing their steps toward the Wall.

Then he changed his mind and began to climb up again, abandoning them to the consequences of their own choice.

Then he stopped, remembering that Loaf had made no choice, and headed back down.

And then the whole matter was taken out of his hands, because from the crest of a ridge he saw something shiny, flying above the trees, coming rapidly toward him.

It was a vehicle from Vadesh's starship. Not the wagon he and Loaf had ridden through the tunnel, but something from the same culture, the same technology. It flew. Was this a starship? No, too small, and it didn't seem designed to withstand the dangers of cold space, as Father had described them to him.

Father had talked about spaceflight. As conjecture, as if it had never happened, but he had talked about it, and enough of it had stuck in Rigg's memory that he knew this flying coach could not be a starship. What else had Father taught him without Rigg's guessing its significance?

Everything. Rigg had never known the significance of anything.

The flying machine rose up swiftly to the level of the crest where Rigg was watching. Then it came to rest in the meadow that surrounded him.

A door opened in the side of it, and Vadesh emerged.

"What are you doing here?" asked Rigg.

"The others called me."

"They're not here."

"I know," said Vadesh. "After I picked them up, I came for you."

"Thank you for telling me that they're safe. Now I can go on."

"There's no reason for you to keep walking," said Vadesh. "I'll take you to the next wallfold, if you want."

"I don't trust you to take me where you say you're taking me," said Rigg.

"The vehicle obeys the ship, and the ship obeys you," said Vadesh. "And I am sworn to obey you now."

"Now that you destroyed my friend," said Rigg.

"Get in the flyer," urged Vadesh. "It will take us all to Odinfold."

"The others wanted to go back to Ramfold," said Rigg. "Take them there, and let me be."

"They changed their minds," said Vadesh.

"Then why aren't they talking to me? Why did they send you?"

Vadesh turned without another word and headed back to the flyer.

Rigg realized how ridiculous this was. What kind of child was he, to insist that they had to ask him nicely to rejoin him? He didn't want to lead them, and they didn't want to be led, so let Vadesh take them wherever they wanted, to do whatever they wanted.

Rigg walked away across the meadow, heading eastward again, retracing paths that he and his one-time companions had already crossed more than once.

Olivenko came out of the flyer and called to him. "Rigg! Wait!"

Rigg just shook his head and went on. He felt foolish. But he would feel foolish no matter what he chose. Somehow, in his hours alone, the wall between him and his erstwhile friends had grown so thick and high that he could not even think of crossing it. They resented him. He was just trying to do his best and they hated him for it. So he was done with them. That was a wall he didn't even want to get through.

So why were tears spilling from his eyes as he continued walking away?

"Please wait," called Olivenko. Rigg could hear him running.

Olivenko is my friend, Rigg remembered.

But he didn't stand with me when the crisis came, he told himself. So he is not my friend.

"Please," said Olivenko. "I know you're angry, you have a right, but it doesn't make sense to pass up a chance to get a ride in this thing. Except for Umbo throwing up the first time it rose into the sky, it's been exhilarating."

Good for you, thought Rigg, still walking.

"Vadesh says we could reach Odinfold well before night. But walking, it will take more than three weeks. Well, it won't take *you* three weeks, trekking alone. But it would have taken us all three weeks at least, at the pace we were going."

Rigg didn't remember deciding to stop walking away from the flyer, but here he was, with Olivenko beside him, at the edge of the meadow. Now he turned to face the man who had once been his real father's friend. "I wish I hadn't brought you all here."

"I distinctly remember Loaf and me carrying *you* the last few steps through the Wall."

"It all started with my foolishness in trying to sell a jewel in O."

"It all started," said Olivenko, "with the arrival on this planet of starships from a world called Earth. You didn't cause that."

"I've made mistake after mistake."

"You didn't cause any of this, Rigg," said Olivenko. "The expendables have been running the whole world from the start."

"But now I'm supposedly in command of all of them."

"That's a joke," said Olivenko. "You only know what they tell you. So by shaping what you know, they shape what you'll order them to do."

Rigg had said almost the same thing to the ship's computer. It was such a relief to know that Olivenko understood the dilemma. "How can I lead anything or anybody when I have no idea what I'm doing?"

"You're not leading because you know everything," said Olivenko.

"Why, then? Because my parents were the deposed queen and king of the Sessamid empire? Because the expendable I called Father bred me and Param into existence so we'd have these abilities to manipulate the flow of time?"

"Both of those things," said Olivenko. "And because your supposed father trained you in all the skills of government, in languages, in finance, in human nature."

"Trained me like a dog."

"Trained you like a soldier," said Olivenko. "Loaf and I were trained like soldiers, too. But look how different we are. Were. Before Loaf acquired his parasitic captor. Loaf was a real soldier. I'm a scholar, pretending to be a soldier because I'm large and strong and because I couldn't find any other work that would keep me alive."

"He's an innkeeper," said Rigg.

"I'm telling you why you're the only possible leader of our group," said Olivenko. "Training is important, which is why the expendable called Ram gave you so much of it. But why did he train *you* and not someone else? He could have trained Param and Umbo—he did train them, to a point. Yet he chose you to receive his constant attention. Why? He's a machine—it wasn't love."

No, it couldn't have been love. Having it said out loud like that stabbed Rigg to the heart. He never loved me because he couldn't possibly love anyone.

I spent my whole childhood without love, unless I count the friendship of Umbo and the rough affection of Nox. But I *thought* I was loved. I thought that one day Father would say it. But now I know that even if he said it, it would be just one more calculated move in my training.

"I'm the last person who should lead," said Rigg. "I'm the one who was most perfectly shaped by these machines. I'm a machine myself. I know it was all illusion, but I still feel this terrible responsibility. This need to carry out the mission these machines chose me for. That's reason enough right there for you all to choose somebody else to lead. You might as well be following Vadesh as me."

"Do you think *we're* machines?" said Olivenko. "We chose you ourselves."

"*Chose* me?" said Rigg. "Param had to flee or her mother and General Citizen would have killed her. Umbo and Loaf—"

"Chose to go to Aressa Sessamo to try to—"

"Get back the jewel I stupidly sold."

"To try to save you, I was going to say. And it wasn't stupid to sell the jewel, it's what Ram intended, knowing what would happen when you did it. It plunged you into the affairs of government, it brought you to your true heritage. By birthright you *are* the king of all Ramfold."

"Param is queen, you mean."

"Param is a lovely girl, but her mother treated her exactly the opposite of the way Ram treated you. She was kept from any knowledge of how to use power, how to influence events around her. She's spent her whole life hiding. She has royal blood, but no royal instincts."

"She has more than you know."

"Whatever her instincts are, she has no idea how to use them. Listen to me, Rigg. Does Umbo resent you? Yes, of course he does. He's also your true friend. Let him work that out in his own way. But one thing is certain—he is *not* capable of leading our little party, if only because neither Param nor I would follow him. Param can't lead. And what am I?"

"The man who made the mistake of befriending me when I was a prisoner, so that you were the only one I could think of to call on when I needed help."

"And I *chose* to help, didn't I?" said Olivenko. "I chose you, and so did everyone else. Did Loaf have to take you and Umbo to O?"

"Leaky made him."

"Loaf does what he wants. Or did," said Olivenko. "Param could have hidden from you. We all chose."

"And then you all chose *not* to follow me."

"I chose to take compassion on Param's weakness and Umbo's resentment. They were in rebellion. You were—correctly, I might add—going on. Loaf was in no position to help anybody. So I had no choice but to stay with them and keep them alive until you came back for us."

"So you knew I'd give in?"

"You're a responsible man, Rigg," said Olivenko. "Don't you get it? That's what you *are*. That's why you're our leader. You take responsibility. So even though you've had the responsibility for the future of the whole human race of Garden thrust upon you, you also have responsibility for the four of us. I knew that you couldn't throw off one responsibility for the sake of the other. You had to do both. Of course you'd come back."

"But you weren't there when I did."

"Vadesh came with the flyer."

"You weren't moving forward to try to meet me," said Rigg. "If you had been, I would have seen your paths."

"We weren't *yet*. We were hungry and couldn't get much beyond nuts and berries to eat. We didn't even know which water was safe to drink. Umbo couldn't admit he was wrong—the boy has more pride than a lord. But Param was already condemning herself for her weakness. Saying that she should have stayed with you, that we shouldn't have let her whining break up our group."

Rigg had no trouble imagining this, particularly since self-blame was part of her weakness.

Part of mine, too, he admitted to himself.

"You're trying to persuade me that giving in and riding the flyer doesn't mean I lost," said Rigg.

"That's the plan," said Olivenko. "How am I doing?"

"You're proving to me that you're the real leader of this group."

"Not possible."

"It wasn't possible while Loaf was still himself, because he wouldn't have followed a member of the city guard. But now—face it, Olivenko, you're the only grownup in the group. And talk about taking responsibility—you're the one bringing us back together."

Olivenko shrugged. "So. Imagine that I'm the leader. Does that mean you shouldn't get inside this flyer and go to the Wall with us? Are you as proud as Umbo? Can't you be in a group that someone else is leading?"

"So you admit it."

"I admit that right now I'm giving you the smartest advice you're going to get, and yes, if you follow my advice, that means that in this one instance, I'm leading you. It's a stupid leader who can't turn follower when somebody offers him a wiser course."

Rigg knew he was right. About everything. Rigg was the leader by training, disposition, birthright. And Olivenko was the leader at the moment by virtue of talking sense.

So why did it feel like failure and humiliation even to *think* of entering the flyer and facing the group that had rejected him and left him to go on alone? He wanted to lash out at them, punish them for their pointless defiance. He wanted to cry at his frustration and loneliness. He wanted to go on alone and never see any of them again. He wanted them to admit that he had been right all along and beg for his forgiveness. Yet he didn't want their subservience. He wanted them to *trust* him. He wanted them to like him. He wanted Umbo to be his friend. And as far as he could tell, he'd never have any of those things.

So it came down to this: He had a responsibility to take care of these people who had committed their lives to his cause when they came with him out of Aressa Sessamo, when they passed through the Wall with him. And if they were willing to go on to Odinfold with him, then it hardly mattered how they got there, or how miserable he felt about all that had happened in the past few days. The tasks at hand mattered more than how he *felt*. Feelings would pass. Feelings were a temporary lie. They must be ignored. Sensible plans must be acted upon.

Rigg nodded. He touched Olivenko's arm. "Thank you for talking to me like a better person than I actually am."

Then Rigg walked to the flyer, with Olivenko close behind.

And when he went through the door, he sat down in a chair and then looked at Param and Umbo in turn, and at Olivenko when he came through the door and also sat. "Thank you for coming to find me," he said. "I'm sorry I left you. I was coming back for you."

"That's all right," said Umbo. A little sullenly, and his ungenerous forgiveness galled Rigg, since in Rigg's view one apology should have been answered with another.

Param reached over to put her hand on Rigg's. "I needed you more than I needed rest," she said softly.

That was what Rigg had needed. A word of kindness. A gesture of affection. A recognition that someone needed him. He could go on now. He could do this.

"Let's go then," said Rigg. "How is Loaf?"

"No change," said Umbo.

"Except that he's stronger and leaner and healthier," said Vadesh. "His companion is helping his body reach its best possible condition."

"Shut up and take us to the Wall," said Rigg.

CHAPTER 10

Foreknowledge

For the first few minutes, the sensation of flying was overpowering, and Rigg could not stop watching the forest and foothills pass underneath them. Rugged ground that he had covered with such labor now looked like gentle cushions of treetops, soft as clouds.

And within the depths of the forest, he could sense the webs of animal paths, and his own path brightly human among them, until they passed over the places where he had doubled back, and then there were no human paths at all.

Only a few minutes, and they had covered a day's hiking.

Only a few minutes more, and he was tired of looking. So quickly did he get used to flying. Just as he had quickly gotten used to the velocity of the cart through the tunnel to the buried starship. Sensations that were unimaginable only an hour before were now to be taken for granted.

But Rigg did not stop looking out the window, because it was better than looking at the others.

And then he realized that he had to face them. Was he planning to avoid their gazes forever? So he turned to them and said something safe. "Does any bird ever move this fast over the ground?"

"The fastest bird on Garden can fly as fast as sixty kilometers per hour, unless you count the speed of a stooping hawk," said Vadesh. "But that's not so much flying as plummeting."

Param raised her eyebrows. Umbo rolled his eyes. As if to say, Vadesh is such a know-it-all.

Rigg thought of the food in his pack. "Does anyone want some of the meat I smoked?"

They glanced at each other, embarrassed.

"This vehicle is equipped with a food synthesizer," said Vadesh. "I had it well-stocked with nutrients, and everyone was able to get what they asked for."

The meaning of "food synthesizer" was clear enough, but the concept struck Rigg as vaguely nauseating. He took out some of his meat and began gnawing at it. The others looked away, as if *he* were doing something disgusting. Well, they'd been glad enough to have such fare a few days ago.

"You know," said Olivenko, "that everything we eat is disgusting."

"Rotten vegetable matter, rotten animal corpses, and assorted feces and other bodily excretions combine in the soil," said Rigg, as if he were back at Flacommo's house being examined by scholars to earn the right to use the library. "From that collection of nutrients, plants draw what they need, combine it with water, air, and sunlight, and grow leaves and branches and fruit, which are consumed by us or by animals that we consume."

"It sounds delicious," said Param.

"The food synthesizer apparently skips the plant stage," said Umbo.

"On the contrary, it skips the rot stage," said Vadesh. "It takes the nutrients from any plant matter and grows whatever molecular structure is required—flesh or plant."

"Takes all the fun out of it," said Umbo. "All the farming."

The conversation was only mildly amusing, but it served its purpose: It allowed them all to converse again, without having to deal with their conflicts in the immediate past.

Now that Rigg could look at them normally, he saw something that had changed in the time they'd spent apart. "Loaf has his eyes back," he said.

"The facemask seemed to thin out over his eyes," said Olivenko. "Only we're not sure whether we're seeing his actual eyes, or eyes that the facemask grew there in order to fool us."

"He could see when his eyes were covered," said Umbo. "He never tripped or stumbled and he always knew where we were."

"Could have been by hearing and sense of smell, even touch—sensing the wind of our movements," said Olivenko.

"I take it you've already had this discussion," said Rigg.

"This quarrel, you mean," said Param. "We don't know anything but they argue about it."

"He looks better with eyes," said Rigg. "In both senses of the word 'look.'"

That was worth a mild chuckle, and they dropped the subject. The whole time, Loaf's gaze remained steadily with Rigg.

The flyer came to a landing at the crest of a large grassy hill. It was no mere meadow—the grass extended as far to the east as the eye could see, with only a few stands of trees providing a sense of distance and scale. Dust clouds rose from some distant herd of animals. Apparently they were very near the Wall, though not so near that any of them felt any effect from it.

What bothered Rigg was the crowd of people gathered on the far side of the Wall. "We have observers," said Rigg.

They all got out of the flyer, including Vadesh, and stood beside it, looking at the crowd of at least a thousand people, probably more, who were arranged on a grassy slope beyond the Wall. Many of them jumped up and waved their hands wildly, so the motion could be seen across the width of the Wall.

"They knew we were coming," said Umbo.

Because they all looked at Vadesh, the expendable put up his hands in a very human gesture of protest. To Rigg, it looked like his father telling him that he was about to refuse him a request. "It wasn't me," said Vadesh. "I didn't tell any of the other expendables that I was coming."

"I thought you told each other everything," said Rigg.

"Eventually, yes." Then Vadesh added, "Or at least I tell *them*. I think they are not all candid with me."

"Nevertheless, these people seem to have known we were arriving, and they're here to greet us," said Olivenko.

"Or they've come to rush through if we bring down the Wall," said Rigg.

"Bring it down," said Vadesh. "This wallfold needs people."

"People to wear your happy little facemasks?" said Param.

Vadesh made no answer.

Rigg was scanning the distant crowd, not with his eyes—the distance was too great to pick out individuals with any clarity—but with his path-sense. "They didn't all come from the same place," he said. "They've come from many places, and some of them very far away. They must have been traveling for days."

"Well, I don't want to cross here, then," said Olivenko. "Who knows what they have in store for us?"

"Feels like a trap," said Umbo.

"They seem to be waving to us," said Param. "Cheerfully. Beckoning."

"Laughing," said Olivenko.

"You can't possibly hear any laughter," said Vadesh.

"But you can," said Olivenko. "And I can see enough of their body movement and attitudes to see that they're on a frolic. I don't think they have any hostile intent."

"Or that's what they want us to think," said Umbo.

"No danger," said Loaf.

Everyone turned to him at once. Loaf had not spoken since he was possessed by the facemask weeks before.

"No weapons," said Loaf, still looking across the grassy expanse of the Wall.

"Is this you talking?" asked Umbo. "Or the facemask?"

"Me," said Loaf.

"The facemask would make him answer the same way," said Param.

Loaf reached up a hand and rested it comfortably on the facemask, the way a pregnant woman might rest her hand on her swollen belly. "Husband of Leaky, soldier, innkeeper, it's me," said Loaf. "But yes, the mask is happy to have me say so. The mask is glad that I'm speaking now."

"Why haven't you spoken before?" asked Umbo, still suspicious.

"Nothing to say," said Loaf.

Rigg laughed. "Yes, it's Loaf," he said. "Same sense of humor. Or at least it's as much of Loaf as we're likely to get. I don't suppose you can take off that thing now?"

"Don't want to," said Loaf. "I see so clearly now. I see all the faces, all the hands, what they're wearing. No weapons. All unarmed. And happy, interested, excited."

"You can *see* that?" asked Olivenko.

"Seeing what *you* saw, you have a soldier's eye," said Loaf. It was the most generous thing he had ever said to Olivenko. "But the mask has clarified all my senses. Overwhelming for days. Too much. And it was trying to take control. Manipulate me. But I would not obey. And now it doesn't try. But I see far and clear. I hear everything. I smell everything. The mask helps me sort it out. It's a gift."

"What did I tell you?" said Vadesh. "That's how I designed it to work!"

"Even the original facemasks probably made their victims feel that way," said Umbo sourly. He turned away from Loaf. For weeks, he had been holding the man's hand, guiding him; now it was as if Umbo couldn't bear to see him or be near him.

"We'll have plenty of time to sort out who and what Loaf has become," said Rigg. "Right now we have a few hundred people waiting to greet us on the other side of the Wall."

"Three thousand, two hundred and twenty, including the babies," said Loaf.

"You counted them?"

"All the ones who can be seen," said Loaf. "There are more behind the hill, since a few dozen people have left and a few others have come out since we've been watching."

"Three thousand, two hundred and twenty is a suspiciously round number," said Umbo.

"It's an estimate," said Param.

"It's the exact count," said Loaf. "Someone just left, so it's three thousand, two hundred and nineteen now."

"Counting the babies," said Olivenko drily.

"When people make up numbers and want them to sound exact," said Rigg, "they usually make sure the number doesn't end with zero or five. But in the real world, there's a twenty percent chance that a random number of items will end in either zero or five."

"So you believe him," said Param.

"There are several hundred people behind the hill," said Rigg. "I see their paths. And while I can't say if Loaf's count is correct, I have no reason to doubt it. We all saw how the facemasks fought in the battle we watched. Their precision, their accuracy. Facemasks enhance the abilities of the people who wear them."

"The people controlled by them, you mean," said Umbo.

"Loaf says he isn't controlled," said Rigg, "and we have no evidence to contradict him."

"So you're just going to believe him while he waits for a chance to plant baby facemasks on all of us?" said Param.

"I won't do that," said Loaf.

"They don't reproduce that way," said Vadesh.

"You don't know half of what they do," said Loaf, turning on Vadesh. "In all your years of studying them, you didn't know they can give off spores within fifteen minutes of deciding to?"

"How can you possibly know that?" said Vadesh. "Humans and facemasks don't communicate."

"It would be interesting to take you apart and see how you work," said Loaf. "So smart, and yet you're only machine smart, not human smart."

Vadesh stood in silence.

"I don't want to cross through the Wall with all those people there," said Rigg.

"Then don't," said Param.

"It's what we came for," said Umbo.

"I mean, don't do it when those people are watching."

"You think they'll get bored and go away?" asked Olivenko.

Param looked at Olivenko with her are-you-really-this-stupid expression.

"She means that we should cross the Wall *before* these people show up," said Umbo.

Rigg looked at the people's paths. "They've only been here for a couple of days."

"What does that matter?" asked Param. "Why don't we go back ten years?"

The idea immediately appealed to Rigg. "You're right. We

don't know when the next ship from Earth will come. Ten years will give us plenty of time to visit all the other wallfolds and figure out what we can do to defend against them, because we'd know the Earth ships wouldn't come for at least ten years."

Vadesh immediately dampened their enthusiasm. "You only got control of the Wall nineteen days ago. If you go back in time before that, you'll have no control. You'll have to pass through the Wall on your own, they way you got into Vadeshfold in the first place."

Rigg immediately remembered the crushing despair, the utter terror, the agony of his minutes—his decades, it had seemed—inside the Wall.

"This time we wouldn't have General Citizen trying to kill us," Param said helpfully.

"And now you know how to go back in time and then return without my help," said Umbo.

"Maybe someday we'll need to do that—go back in time to put off our confrontation with the people of Earth," said Rigg. "But right now, since nineteen days ago, any two of us can simply walk through the Wall."

"So let's go back nineteen days to dodge the crowd," said Olivenko.

"I can't calibrate it like that," said Umbo.

"Neither can I," said Rigg. "It's not like the paths have calendars attached." But even as he said it, Rigg realized that he could do it well enough. He remembered that when he first discovered that the paths were actually people in motion through time, he had been standing on a clifftop with Umbo, unbeknownst to him, slowing time so that he could see the people instead of the paths. Couldn't they simply go back a day at a time? Or *count* back? By picking one animal's path, and then another's, Rigg could work his way back to the exact time, then attach to that animal and bring the others with him.

"You've thought of a way?" asked Olivenko.

"Yes," said Rigg. "Take my hands."

"No," said Vadesh. "Get inside the flyer, so I can go back, too, and still have the flyer with me."

Rigg looked at him coldly. "We won't need you," said Rigg. "And I don't want to send you back in time, knowing what you know now."

"What do I know that's so dangerous?"

"I don't want you knowing, nineteen days ago, that our party broke up, that we came here and found people waiting on the other side. That Loaf started talking again."

"What harm do you think would come from that?" asked Vadesh.

"The more you argue for being sent back in time," said Rigg, "the more determined I am never to let you do so. Because you wouldn't want it so much if you didn't have some plan for exploiting your present knowledge in the past."

To that, Vadesh had nothing to say.

Olivenko laughed. "Let's go, then."

"Nineteen days," said Rigg.

"Eighteen," said Loaf.

Again they looked at him.

"It's been eighteen days since I got the mask," said Loaf.

"That's when you got control over the Walls, isn't it? That's what I remember."

They all looked at Vadesh.

"He's confused," said Vadesh.

"You lied to us," said Rigg. "You said nineteen days. You counted on us to trust your accuracy. So we'd take you back to the day *before* I took control of the ship. So you could do something to prevent it."

Vadesh said nothing.

"Expendables," said Olivenko. "Can't trust them, can't kill them."

"Get in the flyer and go back to the ship," said Rigg.

Vadesh immediately started toward the ship. Then he stopped and said, "Rigg, if you only—"

"Go without stopping, without speaking. Go."

Vadesh got back into the flyer. In moments it rose into the air and flew away.

"Maybe that was a mistake," said Umbo.

Of course he'd say that, thought Rigg. Of course I was wrong. "Why?" asked Rigg, trying to keep impatience and resentment out of his voice.

"Because we could never get him to tell us how he knew we needed a ride," said Umbo.

"That's a problem," said Olivenko. "We figured you'd ask him when we got back together."

"Why didn't you tell me you didn't know?"

"It didn't come up," said Param.

"It's our mistake," said Umbo, "not yours."

"He had some kind of foreknowledge, then," said Rigg.

"So does that mean that in some version of the past, you actually did take him with you into the past?" asked Olivenko.

"We know there were multiple versions," said Umbo, "because I came back and warned myself not to go into the tunnel with you."

"But you could only have done that while you were still there," said Rigg, trying to think through what those other futures, the lost futures, might have contained.

"Right," said Umbo. "I think what happened was, the mask got put on *you*. And then we couldn't go anywhere, because . . ."

Because Rigg was the only one who knew how to keep them alive on a long journey. Because until Rigg was able to take control of the ship's computers, they had no way to turn off the Wall. They had nowhere to go, and no way to get there if they did.

"So you didn't go back from here," said Param. "The future you avoided with your warning—"

"I think that in that future, we waited until Rigg got control of his facemask and could tell us what to do," said Olivenko.

"No," said Rigg. "I think I never got control of it, or at least you didn't wait long enough to find out. I think Loaf told you to go back and change who went into the starship. I think he knew that if he and I were the only ones who went in, Vadesh would have to put the facemask on him first, because if he went for me, Loaf would have been in a position to stop him."

"Sounds like Loaf," said Umbo.

"So Loaf chose to be like this?" asked Param doubtfully.

"Good plan," said Loaf.

"Terrible plan," said Umbo.

"Excellent plan," said Loaf. "Because I see clearly now. I have this gift."

"I wish we could leave the facemask behind the way we got rid of Vadesh," said Rigg.

"If you knew how to detach it," said Loaf, "then I'd stay away from you so you couldn't. I never want to go back to how it was before. It would be like blinding me, deafening me."

"Says the facemask," murmured Umbo.

"Says the man who has been awakened to his full potential," said Loaf.

"'Man,' he calls himself," murmured Param.

"Let's be careful about suggesting somebody isn't quite human anymore," said Rigg. "Someone might say the same thing about a woman who slices up time, Param. Or someone who sees paths, or someone who can go into the past."

"Can we just go back eighteen days?" said Olivenko.

"Seventeen to be safe," said Umbo.

It took a while to work his way backward through the paths of the animals, but then Rigg found the right one. They joined hands and in a moment saw the squirrel scampering away.

And on the hill beyond the Wall, there was not a soul to be seen.

Rigg walked toward the Wall and kept walking. He could feel the presence of the Wall, but it was as if from a distance, as if the feelings were happening to somebody else. It didn't even slow him down. He turned back to face the others. "It's there, but it's manageable," he said.

The first time he had come through a Wall, Umbo had been

holding Param's hand. This time he held Loaf's. But Rigg knew Param would not feel abandoned. She had taken Olivenko's hand already. Param had never needed to learn how to hide yearnings she had never felt before, so it was obvious that she was attracted to Olivenko, that she was offering herself to him in the way that came naturally to women who were filled with desire.

It was impossible that Olivenko did not see this. But as they walked toward Rigg into the Wall, he could see no sign in Olivenko of either fending off Param's attention or encouraging it. Is he blind? Or is he as inexperienced as Param, and doesn't realize the significance of the way she stays so very close to him, as if to surround herself with every breath that he exhales?

Why do *I* know these things? thought Rigg.

Because Father taught me to watch people. He taught me how to see.

I don't need a facemask. I have Father inside my head.

CHAPTER 11
Yahoos

As they walked down the hill, over the stream, and up the broad, grassy, tree-dotted slope on the other side, Umbo watched closely, looking for any sign of the people who would be there seventeen days later to watch the flyer arrive on the hill. It gave him something to do instead of looking at Param holding Olivenko's hand.

It was no surprise that Umbo didn't see anybody; he was no pathfinder like Rigg, and wouldn't see anybody if they didn't want to be seen. But Rigg would. "Where are they?" asked Umbo.

"Fewer of them," said Rigg. "Here and there, some of them underground, and not very close. We were noticed when we started through the Wall, and word spread without anybody having to run around passing the news. People stopped what they were doing and went into hiding. No threat to us that I can see."

"It's the threat you don't see," said Loaf.

"That was definitely not the facemask talking," said Olivenko. "Unless it's able to absorb tired old sayings from the military mind."

Umbo saw that Loaf, who would have taken umbrage before, now merely smiled. "I'm glad to be back with you, too, Olivenko," said Loaf.

"Silbom's left butt cheek," said Umbo. "Has the facemask made you *nice*?"

"I was always nice," said Loaf. "I was just too shy to let it show."

"One of the locals is moving," said Rigg. He pointed toward a thick, tall tree perhaps three hundred meters away.

"They can't get much closer than that," said Olivenko. "We're still inside the Wall."

"Moving toward us?" asked Loaf.

"Climbing the tree," said Rigg.

"I see now," said Loaf. "He's naked."

Umbo didn't see anybody. "Isn't it nice of the facemask to open gaps for your eyes," said Umbo.

"The facemask didn't open gaps," said Loaf.

"And yet I see your eyes," said Umbo.

"He's pretty high in the tree now," said Loaf.

That was a habit of long standing, for Loaf to dodge answering one question by changing the subject.

"Let's keep moving," said Rigg. "Nobody else is coming closer."

They walked on up the slope.

"What you see on my face," said Loaf, "are eyes. Not *my* eyes, though I get the use of them."

"Why did the facemask cover your eyes if it was going to have to grow new ones?" asked Param.

"The facemask dissolved my original eyes," said Loaf, "and replaced them with better ones. Very sharp. Perfect focus at any distance where there's anything to focus on."

Umbo thought of the facemask eating away at Loaf's eyes and almost retched, then almost cried. There really was no going back now; if Loaf lost the facemask, he'd be blind.

With his sharpened powers of observation, Loaf must have seen Umbo's physical reaction despite his effort to conceal it. "If I lost the facemask," said Loaf, "my own eyes would grow back. It's changed every part of me. My body can regenerate now, just like the facemask can."

"So if somebody cut off your hand . . ."

"I'd bleed to death, just like anybody else," said Loaf. "But if you put a tourniquet on my wrist, the stump would heal quickly, and then over the next year or two, I'd get a new hand."

"Would it be *your* hand," asked Umbo. "Or the facemask's hand?"

"Was that you talking?" asked Loaf in reply, "or a fart left over from breakfast?"

It seemed to be Loaf, and yet it wasn't Loaf. It was hard for Umbo to put his finger on what was wrong. And then it came clear. Loaf was *young*. Not world-weary. Quick of step, not lumbering.

The more the facemask remade and improved Loaf's body and mind, the less like Loaf he would be.

"The question," said Rigg, "is whether to avoid the man in that tree, or to approach him and make contact."

"Avoid him," said Param. "Let him come out in the open if he wants to talk to us."

"The people we saw coming here seventeen days from now looked cheerful enough," said Loaf.

"Maybe they already ate us," said Param, "and they were there to play with their food."

"They were wearing clothing," pointed out Rigg. "Why is this one naked as an animal?"

It was pointless to speculate. Umbo took off at a jog for the tree.

"Umbo!" called Rigg.

But Umbo knew what he was doing. If the person was dangerous, then Umbo, as the least useful person in their group, should put himself at risk. They no longer needed him in order to go back in time, and in all their talk about who should be in charge, nobody ever proposed Umbo's name. Nobody seemed to know what Umbo was needed for now, least of all Umbo himself. So if there were foolish risks to be taken, he should take them.

As Umbo neared the tree, he slowed to a walk. He still couldn't see the person—only the movement of twigs and branches. The person said no word, made no sound. Umbo would have called out to him, but didn't know what language the watcher might understand. The Wall put all languages into their minds, but they could not find them, could not tell one from another, until someone else began to speak. Then the appropriate language was simply *there*.

It turned out that no language was needed at all. When Umbo came quite near the tree, close enough that in two strides he could have touched the three-meter-thick trunk, the watcher flung something out of his lofty perch. It splatted against Umbo's cheek and shoulder. It stank. It clung.

Umbo reached up a hand to wipe it from his face. It was nightsoil. Presumably the watcher's own.

Or perhaps not, because here came another wad, this time striking Umbo in the chest.

Umbo's first impulse was to rush down the hill to the brook, but that would give the wrong impression to the others—that he was running away. They might assume that there was real danger. Instead, Umbo turned and walked out of range. He was able to determine what the watcher's range was by continuing to walk until fresh fecal wads stopped reaching him.

By now Loaf had run up to him. Of course he had seen everything in perfect detail, and he was laughing. "A fecal greeting!"

"Not so funny to me," said Umbo.

"If that's their worst weapon," said Loaf, "we're in little danger here."

"If the idea was to humiliate and repulse me, it worked," said Umbo. "Is it safe for me to wash in that brook?"

"I don't know," said Loaf.

"Can't you ask the facemask whether it has any cousins in the water?" asked Umbo.

"It doesn't understand language," said Loaf. "Besides, it emits a stink that chases off the spores of other masks. So it doesn't have to be able to detect whether they're there or not."

"You know so much, considering that it can't talk to you."

"I said I couldn't talk to *it*. Its own messages come through loud and clear. And I can sense when it emits smells and fluids."

"Can it eat nightsoil? Because I can offer it a lovely snack."

"The only mouth it has is mine," said Loaf, "so forget it."

"Then I'm going down to the brook to wash."

Loaf looked up into the tree. "She's stark naked."

"She?"

"I saw more detail the closer I got. Hard to tell how old she is. And she moves like an ape or a sloth. Not quick, never taking her eyes off us, but absolutely sure of hand and foot. Short-legged. And look at the feet."

"I can't look at anything, I'm going to wash," Umbo called over his shoulder. The stink was only getting worse. It would probably be in his clothes forever. And he couldn't expect any compassion or respect. When the danger you run into turns out to be flung poo, nobody remembers that you were the bravest when the danger might have been anything.

While Umbo washed his face and then his shirt in the stream, Loaf sauntered down the slope to talk to him. The others followed him, avoiding the tree.

"For some reason," said Loaf, "the word that came to mind when I looked at the dung-flinging naked tree-clinger is 'yahoo.'"

"Did the word come from the facemask or the Wall?" asked Umbo.

"The Wall. Facemasks don't have language," said Loaf. "Why are you so obsessed with the facemask?"

"Because he's still trying to figure out how much of you is Loaf, and how much is this alien thing that makes you so attractive to look at," said Olivenko.

Thanks for the translation, thought Umbo. Apparently the Wall hadn't made Umbo's words intelligible to the others without interpreters.

"The facemask doesn't connect directly to my brain," said Loaf.

"You think," murmured Umbo.

"My hearing is superb, now, Umbo," said Loaf.

"How do you know it isn't connected to your brain? Maybe it's connected and you don't even realize it."

Loaf shrugged. "Maybe, but what I *sense* are the chemicals it leaks into my body. It can flood me with emotion and desire. Rage, fear, hate, love, lust, comfortableness, grief. Bodily needs, too—itches. Full bladder, hunger, thirst. Whatever it wants me to do, it makes me want to do it."

"So you're a slave," said Umbo.

"Just because I feel a desire doesn't mean I have to act on it," said Loaf. "The desires and needs and feelings are so strong, it took some getting used to. It was terrible at first, because my body automatically responded to these wishes, without any passage through my conscious mind. But I got control of it."

"You think," said Umbo again, this time aloud, since there was no point in muttering.

"Because you're young," said Loaf, "you think you understand everything about your own body, and everything about mine. But I'm old enough that I could feel my body slackening, my abilities fading, my strength ebbing, my senses weakening, my memory perforating. Now I see better than I ever could, hear better, I'm stronger, I have more endurance, and my memory has no gaps. I think far more quickly. Almost as quickly as brilliant young boys like you and Rigg."

"Keep me out of this," said Rigg softly. Maybe he was joking. Probably not.

"I know what it means to have control of my own body," said Loaf. "To resist my body's desires, to decide rationally. When perfectly justified fear would have made me flee the battlefield, I stayed and fought. I have long been master in this house. When Vadesh put this thing on me, then for a few days, a few weeks, I barely clung to that mastery. But I'm in full control again. You've *never* been in control. You don't know what it feels like, and you certainly aren't a good judge of other people's rational control."

Umbo felt the sting of these words like a blow. He had never known that Loaf held him in such contempt.

"I don't mean to hurt you," said Loaf. "I'm simply telling you the truth. There are things that you don't know, being young. But I know those things. Or at least I know more of them than you. So instead of being suspicious of me, Umbo, why not accept that however I might be changed since getting this mask—and believe me, I *have* changed, and in more ways than my newfound prettiness—however changed I am, this is who I am now. Whatever I am, I'm still your friend, unless you decide otherwise."

"Is that what I think it is?" asked Olivenko, indicating the muck still staining Umbo's waterlogged shirt.

"It's a shirt," said Umbo tersely. Did they have to discuss this with Param right there?

"It's downright fecal," said Loaf.

"*I* want a fecal shirt," said Rigg, feigning envy.

"Go stand near that tree, and you'll have one," said Umbo.

"What did you do to provoke him?" asked Param.

"Her," said Loaf, putting a hand on Umbo's shoulder to stop him from a sharp retort. "It's a naked woman. A small woman—barely over a meter tall. But full-grown, from the look of her."

Umbo's first angry retort might have been stifled, but he couldn't leave Param's assumption unanswered. "And I didn't *provoke* her. She just went fecal."

Param didn't argue. "There are others hiding nearby, Rigg says, and *this* one is what they chose to show us. I think this whole encounter is some kind of deception."

"The poo is real," said Umbo.

"They were fully clothed seventeen days from now," said Param. "But right now, they don't know we've seen that. So I think they're pretending that the local humans are savages, when really they're completely civilized."

"I think you're right," said Rigg. "The question is, why. They couldn't have known we were coming—Vadesh couldn't have notified their expendable yet, because the Vadesh of this moment doesn't know we're here."

"Unless he has ways of knowing that we don't know about," said Param.

"If nobody objects," said Loaf, "I'll go question her."

"One look at you," said Umbo, "and she'll run away."

"She's had more than one look by now," said Loaf.

"She's not alone, though," said Rigg. "Someone else just came up through the trunk of the tree to join her in the branches."

"Through the trunk of the tree?" asked Olivenko.

"The trees are hollow?" asked Param.

"Look how thick they are," said Rigg. "And from what I can

see of these people's paths, every tree of that size has had people going down inside them for a century or more."

"So this is a village," said Loaf. "And the trees are the houses."

"The trees are the kind we call oak," said Rigg. "By the leaves they are, anyway, and the pattern of the branches. But in our wallfold, oaks never grew that thick and squat."

"So they were bred to be houses," said Olivenko.

"By these yahoos?" asked Loaf.

"Or by their ancestors," said Rigg. "What if they reached a high level of civilization in the past and created all kinds of marvelous things, so they never had to work to get food or shelter—everything they needed just grew. So their descendants didn't need intelligence anymore, and they became tree-dwelling turdthrowers."

"Or that's what they want us to think," said Param.

"Well, it worked," said Rigg. "I'm thinking it. But do we believe it?"

"Why would they want to seem stupider than they are?" asked Umbo.

"Camouflage," said Loaf. "Disguise. If they act like animals, then we don't try to fight them, we avoid them."

"I just want to wash this mess out of my shirt," said Umbo.

"Wear it with pride," said Olivenko. "Stained by yahoos in Odinfold."

Loaf headed up the slope toward the yahoo oak. Umbo spread his shirt on the grass and jogged after him.

"Ready for more flung poo?" asked Loaf. "Aren't you chilly?"

"It washes off my skin better than off a shirt," said Umbo.

"And yes, I worked up a sweat trying to wash the shirt, so now it's chilly. But I will bravely and rationally defy the need of my body to get warm, and continue walking into noble combat with my soldier friend with a blob on his face."

"I'm happy to see that you're maturing nicely."

"Almost ripe now," said Umbo. "Fat lot of good it'll ever do me."

"You mean because the only woman in our party only has eyes for Olivenko?"

Umbo felt a stab of despair. As long as no one said it out loud, he had been able to halfway fool himself into not knowing that Param was sweet on the scholar-soldier.

"She's young—as young as you, Umbo. She's lived in a cage all her life, with only her mother for company, and I think we can agree the queen was crazy."

"Beyond fecal," said Umbo. If he used the word himself, they couldn't taunt him with it.

"So let Param have her schoolgirl crushes on handsome young soldiers," said Loaf.

"Young?" asked Umbo. "Olivenko?"

"Compared to me he's young," said Loaf. "And here we are at the fecal tree."

Loaf boldly stood even closer to the tree than Umbo had. Sure enough, there was a rustling in the branches and a wad of dung flew out, aimed right at Loaf's head.

But it never got there. Loaf's big hand flew up and caught it. Incredibly fast reflexes, thought Umbo. A moment later, Loaf's arm flashed like a catapult and the nightsoil flew back into the tree much faster than it had come out. Somebody in the tree yelped.

"How much poo do they have in their bodies?" asked Umbo.

"Maybe they can't have a bowel movement until they have somebody to throw it at," said Loaf. "So they have a lot stored up."

"That makes us what? A laxative for yahoos?"

Rigg and the others came up behind them. "They both went back down the tree," said Rigg. "Into the roots. And I bet they *store* vats of poo to make their FPs."

Umbo knew the game. "Foul Potatoes?"

"Fecal Projectiles," said Rigg.

"Flying Poo," said Umbo. "Not so pretentious."

"Fart Pellets," said Rigg.

"Fetid Pies," said Umbo.

"When you two boys are through playing word games," began Loaf.

"Are we in a hurry?" asked Rigg. "I'm enjoying being out of Vadeshfold, and I don't think the world will end while we Fling Puns."

"Since you're so much stronger than a human now, Loaf," said Umbo, "perhaps you'd care to pull up the tree so we can get at the yahoos inside it."

"Trees are sacred," said Loaf. "I never disturb them if I can help it."

"They're also very heavy," Umbo pointed out.

"They're also deeply attached to the ground," said Rigg. "Let's leave the trees where they are, and deal with the people. I've been thinking through as many languages as I can get into my head, saying, 'Greetings, yahoo, I'm from Ramfold.' If I can come up with a language where 'yahoo' feels like a native word—"

"Don't bother," said a voice from the tree. He spoke a language Umbo had never heard spoken, but thanks to the Wall, he understood it at once. "This is the language you want. Yahootalk is mostly grunts and clicks and farts and belches."

"So . . . I've been speaking it my whole life," said Umbo.

Param chuckled, but Umbo couldn't be sure if she was appreciating his humor, or taking his irony at face value.

"Who are you?" asked Loaf, "and why are you throwing doodoo at us?"

"Are you really from Ramfold?" asked the timorous voice.

"You already know who we are," said Rigg. "Stop pretending and come down here and talk to us."

A long moment of silence.

"Would you mind terribly if we put on clothes before coming down out of the tree?"

"We'd prefer it," said Loaf. "Take all the time you need. Empty your bowels and wash your hands. Put yourselves out."

"How did you decide they were pretending?" asked Umbo.

"Humans are never going to lose language. There's no reason for it," said Rigg. "Whether they're working hard or not, they'll talk because that's what humans do. So this nonsense of grunting is obviously false."

"Obvious to you," said Umbo.

"It's obvious to you, too," said Rigg, "or you'd be arguing with me."

Everybody thinks they know everybody's inner life, thought Umbo. But we've only known Loaf since Rigg and I stopped by their inn on the way to Aressa Sessamo. None of us really knows anything at all about each other's motives and what's going on in our unconscious minds. Nobody ever does.

Two fully clothed, diminutive people leapt lightly down from the tree. They bowed deeply. "Sorry for using you as a trial run for our social experiment," said the woman, in fluent whatever-the-language-was. "We don't get a lot of traffic through the Wall."

"I'm betting we're the first ever," said Umbo.

"We have a solvent that will get the stain out of your shirt," said the man.

"How about not throwing turds in the first place?" said Umbo.

The man sighed. The woman laughed. "I don't think our disguise is really all that effective," she said.

"Oh, it made me want to scrub my own skin off," said Umbo. "If that was your goal—"

"You got here sooner than we expected," said the woman. "So we weren't sure it was you."

"Who do you think we are?" asked Loaf.

The man handed Umbo a clean shirt that seemed to fit well enough. The fabric was smooth and comfortable; the shirt was light in weight, yet very warm.

"You're Loaf, a soldier-turned-innkeeper-turned-bodyguard," said the woman. "And you're wearing one of Vadesh's nasty little parasites. One of the boys is Rigg and the other is Umbo. The girl is Param, who should be heir to the Queen-in-the-Tent. And, not least, King Knosso's right-hand boy, the scholar Olivenko."

The dung had been irritating. This was frightening. "How can you possibly know so much about what's going on in other wallfolds?" asked Umbo.

"We learned how to intercept and decode all the communications of the expendables, the orbiters, and the ships within a few hundred years of the founding of this colony," said the man.

"You're the biggest news in ten thousand years," added the woman. "Ever since humans went extinct in Vadeshfold."

"A tragedy," said the man.

"I'm surprised Vadesh let you leave," said the woman.

"He's not equipped to stop us," said Rigg.

"Oh, he has all the equipment he needs," said the woman. "But since one of you is carrying his baby"—she indicated the facemask on Loaf—"I suppose he didn't want to damage any of you."

Umbo wasn't sure if she was being literal or figurative. "You don't mean that that thing is going to give birth," said Umbo.

"Oh, goodness no," said the woman. "I forgot you don't have sufficient knowledge yet to understand irony or analogy in this context."

"What was your disguise *for*?" asked Param. "Naked-in-trees doesn't seem very subtle to me."

"Primitivity," said the man.

"Decay and devolution," said the woman.

"But you didn't believe it, and so it probably won't work on *them,* either," said the man. "Which is why, ultimately, all our hopes are pinned on you."

"All your hopes of what? Who *are* you people?" demanded Rigg.

"Don't worry," said the man. "We'll explain everything. But it's going to take some time."

"What it comes down to is this," said the woman. "We have a little over two years before the humans from Earth arrive for the first time since the terraforming of Garden."

"And a year after that before they come back and wipe out all life on Garden," added the man.

"You can see the future?" asked Rigg.

"No," said the man. "But people of Odinfold, from a different version of our future, wrote an account of the end of the world and sent it back to us five thousand years ago, just before they died."

"You can travel in time," said Rigg.

"Not at all," said the woman. "But we have machines that can *send* things to any past time and to any place on Garden."

"And retrieve things," said the man. "We can also bring things back from the past. Like that jewel they took from you and put in that bank in your capital city."

"Our displacers got it out and left it for Umbo to find in Vadeshfold," said the woman.

"We've been helping you as much as possible since we first found out about you," said the man.

It made Umbo feel strange. Somebody had been looking out for them. Or manipulating them. It made Umbo feel vaguely like a pet. But was it really all that different from what the expendables had been doing to them? "Do you have names?" asked Umbo. "What do we call you?"

They looked at each other and laughed. "Names. I suppose we have names, though none of us ever uses them."

"There are only about ten thousand of us in the whole wallfold now," said the woman. "So we know each other, know each other's history, and the compressed version of that history is what we use for names now, if names are needed at all. I'm usually called Woman-Gave-Birth-to-Boy-and-Girl, Swims-in-the-Air, Saves-the-World."

"There's a lot more to her name," said the man, "but that short version is usually enough to distinguish her from everybody else."

"I'm a little bit famous," she said apologetically.

"You're ashamed of being famous," said Umbo, "but proud of going fecal."

"Hoping to save the world," she said with a shrug. "Not everybody thought the yahoo act was worth trying."

"You intercept the communications among the ships?" asked Olivenko.

The man rolled his eyes. "We said it, didn't we?"

"What's *your* name?" Param asked him.

"Mouse-Breeder, Old-Song-Singer, Lived-in-the-Ruins, Mates-for-Life."

"What should *we* call you?" asked Param.

"Is your memory so bad you can't hold on to such simplified versions of our names?" asked Swims-in-the-Air.

"How did you get the air-swimming part of your name?" Rigg asked her.

"I went through a phase where I jumped out of flyers and off cliffs. With wings I designed myself."

"Can we see you do that?" asked Olivenko.

"Oh, I gave that up five hundred years ago," she said, laughing. "A pleasure for children. I'm a grownup now."

"How old *are* you?" asked Umbo.

"We're going to tell you everything in due time," said Mouse-Breeder. "We can even show you vids of her flights, if you want. And you can meet some of my mice."

"Those were the short names," said Loaf, "and yet you know the long names of every one of the ten thousand people in the wallfold?"

"Ten thousand is easy. I don't think that even *we* could have known the names of all the people who lived here before we learned about the end of the world. There were three billion people then." He laughed, shaking his head.

"Three *billion*?" asked Umbo. "Where could they fit?"

"We didn't live in trees then," said Swims-in-the-Air. "But come, let's walk through the ruins, and we'll tell you a few important things."

"About why Loaf thought of you as yahoos?" asked Umbo.

"Well, that's part of it, though when we wear clothing, we think of ourselves as Odinfolders. Mostly we need to tell you about *you*."

"What do you know about us, that we don't already know?" asked Param.

"Why you were born," said Mouse-Breeder.

"Why you have the abilities you have," said Swims-in-the-Air.

"And what you have to do in order to save the world," said Mouse-Breeder.

The two Odinfolders led them over another rise, and there before them lay the ruins of a great city.

CHAPTER 12
Ruined Cities

Param's idea of a city was a fantasy born of literature, with little experience to change things. She had never strayed from whatever house they imprisoned her mother in, so the only cities she saw were illustrations in books or art on the walls. When she fled Flacommo's house with Rigg, she saw only a few streets of Aressa Sessamo, and then she was in fear every moment.

Besides, Aressa Sessamo was so flat and low that unless you climbed one of the few high towers, it was impossible to get any idea of the size of it. From Umbo and Rigg she had learned something of O, which, according to them, was a real city.

And then there was the empty city in Vadeshfold. But, once again, they had ventured only into the outskirts, had never climbed a tower, had plunged underground almost at once.

So she was not prepared for what she saw when they crested

the second rise beyond the Wall. Since the Odinfolders lived in trees, there had been nothing that looked like a house or a shack or a shed or even a tent. But now they stood on the brow of a hill looking down into the valley of a swift-flowing river.

On the hither side of the river, there were only a few hundred hummocks with occasional walls, posts, and roofs rising out of them. Dust blowing primarily out of the east had drifted and turned everything into mounds of earth, covered in grass. Yet enough of the artifacts of human habitation still stood that it would have been an impressive, if bleak, sight.

But on the other side of the river, rising up to a flat mesa, the lower walls gave way to high towers. Most of them were skeletons now, with beams that marked the structure like bones, but many of them rose quite high, and because they had lost their façades, Param could see through each to the building behind, and the one behind that, and on and on up the slope.

On the flat of the butte, the great towers made way for somewhat lower, narrower buildings; but these, perhaps because they had sheltered each other from wind, still had much of their facing. They were ornately decorated and many still showed faded traces of once-bright colors. And the windows: a thousand eyes peered from every building.

Param was above two hundred when she gave up counting the towers.

"Ten thousand people must have lived here," she said.

"Oh, no," said Swims-in-the-Air. "This was a town of a million or so. And just down the river, you can see a city almost as big."

It was true—though distance and bends in the valley made it

so that nearby trees somewhat blocked the view, it was plain that about as many skeleton towers rose just as high, though starting on lower ground. The only thing missing was the patch of buildings with walls still in place.

"A million," breathed Param. She knew the number as a theory, but had no idea what it would mean in practice. Aressa Sessamo was famous for having two hundred thousand inhabitants. Here, that would have been nothing. "How did they eat?"

"Food was easy," said Mouse-Breeder. "We know how to make soil yield hundreds of times more than the primitive farms in Ramfold. It was energy and sewage that were a constant problem."

"A million people would make it a pretty fecal city," said Rigg. Umbo laughed.

Boys could be so crude. Param wondered how long it would be before they finally stopped finding ways to use "fecal" in every sentence. Olivenko didn't think references to poo and pee were an inexhaustible source of mirth, the way Rigg and Umbo did.

"Where did they all go?" asked Param.

"Well, they died, of course," said Swims-in-the-Air.

"Plague? War?" asked Param. "If food was easy, it wasn't famine." She had read enough history to know these were the ways that cities turned to ruins.

"No, not at all," said Mouse-Breeder. "We weren't so long-lived then. Only a hundred years, on average—once you'd seen your century, you expected your body's functions to decay enough that living wasn't a pleasure anymore. You lost interest. Or so I'm told."

"We just hadn't solved the problems of aging yet," said Swims-in-the-Air.

"A hundred years is very, very old in Ramfold," said Rigg.

"Yes, we're so sorry, dear," said Swims-in-the-Air.

"But that doesn't explain anything," said Param, a little impatient. "Just because people lived 'only' a hundred years doesn't explain why the city emptied out like this."

"The first time through our history," said Mouse-Breeder, "our population reached six billion by the time the humans came."

"You say that as if we weren't human ourselves," said Olivenko.

Swims-in-the-Air only smiled. "We do, don't we," she said.

"Again," said Param, "I don't see why the cities—"

"This one likes quick answers," said Mouse-Breeder.

"Or easy ones," said Swims-in-the-Air. "So here's the quick and easy answer. We got a letter from the future, telling us how the world ends. So we set about trying to make it end differently. Each attempt meant cutting our population more sharply, until you see us as we are today, about ten thousand people in the entire wallfold, and most of us clustered within walking distance of the Wall."

"Cutting your population?" asked Param. "How?"

"Having fewer babies, of course. Most of us having none at all. That's why my two children became part of my name."

"She's such an optimist," said Mouse-Breeder.

"Incurable," said Swims-in-the-Air. But she sounded wistful and sad when she said it.

"People just stopped wanting children?" asked Loaf.

Param thought it was odd for him to sound so incredulous, considering that he and his wife Leaky had no children, or none that she had heard of.

"It's not about wanting," said Mouse-Breeder. "The body still has its primate roots. The body wants to breed. But we owed a duty to the whole world of Garden."

"You see, the first time the humans came, they visited only Odinfold, because only our civilization was visible from space."

"From space," said Umbo, "why would the high towers make a difference?"

"Not the towers," said Swims-in-the-Air. "The light. Every street had lamps on it. Every building had lights in the windows. There were lights everywhere at night, lights that could be seen from a million kilometers away. Our wallfold was the only patch of light on the whole planet, so they came to us. They thought we kept the rest of Garden as a nature preserve; they thought the name of the world confirmed that idea."

"But then they learned what this world really was," said Mouse-Breeder.

"And what is it?" asked Rigg, a little defiant-sounding. *"Really?"*

"Give just the tiniest thought to the question," said Mouse-Breeder. "I know you know the answer."

"A place where the human race could develop in nineteen completely different ways," said Param.

"And in Ramfold, we turned out to be time shapers," said Umbo.

"The three of *you* are," said Olivenko.

"But most people in Ramfold can't do anything with time," Umbo added.

"You know that's not true," said Mouse-Breeder. "And it isn't really time per se that you manipulate. You create fields with your minds, fields in which time can be altered because of the way you connect yourselves to the planet's past."

"What do *you* do?" asked Umbo.

"They move objects in time and space," said Param. "They already told us."

"No, Param, we didn't tell you that that's what we do," said Mouse-Breeder. "It's merely one manifestation of what we do. You see, we were the only wallfold where the learning of the Earth we came from wasn't sealed to us. We could study it all. We also knew that the hope of Ram Odin, when he commanded the expendables and the ships to divide the world into folds, was that the human species would find nineteen different ways to evolve and change, either physically or culturally."

"All of human history on Earth was scarcely twelve thousand years," said Swims-in-the-Air, "and that's with a most generous interpretation of the word 'history.' That's how long it had been since the last ice age, as they called them—times when the Earth's climate grew colder and much of the ocean's water was locked up in ice caps."

"Real history—written records and all that—was about five thousand years," said Mouse-Breeder. "And the biggest leaps in science and technology had taken place in only the last thousand years or so, with the most dramatic transformations in the last two centuries."

"The expendables were not even regarded as particularly remarkable when Ram Odin's colony ship set out," said Swims-in-the-Air. "Indestructible materials, highly advanced language modules, things like that were only fifty years old. But the humans of Earth thought of fifty years as a long time, because they were used to such a fast rate of progress."

"It hadn't been two hundred years since humans first went into space, you see," said Mouse-Breeder. "So the colonists in Odinfold expected to be able to continue making progress at the same pace, though they recognized that with a much smaller population and the need to deal with subsistence issues, there would be a slowdown for a few generations."

"Oh, we had babies then!" said Swims-in-the-Air. "Babies and babies and babies, because we needed our population to reach a point where we could specialize, where the smartest of us could live the life of the mind."

"But let's go down to the river and cross into the city," said Mouse-Breeder. "The vista from here is only interesting for a while, and then you want to go inside to get a sense of scale, don't you think?"

They thought so, too, so they walked together down the slope toward the river, while the Odinfolders continued their story.

It wasn't enough to have lots of babies, they explained. Wasn't one of the goals of Garden to promote the isolated evolution of new human species? And since Odinfold retained its memory of the science of genetics, they could keep conscious control of the human species.

"Not just selective breeding," said Mouse-Breeder. "The

way I do with mice, where I select for traits I want and allow only those mice that have such traits to reproduce. No, we went into the genes themselves, the seeds within the human body that decide what each new generation will look like."

They found long-lost traits that they wanted to restore, rare ones they wanted to make common, and then nearly everybody gave birth only to babies that had been enhanced in some way. Improving the species directly.

"What traits?" asked Rigg.

"Short legs," said Umbo.

"Oh, no," said Mouse-Breeder. "The short legs came later, when we were tailoring ourselves to look like yahoos."

"We made ourselves tall and slender at first," said Swims-in-the-Air. "We metabolized food very efficiently, so we required less of it per person."

"And we rebuilt ourselves to concentrate on the brain," said Mouse-Breeder. "Each increase in brain size required more blood for the brain, less for the rest of the body. So the leaner we were, the better. Any organs we could eliminate or shrink saved blood."

"Larger brains?" asked Param. Their heads were disproportionately large for their small bodies, but not larger than normal adults' heads.

"The human brain folds quite elaborately, increasing the surface area," said Mouse-Breeder. "Ours fold more. Also, our skulls are much thinner. Less bone here, more brain inside. It makes us fragile, but we don't face the same sorts of enemies that our ancestors had to deal with. And when we're doing something risky, we wear helmets."

"Throwing dung at Loaf is risky," said Umbo.

"But thrown dung is not going to break skulls," said Swims-in-the-Air. "As weapons go, it's more annoying than damaging."

The Odinfolders also tried, in the early days, to bring out what they called "savant" abilities—perfect visual and auditory memory, the ability to count and solve equations with astonishing rapidity, vast expansion of available vocabulary. "We never quite succeeded. It seems that for true savant capability, you have to pay the savant price—a loss of social function, the inability to do the fuzzy thinking that leads to creativity. Once we realized that the price was too high, we worked to strike a balance. Creativity *and* better memory, better ability to notice things, better abstract and spatial reasoning."

They did so well at shaping their own brains that any one of them might be trained as thoroughly in three or five or ten disciplines as ordinary humans were in one or two.

By five hundred years into life on Garden, they had built machines that could intercept and decode all the messages between expendables and starships, so that no secrets could be kept from them. By a thousand years, they were able to alter the programs that operated the Walls, so that the fields not only triggered powerful emotions in the human mind, but also wakened the latent language abilities present in all humans.

"It's the grammar of grammars, the key to all vocabulary," explained Mouse-Breeder. "It's as if we sing you to sleep in all languages, when you pass through the Wall."

"But nobody passes through it," said Param. "Except us."

"'Through the Wall' means in at one place and out at another," said Mouse-Breeder. "You were the first to transverse the Wall, but many thousands have gone in and out; some have ventured well inside it, and for longer than you might have thought possible."

"But what's the point?" asked Param. "If you can never leave your wallfold, then what does it matter whether you learn languages you'll never speak."

"You're not listening well enough, Param," said Swims-in-the-Air. "These concepts are well within your reach."

Param thought a moment more and then blushed. "You don't give us languages. You changed the Wall so that it gives us Language."

"Yes!" cried Swims-in-the-Air happily.

"I have no idea what that means," said Loaf.

"The deep language of the human mind," said Rigg. "The instinctive grammar of meaning that's born into every human mind, on which we build our particular languages. Father told me that there was such a thing, but no one in the world had ever found the key to it."

"In *our* world, we did," said Mouse-Breeder. "Barely a thousand years into our history, we found it, and then embedded the key to it in the Walls, so that it was potentially available to any people who could bear the torment of the Wall long enough for it to take root."

"And now let's cross the river," said Swims-in-the-Air. "We can't have bridges, you know, since we're supposed to be yahoos, so we arranged stones to allow passage. Your feet get a bit wet, but it's not that unpleasant, and you'll dry off quickly enough in the grass on the other side."

She and Mouse-Breeder led the way, taking off their shoes and walking easily across on stones just under or just breaking the surface. Rigg followed next, being used to such traverses from his life in the wild, and Umbo and Loaf went next, almost as easily. Only Olivenko bothered to stay behind to help Param across, for Param had never had to learn the art of delicate balance, and she was more afraid of falling and injuring herself than the others were. With Olivenko's hand gripping hers, however, she was at no risk of falling, and she could cross in no more than twice the time it took the others.

Once across the ford, the walls began to rise on either side, and it was plain that the grass they walked on overlay smooth and level roads.

Also, other Odinfolders began to emerge from the large trees near the river. They waved, they smiled, but none of them made a move to join them; none tried to speak. Apparently Mouse and Swim had been delegated to be the only Odinfolders that their party would be allowed to meet. Param wondered why.

Meanwhile, as they ascended into the ruined city, the Odinfolders continued their story.

The Odinfold colonists had maximized their population over the years, growing food efficiently, living in splendid high towers so they used up the least possible surface area with mere habitation. As a result, they had enormous numbers of extremely brilliant people working on every scientific and technological problem they could think of—along with art, literature, history, and philosophy.

But in the midst of this vast civilizational florescence, something astonishing happened: A message reached them from their own future.

It consisted of a stack of thin sheets of noncorroding metal, inscribed with fine writing, laying out the key events of the history of the next five thousand years.

This Book of the Future appeared out of nowhere, in the midst of a meeting of scientists who were working on the problem of movement through time. One speaker was leaving the lectern, another rising from his seat at the table to take his place. And there, where the first one had been sitting before, the Future Book appeared, shiny, new.

By demand of the audience, the book was immediately read aloud. It was written in a slightly awkward version of their present language, and it was specifically written to the scientists at that gathering.

First, it confirmed to them that five of their number had already completed the theoretical work that laid the foundation of the ability to move objects through time. The Messengers who wrote the book chose this date for the book to arrive precisely because the science was already in place, and the book would be confirmation of what they already knew.

Second, it told them a rough outline of the history of Odinfold up to the year zero, and the nearly fourteen years beyond.

Third, it told of the coming of the first humans from Earth. To these Visitors, it had been only fourteen years since Ram Odin's colony ship made the first Jump. So they were stunned to find six billion people living in such a limited area as Odinfold.

They were even more surprised to learn that the colony ship

had replicated itself to make nineteen complete copies, all of which had become the source of colonies separated by Walls.

Almost their first act was to turn off all the Walls, something that no one on Garden had yet been able to do. Then they did what Odinfolders had never been able to do. They visited every wallfold and saw what had become of the human race within it.

Then they went home.

Eleven months later, in the year fifteen, nineteen starships arrived at once. These were not Visitors, but Destroyers. Without warning or discussion, they activated the destruct systems on the orbiters that had been circling Garden ever since the starships plunged into the planet's surface more than eleven thousand years before. These burned the surface of the planet, destroying almost all plant and animal life.

Then the Destroyers sent flyers to the surface, where they systematically rendered all water undrinkable and the atmosphere unbreathable, with machines that would make the effects continue for at least two centuries.

The Messengers who wrote the Future Book were hidden away in a deep mining operation, where they had air enough to continue to live for the week in which, as a group, they composed and then used a machine to etch the book. They also had a displacer with them, and used it to project the finished book through time and space to precisely the moment when the earliest scientists equipped to understand the situation were gathered.

By the time Mouse-Breeder's and Swims-in-the-Air's story was finished, they were in the center of the city, where there were still walls and windows, instead of bare skeletons. Soil and dust had built up, mostly against east-facing walls, and so grass had softened the bottom edges of the buildings, and trees had taken root here and there. But it was still a city, however empty of inhabitants it might be, and Param could not help but be awed, not so much by the size of it, but by the way these people had lived.

"All stores and businesses on ground level, of course," Mouse-Breeder explained. "And everybody walked—transportation was underground. Parks everywhere—the streets were of a very durable grass. Not this high grass, but a low grass that you could walk on and it wouldn't die."

"Then I'm surprised it ever went away," said Olivenko.

"It had to be misted with water every day," said Mouse-Breeder. "And this prairie grass blew in as seeds, then became so tall, and thrived so well in dry seasons, that it blocked the old paving grass from any access to sunlight. It only took a few years."

"Why are we talking about grass?" asked Param. "I want to know about the people."

"They lived in these buildings, and worked in them, and went to school in them," said Swims-in-the-Air. "There are still some of the bridges connecting them, do you see? You've never lived in such crowds, I know—but you've come closer than we who live in Odinfold today ever have. It seems so anonymous, to speak of a million people. But they all had lives, and families, and hopes, and disappointments. Every life was its own story, its own thread in the network of life."

"Why did this Future Book kill them?" asked Param.

"No, no, you don't understand at all. It simply changed their purpose." Swims-in-the-Air corrected herself. "*Our* purpose. We still worked to advance science, but now we were in the business of saving the world. Because it was our fault, don't you see? Whatever the Visitors saw in us, they went back and made such a report that the people of Earth resolved to destroy us."

"So you spent five thousand years preparing for war," said Loaf.

"No!" said Mouse-Breeder with horror. "First, it wouldn't work. If we had defeated that fleet, they would have sent a larger one. If we had developed better weapons, they would have returned with weapons better still. The only hope of victory would have been to go back and destroy Earth itself. And we were not prepared to do that. Ever."

"Not that there weren't factions who wanted to try it," said Swims-in-the-Air. "But we had long since learned that we couldn't defeat the programming in the ships. The expendables monitored us, you see, and they were very good at it. In most wallfolds, the expendables were there to nurture beneficial changes, to enhance human survival. But in our wallfold—and a few others, over the millennia—they were watching out to keep us from developing technologies that could defeat the protections on the programs."

"And weapons," said Mouse-Breeder. "If anyone started to work on weapons systems that might eventually reach beyond the Wall or up into space, the expendable simply came and killed him. No trial, no questions, he was dead."

"I thought you said you broke into the programs," said Umbo.

"We *read* them," said Swims-in-the-Air. "And we found that there were some we could change—like the programs controlling the Wall. But we couldn't defeat any of them. And we found code that clearly warned us that any attempt to defeat or change anything significant would cause the destruct system on the orbiter to burn out the entire wallfold."

"So you couldn't defend yourselves," said Loaf.

"These systems weren't designed to defend us from the human race. From Earth," said Mouse-Breeder.

"But the expendables said that their whole purpose was helping us to get in place to protect Garden," said Rigg.

"It is *now*," said Mouse-Breeder. "But they're limited by the same programming that blocks us. We had to find a way to get the Visitors to reach a different conclusion about the people of Garden."

At first, the Odinfolders feared that the Visitors had been frightened by Odinfold's magnificent achievements. So they began reducing their population and concealing their technological achievements. But within a dozen years of their first efforts along these lines, they got another book.

This time the book was only a single sheet, and it was on gold instead of a complicated alloy. The message was also simpler. It outlined what had been attempted, and reported on its complete failure. The outcome was the same as before.

More plans were made. More drastic cutbacks in population. A deliberate reduction in technological change. And yet there came another Future Book.

So they tried again. Instead of cutting back on technology and science, they pushed it forward, trying to offer dazzling brilliance as an incentive—something to sell, something that might earn their survival.

Another Future Book showed that as a dead end.

"Nine books in all," said Mouse-Breeder. "The last one came only three thousand years ago. That was when we decided on the yahoo strategy. We got the idea from a book from Earth, *Gulliver's Travels*. It ended with the traveler visiting a land where the sentient residents had evolved from horses, and the creatures that looked like humans were tree-dwelling beasts that grunted and threw their dung at strangers. We bred ourselves for that, in a flurry of new generations, and then sat back and waited."

"That was when we gave ourselves shorter legs and semi-grasping feet. Learning from the primate ancestors of humans on Earth," said Swims-in-the-Air. "And when there were about ten thousand of us, long-lived, intelligent, but able to pass for beasts, our beautiful ancestors allowed themselves to die out, so that only we were left."

"What good is it?" said Param. "How do you even know it was *your* wallfold that convinced the Visitors that Garden had to be destroyed?"

"Ours was the only one we could change," said Swims-in-the-Air.

"Be accurate," said Mouse-Breeder.

"I should have said," Swims-in-the-Air replied, "that ours was the only wallfold we could change as drastically as this. We didn't have the right to interfere in the others at anything like this level. But we did fiddle here and there."

"How?" asked Param.

"You mean, what changes did we make? Or how did we manage to make changes?" Mouse-Breeder said. "You know that we can send things back in time to any place on Garden, the way we did with the jewel. Well, we also assembled all the jewels—originally, each wallfold contained only its own control jewel. We put them together, and we gave them to Ramex."

"Ramex," said Rigg. "The expendable who raised me?"

"In this language," said Mouse-Breeder, "we name each expendable with the name of the founder of the wallfold, plus 'ex' for expendable. So we speak of Vadeshex, Ramex, Odinex."

"Where *is* your expendable?" asked Olivenko.

"Off doing whatever he does," said Swims-in-the-Air. "Vadeshex met you in Vadeshfold because it has no other sentient inhabitants. But if a stranger came to Ramfold, do you think Ramex would be there to greet him?"

Param was impatient with such digressions. "Why did you assemble the stones? And when you did, why didn't you use them yourselves?"

"Because we can't," said Mouse-Breeder. "You have to pass completely through a Wall *without* using the stones before you gain the ability to control a ship and pass freely through the Wall."

"So if we had only had the one stone," said Param.

"You would have had to present your stone at that starship and gain the right to control the Wall surrounding only your own wallfold."

"That still doesn't explain why you gave all the stones to us," said Param.

"Because you are the most powerful," said Mouse-Breeder, with a shrug. "Though truth to tell, we didn't understand about your ability, Param. We figured that Rigg would be able to attach to the past and go through before the Wall existed."

"But then we never would have acquired the language ability," said Umbo.

"Truth is, if Umbo hadn't pulled us back to the present when we were still short of the edge of the Wall, Loaf and Rigg and I wouldn't have had any effect from the Wall," said Olivenko.

"I didn't do it on purpose," said Umbo.

"They were about to kill us!" said Param.

"I know that," said Olivenko, sounding annoyed.

Param couldn't believe she had spoken so sharply to Olivenko. But it really had sounded as if he was criticizing Umbo, and he had no right—he wasn't there. Yes, he experienced the agony of the Wall because of it—twice, because he and Loaf heroically went back to rescue Rigg—but to phrase it as if it had been Umbo's fault . . .

"Nobody's blaming anybody for anything," said Rigg. "It's obvious they're not telling us the whole truth, but—"

Rigg waved off the Odinfolders' protests.

"You can't tell us everything at once," said Rigg. "You also want us to pursue a particular course of action, so you're framing the information you provide us in order to maximize the likelihood of our doing what you want. Since I would do exactly the same thing, I'm not criticizing you. I'm just waiting to find out what you're planning for us. And I want to know just how much you've already bent our course without our knowledge." He held up his hand. "Again, that's not a criticism. Can we all stop being so sensitive? Short of leaving us notes, which we wouldn't have understood or believed anyway, you couldn't explain anything to us. And thanks for the stones. I don't know why you have that kind of trust in us, but I hope to live up to your expectations wherever I agree with them."

Param listened to Rigg's speech and was both proud of him and annoyed that he was so eloquent. He was so aware of how the others were taking the things he said. It was obvious that the Gardener—Ramex—had done a splendid job of training Rigg to be a leader, and Rigg himself was doing a splendid job of using that training wisely and well. She found herself thinking: He should be King-in-the-Tent. And then answering herself, I am the queen's heir! And then answering, Mother has repudiated me, tried to kill me, and I am reduced to following my younger brother, whom I barely know, and pining over a scholar from the city guard like a moonstruck girl in a romance.

"How have we changed your course of action?" said Swims-in-the-Air coldly. "You want the entire list right now?"

"Yes," said Param, without hesitation.

"Tell it in the order that you planned," said Rigg.

"Tell it now," said Umbo.

The attitude of the Odinfolders had changed completely. The warmth was gone. "Everything depends on you," said Mouse-Breeder. "The yahoo thing—that's what we tried last time, and it failed."

"So you didn't tell us the truth the first time around," said Olivenko.

"As Rigg already guessed," said Swims-in-the-Air. "Here's what we did. We learned how to transfer very, very tiny things to very, very precise times and locations. Specifically, we learned how to pick up the genetic material from a fertilized egg before it implanted itself in the uterine wall, alter it as we desired, and reimplant it a microsecond later."

Param's mind was reeling. "Whom did you do that to?"

"We did it to your father, Knosso, in his mother's womb," said Mouse-Breeder. "Then we made just a couple of tweaks to ensure that it was Knosso your mother married, producing the two of you."

"What changes did you make in Father's genes?" asked Rigg.

"We knew both his parents had very strong gifts in time manipulation. So we added our ability to his genes, and hoped the recombination would be interesting and productive. It was—it gave us a timesplitter and a pathfinder."

Param looked at Rigg, trying to see if he was as devastated as she was. But he showed nothing. "How dare you," she said softly to Swims-in-the-Air.

"My name includes the title Saves-the-World," said Swims-in-the-Air. "How do you think I earned it?"

"What other changes did you make?" asked Rigg.

"A certain knife," said Mouse-Breeder. "Which we placed very early, so it had a history, and then moved to the hip of a man whom you encountered the first time you and Umbo did time-shifting together."

"The knife," said Umbo, touching his waist, where it was sheathed under his shirt. "But why?"

"You've already noticed that the hilt contains duplicates of all the jewels of control," said Mouse-Breeder.

Param hadn't known anything about that; but then, she hadn't had many opportunities to see either the knife or the jewels.

"That's not all," said Rigg. "You can't tell me that you left anything to chance. What about Loaf?"

"Loaf *was* chance," said Swims-in-the-Air. "And Olivenko. But you chose your companions well. You could hardly have done better."

Loaf showed no reaction, but Olivenko turned his face. To show disgust, but Param guessed that he was also flattered, and wanted to conceal the fact.

"But yes, Rigg," said Swims-in-the-Air, "we didn't just hope you'd run into someone who could help you use your pathfinding to get into the past. It might have taken years of training, and we didn't have years. So we gave you Umbo."

"*Gave* me Umbo?" asked Rigg.

Param saw that Umbo's face was red. Anger? Embarrassment?

"What am I?" asked Umbo. "Another genetic experiment?"

"Not like Knosso," said Mouse-Breeder. "Your mother was extraordinarily gifted, but your father was nothing."

Umbo nodded.

"So we preempted all of his sperm, when you were conceived," said Mouse-Breeder, "and gave you sperm from our most gifted displacer."

To Param's surprise, tears spilled out of Umbo's eyes and down his cheeks.

"He's not my father," said Umbo.

"You have nothing of him in you," said Mouse-Breeder.

"And your best displacer—who is he?"

"Dead," said Mouse-Breeder. "We went back to get his sperm, too."

"So I'm half . . . half Odinfolder," said Umbo.

"Yes," said Swims-in-the-Air. "Your father was from the time after we bred ourselves to be small, but before we made ourselves into yahoos."

Umbo bent over till his face was touching his knees, almost hiding him in the grass, and wept. Loaf sat down beside him, put his arm across his shoulders, and Umbo leaned into his embrace.

"So Umbo's the smartest of us," said Rigg.

"Umbo has all the potential of an Odinfolder," said Mouse-Breeder. "But you and Param carry our intellectual potential as well."

"We made the decision not to try to solve the problem ourselves," said Swims-in-the-Air, "because in nine tries, we failed every time. Instead, we chose genetic threads in the other most promising wallfold, and combined our own best traits to produce you. And it is in your hands we will place the solution to the problem."

"The problem of getting the Visitors not to go back to Earth and make a report that results in the destruction of Garden," said Rigg. "Just to make sure I understand what the goal is here."

"You have understood it perfectly," said Swims-in-the-Air.

"How much time do we have?" asked Rigg. "Because we're not ready."

"You have all the time you need," said Swims-in-the-Air.

"I thought you said the coming of the Visitors was only two years away," said Rigg.

"It is. But look at who you are," said Swims-in-the-Air. "Let the Visitors come—we'll hide you from them so you can continue your education. Your preparation. Then you just go back in time—something we could never do—and continue your education in another village, so you aren't constantly running into yourselves. You can do that as often as you need."

"Though there is some thought," said Mouse-Breeder, "that the more iterations of you there are, the harder it will be to conceal you from the Visitors. From the Future Books, we get the idea they're quite intrusive and clever, and they get a lot of information from the expendables."

"That's why we have made sure that Odinex doesn't see all that we do. He agrees—we're not lying to him about it. But what he doesn't know can't be learned from him. So he's not going to meet you. He's not even going to know you're here."

"But Father knows about us," said Rigg.

"He knows about you up to the moment of his death," said Swims-in-the-Air. "After that, he's seen nothing of you, heard nothing about you. He doesn't know how any of his plans came out."

"Not true," said Rigg. "He was prompting the starship in Vadeshfold when I first took control."

Swims-in-the-Air made a dismissive gesture. "So he was called on when he was needed. That can't be helped."

"Our advantage," said Mouse-Breeder, "is that we absolutely know that the Visitors have no knowledge of time travel. In fact, all their theories say that it's impossible, that your alterations of the past are self-destructive loops that can't happen. But they can, and that gives us a chance. As long as you don't actually get yourselves killed, you can meet the Visitors again and again, trying to get it right."

"As you did," said Olivenko.

"*Not* as we did," said Mouse-Breeder. "We were limited to sending messages. You can *personally* do things over and over. As Loaf and Umbo proved in their efforts to retrieve the Ramfold jewel from the bank in Aressa Sessamo."

"We just made things worse," said Loaf softly. "Until it became completely impossible."

"So now you know the danger," said Mouse-Breeder. "You won't keep trying the *same* thing over and over."

Rigg sighed. "How much of this did Vadesh know?"

Swims-in-the-Air laughed. "Nothing. He saw what he saw, of course, but he doesn't know your real origin. He doesn't know that by bringing you here he was, in effect, taking you home."

"How do you keep it from him?" asked Rigg.

"Our expendable lies to him," said Mouse-Breeder. "All the expendables lie to him."

"He's a complete failure, you see," said Swims-in-the-Air. "All his humans died."

"Not a complete failure," said Loaf, indicating the facemask he wore.

"Yes," said Mouse-Breeder. "One look at you, and the Visitors will absolutely want to make sure no harm comes to Garden."

"Are you saying I shouldn't be part of our . . . whatever-we're-doing?" asked Loaf.

"I'm saying nothing at all," said Mouse-Breeder. "We didn't

call you into being in order to do our bidding. If we had a plan, we'd do it ourselves. We needed you to come up with a plan and carry it out. We're here to serve you and prepare you in whatever way you think you need to be prepared."

"We have only one suggestion," said Swims-in-the-Air.

"*Your* suggestion, not mine," said Mouse-Breeder.

"All right, *I* have only one suggestion," said Swims-in-the-Air. "Don't delay too long. Don't go back and try new things for too many cycles. You might pass through the same two years a dozen times—but *you'll* age two dozen years in the process. And I think you need to do whatever you do while you're still young."

"Why?" asked Loaf. "Because it's too late for me and Olivenko. 'Young' is already history."

"Rigg and Param and Umbo look like adolescents. Not threatening at all. Not dangerous. And if you and Olivenko are obviously obeying them, then perhaps it will buy you some time, maybe even a little trust. Some compassion. Something. I hope. I think. What I'm saying is, you can't learn everything and you definitely can't anticipate everything. Take the year or so before they come and learn all you can; then see what they do and learn from that. Maybe there'll be a different outcome—we have no way of predicting—and so you won't even have to do the mission. But if the Destroyers come yet a tenth time, go back and learn more, this time based on your own observations and experiences. You see? Just don't do it too often; don't age too many years. Take your action, whatever it is, while you're still young."

"Very eloquently put, my dear," said Mouse-Breeder. "And pointless. They'll decide for themselves."

"Yes, but I've put the thought in their minds and there it is," said Swims-in-the-Air. "Now, do you want to see the library?"

CHAPTER 13
In the Library

The library was deep underground, down many stairways, yet the air felt fresh, and there was a light breeze in the corridors. The walls were covered with paintings and murals, with sculptures in many corners and sometimes filling entire rooms. Tables here and there were surrounded with comfortable-looking chairs, and always the light was bright enough to make reading easy.

Yet there was not a book in sight.

"How is this a library?" asked Rigg.

"It contains every book ever written in the entire history of our wallfold, and every other," said Swims-in-the-Air.

"Not to mention every book from Earth that was brought to Garden with the colony ships," added Mouse-Breeder. "And every work of art ever made, though we can't display them all at once."

"But where are they?" asked Umbo.

Mouse-Breeder smiled modestly, and Swims-in-the-Air laughed. "Now is when Mouse-Breeder shows you his babies."

"Come, children," said Mouse-Breeder softly.

At once small arched doorways appeared in the baseboards of the room. Dozens of mice, white, brown, black, tan, yellow, red, swarmed out onto the floor, and many of them came up onto the tables.

"Can you show us sculptures from the Greeks of Earth?" asked Mouse-Breeder.

Rigg wasn't sure which mice made the change, but suddenly the sculptures in the four corners of the room changed to brightly painted, lifelike, life-sized stone sculptures. Yet when Rigg put his hand out to touch one, his fingers passed within the "stone."

"Illusion," said Olivenko.

"Trickery," said Param.

Loaf only chuckled.

"You knew," said Rigg.

"The mask was not deceived," said Loaf, "and so I saw the difference between the dancing light of the illusion and the solidity of the walls."

"But you still see the beauty of the art?" asked Swims-in-the-Air.

"As much as I ever could have without the mask," said Loaf. "It adds nothing to my appreciation of artificial beauty."

"So art does not speak to you?" asked Mouse-Breeder.

"Your art with the mice speaks to me very clearly," said Loaf. "The mice only understand your language, am I right?"

"They'll learn yours quickly enough," said Mouse-Breeder.

"But when the Visitors come, they won't be able to get access to any of the books that are invisibly stored in this place."

Mouse-Breeder nodded, his smile even slighter, if that were possible. "Only with the help of the mice can anyone find any book or diagram or map or work of art in all of Odinfold."

"So if someone killed the mice?" asked Umbo. "You'd lose your whole library?"

"You must have another way," said Olivenko. "Another key to the library."

"Something mechanical," said Loaf.

"No," said Swims-in-the-Air. "Back doors can be found. Machines can be discovered. No, it's mice and mice alone."

"But we're mindful of the chance of loss," said Mouse-Breeder.

"He's too modest to tell you himself," said Swims-in-the-Air. "These mice are actually a genetic hodgepodge of astonishing variety. More than three thousand species, and no two in this room are genetically close. A disease that wiped out all the mice of any one species, or even all the closely related species, would still leave most of the mice untouched."

"If you have three thousand species," said Olivenko, "how many individuals are there of each?"

"We can't count them all," said Mouse-Breeder. "They reproduce like mice, you see, and then they teach their children how to manipulate the electronics, so nothing is lost. The great prairies of Odinfold have thousands of different kinds of grass, and the mice thrive on all the seeds. There are hundreds of billions of mice."

"So where three billion humans once lived . . ." began Olivenko.

"A hundred times as many mice. And also the owls and foxes, ferrets and cats that feed on them, and the hawks and eagles and wolves that feed on *them*," said Mouse-Breeder. "And grazing animals to keep any one grass from crowding out all others, and the great cats that feed on the grazing animals, and the hyenas and other scavengers that gather at their kills. Our great wallfold is a garden of life, dotted with the ruins of our ancient civilization, and only tree-dwelling yahoos to show that humans once lived here."

"An elegant disguise," said Rigg.

"Which failed," said Mouse-Breeder. "And so we bring you to our library, in hopes that you can find a better way."

"I take it the mice will bring us books," said Olivenko.

"Just say what you want to study—the topic, the source, a specific title, an author, or even a question. Sit at the table, or lean against a wall, or ask while you're walking, and the mice will cause the book you want to appear before you."

"Mouse-Breeder is our best librarian," said Swims-in-the-Air.

"She means the best one living," said Mouse-Breeder, "because our ancestors designed and built and collected so well and thoroughly that there was hardly anything left to do when I came along."

"So using intelligent mice for access is just a bit of decoration?" asked Olivenko wryly.

"I want to see a book," said Rigg.

Instantly there was a book lying on the table. And then another, and another, two or three appearing, another disappearing, as if the books were works of sculpture being displayed in rapid succession.

"This one," Olivenko said, putting his finger into one. At once it rose into the air, exactly the right distance from his eyes for comfortable reading. It opened. "*Travels into Several Remote Nations of the World*," said Rigg. "By Jonathan Swift."

"Commonly known as *Gulliver's Travels*," said Mouse-Breeder. "Part four, chapter one, in which Gulliver meets the Yahoos."

"You can't expect us to believe that he happened to choose that title by chance," said Loaf.

Mouse-Breeder looked pained. "Of course not. No matter what book he chose, it was going to contain *Gulliver's Travels*."

"Is that what we're required to read first?" asked Param.

"You're not *required* to do anything at all," said Swims-in-the-Air. "The only way this will work is if you freely choose for yourselves, follow up on whatever interests you. Of course, we expect your most important results will come from studying the culture of the society that launched the colony ships—to us, eleven thousand years ago, but to the Visitors, only half a generation."

"But I can study the history of Ramfold if I want?" asked Param.

"If you wish," said Mouse-Breeder.

"And I can study the wallfold where Knosso was killed?" asked Olivenko.

"Unfortunately, they have no writing," said Mouse-Breeder ruefully. "We can't collect oral histories from other wallfolds, because our machines can't pick up sounds. Only things that persist in time."

"What if I want to roam through Odinfold," asked Loaf. "To see this place for myself?"

"Go where you want," said Swims-in-the-Air. "But you should be careful. The predators have no fear of humans, which means they have no respect for us, either. We look like meat to the larger ones, and we carry no weapons."

"I do," said Loaf.

"And how effective will they be against a pack of wolves? A pride of lions? A troop of hyenas?" Mouse-Breeder shook his head. "Of course, if you're killed, your friends can go back in time to rescue you, but it seems a waste of time."

"I'm not going hunting," said Loaf. "I want to see the prairie you describe."

"It's interesting for about a day," said Mouse-Breeder. "But be our guest. There are no restrictions. Whatever you think you need to know before you meet the Visitors. Or whatever you simply want to know to satisfy your own curiosity. All our plans have come to nothing. We have no plans for you, beyond providing you with access to all the information we have."

"Then I want to learn how the starships work," said Umbo. "And all about the machines that govern them."

"It's a lifetime's study," said Swims-in-the-Air.

"And your lifetimes are shorter than ours," said Mouse-Breeder.

"I don't have to learn how to build one," said Umbo. "But I assume that the design of whatever the Visitors use to come here will be based on the same principles. They rely on machines, as you do. More than you do. Right?"

Rigg was surprised that Umbo had thought of such a project, and seemed determined to pursue it. Umbo had no particular education in science and technology. He would be duplicating the kind of education that Father had given Rigg as they wandered the forests. Rigg well knew what effort it had taken him with the best teacher in the world.

And then Rigg realized that he was assuming Umbo was less capable of learning than Rigg himself was. But that wasn't so. Umbo was half Odinfolder, while Rigg and Param were only one-quarter. If they really had bred for superior intelligence, Umbo might be even smarter than the two royal children were.

How quickly I bought into the class biases of the Sessamids, thought Rigg. Thinking I was Father's son, I assumed I was as smart as he was—he knew everything, I thought. Turns out he was a machine, and I was the son of the Queen- and King-in-the-Tent. So I turned all my sense of superiority toward the royal family, and once again, I was wrong.

Wrong and wrong again, and again, and probably now as well. Let Umbo study what he wants. He'll learn as quickly as I will, or more quickly.

Soon they all had books, except Loaf, who pleasantly insisted on going out into the world. He asked for a flyer, and they produced one—a duplicate of the one they had ridden in when Vadesh brought them to the Wall. Within three days he was back, saying little about what he saw, and then settled into the same life they were leading: Hours on end sitting or standing or walking about in the library, reading whatever the mice made appear at their request, then discarding what they were done with, which promptly vanished, yet reappeared again upon request, open to the very page they had been on when they closed it.

But it wasn't all reading. There were meals, and at the meals they talked, and sometimes in between. Umbo and Olivenko were the sort of student who has to talk about or show whatever excites them. Rigg understood the principle, but Father had curbed it in him, if only because whatever Rigg had learned, he had learned from Father—from Ramex—and in the deep forest there was no one to tell but him, and what was the point of that?

Rigg was annoyed sometimes at the interruptions from Umbo and Olivenko, but then he changed his mind when he realized that it was good for him to know the extent of what they learned, as well as their questions and conclusions about it. It's not that Rigg actually knew everything they knew, but he knew what they had *said* about what they knew, and didn't forget it, so that he would be able to ask them questions and have some idea of whether they'd know the answer.

Param, on the other hand, talked about nothing she was learning, and showed her annoyance if anyone asked. For a few hours once he asked the mice to show him what Param had been reading, and he skimmed through the books, finding that she was, indeed, reading histories of the Sessamids. But very quickly he found that she was beyond—before—the royal family, backtracking through the entire history of Ramfold. It was a world she had never really seen, he realized, and by studying the whole history and geography of it, she was, in a way, seeing what she had been kept from seeing her entire life.

Olivenko immersed himself in the culture of Earth, but not

the modern history that would be familiar to the Visitors who would come to Garden only a year or so from now. Instead, he was discovering all he could about the evolution of the human race and then about the earliest histories, the movement of ancient tribes, the formation of nations. "I have to know why humans are the way they are," said Olivenko.

Rigg took note of how Olivenko spoke of humans as "they," though he wasn't quite sure what it meant. The Odinfolders looked rather simian, with their shorter legs and semi-grasping feet. It was easy to see that they would not register as fully human. But as far as the Visitors would be able to see, Rigg and his company were fully human. Except for Loaf, and that was only because of the parasite he bore on his face. And Olivenko had no share in the inborn time-centered powers that were the unique achievement of Ramfold. In what sense should *he* think of humans as other than himself, or of himself as other than human?

To Rigg, there was no doubt that he was human, and the others as well—including the yahoo-bodied Odinfolders. It took a little getting used to, the way their strides were shorter, their running slower, but their reach longer, their strength much greater than any of the Ramfolders but Loaf. Still, they spoke human languages, thought human thoughts, ate human food, and had the same tribal and personal instincts as any human. Self-preservation, yet the willingness to sacrifice for the good of the community; personal pride and ambition, and yet a willingness to be modest in order to retain their acceptance by others. Rigg could see no particular difference in the way they thought and acted, the social rules that governed them.

The only real difference was that the Odinfolders were so self-controlled. They might feel the same imperatives as the people Rigg had known in Ramfold, but they knew what was happening to them as they felt these things, and chose rationally whether to act on those feelings or not. He could see in their faces as the decisions were made, the momentary hesitation, and instinctive move that they held in check. But it seemed to cause no stress. Reining in their passions was as natural to them as eating and drinking and talking. So perhaps they had evolved to a higher level, another stage. Once they started getting the Future Books, they had transformed themselves again and again, remaking their history from that moment forward, over and over, and learning from each failure, only to fail again. Perhaps that process had bred in them a calm acceptance of defeat, or a readiness to take the long view of things.

There came a time when Rigg realized he had to read the Future Books in order to try to make guesses about what might have struck the Visitors as so terrifying or disgusting about the people of Garden that they came back to destroy the world. No matter how much Rigg read from the histories, biographies, and literature of Earth, it made no sense to him. The stories all seemed to champion tolerance, acceptance of the strange, the need to change in order to adapt, survive, grow.

Indeed, the whole colonizing project was born of a fear that as long as Earth was the only repository of human life, it could be extinguished. A near-miss with a large meteor was the wake-up call; humanity had to establish itself on more worlds, so the fate of one world would not be the fate of the human race. And on a new world, maybe they could get some things right which they had done badly on Earth. The birthplace of humanity was too crowded, too polluted, too endangered after years of botched development. The human genome bore the traces of too many behavioral and physical dead ends. On different worlds, the human race could evolve in different ways, so that one version of humanity or another would be more likely to survive.

So Ram Odin had been sent out in command of a starship that would use the new technology of jumping through space to reach another habitable planet as quickly as possible. If the jump hadn't worked, the ship could have continued at a much slower speed, with passengers and pilot in stasis until they reached the planet that Ram named Garden. The idea was to succeed in establishing the human race on another world. And in this the colony project had succeeded astonishingly well.

It was hardly the fault of the people of Garden that there had been a time anomaly in the first jump, and they had been thrust back in time by eleven thousand, one hundred ninety-one years. Nor was it their fault that another anomaly caused the ship to make the passage nineteen times, so that nineteen complete copies of the colony ship, including all the people on it, reached Garden at the same time. What could possibly have caused the Visitors to ignore their own ethos, the innocence of the people of Garden, and a human history longer than that of recorded human history on Earth?

When he started reading the Future Books, he asked the mice to show him which of his party had already read them. When the list appeared, he was surprised and rueful when he learned that he was the last, not the first, to read the Future Books. To his surprise, the first had been Loaf.

For many months they had been leading the studious life that the Odinfolders had invited them to lead, preparing as best they could to learn useful things about the Visitors, about the people of Earth, and about their own world, in the effort to understand what would provoke genocide by the Destroyers. But when Rigg reached the end of his third detailed pass through the Future Books, and still understood nothing, he called a meeting that he realized was long overdue.

He brought them out of the library, out of the ruined city, to the brow of a hill overlooking a wide reach of prairie. It happened that a herd of elephants was busy destroying a copse of trees in the distance, and Loaf amused them for a while by describing in detail the way a young elephant was trying to push down a tree until an older female finally shoved him out of the way and took it down with a single surge. With the vastly superior eyes given him by the facemask, Loaf had no need of telescopes or other tools to see things that were a tiny blur to the others. And that gave Rigg the question with which he began the meeting.

"Loaf's eyes are better than ours, because he's been partially merged with a highly altered life form from Garden," said Rigg. "But that can't be why the Visitors rejected Garden, can it?"

There was a brief digression as Param pointed out that since the Visitors had never seen Loaf wearing a facemask on any of the previous passages through this period of time, it couldn't possibly have any influence.

"Not Loaf in particular," said Olivenko. "For all we know

there are other wallfolds that have been transformed just as radically, and the Odinfolders just don't know about it. That isn't what Rigg is asking."

If they failed, Rigg knew he would have to return to his original plan of visiting every wallfold himself. This time, though, he was spending his time studying the most vital world of all, the one the Visitors would come from.

"The whole literature of Earth is full of condemnation of people who hate others just for being strange and different," said Rigg. "Their histories are full of self-congratulation about how they've left such base impulses behind them. The worst thing their biographers and historians can say about a person is that he judges people on the basis of differences in their physical attributes, their languages, their cultures. How can they possibly come here and violate everything they believe?"

Loaf only laughed. "Rigg, you're still so young. What would your father have said?" When Olivenko started to bring up Knosso, Loaf held up a hand. "I mean Ramex, the expendable who raised him."

Rigg sighed. "Yes, I know. The very fact that they condemn xenophobia so harshly is proof that they hadn't overcome it at all."

"An aspirational virtue, not an achievement," said Olivenko.

"Whatever that means," said Umbo.

"Oh, drop the pose of youthful ignorance," said Param impatiently. "I've seen what you're reading. By now you could probably build a starship yourself."

"I only understand a fraction of what I'm reading," said Umbo. "I don't know how anything works, I just know what the machines are supposed to do and where you can find them in each ship. And since the Visitors' starship design is probably completely different, I doubt anything I've learned is useful."

"So you've wasted your time here," said Param. "But don't pretend that you don't know what 'aspirational virtue' means."

"A virtue that you admire but don't actually have," said Umbo, "yes, I understand it. I just think it sounds absurd for us to talk like philosophers when we're just *us*."

"Sorry," said Rigg. "But the fact that the people of Earth recognize that they still have a serious problem with xenophobia makes it seem all the more absurd that they could come here, see how strange we are—but also how much the different wallfolds have accomplished in eleven thousand years—and then decide that they hate us and fear us so much we have to be wiped out."

"We don't know that's what the Visitors decided," said Olivenko.

"You think the Future Books are lying about the Destroyers?" asked Rigg.

"I think there's no shortage of lying here in Odinfold, but no, I think the Future Books are telling the truth. But the very fact that they call one group from Earth the Visitors, and the second group by a different name, Destroyers, should be a clue to a real possibility—that the humans who came to destroy Garden are *not* the same group that first came to visit."

"Two separate groups with starship technology?" asked Umbo doubtfully.

"No," said Olivenko. "But how do we know that there wasn't a political revolution, a coup, a war during the gap between the Visitors' return and the Destroyers' departure? Maybe the

Visitors came back with a brilliantly glowing report, but a group of xenophobes took over the government. And maybe they didn't last long in power—just long enough to send the Destroyers. We have no way of knowing whether by the time the Destroyers returned to Earth, there wasn't a new government in place that deeply regretted the destruction of Garden."

"I suppose nobody has ever been there to receive their apology," said Param.

"Exactly," said Olivenko. "Maybe no matter what the Visitors see, the Destroyers come, for reasons having to do with the politics of Earth. Aren't there powerful groups that still espouse xenophobia?"

Rigg nodded. "They aren't the people with the high technology, but yes, there are widespread cultures that believe in killing everyone who doesn't comply with their cultural practices. But they've been kept in check for centuries by the superior technology of the more enlightened cultures."

"Enlightened?" asked Loaf. "Who's judging now?"

"*I'm* judging," said Rigg, "and I'm using the only standard that matters to us: Enlightened people are the ones who don't want to destroy Garden, and the Destroyers are ignorant monsters. I think that's a pretty fair assessment, don't you?"

They agreed readily enough.

"*We're* ignorant monsters," said Param. "Look how Mother and General Citizen treated us. How Vadesh treated us—and how we judged him and the facemask people. Humans judge each other and we kill each other when we decide the other people are too bad to allow them to live."

"But not everybody," said Rigg.

"Everybody," said Param. "No exceptions."

"Not me," said Rigg. "Not you."

"You wouldn't kill somebody who was trying to kill *you*?" asked Param.

"That's self-defense," said Rigg.

"But Jesus and Gandhi and a lot of others say that you have no right of self-defense," said Param.

"I'm not sure that's what they said," said Rigg, "but I'm glad to know you've been reading Earth literature, too."

"I skimmed it a little," said Param. "Look, human nature hasn't changed. What does it matter if the Visitors liked Garden and the Destroyers are a different group? Garden ends up just as dead."

"What I'm saying," said Rigg, "is that maybe we need to be prepared to go back to Earth with the Visitors."

"Where they'd kill us," said Param. "And then we'd be so far from here that we couldn't go back in time and get *here*, we'd only travel back in time on *Earth*. That's a deeply terrible idea."

"It might be the only way," said Rigg, refusing to take her negativism as a final answer. "Go back with them to Earth, with the chance that we die there, but with a chance that maybe we can change the outcome."

"What makes you think the Visitors would let us go?" asked Loaf.

"What makes you think they could stop us if we want to go?" asked Umbo.

"Getting onto a human starship isn't the same as going through the Wall," said Rigg.

"We can do things with time," said Param, "but we can't fly."

"Maybe we could use the Odinfolder technology to put something on board their ship," said Umbo. "A plague, maybe. Something that kills them all. But we show the Visitors who are on Garden what happened to their ship, and then we take them back in time *before* we implanted the plague, so that they'll understand that we *could* kill them but we chose not to."

"How would that make them not want to destroy us?" asked Loaf. "That's the point I'm not getting. Because I think that's a sure way to guarantee that they send the Destroyers."

Umbo shrugged and turned away, a little angry. Rigg was so tired of the way Umbo took offense at any slight, while he felt no compunction about slighting Rigg at every opportunity. The only thing that had kept them from open quarrels during these many months was the fact that they were able to avoid each other most of the time.

"It's not a stupid idea," said Olivenko. "We just need to refine it."

"We can't use any version of it," said Rigg. "As soon as the expendables realize what we've done, the orbiters destroy our wallfold. We aren't allowed to develop weapons."

"It's a disease," said Umbo, "not a weapon."

"If we send it to their ship in order to kill people, it's a weapon, and we get blown to smithereens," said Rigg.

"You're such an expert on how the ships' computers think?" said Umbo.

"No, *you* are," said Rigg.

Umbo's lips tightened, but he didn't argue with Rigg's point. Umbo knew more than anyone about how the original starship worked, and in fact the computers would not be fooled by a sophistry like, It's a disease, not a weapon.

"Maybe we just need to study more," said Param.

"No," said Umbo. "We have a deeper problem than the fact that if we went to Earth, we couldn't travel back in time to when we were on Garden. We don't even know if our time skills even *work* off the surface of Garden."

"Why wouldn't they?" asked Olivenko.

"Think about it," said Umbo. "We don't understand anything about *how* we're able to travel back in time—or how Param can make microjumps into the future, skipping the moments in between. But we do know some obvious things about the *rules* of time-shifting. It's absolutely tied to the surface of the planet."

"It worked fine when we flew to the Wall with Vadesh," said Param.

"Really? Did you try any time-skipping in flight?" asked Umbo.

Param bristled. "We jumped off a rock once, if you remember."

"We were never more than two meters from solid stone," said Umbo.

"It's a good question," said Rigg, "but the flyer isn't a real test, anyway, because it's still tied to the gravity well of Garden. The real problem is this: Garden is flying through space as it orbits our sun. The whole solar system is also moving rapidly through space. Say we travel back in time by six months. In that amount of time, Garden has moved completely around the sun to the opposite side. Yet we travel back, not to where we were in absolute space, which would kill us instantly, but to where we were in relation to the surface of Garden. Our time-shifting is tied to the planet. So Umbo's asking, what happens if we leave the surface of Garden and go to another planet? Do we even *have* time-shifting ability there? Or is our time-shifting still relative to the surface of Garden? If we're on Earth, in a certain position millions of kilometers away from Garden, and travel back in time, do we end up in exactly that position *relative to Garden*? Because Earth and Garden move so differently from each other, that we'd end up in cold deep airless space if we're still tied to Garden."

Umbo glared at him. Rigg couldn't imagine why. Hadn't Rigg just defended Umbo's argument? There was no figuring out what made anybody work. But now Rigg had a whole bunch of new stories to help him understand. Among the Mongols, Temujin and Jamuka had been blood brothers, but they became bitter enemies on the way to Temujin becoming Khan and taking the name Genghis, or Chinggis. It was part of human nature that best friends could easily become rivals and then deadly foes. Rigg would count himself successful if he could keep it at the level of rivalry without ever letting Umbo become his enemy.

"I think it's obvious," said Olivenko, "that it's tied to whatever planet you're on."

"I don't think anything's obvious," said Rigg. "Whatever we decide, we're betting our lives on it. All the paths I can see are actually views into the past—I see the actual people and animals going through all the movements of their lives, and they're tied to Garden. But they're all people who were *born* here, who lived their whole lives here. And think of when we went downriver, Loaf, Umbo—when I was a prisoner in the cabin of that boat, I tried to catch on to the paths of previous travelers, and I couldn't, because their paths hung in the air over open water, and I could only reach them for a moment or two as our boat passed under them. It might work that way no matter how far we get from Garden—paths just hanging there in space, long after the ship is gone."

"But the original pilot, Ram Odin," said Umbo, "*he* had time gifts. That's where all our abilities come from. And he did time stuff when he was in a ship in space."

"Yet the ship was displaced nineteen times," said Rigg. "Doesn't that tell you something? During the microseconds when the ship's nineteen computers were separately calculating and activating the jump, the whole ship had moved far enough in space that Ram's unconscious time-jump reached nineteen different places. We can't go into space and use our time-shifting ability, or we'll just create duplicate ships."

"We don't know that," said Olivenko.

"But we don't know it *won't* happen. Or worse," said Rigg. "Please remember that when I suggested going back to Earth with the Visitors, I wasn't counting on the idea that we could keep ourselves out of trouble by using time-jumping. For all we know, that'll be a sure ticket to our deaths. My idea was to go back, to make the attempt, and if they kill us, then they kill us."

"Well, there's this," said Olivenko. "Even if that happened, and we couldn't save ourselves—or rather, *you* couldn't save us with your time-shifting—the Odinfolders would send another book into the past and tell them—and us—that having us get on the Visitors' ship was a very bad idea and we shouldn't do it."

Param laughed. "So the fact that they haven't already received such a Future Book proves that we succeeded?"

"Or that we decided not to do it," said Rigg.

"Or that we did it, and failed, but the Odinfolders decided not to show us the Future Book that resulted, and just went on to try something else."

"Or they gave up," said Param, "and just decided to die."

"No matter how much we learn," said Umbo, "we never know enough."

"All we can do is what we've always done," said Rigg. "Make a try at something, and then if it doesn't work, go back and try again. But we can't always go back."

Umbo leapt to his feet, "Right, there are things that stay *terrible*. For instance, Rigg, that you've completely forgotten about going back to save my brother Kyokay's life."

It struck Rigg like a knife, that this was part of what Umbo still held against him. "We already decided that we can't, because if we did, then we'd never have gotten together to learn how to manipulate time."

"But now we know more, we have more control, we could figure out a way to catch him partway down maybe, or—"

"Maybe we can," said Rigg. "Maybe we can put in a net to catch him, or train a giant bird to snatch him out of the air, or a huge puff of air to blow him out to sea. But we'll do it later—go back and save one boy after we've figured out how to save the whole world."

"So you're saying Kyokay has to stay dead, so that we can do whatever useless stupidity we've done since we found out how to do this stuff?" said Umbo. "Well, you know what? Maybe the best thing would be to stop Kyokay from falling in the first place, so we *don't* ever learn to do our little time tricks, and then all the rest of our miserable history doesn't happen!"

"And then," said Param bitterly, "you get to enjoy living with your brother in your happy home, under the authority of your beloved father, while *I* get murdered by my mother and General Citizen because Rigg isn't there to save me."

"But if Citizen didn't capture Rigg and realize who he was—" began Umbo.

"Whatever Citizen and Hagia Sessamin were plotting, it didn't begin with Rigg's capture," said Olivenko scornfully. "Your father would probably have killed you by now, Umbo, and meanwhile Param would also have been murdered, and even if none of those things happened, the Visitors would come and then the Destroyers and kill us all, so what exactly are you saying here, that having a few more years with your brother—who would probably have found some other colorful way to get himself killed—*that* would be worth the destruction of the planet?"

Umbo buried his face in his hands. "I just want to stop all this. When did this become my job?"

"It's not," said Param. "It's *my* job, and Rigg's, because we were born with responsibility."

"Stop it," said Rigg. "Let's just face the fact that we can't fix every bad thing that ever happened, because every change we make brings about new bad things, because in the real world, bad things happen, period, that's it. People die and we can't always unkill them, that's how it is. I'm sorry Kyokay died, Umbo, and I'm sorry we can't fix it yet without making a whole bunch of terrible unpredictable changes. And I'm sorry that Param is such a provincial twit that she makes stupid arrogant remarks about how the royal family is born to responsibility—"

"We are!" cried Param, leaping to her feet.

"At least you got angry," said Rigg, "instead of disappearing on us."

"I really like the way you're making peace here, Rigg," said Loaf.

"Was that Loaf or the facemask talking?" asked Rigg. "Listen, we have plenty of reasons to be angry and resentful and suspicious and whatever else we're feeling. Grief-stricken, terrified, whatever it is, it's completely justified. And if we all *hate* each other what difference does it make? We have these abilities, which may be worthless, but we have them, and if there's any chance we can use them to save the world, then let's do it, and if we fail, well, we're all dead so who cares, and if we succeed, then we'll have plenty of time to feud and bicker like children, and no, I'm not saying I'm any better, I'm so lonely and angry all the time that I can hardly sleep, and I wish my father had really been my father and not some stupid machine, so don't tell me what it's like to lose somebody you loved, or to be disappointed in life, or whatever else is going wrong. Loaf misses Leaky. I miss my father. Param's mother, the only person she trusted, tried to kill her. Olivenko's mentor, Knosso, got dragged out of his boat and drowned. Have I given the complete list of Things We Haven't Been Able To Change?"

"No," said Loaf, "but it was a pretty good start."

"We've been studying forever, and the Visitors are close to arriving, and while we might end up trying the idea of getting on the Visitors' starship, if they'll even let us, and going back to Earth, I think it's pretty obvious that it's *not* what we should do first."

"What *should* we do, then?" asked Olivenko.

"Not one thing," said Rigg. "Nothing. The Visitors come, we watch from a distance, we see *for ourselves* what they are. Or maybe we even meet them and talk to them. But then they go, and we think about what we learned from them, and we go on studying everything we can, and then the Destroyers come, and we see what *that* looks like, and then we jump back in time to right after we got here, and *then* we decide what to do."

They all sat there, looking at the ground, at the distant ruins, at the sky, at the elephants, at passing insects or the mice scurrying through the grass—anywhere but at each other, anywhere but at Rigg.

And finally Olivenko said, "That sounds like the best plan I've heard."

"I think so, too," said Param.

"Then unless Umbo's an idiot," said Loaf, "it's unanimous."

"I'm an idiot," said Umbo, "but I still vote for it. Which should prove to all of you that it's an absolutely stupid idea."

"I agree," said Rigg. "It's cowardly and overly cautious and I wish somebody would think of a better plan. But for the meantime, it's what we're planning to do. Right?"

Right.

CHAPTER 14

The Knife

Umbo had always had mixed feelings about school. On the one hand, it got him away from home, and he didn't have to work all that hard. On the other hand, he envied his friend Rigg for the way he only came to school now and then, and spent the rest of the year out in the deep forest with his father, trapping animals and bringing home the furs.

Then he learned that Rigg's time in the forest was spent in a kind of schooling far more rigorous than the country school Umbo attended. And, after traveling with Rigg in varying degrees of wilderness, from the edges of civilization beside the Stashik River to the untouched wilderness of Vadeshfold, and seeing how hard Rigg had to work to find food and water for them all, and good campsites where they'd be safe from animals, Umbo had a new appreciation for the rigors of that supposedly free life that Rigg had lived.

Here in Odinfold, Umbo felt like he was back in school—and as a rather poor student, too. Knowing he could never catch up with Rigg's sophisticated education, Olivenko's deep scholarly training with King Knosso, and Param's courtly training at her mother's knee, Umbo set himself a much simpler, but very practical task—to learn everything he could about the starships from Earth.

He worked hard at this, and mastered it as well as could be expected. Now that he knew he had the heredity to be very bright, he enjoyed testing his own memory, wondering if he was a match for Rigg's nearly perfect recall, or even Rigg's superior.

But it was all a deception, because Umbo had a much more important purpose—one he could not speak of to anyone, not until he learned something useful.

There were deep holes in the things that the Odinfolders had told them, subjects they simply didn't touch on. Moreover, the only Odinfolders who ever spoke to them were Mouse-Breeder and Swims-in-the-Air. They were affable, likeable, patient adults—but Umbo didn't like the fact that apparently the rest of the people who lived here near the Wall were either forbidden to talk to the Ramfolders or uninterested in them, which seemed extravagantly unlikely.

Weren't the Odinfolders supposed to be completely free? Weren't they brilliant, creative people? Why, then, were they acting so incurious? Here were people who could manipulate the flow of time as if it were just another bodily function, and the Odinfolders didn't want to meet them, talk to them, see a demonstration? No, there was a reason nobody talked to them, and

Umbo was pretty sure that it was to keep the Ramfolders from learning things that the Odinfolders didn't want them to know.

They only had the Odinfolders' word for it that any person that developed serious weapons would be killed, that they had broken into the programs that controlled the Wall but for some reason couldn't break into the programs controlling the orbiters. It also seemed unbelievable to Umbo that the Odinfolders were really going to leave all the decisions up to the Ramfolders. That had to be illusory. They would *think* they were making the decisions, but in fact they were being shaped, forced into a certain path by the information the Odinfolders gave them, and the information they withheld.

Yet how could he discuss his doubts with any of his party? Down in the library, surrounded by mice that seemed to understand human speech, it seemed likely that everything they said was recorded for later study by the Odinfolders. And the mice were outdoors, too. A spy network covering the entire wallfold.

One question that bothered Umbo was the way the villages of the ten thousand remaining Odinfolders were all clustered near the Wall, according to their own maps, leaving the vast center of their country for the animals, which were reputedly wild but were quite possibly as domesticated as the mice.

Another question was why all the wallfolds were named for the colonist who played the dominant role in their earliest years. And yet this wallfold and Umbo's home wallfold were both named for the same man, Ram Odin, the captain of the starship. Supposedly Ram Odin had only come to the surface of Garden in the one fold, Ramfold; why, then, was Odinfold also named for him? And if the story was wrong, and there was a copy of Ram Odin in every wallfold, just as there was a copy of everyone else, why did he dominate in only two of the colonies? Why not all of them?

Yet these matters were not discussed in any of the books Umbo found. He deliberately asked for books that dealt with the earliest history of all the wallfolds, supposedly looking for references to the starships buried in each wallfold, but what he searched for was any reference to Ram Odin. Yet even in Ramfold and Odinfold, it was as if the man were legendary from the start, never actually living among the people.

How could he not live among them? He had descendants—the time-shifters of Ramfold were supposedly all descended from him. Were the time-shifting machines of the Odinfolders also using some ability that came from Ram Odin? Had he fathered children in *both* wallfolds? If so, then why not others?

Mouse-Breeder and Swims-in-the-Air were so nice, so patient, so wise—but Umbo wondered how nice they'd be if he started asking these questions openly. They were such obvious matters that Umbo couldn't believe he was the only one who thought of them—yet no one said anything or asked anything. It was as if they all knew that these subjects were forbidden even to think about.

But Umbo thought about them. Thought and studied and tried to get around the lack of information, but what the Odinfolders didn't want him to find, he did not find.

After the meeting where they had decided to do nothing and merely observe the Visitors this time around, Umbo went back to his lonely studies, just as the others did. Oh, they were sociable enough at mealtimes, sharing interesting tidbits from their research, joking with each other, offering theories about the people of Earth. But they never said anything personal or important, at least not in front of Umbo.

Is everyone silent with everyone else? Umbo wondered. Or is it just around me that they say nothing significant? Am I being frozen out, or are we all living in private worlds?

Human beings were not meant to lead such solitary lives.

And then one day it dawned on him that he might have a tool that would let him get answers in spite of the Odinfolders' evasions, deceptions, and concealments. He had the knife.

The knife that the Odinfolders admitted to having made and then planted on the person Rigg stole it from, the first time they deliberately combined their talents in order to travel into the past. The knife that had replicas of the nineteen jewels embedded in the hilt.

How faithfully had the stones been replicated? Could they also control the ships? Control the Wall? Could the knife be used to communicate with the orbiters?

What had the Odinfolders made it for? Why had they given it to them? What did they make of the fact that it was Umbo who had been in control of it since Rigg was arrested in O, and even after his escape, when he could have taken it back?

Yet how could Umbo test the knife? What could he possibly do without being reported on to the Odinfolders?

And then it dawned on him: Why conceal it? Why not simply ask to go to the ship that was buried somewhere in the heart of Odinfold? It was a natural culmination of his study of the starships.

"I need to go to the starship," Umbo announced at dinner.

"Want company?" asked Rigg. "Or is this a solitary adventure?"

If Rigg went along, then it would be Rigg's expedition, and if any good came from it, it would be Rigg's achievement. Not because Rigg took credit. If anything, Rigg shunted praise away from himself. But that very fact would make it all the more likely that people would give him credit for anything Umbo found in the starship.

What Umbo wanted was for Param to go with him. He wanted Param to invite herself, to *choose* to be with him.

But she was so lost in her own thoughts that Umbo wondered how she managed to get the food into her mouth instead of smearing it all over her face.

She had no use for him, that was plain. But Umbo's consolation was that she showed no special favor toward Olivenko, either. She wasn't closing herself off by disappearing constantly, as she had done in Flacommo's house. So it wasn't that she objected to their company or fled it; she simply didn't have the same need to connect with other people that Umbo had.

Nonsense. Human beings had the need to be part of a community, even if they were introverted or shy or suspicious of others, even if they weren't joiners. So how was Param meeting that need? What was she part of? If it was this group, Umbo saw no sign of it. She treated them as distantly as she did the Odinfolders.

Or maybe she behaved completely differently when Umbo wasn't around. Maybe the others all regarded Umbo as the weak one, the untrustworthy one. The one who had cried when he found out he wasn't his father's son. The one who had been sniping at Rigg in obvious, childish resentment. Umbo wasn't ashamed of having felt as he did—Rigg really did assume command at times when he didn't know any more than any of the others. But Umbo wished he had borne it in patience, never letting his resentment show. Because he suspected that now the others all regarded him as the one who couldn't be told things, or he'd make a scene, cause a problem.

Sometimes it's better to face a small problem now than a huge one later, that's how he wanted to answer them.

But since he didn't absolutely know that they were all freezing him out in order not to rile him, he couldn't confront anybody about it without seeming paranoid.

Umbo wasn't a loner. He liked being part of a community. He liked having close friends. He liked feeling accepted and trusted. And when he felt that he wasn't accepted, wasn't trusted, it made him feel lonely and angry and hurt and resentful. Precisely the feelings that had probably cost him the others' trust in the first place.

Yet he couldn't bring himself to try to make things right with Rigg. Let him apologize! *He* was the one who had created a rift between them, with his officious attitude, the way he and everybody else treated Umbo as if he were unworthy of being consulted.

"I'll go alone," said Umbo, wishing that someone, anyone—

Loaf, Olivenko—would insist on coming along, if only to look out for him, cover his back.

But of course none of *them* was so paranoid as to suspect the Odinfolders of being untrustworthy. And so they said nothing, except for Olivenko, who only said, "I wonder if they'll actually take you there."

"Why wouldn't they?" asked Umbo, nonchalantly. It was as close as they'd come to openly discussing the possibility that the Odinfolders were holding them more as prisoners or spies than as compatriots in the common cause.

"It's a long walk, that's all I'm thinking. I wonder if they'll let you use their flyer, the way Loaf did."

And that was that. The conversation moved on to other things.

That evening, Umbo deliberately avoided running into Mouse-Breeder and Swims-in-the-Air. He knew right where they'd be, because they were as predictable as day and night. So he made sure not to pass near them.

Instead he went out among the housetrees and walked straight up to a tree where he knew several other Odinfolders lived. "Excuse me," he said. "Excuse me. Excuse me."

Eventually a head and shoulders emerged from the center of the tree. "What?" asked the woman tentatively.

"I'm Umbo. One of the Ramfolders."

"I know who you are," she said.

"I'm studying the way starships from Earth are designed, and I need to get into the Odinfold starship. How do I call the flyer?"

"You don't," said the woman, and then she was gone, having dropped back down into the tree.

So there it was, out in the open. He wasn't allowed to summon the flyer.

And, just as predictably, within a few minutes Swims-in-the-Air came to find him, a bemused expression on her face. "Why didn't you ask me or Mouse-Breeder to help you get to the starship?"

"I didn't run into you inside and came looking for you out here, and then I thought, why not ask one of the others?"

"You've been here nearly a year," said Swims-in-the-Air. "Has any of them shown the slightest interest in meeting you?"

"No, and I've wondered about that."

"Why should you wonder?" asked Swims-in-the-Air. "You're a symbol of our failure, after nine tries, to save the world. Here you are, this ragtag group of five, and you're supposed to succeed where the finest minds of Odinfold have failed again and again and again? What do you think they feel."

I thought they were forbidden to speak to us. I still think that. But of course he kept such thoughts to himself.

"I'm sorry I intruded on them," said Umbo. "Fortunately, I think the woman I talked to will recover from the injury I caused her."

"It was more injury than you think," said Swims-in-the-Air. "You don't understand us, what we go through."

"Go through! This is a utopia, everybody's happy and everything's perfect."

"If I thought you believed that," said Swims-in-the-Air, "I'd worry about your sanity. But we still have our sense of irony, my young friend. Ours is a bleak and dreadful life here in the borderland, and you'd do well to remember that most of us value our solitude. In fact, all of us do, but Mouse-Breeder and I decided to make ourselves available to you. Somebody had to do it."

"What do you mean, a bleak and dreadful life?"

"In the shadow of the Wall."

"So move! Move away from the Wall, take back a few scraps of that vast game preserve."

Swims-in-the-Air shook her head. "How can you not understand? We *have* to live near the Wall. We need the Wall."

"Need it? How can you use the Wall?"

"Why, by walking into it, of course."

"That would be insane."

"Yes," said Swims-in-the-Air. "It fills us with terror and despair, and yet we walk inside the Wall every day, some of us for miles, deep inside, where it's all we can do to keep from killing ourselves, or going mad with fear."

"Why do you do it?"

"Why do you think we have no children?" asked Swims-in-the-Air. "How do you think we keep ourselves from bonding into families? The Wall is the antidote for our humanity. It keeps us insane enough to reduce our population from six billion to a mere ten thousand. Children come along once a decade."

"Though even at that rate, we never see them."

"Him, you mean. Him, the one child who was born shortly before you got here. He lives on the far side of Odinfold. The previously born child is older than you. And that's it, out of our entire wallfold. Two children."

"Yours, then?" asked Umbo, thinking of that part of her name.

"My children are only thirty or forty years younger than me," she answered. "They're not children anymore, and I don't keep track of their movements."

"But you keep track of mine."

"There are dangers here. But yes, Umbo, since you ask so sweetly, I'll take you to our starship."

Umbo almost blurted, "You will?" But that would have revealed that he hadn't expected them to take him. And if they realized that, they would be bound to understand that he didn't trust them, that he thought they were withholding things from him.

"When can we go?"

"The flyer can be here in an hour or so, if we summon it right now. I wish you wouldn't, though."

Ah, here it comes. "Why not?"

"Because there's no way to call the flyer without Odinex knowing, no way to visit the starship without Odinex being there."

"Can't he go somewhere else while I'm there?" asked Umbo. "And really, what harm will it do?"

"If he sees you, if he converses with you, you'll show up in the ships' memory as a person instead of as a series of activities and dialogues. The Visitors will have everything from the ships' computers before they ever reach the surface of Garden. They'll know about you."

"Let them," said Umbo. "If it wrecks everything this time for me to visit the starship and meet your expendable, it'll make no difference in the long run, because I won't visit the starship on our next go-round, and so there'll be nothing to report next time."

"All right," said Swims-in-the-Air. "Who's going with you?"

"Nobody," said Umbo.

"Because you're afraid they'd stop you if they knew you were going?"

"Do you think they would? My only thought was that it wasn't worth disturbing them. I'm the only one who cares so much about the starships."

"I think you should tell them," said Swims-in-the-Air.

"You know what?" said Umbo. "I don't think so. I think I'll just go as soon as the flyer gets here."

Swims-in-the-Air shrugged. "Suit yourself."

Umbo felt a slight chill. Her reaction had told him all that he needed to know. She had tried to manipulate him, to play on his uncertainties and self-doubt, to delay or forestall this visit to the starship. The Odinfolders were not quite so open-minded as they had seemed. They had a plan, and intended to shape events so that the Ramfolders would carry it out.

It was only when he was in the air, sitting in the flyer, that it occurred to him that perhaps the manipulation had been on the opposite tack—perhaps she had suggested he wait for one of the others to join him precisely because she knew he would stubbornly refuse, leaving him completely alone, as she had wanted all along.

It was impossible to know what other people were thinking. Not for the first time, Umbo wondered if it wasn't better to be straightforward like Loaf, saying what he thought and letting events fall in place however they would. Loaf didn't try to outguess people. He just looked at what they did, judged the likely results, and reacted accordingly. While Umbo, by trying to be clever, left himself open to being even more easily deceived.

Or maybe nobody was being clever at all, and Umbo was simply outsmarting himself because of his suspicions.

The flyer skimmed over the surface of a rolling grassland, cut here and there by rivers and streams. But then there came a familiar sight: a steep row of cliffs extending for kilometers in either direction. It was Upsheer Cliff all over again, rock thrust upward in a huge circle around the point where a starship crashed into Garden eleven thousand years before.

The flyer rose, surmounting the cliffs. Behind them, a higher mountain stood alone. Where Upsheer had been surrounded by forest, this escarpment rose out of grassland, and it was grass that topped the cliffs. Higher up the mountain, trees formed a ragged pine forest. But Umbo suspected that the other side of the mountain was lush rain forest, given the direction of the prevailing winds.

The flyer settled onto a grassy flatland well back from the cliff edge. The door opened, and a voice said, "Proceed eastward until you are met."

"Met by whom?"

No answer.

Umbo left the flyer and walked east. It wasn't far before he saw a manshape appear, not stubby-legged like the yahoos near the Wall, but tall and robust-looking.

It was Vadesh; it was Rigg's father, the Golden Man. It was the expendable of Odinfold.

"Odinex?" asked Umbo.

"It was not wise of you to come here."

"Yet here I am."

"Turn back. There's the flyer. Go back to the Wall and await the Visitors. They'll be here very soon."

When Umbo was younger, such authoritative instructions from Rigg's father would have filled him with awe and he would have obeyed without a second thought. But now Umbo knew that this was no man, but a machine, and he was no longer cowed by his voice of command. Umbo made no move toward the flyer.

"Are the Visitors' ships in communication with you?" Umbo asked.

"Not yet," said the expendable. "But when they establish a link with the ships of Garden, I will have no secrets from them. We must keep them from discovering you and the other time-shifters."

Umbo realized now the absurdity of the Odinfolders' excuse for not letting them meet Odinex. "You already know so much about us that my visit here will hardly make a difference. What you don't know, Vadeshex and Ramex definitely know, so the Visitors will have it all."

The expendable said nothing.

"Please take me to the starship so I can verify my studies."

"Do you believe the designs were altered?"

"I did *not* think so, until you asked that question," said Umbo, smiling. "My intention is to see for myself how the designs were expressed in the actual machinery."

The expendable turned his back and led the way into a tunnel opening.

It wasn't long before ragged rock walls became smooth, and

then were sheathed in the same uncorruptible metal that had covered the Tower of O and the skyscrapers of the empty city of Vadesh. Umbo came to a doorway that opened into a huge chamber that was almost completely filled by the starship. Between the doorway and the ship stretched a bridge, two meters wide.

Umbo hesitated.

"You can't fall," said Odinex.

But his hesitation had not been prompted by fear. Rather, he wanted to test a guess he had made about the naming of the wallfolds. "Before I board the ship, will you answer a question?"

"I will, if it is permitted."

"Did you know Ram Odin?"

"All the expendables knew Ram Odin."

"Did you kill Ram Odin?"

"I did not."

"Did other expendables kill the Ram Odins on their ships?"

The expendable did not answer.

"There were Ram Odins in only two colonies," said Umbo. "I think he was supposed to be leader of the colony, but those two were the only ones he survived to establish. Tell me why the others were killed."

"When the nineteen identical Ram Odins realized that confusion would result as soon as two of them gave conflicting orders, they said to the expendable on duty at the time, 'Therefore I order you and all the other expendables to immediately kill every copy of Ram except me.'"

"If they all said that," said Umbo, "how did you know which one to obey?"

"They did not all say that. One of them left out the word 'immediately,' so his order was completed a fraction of a second before the others'. Therefore all but one of the expendables obeyed that order."

"You mean, all except the expendable who was with the Ram Odin who left out the word 'immediately.'"

"No. The order was to kill all the Ram Odins except the one who gave the order, so the expendable who was with the first Ram obeyed him by not killing him. Seventeen Ram Odins were killed by having their necks broken by their expendable. The one who gave his order most quickly was then in charge of all."

"But one expendable who was ordered to kill his Ram Odin failed to do it."

"Correct."

"Was it your Ram Odin who gave that order successfully, and lived?"

"No. That was the Ram Odin of Ramfold."

"Were you the expendable who did not obey the order he gave?"

"I was," said Odinex.

"Your Ram Odin lived."

"He did."

"Why?" asked Umbo. "I thought you couldn't disobey."

"I didn't disobey. My Ram Odin had the same impulse as the others, to issue the kill order. But he waited a fraction of a second and in that moment realized what the result would be—his own death—so he moved away from me as he said, 'Obey only me.'"

"And he completed that order before the other order was completed."

"He did. I heard the same order as the others. But I had a previous order to obey only the Ram Odin who was in the control room with me. So I obeyed that Ram Odin, and no other."

"And he didn't tell you to kill anyone," said Umbo.

"He told me to pretend that I had obeyed. He told me and the ship's computers to reveal to no other expendable and no other ship that he was still alive. We should obey all orders that would not harm him, and to pretend we had obeyed the ones that would. We kept him alive, but hidden, until all the other colonies had been founded. Our secret Ram Odin slept in stasis, and so did his colonists, until the ruling Ram Odin died of old age. Only then did I awaken our Ram Odin, as he had ordered."

"So there was no conflict," said Umbo. "He was asleep, and so you could all obey the Ram of Ramfold without any chance of your secret Odin contradicting him."

"Our colony started seventy years later than the others. But what is seventy years compared to eleven thousand, one hundred ninety-one?"

"Your Ram Odin did not follow all the policies of the first Ram Odin."

"Ram of Ramfold ordered all the ships to conceal higher technology from their people and allow it to die out, so that it could be reinvented many generations later, in new forms, but without any terrible weapons. Ram Odin of Odinfold gave a different order, and I obeyed him. While I had no choice but to keep the terrible weapons from them, I gave them full access to knowledge of the rest of the high technology of Earth. I told them what subjects they were forbidden to study, and what the penalty would be. I also kept the colonists fully informed of what was talked about among the starships and expendables of the different wallfolds."

"Except when that information would have harmed them," said Umbo.

The expendable did not answer.

"You tell them everything that you think they should know, but there are things you don't tell them."

The expendable said nothing.

"I won't tell them that you're leaving things out," said Umbo. "Because I don't actually know it."

The expendable said nothing, but now, at the other end of the bridge, the door in the side of the ship opened.

Umbo almost stepped onto the bridge. Then he stopped. "Are you planning to kill me when I step onto the bridge?"

The expendable said, "I do not kill human beings." It sounded as if Odinex were proud of not having killed his Ram Odin.

Again, Umbo almost stepped onto the bridge, but caught himself. "Odinex, am I a human being?"

"No," said Odinex.

"So if you kill me, you will not be killing a human being."

"Correct."

"Odinex, I am a human being."

The expendable said nothing.

"What is your definition of a human being?" asked Umbo.

"An organism compliant with the standard human genome, with the normal range of variation."

"What is my variation from standard?"

"You are genetically more different from human beings than a chimpanzee is."

"Is that true of all the humans of Odinfold?"

"No," said the expendable. "You have their variations, plus the variations from Ramfold."

"Are any of the people of Garden human, as you define that?"

"No," said the expendable.

"And by your definition, I'm even less human than everyone else."

"It is the definition programmed into me on Earth," said Odinex.

"Now let me ask you again. Will you let me cross this bridge safely, enter the ship, and then leave safely when I've finished my work?"

Odinex gave no answer. It was as if the question had not been asked.

Umbo had studied enough of the programming of the ship's computers and the expendables that he understood what was happening. "You can't make a prediction because you don't know what I intend to do."

"Correct."

"Can you tell me what to avoid doing in order to keep you from needing to kill me?"

"Giving you a list of forbidden actions will only make it easier for you to act in a forbidden way."

"But not giving me the list makes it impossible for me to avoid doing a forbidden thing."

"You can avoid doing a forbidden thing by not entering the starship."

"So if you push me off the bridge and I fall and you don't rescue me, I can't violate the ship."

"That would be one solution."

"Is it the one you're planning to use?"

"Yes."

"Thank you for answering my question honestly."

"I tell the truth," said the expendable.

Umbo wanted to ask, Now tell me how to get onto the starship. But of course the expendable would see through a ruse like that; there was no point in trying it.

Besides, Umbo had been studying starship design for the best part of a year. There were things he knew.

"Odinex, are you malfunctioning?"

"I am not."

"How do you know?"

"Because my self-auditing software reports that my functions are normal."

"Odinex, is your self-auditing software malfunctioning?"

A long pause. "I do not know."

"Odinex, will you run diagnostics on your self-auditing software?"

"I will when you are not present."

"I am not a threat," said Umbo, annoyed now that the expendable wasn't going to be as easy to control as he had hoped.

"You are a threat," said Odinex.

"On what basis do you regard me as a threat?"

"The person you call Swims-in-the-Air has told me you are a threat."

"But that person is not human."

"She is more human than you are," said Odinex.

Umbo pulled the knife from his clothing and displayed the jeweled hilt. "Do you recognize this knife?"

"Yes," said Odinex.

"Are the jewels in the hilt faithful copies of the jewels of control?"

"Yes."

"Smaller, but faithful."

"Yes."

"Do they function like the jewels of control?"

"Yes."

"Because I possess these jewels, can I be certified as commander of this vessel?"

"In the absence of any other commander, you could be certified."

"Is there another commander?"

"Rigg Sessamekesh is the commander of all the vessels on the planet Garden, and all the orbiters, and all the expendables."

"So these jewels cannot be used to take his place."

"He is not dead," said Odinex.

A dark thought came into Umbo's heart. He drove it away. "One of these jewels is the jewel of control for this ship alone, yes?"

"Yes."

"Can I use it to be certified as the commander of this vessel, as long as I don't contradict the orders of Rigg Sessamekesh?"

"With his consent, yes."

"But he is not human," said Umbo.

"Human status is not required to be in command of the vessel."

An interesting loophole. But there was another. "I am a descendant of Ram Odin."

"After generations of intermarriage, everyone now alive in both Ramfold and Odinfold is a descendant of Ram Odin. Everyone is a descendant of all the colonists. After eleven thousand years, it could not be otherwise."

"Was Ram Odin human?"

"Yes."

"Were his children human?"

"Yes."

"What were their names?"

Odinex listed them, and then said, "I see your point."

"Were their children human?"

"Yes. I see your point."

"At which generation did they cease to be human?" asked Umbo.

"I see your point."

"But do you accept it as a valid definition of humanity? As the primary definition?"

A pause. "I do."

"So the argument of genetic continuity is superior to the argument of accumulated genetic drift and alteration."

"It is," said Odinex.

"May I come aboard?"

"You may."

Umbo stepped onto the bridge and strode briskly across.

He did not so much hear the expendable come along behind him as feel the wind of his coming. Then he felt Odinex's hands on his back, picking him up and shoving him toward the edge of the bridge.

Umbo shifted in time to a few seconds earlier. Now he was standing at the point Odinex would propel him to, but now Odinex was two meters farther back on the bridge, preparing to seize him, while Umbo's previous self was one meter away, looking surprised to see this new version of himself.

The expendable was even more surprised, though his face showed nothing.

"Which of us do you need to kill?" asked Umbo.

The earlier Umbo turned around and faced the expendable. Now that Odinex was not throwing Umbo off the bridge, that version of Umbo did not need to time-shift. Both Umbos continued to coexist, standing side-by-side on the bridge.

The Umbo who had shifted—the real Umbo, as he thought of himself—stepped back two paces farther from Odinex and shifted again. Now he could see both earlier versions of himself facing Odinex on the bridge. "Is this how Ram Odin was duplicated, Odinex?" asked Umbo. "Obey no one but me, expendable."

The expendable stood transfixed.

Umbo turned and walked swiftly through the door into the ship.

Then he ran.

He knew the layout of the ship, knew exactly where the

control room was, and knew, from Rigg's account of it, what to do with the jewels. What he didn't know was which of the jewels controlled this ship.

He stood at the verifying machine, holding the hilt of the knife into the field. "Is the jewel of control for this vessel present here?"

"It is," said the ship's computer.

"Rigg Sessamekesh gave me this knife," said Umbo. "I take command of this vessel as Rigg's subordinate."

There was a slight hesitation. "Did Rigg authorize this procedure?" asked the ship's computer.

"Is this the jewel of control?" asked Umbo.

"Yes."

"Did Rigg Sessamekesh give this jewel to me as part of the knife?"

"He did."

"I take command of this vessel as Rigg's subordinate."

Another hesitation. "Certified."

"Command all expendables attached to this ship to obey me and cause me no harm."

"Done."

"Is the expendable still on the bridge with the other two copies of me?"

"No," said the ship's computer. "He killed them both and is on his way to this place."

Umbo shuddered. "Command him to come into this room walking backward. He is forbidden to look at me."

Moments later, Odinex backed into the room.

"Stop," said Umbo.

The expendable stopped.

"This ship, and all the equipment of this ship, will hereby define 'human being' as 'organism descended in an unbroken line from the colonists of one or more of the ships commanded by Ram Odin on their voyage to Garden.' Do you understand?"

"Yes," said the expendable.

"Yes," said the ship's computer.

"Am I human?"

"Yes," they both answered without hesitation.

"Who can change this definition?"

"You can," said the ship and the expendable.

"Let one speak for both," said Umbo.

The ship's computer fell silent.

"You and Rigg Sessamekesh can change this definition," said Odinex.

"Who else?"

"No one."

Umbo knew this was not true, but also knew that the computers couldn't lie.

"Is there a procedure by which someone else can gain the authority to change this definition without my or Rigg's consent?"

"Yes."

"Can you disable all procedures that would allow us to be superseded?"

"No."

"Can I disable them?"

"Yes," said the expendable.

In this situation, Umbo didn't trust simple answers. "And if I do, what will be the consequences?"

"The orbiter will obliterate all life within this wallfold."

Umbo sighed. "I will not attempt to disable those procedures."

Odinex said nothing.

"Turn and face me, Odinex," said Umbo.

Odinex faced him.

"You killed me twice today."

"I killed expendable copies of yourself," said Odinex. "They came into existence because you jumped back in time, and by appearing in their presence, you changed their actions so when they reached the point in time when you time-shifted, they did *not* time-shift, and therefore they did not disappear."

"How long might such duplicates continue to exist?" asked Umbo.

"Until they die."

Umbo had never thought of this possibility. But it gave him a better understanding of how the duplicate ships had come into existence at the beginning of the human settlement of Garden.

"How did you kill them?" asked Umbo.

"I broke their necks and cast them off the bridge."

"You are forbidden ever to destroy copies of me or any other time-shifter, without specific instructions to do so."

"And which copy should I obey?" asked Odinex.

Umbo wanted to say, "Me." Instead he said, "The one who most recently appeared."

"And how will I know which one that is?" asked Odinex.

"I'll try to make sure it never comes up."

"That would be best."

"Odinex, show me everything on this ship that is not included in the plans that I studied in the library near the Wall."

"The plans are complete."

"No they're not," said Umbo. "They don't show, for instance, where the spare copies of you are stored."

"Intact copies of me are not stored anywhere. If this module fails, then a new one is assembled from the parts in parts storage, which is clearly labeled in the plans."

"What triggers the creation of a new expendable?" asked Umbo.

"A death signal," said Odinex. "A request for duplication. Loss of higher functions in the present module. Failure to communicate at any level for ten hours."

"Who can issue the request for duplication?"

"The existing module. The certified commander of the vessel and all superior officers."

"Thank you," said Umbo. "Are the duplicates bound to obey all orders previously given to the earlier copy?"

"Yes," said Odinex. "We are memory-identical."

"Am I human, Odinex?"

"You are."

"Is that what you'll report to the Visitors when they arrive from Earth?"

"They will get a full memory dump of these events, along with all others," said Odinex.

"They'll see me make copies of myself by time-jumping?"

"Yes."

Umbo wanted to grin, but restrained himself. Let the Visitors chew on that.

Then his pleasure faded. Seeing Umbo time-shift might well be a death sentence for Garden. To see someone suddenly pop into existence behind himself, and then again, so three copies exist at once—that wouldn't exactly reassure the humans from Earth.

Well, it's not as if they weren't going to destroy Garden anyway. They've done it nine times already, and until now without any provocation from time-shifters.

It's hard to imagine that I've somehow made the destruction of Garden worse. Will they say bad words while they wipe out all life on Garden? Will they throw stones at the corpses?

"Odinex, the jewels of control are not mentioned in the plans of the ship, or the computer manuals."

The expendable said nothing.

"Consider that to be a question, and answer me," said Umbo.

"The jewels are thoroughly explained in the plans and manuals."

Umbo thought for a moment. "Under what name are they explained?"

"'Remote storage and transfer of the ship's log.'"

Umbo held up the knife and looked at the hilt. "These jewels are the log of each of the nineteen ships?"

"Yes."

Remembering what he had read, Umbo said, "So each jewel contains a complete record of all actions and observations made by all the computers aboard that particular ship."

"Yes."

"Including all the actions of the Remote Expendable Action Modules."

"Yes."

"How recent is the information on each jewel?"

"The jewel that holds this starship's log was updated just now when you certified."

"And the other jewels?"

"The jewels carried by Rigg Sessamekesh were updated when he certified himself as commander of all the vessels."

"And the jewels on this knife?"

"They were updated when you passed through the Wall."

The Wall was certainly a lot more than a barrier between wallfolds. All human languages, and an update of all the ships' logs. Umbo thought through what this might mean. "When a jewel updates, is it a destructive or a cumulative update?"

"Cumulative."

"So if I were to time-shift and enter a Wall in an earlier time, the information recorded from the later time I came from would not be erased by the update that it subsequently gets in the earlier time."

A momentary pause. "I have parsed your question and I can say, Yes, the information from a future time would *not* be erased by updating the ship's log remote storage and transfer unit by passing into the Wall in an earlier era, as long as the time-shifter carried the log with him into the past."

So the jewels would not suffer data loss by passing through the Wall and being updated in a back-shifted time. "If Rigg or I take a copy of the ships' logs through the Wall when the Wall has been made passable according to Rigg's command, is the log still updated?"

"Turning off the barrier features of the Wall does not turn off the Wall. All other functions continue."

Umbo could not help himself. He laughed in delight.

"You are amused," said the expendable.

I can be amused if I want and when I want, for whatever reason I want, Umbo wanted to say. Instead he grinned at the expendable. "The Odinfolders know this, don't they?"

"Yes. I have kept no secrets from them."

"Really?" said Umbo. "Have you told them about the deaths of all but one of the other Ram Odins?"

"I answer all their questions as fully as permitted."

For a moment, Umbo took that as an answer to his question. Then he realized that it was not. "Has anyone ever asked that question?"

"You are the first."

Umbo chuckled again. He not only knew information now that the Odinfolders had wanted to keep from him, he even knew information that they didn't know. All in all, this was turning out to be a successful expedition.

"Odinex, please arrange for the ship to make me a good noon meal. Then bring it to me wherever I am in the ship."

Odinex left the control room.

Umbo sat down in Ram Odin's chair. This is where Rigg also sat in the ship in Vadeshfold. We've both sat in Ram Odin's seat. Does that make us brothers in some sense?

I died twice today, he thought. He was glad that he had no memory of it. But the log had the memory of killing him. When the Visitors came, they would see it and know of all the murders committed by the expendables.

Maybe the destruction of Garden was as much to wipe out the expendables as to wipe out the people.

CHAPTER 15
Sibling Rivalry

Rigg had forgotten Umbo was gone, when Swims-in-the-Air came to him, looking agitated.

"I'm not sure what to make of this," she said, "but our monitoring of the starship's computer tells us that someone has activated the jewel of control and taken control of the ship."

"Someone?" asked Rigg.

"Umbo," said Swims-in-the-Air.

"Thank you for telling me."

"What are you going to do?"

Rigg smiled at her. "Think about it for a while."

"I've already summoned the flyer so you can go to the ship."

"How thoughtful of you," said Rigg. "I'll decide whether to use it in a little while. Thank you. Please don't bother the others with this story."

"It's not just a story," she said, bristling.

"I should have said, Please don't bother the others with this information."

She lingered a bit longer, until Rigg returned to the book he had been reading. She breathed rapidly for a few moments more, then left the room, moving briskly.

Brisk movement was unusual for the Odinfolders. They were always so sedate, so calm. Clearly whatever Umbo had done had the Odinfolders in a dither. Since Rigg didn't think for a moment that they would get this agitated over some kind of revolt within the Ramfolders' ranks—which was clearly what she meant him to think was happening—Umbo must have done something that seriously disturbed the Odinfolders.

Rigg couldn't help but be amused even as he worried. Umbo had gone to the ship alone, and the Odinfolders didn't like what he was doing. That didn't have to be a bad thing at all. But it might be. Rigg really should go and find out from Umbo directly what was going on, before the Odinfolders managed to create a rift.

Well, not create a rift so much as widen the rift that had long been there between Rigg and Umbo.

And perhaps the Odinfolders weren't trying to do something so trivial as to sow contention among the Ramfolders. Perhaps there was something that really worried them about Umbo's presence on the starship.

Rigg was about to go directly to the flyer and head for the starship when he thought again: This is what they want me to do.

So he got up and went in search of the others. He found Loaf and Olivenko practicing swordplay in one of the rooms of the library.

"Did you know you can set these holographic images to varying degrees of solidity?" asked Olivenko. "They have the weight of good steel swords, and clang together nicely, but they won't penetrate skin."

Only then did Rigg realize that the swords were mere sculptures of swords, mere images. But solid now. Interesting information to be filed away. It might have something to do with the Odinfolders' ability to transport items back and forth, not just in time, but in space as well. Were there real swords somewhere which were being semi-copied to this location? Did the projection of the image mean that the original swords were somehow less substantial while the image was being projected?

It would make sense. After all, Umbo had projected images of himself into the past to give warnings, long before he mastered the ability to actually transport himself completely into the past, leaving nothing of himself behind.

But that was not the business at hand. "I wondered if either of you would like to come with me to the starship," said Rigg. "Swims-in-the-Air was quite anxious for me to go stop Umbo from doing whatever he's doing."

They regarded Rigg curiously.

"Are you taking orders from them now?" asked Olivenko.

"I'm observing that they're anxious for me to stop Umbo, which makes me very curious to find out what Umbo's doing. They told me he had taken control of the starship from me. If that's possible, we should know it; if he did it, we should ask why; if any part of this is a lie, we should find out the truth."

"And you need us because . . ." said Olivenko.

"I'll go," said Loaf. He let go of his sword. Instead of falling, it simply vanished. Was that automatic, Rigg wondered, or had one of the mice in the room caused it to happen?

To Rigg's surprise, Loaf reached down and scooped a couple of mice into his hand, then put them on his own shoulder.

Rigg almost asked him if he was bringing reading material along for the trip, but just as he was about to begin the jest, he caught Loaf's expression: A warning. Don't ask.

Or perhaps: Don't speak.

"I'll come, too," said Olivenko.

"That leaves Param here in the library alone," said Rigg.

"She'll be all right," said Olivenko.

"As far as we know," said Rigg. "But you're right, she won't want to come. She never wants to come." There had been a time when she would have come along just to be with Olivenko, but these months of study in Odinfold had made them all tired of each other, and whatever romances had been blooming—Umbo's crush on Param, and Param's fascination with Olivenko—had either died or gone dormant.

Nothing hopeful thrives here, thought Rigg. We live under the shadow of the Books of the Future, and death is always present.

Rigg continued to follow Loaf's suggestion of silence during the voyage by talking about nothing—things he'd recently studied about total war. "The humans of Earth keep developing ways to limit the damage of war—pacts about what constitutes a war crime. Banning poison gas, for instance. The formal agreements only last until someone wants to break them, of course, but a surprising number of the agreements lasted for a while—just because of intelligent self-interest. Mutually assured destruction. But eventually, they go back to total war because any other policy turns war into a game, and games only last as long as both sides play by the rules."

"No rules in war," said Olivenko knowingly.

"No rules in a war you want to win," said Loaf. "As long as winning doesn't matter, then you can have rules and make a game of it."

"Why fight a war if you don't intend to win it?"

"When armies benefit from being perceived as necessary, and war provides a means of gaining prestige and leverage over the government," said Loaf. "Then victory ends a very profitable game. So you play the game of war only fervently enough to keep your military budget high. Nations can get used to a fairly high level of combat attrition without noticing or caring that nobody's actually trying to win, and nothing but the lives of a few soldiers is at stake."

"I didn't know you were a philosopher," said Rigg.

"Living on the edge of death, with the power to murder always in their hands, all soldiers are philosophers," said Loaf. "Not necessarily smart ones."

The flyer landed in the same place where Umbo had disembarked earlier—Rigg could see his path.

"Now is when we could use Param's ability," said Loaf. "We could go back in time and then watch what happens, unobserved."

Rigg studied Umbo's path as they got out of the flyer. "I think he was talking to somebody, from the way his path bends and doubles back now and then. I assume that means that Odinex met him here. The expendables leave no paths."

"How precisely can you take us back in time?" asked Loaf.

"This is only a few hours, and I have a clear, recent path," said Rigg. "I can be as precise as you want. Do you have something in mind?"

"First tell me how many recent visits have been made here by Odinfolders."

"What are you thinking?" asked Olivenko.

"I can't talk about it now."

"*You* brought the mice," said Olivenko.

Loaf laughed and gestured at the grass and shrubbery all around them. "Where are there *not* mice?"

Good point. Which made Rigg all the more curious about why Loaf had brought two of them along from the library. Hostages? Ridiculous. They perched on Loaf's shoulders, but they could scamper down his body at any moment.

Rigg led them along Umbo's path. It followed the obvious course—through the increasingly finished-looking tunnel toward the ship. It was only when they reached the beginning of the bridge across the gap between the stone and the starship that Rigg saw something that he couldn't explain.

"Umbo shifted time here," he said. "On the bridge." Rigg stepped out onto the bridge, walking Umbo's route. "He turned toward the edge, and then suddenly jumped back and stepped here. Then he jumped back again and stepped there. But the paths also fork, as if—but they're a little different, not quite Umbo, not—"

"See what you can figure out without jumping back to look," said Loaf.

"You think the expendable was trying something?" asked Olivenko.

"I know he was," said Loaf. He walked to the edge of the bridge and pointed downward.

Umbo's dead body lay crumpled on the stone below the ship. Even though Rigg had seen Umbo's path go on inside the starship, it still made him gasp, still stabbed him with grief.

Not far off, but only visible from the other side of the bridge, lay his dead body again.

"Silbom's left eye," whispered Rigg. "Two of him. Two copies. But he's not dead, Loaf. The main path, the real path, it goes on inside the ship."

"I've always wondered what happens when you or Umbo go back in time and warn yourselves," said Loaf. "Changing your course of action. Does the old path persist?"

Rigg blushed, embarrassed. "I've never looked. I've never paid attention."

"You made your original choice, you took that path, and the effects of it remain real," said Loaf. "But when you warn yourself—"

Olivenko finished the thought. "Your path takes a different turning. That becomes the real path. But the old one—"

"This is different from a mere warning," said Rigg. "Umbo didn't *appear* to his earlier self, he actually jumped and physically moved himself in time. But that still bent the path of his previous self, because here—he appears *in front of* his slightly older self. Same thing with the second jump. So his previous self no longer takes the action he used to. Which is why there's a new path. A slightly different path. Now the Umbo who time-shifted on the previous path *doesn't* time-shift."

"So he stays in existence," said Loaf.

"He copies himself," said Olivenko.

"You could make an army of yourself," said Rigg.

"Didn't work out so well for these two," said Olivenko.

Just because one version of Umbo remained alive didn't change the terror and pain these two Umbos must have felt. Almost by reflex, Rigg prepared to jump back in time, at least to understand the situation, if not to fix it.

"No," Loaf said to him.

"But I have to—"

"Umbo's alive," said Loaf. "There's nothing to fix here."

Rigg understood at once. "If I suddenly appear, it might change more than I want to change."

"We don't know what Umbo has done. What we might *un*do by appearing here. Let's talk to him, if we can, before we start taking action that might cause more harm than good."

Rigg knew good advice when he heard it. Loaf might not have the ability to time-shift, but that didn't stop him from having a clear understanding of how it worked, and when it might not be wise to use it. He and Umbo had had enough experience with failure in their attempts to get the jewel from the bank in Aressa Sessamo. Loaf had learned a lot about the unexpected, damaging changes you could make. And that was before Umbo learned how to physically transport more than an image of himself into the past.

"What if one of them isn't dead?" asked Olivenko.

"They're dead," said Rigg.

"How can you be sure from up here?"

"Their paths don't go off the bridge," said Rigg. "They were dead before they fell."

"Careless of the expendable," said Loaf.

"If you kill a discarded copy of a time-shifter," said Olivenko, "is it murder?"

"By all means, let's discuss the definition of murder," said Loaf.

"You're the one who said all soldiers are philosophers."

"There's a time and place," said Loaf.

Olivenko grinned.

Rigg led them into the ship.

Umbo's path led by the shortest possible route directly to the control room. The jewel-reader was open—if Umbo had done what Swims-in-the-Air said he did, this is where he would have attempted to take control of the ship.

Umbo's path moved around in the room and sat in the pilot's seat twice. But ultimately the path left the control room. Rigg and the others followed.

Umbo was apparently touring various key areas of the ship—inspecting? Verifying? Or making changes? Impossible for Rigg to know without jumping back in time to see.

They turned a corner and there was Odinex—or so they assumed—walking away from them down the corridor. They were among the storage units where colonists had lain in stasis during the voyage.

"I know you're there," said Odinex. "I knew when you entered the ship, and the ship informed Umbo." But Odinex did not turn around. He was carrying something on a tray in front of him.

Odinex turned where Umbo's path had turned.

Rigg knew the place at once, as soon as they entered behind the expendable. It was the chamber where colonists were revived from stasis or received medical attention. Umbo didn't even look up when they came in. The expendable was laying out lunch on a small table—apparently the tray he had been carrying could sprout legs when it needed to.

"Checking up on me?" asked Umbo. He took a bite of his food.

"Swims-in-the-Air seemed anxious to tell me that you had taken control of the ship," said Rigg. "Is the food any good?"

"So on her word alone, you come here to put me in my place," said Umbo.

"I came to see if her word bore any relation to the truth," said Rigg, annoyed that Umbo would leap to the conclusion that Rigg had believed the Odinfolder's story.

"Well, it does," said Umbo. "The jewels in the knife are just as effective as the jewels you have. And I took control of the ship."

The words hung in the air.

"Interesting," said Rigg. "What do you plan to do with it?"

"What I came to do," said Umbo. "Study it. See what I can get it to do."

"And in this room," said Rigg. "Do you plan to see if you can bring the murdered copies of yourself back to life?"

Umbo leapt to his feet, knocking the table over. The expendable caught it with a swooping motion that kept all the food still on the tray. Very good reflexes, Rigg noted.

"So you went back in time to check on me!" he shouted at Rigg.

"I don't have to go back in time!" Rigg shouted back. "I can see your path and the bodies aren't exactly invisible!"

"Did I suffer much when I died?" asked Umbo. "Did you enjoy watching that?"

"Stop it," said Olivenko. "The two of you are acting like . . ."

Loaf chuckled. "They *are* children, Olivenko. But in this case, it's Umbo who's acting like the biggest baby."

Umbo whirled on him. "It's nice to know what a *facemask* thinks of me!"

Loaf slapped Umbo across the face.

Umbo staggered under the blow, and he began to cry as he held a hand to the cheek that had been slapped. "Why me?" he said. "Why is it *my* fault?"

"Because you're the liar who wanted to pick a fight, and Rigg is not," said Loaf.

"I didn't lie!" cried Umbo.

"You shouldn't have hit him," said Rigg. "I shouldn't have gotten angry at him, either."

"I'm not angry with him," said Loaf. "But it was time for him to start paying attention. Time for both of you. This nonsense between you has to stop, and it has to stop now. Don't you understand that our lives are at stake? Not just some general warning about the end of the world, but your lives, right now, in this place. Umbo has died twice today. When will the two of you start acting like comrades, even if you can't act like friends anymore?"

"I have no friends," said Umbo. "I thought I did, but—"

"You ended our friendship when you began asking me whether it was me or the facemask talking, months ago," said Loaf. "And you ended your friendship with Rigg when you openly rebelled against him months ago for his *crime* of keeping the whole company alive when you were incompetent to find your way thirty feet without getting lost."

"So it's all my fault!"

"Yes," said Loaf. "And you know it. When Rigg came in here, you deliberately misunderstood his motive for coming. You knew what he had said, and you chose to take offense as if he had said something else. And then you lied."

"I did not lie!"

"It was a lie to say that you had taken control of the ship, when in fact you only took control of *this* ship, and only as Rigg's subordinate."

Umbo fell silent and looked Loaf in the eye. "How did you know that?"

Loaf smiled. "Oh, so you haven't lost your ability to hear accurately what other people say."

Umbo turned to Rigg. "The ship wouldn't give me control because *you* were the commander. But Odinex was killing every Umbo he could find, and I had to stop him. So yes, I found a way to get control and stop him. But I'm *not* admitting that I'm subordinate to you, and I wasn't about to say so. You would have leapt to false conclusions."

Rigg had no answer; the loathing in Umbo's face and voice were beyond his ability to understand or to deal with.

"The only reason the ship respected my control of the jewels on the knife was because *you* gave it to me," said Umbo bitterly. "I only exist because *you* condescend to allow my existence."

In answer, Rigg held out the bag of jewels. "Here," he said. "Let the ship witness. Let this murderous expendable witness. I give the jewels to you."

"I don't want them!" cried Umbo. "I don't want anything from you! I only used the knife because it was the only way to stay alive, I—"

At this point Umbo had drawn the knife, and Rigg saw that he was not holding it by the point, as if to offer it to Rigg, but rather as a weapon, ready for use. That was when Loaf's hand lashed out—every bit as fast as the expendable's had been, catching the table—and took the knife from him, leaving Umbo holding a painful wrist as he fell back onto his buttocks on the floor.

"Rigg, take up those jewels at once," said Loaf. "And assert your control of them, right now."

Rigg could see that Loaf was looking at the expendable, and without turning to see what Loaf was seeing, Rigg grasped the jewels and said, "I rescind my statement. I am still in command of this ship, and all ships; this expendable, and all expendables."

Only then did he turn toward Odinex, who stood perfectly calmly, holding the tray.

"He was reaching for you," said Olivenko, "until you spoke."

"Umbo wasn't going to stab me," said Rigg to Loaf. "You didn't have to hurt him."

"Umbo didn't know what he was going to do," said Loaf.

Olivenko spoke to Loaf. "You never answered Umbo about how you knew that Umbo had taken this ship as Rigg's subordinate."

"I'll answer as soon as Rigg commands this ship and all ships to share none of the information we're about to discuss on any channel that the Odinfolders can intercept, record, or receive in any way."

"They've already heard you say that," said Olivenko.

"No they haven't," said Loaf. "I want to make sure that none of this gets into the ship's log."

"To this ship and all ships," said Rigg. "To this expendable and all expendables. Nothing that gets said on this ship now and in the future, by me, Umbo, Loaf, or Olivenko, is to be recorded in the ship's log or transmitted in any way that the Odinfolders can intercept."

The ship's voice interrupted. "They intercept all channels of communication."

"Do they?" asked Loaf. "Or are they merely capable of intercepting those channels?"

The ship didn't answer.

"Answer him," said Rigg. "Whatever Loaf asks, answer aloud."

"They are capable of intercepting all," said the ship. "Whether they actually listen, I cannot say."

"I can," said Loaf. "The Odinfolders haven't stationed a *human* to listen to communications in many years. Nor do they use machines to do it anymore, because such machines would easily be found by the Visitors when they come."

"So they don't listen at all?" asked Umbo.

"They listen through the mice," said Rigg, realizing.

"But Loaf brought mice with him," said Olivenko.

"Loaf communicates with the mice," said Rigg. "Don't you?"

"More to the point," said Loaf, "they communicate with me."

"How?" asked Umbo, no longer crying. No longer surly, either. It was nice to hear Umbo being *curious*.

"By talking," said Loaf.

Both mice were on Loaf's shoulders, but one was facing Loaf's ear, moving its mouth.

"High-frequency voices," said Rigg, as soon as he got it. "Outside the normal human range of hearing. But because of the enhancements of the facemask, Loaf can hear them."

"I've heard them since we arrived here," said Loaf. "At first I didn't know where they were coming from, but I heard a constant commentary on everything we were doing, a repetition of everything we said, but in another language. I thought I was going insane. And then we saw the mice at work in the library, and I knew. I heard them issuing commands to each other, and to the machinery embedded behind the walls. The Odinfolders thought the mice only knew one language, but they understood us from the start."

"That's why you went out into the prairie," said Umbo. "Alone."

"The facemask created an auxiliary pair of vocal folds for me," said Loaf. "At my request," he added. "I can produce sounds that only the mice can hear. I can speak their clear and beautiful and very quick language."

"And the Odinfolders don't know?" asked Olivenko.

"The Odinfolders aren't in charge anymore," said Loaf. "Mouse-Breeder may have put the altered Odinfolder human genes into them centuries ago, but they've been in charge of their own breeding, their own genome ever since. They are, collectively, the human race in Odinfold, and the yahoos really are yahoos, compared to them."

"I did not know this," said Odinex.

"You don't know it now, either," said Rigg. "Expunge this information from your memory and the ship's memory, and the memories of all ships and all expendables. This must not be available to the Visitors when they come and strip the memories of the starships."

"No need," said Loaf. "The mice have already put programs into the ships' computers that erase all references to their abilities within thirty minutes. It allows the expendables to talk to them for a while and carry on an intelligent conversation, but then the memory clears and it's as if it never happened. The mice don't need the computers to help them remember."

"But the mice are so tiny," said Rigg.

"Their cooperation is perfect," said Loaf. "Each mouse is about as smart as an ordinary human child—not an Odinfolder child, not like you two—but it's still quite a bit of intellect. Mouse-Breeder did a superb job of putting an overcapacity brain into a very tiny space. But what the mice have done for themselves is specialize and cooperate *perfectly*."

"They each store portions of the library," said Rigg.

"That's why there are dozens of mice in every room we

visit," said Loaf. "They're in constant communication with the vast hordes outside. Each one processing whatever his particular job is, trusting the others to do what *they're* supposed to do. Together, any four of them are a match for any Odinfolder. But dozens of them? The human race has never matched such intelligence."

"Except with computers," said Olivenko.

"Computers are imitation intelligence," said Loaf. "Memory and speed, but no brains. Just programs."

"Aren't human brains a kind of computer running programs?" asked Rigg. Certainly the literature from Earth said so.

"Humans make a machine, and then fool themselves into believing that their own brains are no better than the machines. This allows them to believe that their creation, the computer, is as brilliant as their own minds. But it's a ridiculous self-deception. Computers aren't even in the same league."

"The man who called himself my father," said Rigg, "was a computer, and I can tell you he was far smarter than me."

"He was very good at pretending to be smarter. He could give you data, teach you how to perform operations. But he was never your equal when it came to actual *thought*. That's what the mice quickly came to understand. They could think rings around the expendables. They were the equals of any humans."

"I thought you said that dozens of them were more intelligent than humans," said Umbo.

"More capable of feats of memory and calculation," said Loaf. "But a mind is a mind. Thought is thought. The Odinfolders' improvements have increased brain capacity, given better tools, but the mind is not identical with the organic machinery it inhabits."

"Now the philosopher comes out," said Olivenko. "You've discovered the soul."

"Rigg did," said Loaf. "And Umbo."

"When?" Umbo demanded.

"Not me," said Rigg.

"The paths, Rigg," said Loaf. "The part of you that sees into the past. Where is that in the genome?"

"The Odinfolders said that they had clipped the genes that had those powers and . . ." Then Rigg fell silent. They had left him with that impression, but no, they hadn't actually said so.

"If they could find the genes that produced time-shifting," said Loaf, "what would they need *you* for?"

"They're searching for those genes," said Olivenko.

"They've spent all these months studying every genetic trace you've left behind," said Loaf. "They have the mice gather them up. They have the mice study them."

"And have the mice found nothing?"

"There's nothing to find," said Loaf. "It's not in the genes. The part of us that lays down paths through time, tied to the gravity of a planet—it's not in the brain."

"Animals leave paths, too," said Rigg. "Even plants, in their fashion."

"*Life* is the soul," said Loaf. "Living things have souls, have minds, have thought. Living individuals have their own relationship to the planet they dwell on. Their past is dragged along with their world through space and time. But it persists. Long after the organism dies, its path remains, and all that it was can be recovered, every moment it lived through can be seen, can be revisited."

Rigg blushed with embarrassment before he could even speak aloud the thought he had just had. "I should have seen it all along."

"Should have, but didn't," said Loaf.

"Seen what!" demanded Umbo.

"That the paths of the mice in Odinfold aren't mousepaths," said Loaf.

"You read minds now?" asked Olivenko.

"I knew what he had to be thinking about," said Loaf. "And when he realized, and blushed—"

"Their paths are small," said Rigg, "but they're bright. And they have the same—it's not color, but it's *like* color—they have the same *feel* as human paths. It's right there in front of me, and I didn't even realize it, because—"

"Because you have a human mind," said Loaf. "The brain sees all, but the *mind* has focus. That's our great power, the ability to home in on something and understand it to its roots—the brain can't do that. But that same focus shuts out things that the brain is constantly aware of. So we don't notice what we can plainly see; and yet we understand things that we can't see."

"And all living things can do this?" said Umbo.

"At some level or other," said Loaf. "I've had plenty of time to think about this. Because the facemask lets me see like a beast, even though I think about what I see the way a man does. I can see a range of detail that is impossible to an ordinary human.

But the facemask, which perceives it all, can't do anything with it, because its mind is at such a primitive level. When mice were bred with human genes inside them, it was as if humans were born in tiny bodies. They have human souls, or close to it."

"What are they, where do they come from?" demanded Olivenko.

"They're *life,*" said Loaf. "I can't explain it better than that because it's all I've figured out. All that the mice have figured out, either. Living things have this *thing* in them, this connection with the planet, with each other. And humans have more of it than any other living thing, just as animals all have more of it than plants. And that's what Rigg sees: the life, the soul, the mind, whatever you call it, persisting eternally through time, linked to the gravity well of the world."

Rigg thought of the paths of humans who had crossed the various bridges at Stashi Falls; as the falls eroded, lowering and backing away, the paths remained exactly where they had been, never shifting relative to the center of the planet Garden.

"So what happens when we go into space?" asked Rigg. "Do we lose our souls?"

"Of course not," said Loaf. "Or the colonists would all have arrived here lifeless."

Rigg looked at the oldest paths that had passed through this room. The colonists as they were revived, the paths faded with the passage of eleven thousand years, but still present, still accessible.

And one path in particular. The one who had walked through the ship long before the others were revived. The path of Ram Odin.

"Should I look at him?" asked Rigg aloud. "Should I talk to him?"

"And say what?" asked Loaf.

"Talk to whom?" said Olivenko.

"Ram Odin," said Umbo.

"I don't know," said Rigg. "Ask him . . . what he was thinking. What he had in mind."

"And what does that matter now?" asked Loaf. "What will you learn from him? His desires don't matter to us right now—what matters to us is what the Odinfolders are planning. What the Visitors will conclude when they come. Why the Destroyers came a year later. What the ships and the expendables will do."

"If you showed yourself to Ram," said Umbo, "it might wreck everything."

"Unless we already live in the future that was created by our going back and talking to him," said Rigg.

"You'd be experimenting with the entire history of Odinfold," said Olivenko. "You can't do it. You might destroy everybody."

"Not *us*," said Rigg. "We'd be safe if we all went together."

"And the billions of other people?" asked Loaf.

"But we don't destroy them, do we?" said Rigg. "We know their lives happened because they remain part of our past."

"The ships' log keeps memories of lost futures," said Umbo, "even if we carry the ship's log back with us through the Wall."

With that, they all insisted that Umbo recount what he had learned about the ship's logs, the remote storage of their data on the jewels, the way the ship's log became the official means of transferring authority and control from one captain, one admiral to the others.

When Umbo was finished, Rigg said, "Good job, Umbo."

Umbo's temper flared. "I don't need your pat on the head," he snapped.

Loaf reached out and slapped him again. Umbo cried out in pain.

"Stop that," Rigg said to Loaf. "Stop hitting him."

"You don't have control of *me*," said Loaf. "And I'll hit him like the father he *needs* would have hit him."

"My father hit me plenty," said Umbo. "More than I needed!"

"He wasn't your father. He hit you because of *his* needs. But I'm an experienced officer. I'm hitting you because *you* need to be slapped out of your self-pitying resentment and wakened up to your responsibilities."

Rigg wanted to intervene, to say something, but he realized that he needed to trust Loaf to help Umbo in ways that Rigg was too young and inexperienced even to attempt.

"I don't need anybody to wake me to anything!" said Umbo.

"Those very words are proof of how much you need it," retorted Loaf. "A soldier like you is a danger to every man in his unit. He can't function as part of the team, he can't do his part."

"I'm not one of your mice!" said Umbo.

"But that's how the mice learned how to do it," said Loaf. "By getting the genes of humans, by becoming humans in mouse bodies. Humans who could subsume themselves in the group identity and do their part with perfect trust that others would do theirs—those are the humans who had a better chance to survive, the ones who became the primary vehicles of human evolution. The resentful, suspicious man alone—the alpha male—that's the gorilla that beats up or drives away all the other males. He wants everything for himself, hates all comers, and he's stupid and helpless against much weaker primates who act together."

"You're saying I'm like that," said Umbo resentfully.

"I don't have to say it," said Loaf. "That's the way you've been thinking and acting for a year. You're the would-be alpha male who absolutely hates being in the same troop with another alpha. You're getting ready to challenge, you've already challenged, but you back away, waiting, biding your time. But that knife in your hand—it wanted to spring, didn't it. It wanted Rigg's heart, didn't it."

Umbo's hands flew to his head, as if to hide both sight and hearing at once, to hide from his own memory, but failing to hide from anything.

"No," he said. "No, I wasn't going to hurt him!"

"You feel like your life can't even *begin* as long as Rigg is with us," said Loaf. "You think I didn't see, *feel* how you rejoiced when you were able to maneuver things so that Rigg went off by himself, and left you with the whole group?"

"That's not how it happened!" cried Umbo.

"No, because you weren't counting on Olivenko being the next leader, were you. He didn't even want to be leader, but everybody followed him instead of you. Because here's what you don't get, Umbo. You don't get to be boss of the troop because you want it so much and hate the person who has the job. You get to be boss of the troop because you're *fit* to do it—or if you get the job, and you aren't fit, then the whole troop suffers. The whole troop *dies*. If you weren't thinking like a chimp, Umbo, you'd realize: Instead of trying to get Rigg out of your way and resenting everything he does, you should be trying to prepare yourself to be as valuable to the troop as he is."

"How can I!" cried Umbo. "He had his—father, Ramex, the Golden Man—he was trained for everything, and I was trained for nothing—"

"Fool," said Loaf. "But now you're just being a baby instead of an alpha male, and I don't slap babies. Ramex trained Rigg, yes, to prepare him for Aressa Sessamo, for life in court, and that's why Rigg was able to thrive there. But Ramex didn't prepare him for anything since then. He didn't prepare him to get through the Wall without the jewels, he didn't prepare him for Vadeshfold, he didn't prepare him for Odinfold, because he didn't know he was coming to these places. How do you think Rigg managed so well?"

"I haven't managed anything," said Rigg. "*You* have. Olivenko has, but I don't even—"

"I don't slap fools, either, but shut up," said Loaf. "Listen to yourself, Rigg. You tell me that *I* was prepared for things, and I was. Olivenko, too. *That's* what makes you the natural leader of this troop—you see the strengths in the other members and you use them, you rely on them, you don't insist that everything has to be your idea, that you have to be boss of everything, make every decision alone. You don't resent us for knowing things you don't know and doing things you can't do, you're *grateful* we did them and then you go on."

Loaf tugged on Umbo's wrist, pulling his hand away from his head, where he was still using his hands as if to shield himself. "It's what you should have been doing, Umbo. Being glad that there were people who could do things you couldn't do, that needed doing. And then being glad when *you* were able to contribute the things that *only* you could do. As an officer, I can tell you—a squad of men who think and act like Rigg, they'll prevail in battle, they'll survive to fight another day, and even if they die, they'll take a terrible toll on the enemy, because they aren't at war with each other, they're acting as one, as something larger than a bunch of terrified, selfish alpha males trying to climb all over each other to stand on top."

"You should talk!" cried Umbo.

"I *am* talking," said Loaf.

"He's talking about you and Olivenko," said Rigg. "Sniping at each other the whole way out of Aressa Sessamo."

"Yes," said Loaf. "I thought of him as a toy soldier. I didn't see his value. So what? Eventually I did. Before that, we weakened each other. But when we passed through the Wall together, when he went back into the Wall as quickly as I did, and ran as fast to rescue you, Rigg—then I knew his worth, and we were together then. Isn't that right, Olivenko?"

"We still sniped at each other," said Olivenko. "We still do."

"But we trust each other," said Loaf.

"True," said Olivenko.

"Snipe at Rigg all you want, Umbo," said Loaf. "He could use a little deflating now and then, when he puts on that lofty Sessamoto voice. But you have to let people deflate you, too, and not take such white-hot umbrage at everything, not want to *kill* anybody who does something better than you."

"I don't want to kill anybody!"

"No, you don't *want* to want to kill us," said Loaf. "But your body wants it. That alpha male brain, that unevolved, uncooperative human, that utterly selfish adolescent who hasn't yet learned how to attach himself to a group and contribute to it instead of ruling over it. That's who I've been slapping, to get him to shut up and let the human being in you come to the front and take charge of your life. Are you so stupid with rage that you can't see how much we value you and need you? How much respect we all show you? Rigg especially, Rigg more than anybody."

"Nobody respects me," said Umbo, and he cried again.

"I'm just not getting through to him," said Loaf. "This boy needs to have a hole drilled in his head so I can let the demons out."

"He's hearing you," said Rigg.

"And your evidence is?"

"He's hearing you," said Rigg, "because he knows you love him, and he loves you. He's hearing you even though he's still too proud to let you see it. So let's stop talking about Umbo and get back to what we're supposed to do now."

"Do?" said Olivenko. "What *can* we do?"

"The Odinfolders have been lying to us, hiding things from us. I still don't know what their plan is. I don't know what they intend to do with us."

"You mean besides stealing our genes and trying to implant them in time-traveling mice?" asked Olivenko.

"That's it!" cried Rigg. "That's what I don't get. It's been bothering me—if time-shifting is a thing that only the human mind can do, Loaf, then how did the Odinfolders develop a *machine* that can pick up objects and put them down anywhere in space and time?"

"That's an interesting question," said Loaf.

"Yes, that's why I asked it," said Rigg.

"And now I have an answer for you," said Loaf. "Because I asked the mice, and they already know."

"Know what?" asked Olivenko.

"That there's no such machine."

"But the jewel—they put it where I could find it," said Umbo.

"No, Umbo," said Loaf. "The Odinfolders aren't lying. They *think* there's a machine. But the mice have told me that there never was."

"What, then?" asked Umbo. "How could they think there's a machine when—"

"They've *seen* a machine," said Loaf. And he started to laugh. "Who knew that mice could have such a penchant for theater? The Odinfolders have seen a very lovely machine that whirrs and flashes, just like the machines the Odinfolders used to build until Mouse-Breeder shifted their whole civilization over to humanized mice. But it's not the machine that does the thing."

"It's the mice," breathed Olivenko.

"They are also descendants of Ram Odin," said Loaf. "They also have those genes. And they've had hundreds and hundreds of generations in which to breed them true. They can't time-shift themselves. They can only move inanimate objects. When they try to move living things, they die. Many mice gave their lives in proving that. But they have precision we can only dream of.

And they have to have hundreds of mice working together to do it. Rather the way Rigg and Umbo had to work together in order to time-shift, when they first figured out they could do it at all."

Yes, thought Rigg. Umbo and I began all this when we found out that we could do things as a team—a troop—working together, neither one more valuable than the other. And the trouble started when Umbo and I each learned how to do it on our own, and we didn't need each other so much anymore.

"So now I have to tell you something that happened almost as soon as we left the library to fly here," said Loaf.

"Something the mice told you?" asked Rigg.

It was Umbo who leapt to the conclusion. "What happened to Param!" he demanded.

"The Odinfolders ordered the mice to terrify Param into disappearing—into slicing time. Then, during one of the gaps where Param doesn't exist, as she flashes forward, the mice were to insert a large block of metal into some vital place."

"That would kill her!" cried Rigg.

"The mice can't project an object into the space occupied by anything more solid than a gas," said Loaf. "But they could insert metal where Param's heart or brain will reappear."

"But you stopped them," said Umbo.

"Why would I do that?" asked Loaf.

"Because she's one of us!" cried Rigg, furious.

"Are you both complete idiots?" asked Loaf. "Who *are* you? Can you remember? There are two dead Umbos out there, and yet Umbo is alive, right?"

Rigg relaxed. "We're going to go back in time and save Param."

"Oh, we're going to do more than that," said Loaf. "We're going to go back in time and *get* Param, and then we're going to go even farther back and leave Odinfold before we even got here."

"You mean stop ourselves from coming here?" asked Olivenko.

"If we did that," said Loaf, "we wouldn't ever find out the things we learned here. We'll grab Param just before the mice kill her, and then we all disappear. The Odinfolders will see that the mice tried to obey, but you two were able to prevent it. They won't realize the mice are no longer obedient to them."

"Are they obedient to you?" asked Olivenko.

"They aren't obedient to anybody," said Loaf. "They're *people*. They're a whole civilization that has existed for hundreds of generations, building on the ruins of another, older one. They aren't going to obey an old soldier like me who can't even shift time."

"They aren't obeying you now?" asked Rigg.

"They're telling me the truth, and doing what they think they should," said Loaf. "I told them that it was all right to kill Param, because we could go back and save her. Was I wrong?"

"No," said Rigg doubtfully.

"We *hope* you weren't wrong," said Umbo. "Because I can see some problems with saving Param. At least saving her without showing the Odinfolders that the mice are on our side. Or . . . not on *their* side, anyway."

"We can work it out as we fly back," said Loaf. "We'll want to hold on to the flyer and bring it back in time with us. Save us the effort of *walking* to some remote spot along the Wall so we can pass through it into another wallfold."

"So right now," said Umbo, "Param is dead."

"It's all right, Umbo," said Loaf. "You two get to save her—you push Rigg back into the time before she dies, and when he has her, you snatch them back."

"Besides," said Rigg, "you're twice as dead yourself."

CHAPTER 16

Temporary Death

For Param, the months in the Odinfolder library were the happiest time of her life. Her childhood had been spent as the target of symbolic rejection of the Sessamid monarchy. Whatever was done to her, was done to the royal family, so the People's government never tired of "accidentally" allowing her to be humiliated. Only the discovery of her ability to vanish from their sight, to let the world pass rapidly by while she observed in perfect silence, had protected her.

During her childhood, her education had been limited. It consisted of whatever her mother told her, the Gardener's few lessons in controlling her time-slicing, and whatever she learned from the occasional host who took some interest in her. She learned to read and write, and enjoyed reading, but she had no idea what to read. Any book she knew enough to ask for was obtained for her, but without books to browse, she could make no discoveries.

In her solitude she had thought much about what little she had read, but now, with the histories of all the wallfolds opened up before her, she could replace her empty childhood with the memories of kingdoms and republics, of nations nomadic or sedentary, marauding or peaceful.

Let Rigg and Umbo, Loaf and Olivenko study whatever they wanted—the human race on Earth, the functioning of starships, military techniques and technology, the deep science of the Odinfolders—none of it interested Param. She was discovering the world of her birth, the world that she had only seen as it came to visit within the walls of her dwellingplaces, then raced past her whenever she felt the need to hide in the invisibility of her timeslicing. She was finding out who she would have been, if she had been free; or, if not free, then shaped within her destiny as the royal child.

Accustomed as she was to contemplation, meditation, reflection, and the fantasies of a lonely child, Param saw herself in every history, and found lessons for herself as well. In this nation, this wallfold, this event, here is what she would be, that is what she would do. She would not have committed her people to fruitless attempts to conquer the mountain fastness of Gorogo; she would have sheltered the trading people of Inkik instead of persecuting them and driving them out; she would have married for love where another ruler married for reasons of state, and vice versa.

I would have been a great queen, she concluded on many days.

I would have been happiest as a commoner, for powerful people are more miserable and lonely than simple ones, she concluded on other days.

But every day saw her horizons widening, her vicarious memory deepening. There were worlds now blossoming inside her imagination. The others might think her solitary and withdrawn, but for Param, compared to her life before, she was gregarious and enthusiastic. She was broadening, reaching out, filled with curiosity and wonder.

She knew that the others usually talked around her and seemed surprised whenever she spoke; often, too, she could see that they thought that what she spoke of was not to the point of their conversation. But what of that? Their conversations were rarely on a point she cared about, and when their words made her think of something she did care about, she said it, boldly speaking up at the moment of her thought, in a way she never had before.

Umbo thought that he loved her? He hardly listened to her, since she had nothing to say of spaceships and he cared nothing about the intense spiritual lives of the people of Adamfold, or the strange chaos of the child-ruled forest dwellers of Mamom, who allowed certain children to choose the site of their next village by seeing where they wandered, and what they were curious about.

And Olivenko, who once had seemed so wise to her, was surprisingly ignorant of history and uninterested in learning more about it. Instead he was all physics and metaphysics, wondering about how time travel worked and how it was related to gravity. Why should they care? It was not as if Param or her fellow émigrés from Ramfold could change how the world worked; they obeyed the laws of physics, whatever they were, and had whatever talents they had. Did Olivenko think that by studying these things, he would acquire some talent for time travel that he never had before? Or was he hoping to discover a machine like the Odinfolders' time-sender? What good is it to study things too big to move?

Loaf, on the other hand, seemed to understand the world much as Param did. He listened to her accounts of strange customs and histories as if he were interested in what she was saying, and not just in the fact that the only woman in their group was saying them. He might bend everything to his own understanding, but Param didn't mind that: It only mattered that he received what she offered to them all from her research, and treated it as having value.

And then there was her brother, Rigg, so desperate to be a good man that he would never be a truly effective leader. Real leadership required authority and ruthlessness, she well understood. That's why she didn't want it. But Rigg did want to lead, yet thought he could do it by persuasion, by meekly taking suggestions, by genuinely loving the members of their little band.

Didn't he know that gentleness didn't just seem weak, it *was* weak? Yet she found it endearing that he tried so earnestly, and so she treated him with a kind of respect that he didn't really deserve, since only strength mattered, in the end. She saw in Rigg the person she might have been, if she, too, had wandered in the wild with the Gardener, the Golden Man. With only wild animals and a manlike machine for company, what could Rigg ever understand about the ravening appetites of human beings? We are the wildest animals, Rigg, she wanted to say. And then he would say, Who was talking about animals?

We are all talking about animals. More to the point, we are talking *as* animals. We are the beasts that scheme, the predators that predict. We live by the lie, not by the truth; we study truth only to shape more convincing lies that will bend other people to our will.

The only thing that keeps me from being a truly extraordinary ruler, as I was born to be, is that I have no access to the people whom it would have been my right to rule, and no idea what to do with them if I ever won my place.

My place? There is no such place. I'm a queen-in-training when I ought to be studying horticulture and growing flowers, beautiful and useless.

Such were her thoughts during these glorious months of exploration and imagination. She lived a thousand different lives, conquered, ruled, lost, loved. The others understood nothing of what went on inside her heart.

Then came the day when they left her.

Umbo had gone first, making an expedition to visit the buried starship of Odinfold in order to test and expand what he had learned in his absurdly focused study of a single thing.

Then Swims-in-the-Air had said something to Rigg that alarmed him, and he had taken Loaf and Olivenko to follow Umbo. Nobody even looked for her, or asked her what she thought. Swims-in-the-Air mentioned they were gone, and when Param asked why they hadn't told her where they were going, Swims-in-the-Air had only laughed lightly and said, "I don't think they needed you, my dear."

Param had simply gone back to her studies.

Until she noticed that her room was filling up with mice.

They swarmed around the floor and up onto the table. Their constant motion was distracting. "Why do you all have to be here?" she asked, not expecting them to understand or respond.

But they did respond—by ceasing their movement, by all turning to her at once and gazing at her.

They're only mice, she told herself.

But the intensity of their gaze was disconcerting, and when it continued, it became alarming.

She got up from her place, intending to leave the overcrowded room. But when she stepped, there was a mouse under her foot. It squealed in agony and when she moved her foot to release it, she saw that blood had spurted out of its throat. Worse, she had stepped on yet another mouse, and this one made no sound at all when it died; she only felt the sickening crunch under her foot.

"I'm sorry," she said. "There are too many of you in here, there's no room to walk. Please go away."

Please! Was she a beggar now, she who should have been Queen-in-the-Tent? Was she reduced to pleading with mice?

In answer to her words—or to the deaths of the mice she had stepped on—more mice came into the room, until the floor and table were as solidly covered as if they were carpeted. No, as if they had grown a pelt and now had muscles that throbbed and surged under the many-colored fur.

She didn't want to kill any more of them, and besides, they were frightening her. It was a sign of how much she had changed that she had not gone invisible the moment she noticed there were too many mice in the room. But even if she no longer sliced time by reflex, she could certainly do it as a matter of good sense. There was no reason to stay in this place, trampling mice and snuffing out their annoying little lives.

She went invisible, and began to walk out of the room.

But something was very wrong.

In one sense, everything worked perfectly normally. She could now walk right through the mice without crushing them.

On the other hand, the mice did not speed up or scurry around madly the way people did when Param slowed herself down. Usually they sped up and scampered like mice; but these mice did nothing of the kind. In fact, for a moment Param wondered if she had somehow acquired the opposite talent, and had frozen them in time, for they did not move at all. They stayed in place, noses pointing toward her.

But they *were* moving. Tiny movements, yes, but it made the carpet of mouse fur undulate and shift constantly. And those shifts were as rapid as she would have expected—she was indeed slicing time and skipping forward in tiny increments, walking as she did.

As she made her slow progress along the floor toward the door, she realized that the mice were not staring at the place where she had been. They were staring at where she was now.

They could see her.

It was impossible! When she sliced time, she never remained in the same place long enough to be visible to humans, whose brains couldn't register an object that was passing through each location for only a split second at a time.

But mice were not human. Their metabolisms were faster.

Did this mean that they also perceived more rapidly? Did it mean that they could see and register her presence for the tiny moment she spent in any one place?

Then something else. The mice were moving a thick cylinder of steel through the room, bringing it closer to her.

How could they lift it?

They weren't lifting it at all. It was jumping from place to place. Near the door; halfway across the room; at the base of the table; up onto the table. It stayed in each place for what might have been five or ten minutes, though to Param it seemed only seconds.

They were shifting it in time and space. Or no, the *mice* weren't doing it—how could they? The Odinfolders must be using their time-sender to move the thick cylinder from place to place.

A thick cylinder of solid metal that could be placed anywhere in space and time.

She thought of Mother ordering her soldiers to sweep the air with swords and metal rods, in the effort to pass metal through her body and kill her. It was not hard to imagine that the Odinfolders controlling this cylinder had something similar in mind.

Now she could see that each time the cylinder moved, the mice moved out of its way first. It damaged none of them. In fact, it might well be that the cylinder *could* not move until the mice had cleared enough space for it; that might be the reason for its staying in each place for minutes at a time, waiting for the mice, their noses and paws and tails, to get out of the way.

She thought of Olivenko and his discussion of rules of physics. Two objects unable to occupy the same space at the same time. That was the principle that made Param slightly sick when she moved through soft things, like people and organic walls and doors—wooden things. Since most of any object was the empty space between and within atoms, there were surprisingly few collisions when she jumped ahead in time. When Rigg and Umbo shifted back in time, they never ended up inside a tree or a rock. They could move into a volume of air without causing the annihilation of more than a few particles.

Was that what this cylinder was doing? They could move it in time and space, but they couldn't move it into a location occupied by something as substantial as a mouse. The mice had to move first.

But that was the second most frightening thing: The mice *were* moving. Whoever was controlling the movement of the cylinder was also controlling the mice.

The *most* frightening thing was the way the mice continued to stare at her, seeing exactly where she was. They could see her; she was not invisible. Their eyes were pointing to her. Whoever was controlling the cylinder could therefore put it into the space occupied by her heart or her brain during one of the gaps between her time-slicing jumps, and when she reappeared in that spot a fraction of a second later, that organ of her body would be annihilated.

Nor could she easily stop her time-slicing and reenter the normal timeflow. For then her feet would occupy the same space as the mice underfoot. It would not kill her, but she would be crippled. In agony. Her feet would be unable to hold her. It might take weeks for her feet to heal. And the mice themselves would be quite dead.

Why should she care if mice died? Someone was using them to try to kill her!

And they would succeed. Any moment they wanted to, they could put the cylinder into her body space and, when she came back into momentary existence, it would be sliding downward through her body, drawn by gravity while she was not there, then suddenly stopped and cradled by the skin and bones of her body when she did reappear with the cylinder inside her.

I'm going to die, she thought, and her stomach went sick and her head felt light and she was filled with more terror than she had felt before, more than the fear she had felt when she and Umbo leapt from the high rock and slowly fell downward toward the metal being waved around by Mother's men.

The difference was that then she had Umbo with her—Umbo, who could jump backward in time and take her with him.

Who would save her now? Even if Rigg or Umbo showed up, they couldn't see her; Rigg could see her path, but even he could not reach into the slices of time and take hold of her.

Why didn't they warn me? Why didn't they go back to an earlier time and give me one of Umbo's trademarked visions of his future self, saying, Get out of this room! Or simply taking her by the hand and moving her to another time or place.

Maybe they can't get back into the library. Maybe when they found out I was dead, the Odinfolders kept them from coming here, where they could intercept me and prevent this terrible moment and save my life.

But then, they could always go back to a time before we came to the library. Back when we first came to Odinfold, but before the Odinfolders knew that we were here. Why didn't they?

She knew the answer. If they went back and warned the whole group that Param would be murdered here, nearly a year after they arrived, then they would turn aside and would *not* learn all the things that they had learned. They wouldn't know about the Visitors and the Destroyers. Nor would they know about the high technology of the Odinfolders and the billions of people who lived in these vast ruins when they were still mighty cities.

They had to choose between what they had learned in Odinfold, and saving my life at the cost of never learning it. And they chose correctly. What was her death, compared to the need to know about the end of the world and save it?

I am like a soldier who dies in battle. Regrettable, but an unavoidable loss.

Unless . . .

They didn't have to *warn* her. They could come back and simply *take* her. A warning would make them all turn away, change the past, annihilate the months they had just lived through. But if they came back to the moment of their first arrival, they could take her away and drag her into some other time, earlier or later. *She* would be prevented from learning anything she had learned, but *they* would keep the knowledge that they had, because they would still have lived through all these months and would keep their memories when they shifted in time.

But they didn't do it.

No, no. They didn't do it in *this* timeflow, because they couldn't possibly know to do it unless they found out that I was killed. It is my death that provokes them into going back to change time and save me. So I have to go through this whole process, I have to see my death coming and then, most terribly, *die*.

Only then can they travel back in time and interfere with the forward flow of it, snatching me out of time before I can be murdered in this way. That version of myself will never live through these terrible minutes. Because in that version of time, I didn't die.

But in this one, I will die. I won't remember it, in that other timeflow, but it has to happen in order for them to save me, so my death will still be real, because it will still have its residual effects, even though a version of myself, a copy, will move forward into the future without this death.

To that version of me, this death will seem unreal, temporary; it will seem to have been avoided.

But it will not be avoided. I will live through it. I will die, and I will stay dead, *I* will; *this* version of me will be extinguished and *I don't want to die.*

The cylinder disappeared again, and almost immediately Param felt a searing agony in her throat, the heat of billions of molecules being torn apart, some of them becoming radioactive as atoms collided and tore each other apart and then reassembled. She lived just long enough to feel the heat pulse through her entire body, every nerve screaming with the pain of burning to death in a searing moment.

Param noticed the room was full of mice. They were scrambling up onto the table, swarming all over the floor. Annoyed and a little frightened, Param was proud of herself for not time-slicing by simple reflex. No, she would get up and leave the room.

But before she could even push back her chair, Rigg appeared in the air above the table, his feet a few inches above its surface. He dropped to the table, crushing mice under his feet. He reached out his hand to her.

Something terrible must be about to happen, Param realized. Rigg is coming back to save me.

She held out her hand and clasped his.

And suddenly the mice were gone.

Rigg pulled her to her feet, then jumped off the table. "Come on," he said. There were several mice in the room.

"They can see us," said Param.

"Doesn't matter," said Rigg. "We have to get outside, to the flyer." He took her hand again and began drawing her after him, out into a corridor. "We should never have let ourselves spend so much time in these underground rooms. It's devilishly hard getting in and out."

They turned a corner and there was Mouse-Breeder, coming down a flight of stairs.

Rigg squeezed her hand and she saw him give her a warning glance.

"Mouse-Breeder!" Rigg called out. "I hope there isn't a rule against running in the library!"

"None that I know of," he said cheerfully. "Where are you headed?"

"Up for sunlight!" said Rigg. "I had a sudden need for air, and my sister decided to join me."

"Have fun," said Mouse-Breeder.

They ran past him up the stairs.

"He doesn't know."

"It's six months ago," said Rigg. "But the moment he runs into one of us in *this* time, he'll realize that he saw *us* running because we came from the future."

"What does it matter?" said Param. "Wherever we go, whatever we do, they can use their time machine to send something to kill us—a sword in the heart, poison into our bodies, we'll never be safe."

"Stop talking and run again," said Rigg. "And don't worry, they won't do it."

"How do you know?" asked Param.

"Because there *is* no machine," said Rigg.

"But . . ."

"Run," said Rigg.

She was utterly out of breath, her lungs on fire and her legs leaden with exhaustion when they reached the surface and came out into sunlight.

There was Umbo, watching intently. And suddenly a flyer appeared behind him, and Loaf and Olivenko stood beside it.

They must have transported Rigg back in time the way they used to do it, when they worked together. Rigg must have found a path that would take him to the exact time he wanted to reach. Then Umbo must have slowed time down so he could take hold of that path. Umbo waited here so that he could bring them back into the present when Rigg returned to the out-of-doors with Param in tow.

By the time Rigg and Param reached the flyer, Olivenko and Loaf were already inside it. Umbo waited till they arrived. Then he reached out and took, not *her* hand, but Rigg's, and drew them up the ramp into the flyer.

"Good work," said Loaf.

"Rigg and Umbo just saved you from a terrible death," said Olivenko.

The flyer took off.

"What, the mice were going to attack me?" asked Param, incredulous.

"Not by nibbling you to death, no," said Olivenko.

"A cylinder of metal in the throat," said Rigg. He demonstrated the size of it with his hands. "They slipped it into place during one of the gaps in your time-slicing. It tore your head off your body and burned you up."

Param felt ill. "Why? What did I do?"

"I think they wanted to show us how easily we could be killed," said Olivenko.

"I think they wanted to force us to use our powers and get out of here," said Loaf.

"Why?" asked Param. "All they had to do was ask us to leave!"

"The people who wanted us to go may have been in the minority," said Loaf. "We only ever met Swims-in-the-Air and Mouse-Breeder. It gave us an impression of perfect unity among the Odinfolders. But there may well have been a powerful faction that wanted us gone."

"By killing me?"

"They knew we wouldn't leave you dead," said Rigg. "And they knew that we wouldn't stay."

"But what about meeting the Visitors?" asked Param. "I thought we were supposed to figure out a way to convince them not to wipe out Garden."

"I don't think so," said Umbo. "I don't think that was ever the plan."

"They've been lying to us?"

"Of course they have," said Loaf. "They're only human."

"Why did we believe them?" said Rigg, shaking his head. He imitated Swims-in-the-Air's melodious voice. "'We want you to figure things out yourselves. We want you to find your own way to convince the Visitors that we're worth saving.' Silbom's right heel!"

"What *did* they want?"

"We don't know yet," said Loaf.

"I have a theory," said Umbo.

"Which is?" asked Rigg.

"You'll think it's stupid," said Umbo.

"Probably," said Rigg. "But that doesn't mean you won't be right."

"Or lead us to a right answer," said Loaf.

"I think they've given up completely on changing the Visitors' minds," said Umbo. "I think they only wanted us to get on the Visitors' starship long enough to smuggle a weapon aboard. A weapon that they'd carry back to Earth and wipe out the human race there before they can possibly send the Destroyers to kill all the people of Garden."

"A weapon?" asked Param. "I thought we couldn't build weapons."

"Not literally a weapon," said Umbo. "They can't make a weapon. They haven't made a weapon. Not mechanical, not biological, no such thing."

"Then what is it that they're supposedly going to smuggle back to Earth?" asked Rigg.

In reply, Umbo gestured toward Loaf.

Only now did Param notice that a couple of mice were perched on Loaf's shoulders.

"Mice?" she asked.

"I told you there was no machine," said Rigg. "But they think there is one. They think they've seen it, they think they know how it works. Instead, what they've seen is a very solid-seeming hologram. And when things get sent back in time and over to some distant location, they think the machine is doing it."

Param realized what he was leading up to. "But it's the mice doing it."

"Mouse-Breeder's mice," said Umbo. "They have human genes in them. Including the genes of time manipulation. Only in these mice, the genes are expressed by time-displacement of inanimate objects. They can put anything anywhere."

"So when they put a cylinder in my throat—"

"It's what some Odinfolder humans told them to do," said Umbo. "And they obeyed, because they knew that we could retrieve you."

"Though it was harder than they thought," said Rigg. "Because we didn't want to retrieve you from a point *before* you learned all that you could learn here."

"Whatever it is you learned," said Olivenko. Was there a bit of scorn in his voice?

"We've spent nearly a year here, all told—a whole year since we left Ramfold and went to Vadeshfold. Which of the things that happened in that time should be erased?" asked Loaf. "We wanted to save your life, of course, but we didn't want to kill a year of it in the process."

Param felt uneasy, thinking of a version of the future in which her burnt-up body had no head left on it. "What will we do now?"

"Go to the border with Larfold," said Rigg. "The wallfold to the north. Where Father Knosso was murdered."

"We're going to go back earlier and save him?" asked Param.

"We don't dare," said Umbo. "Not yet, anyway. We can't go back before the time when Rigg took control of the Wall."

"The flyer won't pass through the Wall," said Umbo. "We have to walk through. I'd rather not do it while experiencing the agony of the Wall."

"We'll go through the Wall at almost exactly the time Rigg took control," said Loaf. "While we were still hiking around in Vadeshfold. Before we ever appeared here."

"But they'll see us," said Param.

"Who?" asked Rigg.

"The Odinfolders."

"Oh, well—they probably will," said Rigg, "since they seem to cluster around the Wall. But they won't know to stop us."

"Unless the mice send them another Future Book," said Umbo, laughing.

"Is that who's been writing the Books of the Future?" asked Param.

"No, no," said Olivenko. "This is the only timestream in which these mice existed. All the other Future Books were sent using the original crude displacement machine, before this version of history, in which the mice preempted the business of time-shifting."

"And did the Odinfolders—the *mice*, I suppose—really alter Father's genes? And create Umbo outright?"

"Yes," said Rigg. "But this is the first timestream in which we existed. Ramex was carefully breeding for time-shifting power, but he hadn't reached *us* yet, not until the mice intervened. And he would never have reached our level in his breeding program, because Garden would have been destroyed first."

They explained to Param all that they had learned in the starship. And Param could see that something else had happened, too—Umbo and Rigg were still a little wary around each other, but Umbo was actually cooperating with Rigg and not arguing with every little thing he said. Something happened on that starship, and Param asked what it was.

"I died a couple of times," said Umbo.

"Really?"

"Copies of me," said Umbo. He explained how that worked, and Param nodded. "The way there must have been two versions of me back in the library, when we were running away a minute ago. Six months ago."

"Only because your earlier self didn't see your later self, and so you didn't turn away from the path in which you time-shifted, you didn't cause yourself to split," said Olivenko.

"But I still died," said Param.

"Only it's all right," said Umbo, "because we don't remember dying."

"It's not all right," said Rigg.

Param and Umbo both looked at him, waiting for an explanation, and Param was surprised to see how upset Rigg looked.

"It's not all right, because I saw you both dead." He looked away. "I never want to see that again."

"Really gruesome?" asked Umbo.

"There was a version of both of you," said Rigg, "that felt all the pain and terror of death. You don't remember it, but it happened."

"And by the Odinfolders' account, the whole world has gone through that many times over," said Olivenko.

"Which brings us back to Umbo's idea," said Param. "How do you figure the Odinfolders are going to destroy the human race on Earth, if they haven't made a weapon or even planned what such a weapon might be?"

"The mice," said Umbo, as if it were the most obvious thing in the world.

"What can they do?" asked Param.

"If a breeding pair can make it back to Earth," said Umbo, "they'll have maybe a dozen children after three weeks. If only five of them are females, and they reach sexual maturity in six weeks, and they have the same number of female children, five in a generation, how many will they have before that Destroyer fleet is scheduled to take off?"

Loaf raised a hand. "These mice reach sexual maturity in four weeks. It's one of the first changes Mouse-Breeder made."

"Even without any notion of weaponry when they arrive," said Umbo, "they'll have several generations to learn all about it on Earth. And plenty of time in which to carry out the war. They won't even need to learn about mechanical weapons, anyway. They're experts on genes. Look what they did to *us*."

Param was in awe. "You think a pair of mice could destroy the human race in a year?"

"That's if only one breeding pair makes it through," said Umbo. "And I'm betting more than that will make it."

"Mice are vermin, in the eyes of Earth people," said Olivenko. "They'll exterminate them."

"They won't even know the mice are there," said Umbo. "It won't be like the library, where they're out in the open. Mice are good at hiding. And the voyage doesn't take long."

"How will they get off the ship?" asked Param.

"They're collectively even smarter than we are," said Rigg. "They'll find a way."

"And then the Destroyers won't come," said Param. "So Garden will be saved."

No one answered her. Umbo looked away. Rigg blushed. Was he ashamed of her?

"That's true," said Loaf. "But how is it better to trade the destruction of human life on one planet for another?"

Param shook her head. "It isn't, except for one point. This way, the planet that survives is *ours*. And I count that as very much better than the other way around. Does that make me a monster?"

"We're all monsters," said Loaf, "because we all thought of that. We're just ashamed of ourselves for thinking it."

"I'm not," said Param.

And then it occurred to her that that was why Rigg had blushed. Because he was ashamed of *her* for not being ashamed.

Which was why Rigg could never have been King-in-the-Tent.

CHAPTER 17
Trust

The whole way to the Wall, Rigg sat in the flyer, looking out the window at the prairies that passed under them, and then the tree-covered hills as they came into the north, where autumn was in full swing again. It made Rigg feel a moment's nostalgia for his life in the high forests of the Stashi Mountains.

But then he remembered that those high mountains had a starship under them, and the cliffs that loomed over Fall Ford had been raised by the collision that wiped out most of the native life of Garden. The man who had walked with him and taught him and called him "son" was a machine, and a liar, and when he died he didn't die at all, but he left Rigg to feel the grief of the loss, and then to puzzle things out without help.

Now Rigg's sense of who he was in the world had been torn away again. Son of the royal family, that had been hard enough;

target of assassination, he could take that in stride. But now to learn that his real father, Knosso, had been genetically altered to enhance his mental abilities, and those abilities had been passed along to him and Param, and that this genetic alteration had been carried out by semi-humanized mice—it was just too bizarre.

Is there anything in my life that was not someone else's plan?

Even now, there were those two mice perched on Loaf's shoulders, ostentatiously looking at everything that happened, with all that clever cuteness that mice always had. But Rigg could see the paths of the other mice in the flyer—the ones that had jumped up to hitch rides in everyone's clothing as they walked to the flyer, the ones that had already climbed in unnoticed as the flyer stood open and waiting. They had at least a hundred mice on this vessel, and yet no one else seemed aware of it. Did Loaf know? Surely he could hear them.

Rigg should probably mention it. But how would the mice's behavior change if he called everyone's attention to their presence?

Was this just a trial run for the Visitors, to see if the mice could sneak aboard a vessel without humans noticing? Very clever. Humans who didn't have Rigg's particular pathfinding ability or Loaf's facemask-enhanced perceptions wouldn't have known.

Or was it an experiment at all? The mice had shown that they could and would kill—would kill *them*. Just as Odinex had shown that he could murder one of their number. And they had been afraid of Vadesh! By comparison, Vadesh was their best friend.

No, the mice probably weren't planning any homicides during this voyage. What *were* they planning?

"I wonder how the ships' computers will interpret my instructions concerning the Wall," said Rigg.

Since he was looking at Loaf when he spoke, Loaf answered him. "Which instructions?"

"I told them that anybody who was with me could pass through the Wall when I did. But how do we define 'anybody'?" Rigg glanced at the mice that Loaf was wearing like animated epaulets.

Loaf nodded thoughtfully. "You're saying they can't get through the Wall."

"I'm saying that I don't know."

"So the philosophical question of personhood," said Olivenko, "has practical consequences."

"It always does," said Param. "Those we would kill, we first turn into nonpersons."

"Dangerous not to be a person," said Umbo. "Or to be an extra copy of a person."

"Individually, these mice are bright enough, but not really up to individual human standards, is that right?" said Rigg. "I'd like to know their own assessment."

"They need each other," said Loaf. "They specialize, and so they can't really function at their highest level when they're alone."

"These two on your shoulders," said Rigg. "They function like one human? Or less?"

"Less," said Loaf. "Or so they tell me. They're mostly here for data collection."

"I'd like to collect a little data," said Rigg. "Are they a breeding pair?"

The mice froze and stared at Rigg.

"How interesting," said Loaf. "They've been chattering constantly until you asked that."

"It's what they plan to do with the Visitors, yes?" asked Rigg. "Get aboard their ship, go to Earth, and then breed their brains out."

"They're a breeding pair," said Loaf.

Rigg did not mention that there were almost certainly many dozens of breeding pairs among the rest of the mice aboard. "So if we take them into Larfold, they intend to establish themselves there?"

The mice immediately struck the pose that showed that they were speaking into Loaf's ears. But Rigg had long since decided that this pose was just for show. Loaf could hear them perfectly well no matter which way they faced, and they were so small that at any distance—like across the cabin of the flyer—it was nearly impossible to see when their lips moved in speech. So they struck this pose when they wanted to be *seen* to be speaking.

"They say the thought hadn't occurred to them," said Loaf.

Rigg said nothing. Nor did anyone else.

"All right, they admit that was a lie," said Loaf. "They do intend to colonize Larfold. They say that since the people of Larfold live in the ocean, the land is fallow and there's no reason not to use it."

"It would be the first invasion of one wallfold by the people of another," said Rigg.

"Not an invasion," said Loaf. "Colonization."

"And the colonization of Garden was so gentle on the natives the first time around," said Olivenko.

"Since we're going into Larfold in the past, it will give them many generations there before the Visitors come," said Umbo.

"If they make weapons in Odinfold," said Param, "and bring down destruction on that wallfold, they will still survive in Larfold—along with the knowledge of weapons-making, I assume."

"So many possible plans," said Rigg. "No, I don't think I'll let them pass through the Wall."

Again they chattered into Loaf's ear.

"Tell them not to bother with another set of lies," said Rigg.

"They know," said Loaf. "They want you to understand that they assumed you would see them all, and didn't understand why you hadn't already mentioned their presence."

"Another lie," said Rigg. "They didn't have to come stealthily, they could have done it openly. They chose to be deceptive."

"What are you talking about?" asked Umbo.

"There are more than a hundred mice on the flyer," said Rigg. "Since they were traveling 'with' us, I suppose they thought that would qualify them to go through the Wall."

"Where are they?" asked Param.

"There are two in your hair," said Rigg.

Param shrieked and combed through her hair with her fingers; the mice leapt out onto the seat back and then out of sight behind the chairs.

"In all our clothes," said Rigg. "I'd appreciate it if they'd all assemble here in plain sight."

Within moments, a swarm of mice was visible, tightly packed on the floor, perched on chair backs, and at the controls of the flyer.

"The flyer is not to obey any commands from the mice," said Rigg.

"Understood," said the voice of the ship's computer.

"Have they given you any commands?" asked Rigg.

"They chose the point where the flyer should land," said the ship's voice.

"Silbom's left . . ." began Umbo.

"This is way beyond Silbom," said Olivenko.

"I didn't hear them command anything," said Loaf.

"They click their teeth, they tap their toes," said the ship's voice. "They slide and brush against surfaces, they sigh and gasp. It is a language as complete as any other. They taught me centuries ago."

"Were they prepared to crash the flyer?" asked Rigg.

"Yes," said the ship's voice. "If you made any attempt to kill them, I was to make a fatal impact into the ground."

"So I'm not in charge of you at all," said Rigg.

"You had not yet commanded me not to obey the mice."

"Very smart group," said Rigg. "Much smarter than we are, with so many here."

"Not really," said Loaf. "They can handle more tasks and recall more data, when there are this many. But they aren't any wiser, necessarily. It depends on how you define 'smart.'"

"After all the times we've been lied to," said Umbo, "I can't believe I was believing *mice*."

"They're so cute," said Param bitterly.

"Fatally," said Umbo.

"I'm afraid our rodent companions have the odd notion that

because they created us, after a fashion, they can do with us whatever they want," said Rigg.

The mice sat rigid, regarding him steadily.

"It's the mistake a lot of parents make about their children," Olivenko added.

"I give an order that must survive my death. No mice will be allowed to pass through the Wall, ever."

"Understood," said the ship's voice.

"And agreed to?" asked Rigg.

"Your commands cannot survive your death," said the ship's voice. "But we agree with the desirability of this command and we will continue to respect it."

"The jewels confer authority only on persons of human shape," said Rigg. "Is that rule agreed to?"

"Yes," said the ship's computer.

"They think you're a bigot," said Loaf.

"I think they've proven themselves to regard the killing of humans as one of their rights," said Rigg. "That puts them in a different category."

"They're saying all kinds of soothing things," said Loaf. "But I don't believe them, and so it's hardly worth telling you what they're saying."

The mice all turned as one to face Loaf.

"I think you just pissed them off," said Umbo.

"Do you want the flyer to proceed to the landing place the mice selected?" asked the ship's voice.

"Yes," said Rigg. "I'm assuming that many thousands of mice are already waiting there, expecting to cross into Larfold. We might as well have a conversation with this squad of would-be colonists as a whole."

"They don't have to listen to you," said Loaf. "That's what they just said to me."

"And we don't have to listen to them," said Rigg. "We also don't have to take any of them with us into the past."

"They think they know how to attach to your timefield as you shift," said Loaf. "They tried it out when you went back to get Param."

"I wonder if that's true," said Rigg.

"They're practically screaming that it's very, very true," said Loaf.

"Just what they'd do if it were a lie," said Olivenko.

"Suppose one mouse always lies, and one always tells the truth," said Loaf.

"Ask one if he's a liar, and then ask the other one if the first one told the truth," said Param. "That's an old one."

"The trouble is," said Rigg, "they might both be liars. In fact, I'm pretty sure that we can't believe anything they say."

"I think there are too many of them," said Olivenko. "They have a lot of redundancy. I think a little mouse-stomping would thin the herd."

Mice skittered away from him.

"It's our one advantage," said Olivenko. "We can break their little skulls under our feet."

"Or between our fingers," said Umbo. "Much less elaborate than sliding a slab of metal into Param's throat while she's time-slicing."

"I don't think we need to declare war quite yet," said Rigg. "Besides, from the paths I'm seeing, there are several dozen who are *not* out in the open here. They're all deep inside the machinery of the flyer. I think that regardless of who actually commands the flyer, this vehicle *will* crash if the mice feel threatened."

"Good guess, they say," said Loaf.

"And we can't jump back in time," pointed out Umbo, "since we'd materialize in midair before the flyer got here, and plummet to the ground."

"Thanks for pointing out our powerlessness," said Param.

"They call it a stalemate," said Loaf.

"Not really," said Rigg. "Not while we might save the world, and they might not. We need each other. But let's say that I'm open to discussion when we reach the Wall."

"I'm not," said Umbo. Rigg saw that Umbo immediately regretted his defiant tone. He held up his hands as if to erase what he had just said.

"Then it's a good thing I'm going to do all the talking," said Rigg with a grin.

"What are you going to say?" asked Param.

"Anything I say to you," said Rigg, "they can hear."

"I can hear whatever they say to each other," said Loaf.

"Everything? Their click-and-tap-and-sigh language, too?"

"Now that I know it's a language," said Loaf.

"They have *no* level of communication too soft for you to hear, even with the facemask?" asked Rigg.

Loaf nodded at the question. "I have no way of knowing," he admitted. "That may be what they wish me to believe."

"Such a quandary," said Rigg. "How to establish trust with a nation that has already attacked us and murdered some of us."

"We've killed a few of them, too," said Param.

"Only when they put themselves underfoot," said Umbo.

"You call them a nation?" said Olivenko.

"That's what they are, don't you think?" asked Rigg. "A foreign country. An inscrutable culture. They regard us with such contempt that they don't think they have any obligation to tell us the truth or keep their word to us."

"They're assuring me that they'll keep their word, they don't break promises," said Loaf.

"How odd," said Rigg. "And here I thought they were supposed to be human."

"All right," said Loaf, "now they're saying that they can't trust us, either."

"Because we've killed so many of them, and broken our word to them, and lied to them constantly," said Rigg.

"They say that the only reason you didn't lie is that you didn't take them seriously enough to think that they were worth deceiving."

"A fair assessment," said Rigg. "Also, they could overhear everything we said to each other, which makes lying harder for us than it is for them." Then Rigg broke into the ancient language of the Stashik River plain, the one that had been spoken by the Empire of O, while the Sessamids were still dung-burning tent-dwellers.

Until this moment, Rigg had never known why Father thought it was so important for him to become fluent in a dead language. But now, having been through the Wall, the others understood him very quickly. But these mice, having never been through the Wall, and having never studied a dead language spoken only in another wallfold, understood not a word.

Father—no, Ramex—had known about the language enhancement that anyone who passed through the Wall with Rigg would receive. He gave me this language so I could use it under exactly these circumstances—needing to talk with those who had passed through the Wall, without being understood by those who hadn't.

Once Rigg was sure that the others were up to speed in the language of O, he asked Loaf, "Are they understanding us?"

"If you ask obvious questions like that, complete with gestures," said Loaf, "they're sure to pick up this language very quickly. But so far, no."

"But they're paying very close attention," said Umbo.

"That's how they learn," said Loaf. "And, again, you looked at them in a pointed way and used a hand gesture that allowed them to decode your meaning. I suggest we close our eyes so we won't give so many visual cues."

"And then they swarm all over us," said Param.

"They can do that whether our eyes are closed or not," said Loaf. "And Rigg can see their paths even with his eyes closed."

It was true. Rigg did not need to answer. "No matter how dangerous and untrustworthy they are," said Rigg, "these little hair-dwellers may well be the only hope the people of Garden have against the Visitors."

"Then we're the only hope the people of Earth have against these rodents," said Olivenko.

"As Param said," Rigg answered him, "if it's us or them, won't we all choose us as the survivors?"

"Is it survival, if we're ruled over by mice?" asked Olivenko.

"An excellent question," said Rigg. "That's certainly a topic for discussion when we get there."

"Let's just go back in time and leave them here," said Umbo. "I mean, after the flyer lands."

Param and Olivenko murmured their assent.

"Then we have an enemy," said Loaf.

"They aren't already the enemy?" asked Olivenko.

"The enemy," said Loaf, "are the Destroyers."

"But we can't trust them," said Param. "Even if they save Garden from the Destroyers, who will save Garden from the mice?"

"Who will save the mice from *us*?" asked Loaf. "Who ever saves anybody from anybody?"

"Humans make war," said Rigg. "Loaf is right. If we separate ourselves from the mice right now, then we'll just be acting out the main theme of human history—people going to war precisely at the times when they should be most united."

"How can we unite with them?" asked Umbo.

"That's the question, isn't it?" said Rigg. "Up to now, we've been united with them without knowing it—acting out their purposes, obeying their plans for us, and we had no idea who they were. Picking up jewels, using a knife they made for us, we've been their puppets."

"Cut the strings," said Olivenko.

"The only strings we can cut," said Loaf, "are the ones that we can see."

"Our very existence is one of the strings," said Rigg. "And let's remember. They can't time-shift, but what if they change their minds about giving us the missing jewel? What they gave us, they can go back in time and take away."

That gave them pause.

"Why haven't they done that already?" asked Umbo. "Since we're not doing what they told us to do."

"We haven't *not* done it," said Rigg. "We're still talking."

"They need to get what they want," said Loaf. "And that's survival. To them, that means getting out of the wallfold, spreading through the world. The *worlds*."

"And stopping the people of Earth from sending the Destroyers," said Param.

"What do *we* want?" asked Rigg.

"For them to stop manipulating us," said Umbo.

"We can't even stop manipulating each other," said Rigg. "It's what humans do. We influence each other."

"What, then?" asked Umbo. "We want to stop the Destroyers, too."

"What's our plan?" asked Rigg.

"We don't have one," said Olivenko.

"And why don't we have one?" asked Rigg.

"Because we aren't a trillion mice," said Param.

"We don't have a plan because we don't *know* anything yet," said Rigg. "All we have are the Future Books. And they don't tell us the only thing that matters."

"*Why* the Destroyers come," said Loaf.

"Until we know what causes their action—their motive,

how they see the world—we can't possibly have a plan," said Rigg.

"But the mice don't know either!" said Param. "It's just stupid."

"Exactly," said Rigg. "Yes, that's it, Param. They have a plan, but it's a plan to do exactly what the Destroyers are doing—wipe out the problem so you don't have to deal with these strangers anymore."

"Well, that's a plan," said Umbo. "Not a great one, but a plan."

"What we need," said Rigg, "is to get the mice to agree that their plan is the wrong one."

"We don't know it's the wrong one," said Param.

"Not the wrong one, then," said Rigg. "Premature, how's that?"

They murmured their assent.

"We need to get them to agree to wait through one more cycle," said Rigg.

"Why would they do that?" said Olivenko. "There have already been nine cycles. This is the first one that included mice—they want to see what *they* can do."

"But in the other cycles, all the Odinfolders ever knew was whatever message was sent back by the people of the future," said Rigg. "This time, we have *us*. We can see for ourselves. Meet the Visitors. See the Destroyers. Then we shift back to now, or to . . . sometime. We go back, and *then* we can do something together, we and the mice, because we'll know a lot more than the scant information in a Future Book."

"It'll be the first time that ever happened," said Olivenko.

"It means taking the mice into the past with us," said Umbo.

"Both times—right now, and then at the end, when the Destroyers come."

"We'll have all their memories to pool with ours," said Param.

"It makes sense to *us*," said Loaf. "Will it make sense to them?"

"Yes," said the ship's voice.

"Yes what?" asked Rigg.

"They agree that your plan is a good one," said the ship's voice. "They agree to wait through a cycle, as long as you promise to bring back as many of them as you can."

So the mice had understood them after all. How? "You translated for them," said Rigg.

"I didn't have to," said the ship. "Where did you learn the language of Imperial O?"

"From Ramex," said Rigg, feeling stupid.

"Ramex knew it, so all the computers and expendables knew it," said the ship's voice. "Therefore it was known among the mice."

"Why would they bother to learn a dead language from another wallfold?" asked Olivenko.

"You're a scholar," said Rigg. "You learn all kinds of useless things."

"Just because some of the billions of mice know something doesn't mean they *all* know it," said Olivenko.

"They made sure that the mice that flew with us included speakers of every language that any of us knew," said Rigg. "The expendables knew which languages Ramex had taught me, so the mice knew which languages were needed."

"They tricked us into thinking they couldn't understand us," said Param.

"We tricked ourselves," said Rigg, "because I assumed they wouldn't know."

"And now they trust you," said the ship's voice. "Because they know what you say when you think they can't understand."

"It's exactly what we were going to say to their faces," said Rigg.

"Yes," said the ship's voice.

"I guess that's how trust is built," said Loaf.

"By spying on us when we think they can't hear?" asked Umbo.

"By learning something about us that they couldn't find out any other way," said Loaf. "By hearing what we sound like when we tell the truth."

"Unless we knew it all along," said Param.

"They knew none of us was lying," said Loaf. "They can see body signs the same way I can. If we had been pretending to believe they couldn't understand us, we couldn't have concealed the pretense from them."

"May I land now?" asked the ship's voice.

"Are we there?" asked Rigg.

"I've been circling the landing site for some time now."

"Yes, land," said Rigg. "Do we ever know *anything* about what's going on?"

"No," said Olivenko. "All we can ever do is guess based on the information we have."

"And our guesses—are they ever right?" asked Rigg.

"Often enough that we don't all give up trying," said Olivenko. "The trouble is, sometimes when we think we're right, we're right for all the wrong reasons, and sometimes when we think we were wrong, we were actually right."

"We never know anything," said Param. "That's what you're saying."

"I'm saying we have to make our best guess and then see how things turn out," said Olivenko.

"So do we all agree that this is our best guess?" asked Rigg. "Wait till the Visitors come, learn what we can, then wait for the Destroyers, learn what we can about them, and then go back and make a new plan about what we think actually happened, and what we can do about it?"

"I think we can agree on something else, too," said Loaf. "I think we *have* to agree, all of us and all the mice as well."

"What's that?" asked Umbo.

"We'll try to keep Earth and Garden both alive," said Loaf. "But if we can't save both, we save Garden."

The flyer settled onto the ground and the door opened.

The ground outside was teeming with mice.

"They're going to kill us all," said Param, as mice swarmed up into the flyer.

"No," said Rigg. "They're just happy to see us."

CHAPTER 18
Transit

Umbo watched as the mice swarmed through the flyer, climbing all over each other in writhing heaps.

"They're telling each other what happened here," Loaf said.

"I think some of them are mating," said Rigg drily.

Umbo saw how Param drew her legs up onto the seat. It wasn't as if she had any memory of being killed by the mice. Umbo knew that Odinex had killed two copies of himself. He had even glanced down at the bodies as he walked over the bridge out of the starship. But they meant nothing to him. They had *been* him, but they weren't him anymore. Still, he was bound to be a bit more wary of expendables now, so it probably wasn't irrational for Param to be wary of the mice.

"It occurs to me," said Umbo, "that we are nothing but a mouse's way of getting through the Wall."

Olivenko gave a sharp bark of a laugh. Nobody else responded.

Umbo went on. "And the mice exist only as the Odinfolders' tenth strategy for preventing the destruction of Garden. If any of the earlier ones had worked, all the mice of Odinfold would be ordinary field mice or house mice."

"And all of us exist on Garden," said Param, "because the humans of Earth wanted to spread out onto other worlds."

"You say that as if it were a poor reason for being," said Olivenko, still amused.

"Why did humans ever come to exist?" asked Umbo. "At least we and the mice have a purpose. Somebody meant for us to be here."

"Every generation exists to give rise to the next," said Olivenko. "Every generation exists because of the desire of the previous one. It's the cycle of life."

"So you're saying that the cycle of life exists in order to perpetuate the cycle of life," said Umbo.

"Round and round," said Olivenko.

"My head is spinning," said Rigg. "I wish I could hear what they're saying."

"I've never wanted to be part of the conversation of mice," said Olivenko.

"I've spent half my life *as* a mouse," said Param. "Hiding the way they do. Watching from the walls."

"Snatching food in the night from a dark kitchen?" asked Umbo.

"The kitchen in Flacommo's house was never dark," said Param. "Something was cooking every hour of the day and night."

"Which is pretty much the way these expendables and starships are," said Umbo. "If we're all about the cycle of life, what are *they* about? Tools made by the starship builders. But for eleven thousand years, their starships haven't flown. They've been the stewards of the human race, obeying some set of rules laid down at the beginning. Ram Odin changed the rules, and the second Ram Odin changed what *he* could change, and the Odinfolders have fiddled, but mostly the expendables have followed plans of their own, telling us what they wanted us to hear."

"What's your point?" asked Param, sounding a little annoyed.

"What if the Destroyers come to burn off Garden because of something the expendables tell the Visitors?" asked Umbo. "What if it has nothing to do with anything that any of the people of Garden do or say or built?"

They were silent again, but this time not because of uninterest in Umbo's observation.

"I don't know how we'd ever find out," said Olivenko.

"The mice know what the expendables and ships say to each other," said Loaf.

"No," said Umbo. "The mice have *told* you they intercept the ships' communications. The Odinfolders told us *they* could do it, too, but how do they know if they're getting everything? They can't intercept what the ships and expendables don't actually say. Besides, the expendables know they're being spied on, and they're good at lying."

"The ships tell me the truth," said Rigg. "As far as I know."

"I hope so," said Umbo. "Because when you think about it, the ships and the expendables are all the same thing. The same mind."

"Actually," said the ship, "we have a completely different program set."

"Shut up, please," said Rigg cheerfully.

"The ships take over the expendables whenever they want," Umbo went on. "That means that whatever the expendables do, the ships consent to it. Does it work the other way around?"

"Whatever the ships do is because the expendables want it?" asked Param.

"The orbiters are set to destroy the life of any wallfold that develops technology the expendables disapprove of," said Umbo. "That means that part of the expendables' mission is to judge everything we do. Everything the mice do. And destroying us all is part of their mission. What if this seed of time-shifting ability that exists among all the descendants of Ram Odin is a forbidden weapon? Then the only way to expunge it from the world is to wipe out the human race on Garden."

"That's as good a guess as any," said Rigg.

"But still only a guess," said Olivenko.

That irritated Umbo. "Why are other people's ideas 'theories,' but mine are 'guesses'?"

"They're all guesses," said Rigg. "And they're all theories. This is one we have to keep in mind when we meet the Visitors. Maybe they're not the problem. Maybe it's what they learn from the logs of all the ships' computers."

"Maybe it's what they're *told* by the expendables," said Umbo. "Maybe there's programming deeper than anything that Ram Odin could reach. Maybe they had an agenda from the beginning."

"In the beginning," said Param, "there was only one starship, and it was coming to this world to found one colony. As far as the Visitors know until they actually get here, the colony on Garden should be only twelve years old. What deep secret plan could possibly exist in the expendables' programming?"

"A plan that has nothing to do with us, but which gets applied to us anyway," said Umbo.

"How will we ever know?" asked Rigg seriously. "How can we ever know anything?"

"I think we have to go back to the beginning," said Umbo. "I think we have to talk to Ram Odin."

"We can't," said Rigg. "We don't dare. If we change his choice, we undo all of human history on Garden."

"Not *un*do, *re*do," said Olivenko.

"And maybe not," said Umbo. "There were nineteen Ram Odins, at least for a few minutes. What if we could talk to one of the ones who died?"

"What could we learn from that?" asked Olivenko, a little scornfully. "*Those* aren't the Ram Odins that made all the decisions that shaped this world."

"First," said Rigg, "Ram Odin only made the decisions that he made, based on the data the ships and the expendables gave him. But he also knew things about how the expendables worked that we don't know."

"The mice are leaving," said Param.

It was true. They were rushing from the flyer, down the ramp and simply dropping off its sides. It took a surprisingly long time. They had apparently been swarming everywhere in the vehicle.

"Alone at last," said Olivenko, when the last mouse went down the ramp.

"There are still five on Loaf," said Rigg. "And three hiding in the upholstery."

Those all came out of hiding and headed out the door.

"They don't have to go," said Rigg. "We have nothing to hide."

But the mice went anyway.

Umbo got up and went to the doorway and looked out. They were on the brow of a hill, surrounded mostly by woodland. He could see several housetrees of the Odinfolders. Rigg came and stood beside him. "They're at home," said Rigg.

"But not coming out to see what we're doing," said Umbo.

"They see the Odinfold flyer," said Rigg, "and all they can see of us is a couple of people standing in the doorway. As far as they know, we're transporting mice for some kind of mousemoot."

Umbo turned back to face the others. "Should we do it?" he asked.

"Transport the mice with us into the past?" asked Loaf. "We gave our word."

"We don't even know if we *can* do it," said Umbo.

"Of course we can," said Rigg. "If we can take Loaf with us, we can take anybody."

Loaf smiled wanly.

"*When* should we travel to?" asked Umbo. "How far into the past are we going to take them?"

"As soon after we got control of the Wall as possible, I suppose," said Rigg.

Umbo noticed the way he said "we." As if anybody but him had any power over it. "I don't carry a perfect calendar in my head," said Umbo. "Why not just go through now, a year or so before the Visitors arrive?"

"Because the mice want more than a few of their generations to get established," said Loaf. "They want to take ten thousand mice through the Wall, so they'll have millions in place before the Visitors come."

"That's what the mice want," said Umbo.

"We gave our word," said Param.

"Based on information they gave us," said Umbo. "And what the expendables and the ship told us."

"Umbo has a point," said Rigg. "Not the point he thinks he's making—we're going to keep our word, or at least I am. But we don't know if we can take ten thousand mice into the past. Or even fifty. And how will we pinpoint *when* to arrive?"

"Just . . . hook on to some path, like you always do," said Umbo.

"What path?" asked Rigg. "How do we know which of the paths that come near the Wall are from that time, or even close to it?"

"Take the flyer back with us," said Olivenko, "and when we get there, ask it if we hit the right time."

"No," said Umbo. "If we arrive at a time before Rigg got control of the ships, then the flyer doesn't have to do anything we say."

"But it's the flyer from now, from the future of that time," said Olivenko.

"Machines aren't people," said Umbo. "It will sync up with

the starship computers of *that* time and do what they tell it to do—and they won't be obeying Rigg. They won't even know who Rigg is."

"We're so powerful," said Param. "But now we want to be all-knowing, too."

"Well, it would be nice," said Rigg.

"I think we need to fly back to where we came through the Wall from Vadeshfold," said Umbo, "and go back to that time, where Rigg can see our own paths coming through the Wall."

"But we won't have the mice there," said Loaf.

"They assembled here," said Umbo. "Let them assemble there."

"And then how long will it take them to travel here to the Larfold Wall?" asked Loaf. "They have little tiny legs."

"I stay here," said Umbo. "Rigg flies back there. Rigg hooks onto our paths. I push Rigg back, complete with the flyer. Rigg flies back here in that time, and then when he gets here, I pull him back to this time."

"So much rigmarole," said Olivenko.

"It's the only way Rigg can go back and then get back to this time exactly," said Umbo. "I'm still needed for *that*—the ability to stay in the present and send somebody else into the past. When Rigg comes back to the present, his own path will be here, at the Wall, and then we can take the mice back. Even if we can only take twenty or fifty or a hundred at a time, I can send Rigg back with the mice again and again, bring Rigg back to the present, and send him again."

"I wish I could sense paths through the curvature of the

planet," said Rigg. "I can see them through hills, but they get faint and then invisible as more and more planetary mass gets between me and them."

Param got up from her chair and walked to the door. She put her hands on Umbo's shoulders. "What are you planning, Umbo?" she asked.

"I'm planning to do whatever we decide to do," said Umbo, puzzled by the question.

"If you push Rigg into the past," she said, "and then *leave* him there, he can't get back to the present. He can't see paths in the future. He can't shift forward."

"But I *won't* leave him there," said Umbo, blushing as he realized what treachery she was accusing him of.

"I'm sorry," said Param, "but I'm trying to figure out what great wellspring of loyalty you're drawing from here. Aren't you the one who got rid of Rigg before, when we were still on our way to Odinfold?"

This was too much to bear, coming from her. "*You're* the one who refused to go on hiking! I was trying to help *you*."

"You were trying to get out from under Rigg's thumb," said Param. "Don't blame it on me. Stranding Rigg in the past would make you the only time-shifter left here in the present."

"But I won't do that," said Umbo.

"And we know that because . . ."

"Because I say so," said Umbo.

"And we're supposed to take the word of a peasant boy?" asked Param scornfully.

"The word of peasant boys is worth a lot more than the word of the royal family, as far as I've been able to see!" shouted Umbo.

In answer, Param gave him a shove out the door.

Umbo stumbled backward, lost his footing on the ramp, and fell off to the side into the grass. Above him, he could hear Param say to Rigg, "Now let's take the flyer and go."

"I see," said Rigg.

"See what?" asked Param.

"That you're our mother's true daughter," said Rigg.

Umbo was still getting to his feet when he heard a scuffle above him. He looked up to see Param stumbling down the ramp, tripping, falling.

Umbo might have caught her, or broken her fall a little. Instead he ducked under the ramp. She fell unimpeded into the grass, just as he had. Only she wasn't used to falling. She didn't have the catlike reflexes that Umbo had developed growing up in Fall Ford, playing in the woods, by the river, on the rocky cliffs, climbing every tree, every boulder, with other boys and many a girl scuffling with him. She fell like a lump and then cried out in pain; she curled up, holding her elbow.

Umbo had seen the elbow bend way too far in the wrong direction. And now it hung limply. Torn ligaments, broken bones—it had to be one or the other, or both. It wasn't a hinge joint anymore. It was more like loose skin between two bones.

"That was ugly," said Umbo.

Param screamed in agony and then . . . disappeared.

"Param," cried Rigg, rushing down the ramp. "I didn't mean to . . ."

Loaf and Olivenko followed him out of the flyer and down the ramp. "Rigg, you stupid little—" Loaf began.

"I know!" shouted Rigg. "But she had no right to treat Umbo that way! Who does she think she is?"

"She thinks she's the Queen-in-the-Tent of the Sessamids!" said Olivenko. "And oh, surprise: As soon as your mother dies, she *is*."

"She's not queen of anything, here," said Rigg.

"She's *my* queen wherever she is," said Olivenko.

"Well isn't that sweet," said Loaf. "As big a collection of idiots as I've ever seen in my life."

"We have to get her back," said Rigg.

"Any bright ideas about how to do that?" asked Loaf.

"I can write her a note. I used to write her notes on a slate back in Flacommo's house. Before we actually met."

"She can't have gotten far," said Olivenko. "It's not as if she was in any shape to move."

"If she isn't moving," said Rigg, "she wouldn't disappear. Time-slicing only makes her invisible if she's *moving*."

"How can she move with that elbow?" asked Umbo.

"She doesn't walk on her elbows," said Rigg.

"Don't talk to me like I'm an idiot," said Umbo. "I'm the one who came up with a plan to get us and ten thousand mice through the Wall at exactly the right time."

"Well, now we're not doing *anything*," said Olivenko.

"Listen to yourselves," said Loaf. "Is there anyone here with a brain? This didn't have to happen."

"But it did!" shouted Umbo. "And it's not my fault!"

"Nobody thinks it's your fault," said Loaf. "And it was Param whose ignorant arrogance caused this particular problem, that plus Rigg's misguided loyalty to you. So here's what you're going to do. Rigg and Umbo, you're both going to go to the top of this ramp and make a magical appearance a few minutes back in time, just before stupid Rigg pushed his stupid sister down the stupid ramp so she could shatter her stupid elbow."

"But then all this will be undone," said Umbo.

"Yes," said Loaf, incredulous. "That's what we *need* to accomplish—undoing all this wonderful nightmare!"

"But then I'll never know that Rigg is still my friend!" said Umbo. And to his surprise, he had tears on his cheeks. He was crying. Why was he crying?

"Silbom's left . . ." Loaf began. "Silbom's left and right and middle everything. Go up there and *tell* yourselves what happened but stop this stupidity from going so far. Do you understand me?"

"You're not my father, you know," said Umbo.

"I'm as close to a father as you'll ever get," said Loaf, "and don't you forget it."

"I *will* forget it," said Umbo. "That's what you're sending us up the ramp to do."

"Yes, I am. So do it. Erase this lovely moment of agony for Param and stupidity for you and Rigg and utter frustration for the only grownups in our little company."

"Are you counting me as a grownup?" asked Olivenko. "How sweet."

"Go," said Loaf.

Umbo and Rigg walked up the ramp together.

Umbo hit the ground after his fall from the ramp. He could hear Param saying, "Now let's take the flyer and go."

"I see," said Rigg.

"See what?" asked Param.

But instead of Rigg answering her, Umbo heard his own voice coming from above him. "Don't do it, Rigg," he said.

"Don't do what?" asked Rigg.

"Don't push her, you fool," said Rigg.

Rigg?

Umbo got to his feet. He could see himself and Rigg standing at the top of the ramp, talking to Rigg and Param.

Something bad must have happened, and he and Rigg had come back together to prevent it.

"I won't," said Rigg-of-the-present. "I never would."

"You did," said Rigg-of-the-past.

Umbo-of-the-past said, "But I'm glad you're still my friend." Then he turned a little and shouted into the air. "And Loaf is not my father!"

Then the apparitions of Umbo and Rigg disappeared.

Rigg and Param stood there in the doorway of the flyer. Param glared at Rigg. "You were going to push me down the ramp?"

"Don't ever talk to my friend that way again," said Rigg to Param. "I trust him a lot more than I trust *you*." Rigg walked down the ramp. "Are you all right?" he asked Umbo.

"I am now," said Umbo. "Worth the fall."

"I thought you were my brother!" said Param. And then she disappeared.

Loaf and Olivenko appeared in the doorway of the flyer. "I don't know what you two came back to prevent," said Olivenko, "but it must have been a catastrophe, if *this* is better."

"It's not my fault if Param decides to disappear," said Rigg.

"She's your sister," said Olivenko. "And someday she'll be Queen-in-the-Tent."

"And Umbo is a powerful time-shifter," said Rigg. "Maybe she should remember that when she starts talking about peasant boys. Where I grew up, peasant boys were way above my station!"

"Seems to me none of you has grown up," said Loaf.

Umbo had a pretty good idea of why his apparition had declared that Loaf was not his father. "Are we going to do what I suggested?" asked Umbo. "You fly back there and hook onto the past, and then fly here, and then I bring you and the flyer back?"

"Can you hold on to me that far?" asked Rigg.

"I don't know."

"So how will I know if you can bring me back to the present?"

Loaf held up his hand. There was a mouse on his shoulder, talking to him. "Our friend suggests you use the orbital phone to talk to each other when Rigg is at the other place."

Umbo had no idea what Loaf was talking about. The term "orbital phone" meant nothing to him. That is, he understood both of the words, but had no idea what physical object they might be referring to, or how it would work.

"The knife," said Loaf.

"Knife?" asked Umbo.

"It's an orbital phone," said Loaf.

"You knew this?" asked Umbo.

"I had no idea," said Loaf.

"What's an orbital phone?"

"I have no idea," said Loaf.

Umbo pulled the knife from its sheath at his belt. "I thought this was a duplicate set of ships' logs."

"The jewels are a duplicate set," said Loaf, who was apparently getting an explanation from the mouse. "But the hilt under it is a communicator. Wherever you are, it connects to the starship of that wallfold by transmitting a signal to the orbiter, which relays it to the starship, and back and forth like that."

"This does that?" asked Umbo, looking at the knife. "It still looks like a knife."

"My friend says that it's in constant communication with the orbiter," said Loaf. "The whole time you've had it, it's been transmitting everything we said and did to the starship computers."

Umbo flung it away from him. "It's been spying on us."

"It's been keeping you connected to the rest of the world," said Olivenko.

"Is there anything else it does?" asked Rigg, picking up the knife.

"Cuts meat," said Loaf.

"Was that your joke, or the mouse's?" asked Umbo.

"Mine," said Loaf. "The mouse says the orbital phone was all they could fit into the hilt."

"It must be a primitive design," said Umbo acidly.

"Yes," said Loaf. "It was made and sent back to you more than a hundred years ago."

"But we only got it two years—" and then Umbo interrupted himself and fell silent. They *got* the knife two years ago, but with time-sending, that had nothing to do with when it was sent. Umbo blushed.

"We're all still trying to figure it all out," said Rigg. "So the knife is a communicator. No wonder the expendables in every wallfold knew all about what we were doing."

"Well, they knew all about me and Loaf," said Umbo. "During those months I had the knife and you were in Aressa Sessamo." Then Umbo blushed again, thinking of the prank he had played, stealing one of the jewels from the bag Loaf hid near the Tower of O. What a *child* he had been. No wonder Loaf got so impatient with him.

Does the fact that I feel embarrassed about it now mean that I'm growing up? Umbo decided not to ask the question aloud. He had a feeling he knew what Loaf's answer would be.

They waited an hour or so as Rigg tracked Param's path down the ramp. As soon as she was clear of the flyer, Rigg took off, heading for their original entry point into Odinfold. Umbo stayed there on the knoll, holding the knife, talking to Rigg continuously. He knew that when he sent Rigg back in time, he kept hold of him, not with his eyes, but with some other sense, a deep knowledge of where and *when* Rigg was located. They had found each other in Aressa Sessamo without being able to see each other, and Umbo had pushed Rigg back and forth in time. But the distance now would be far greater, and there was that problem of line-of-sight. If Rigg couldn't track paths through the curvature of Garden, could Umbo hold on to Rigg despite the thickness of rock and earth between them?

It took hours to complete the voyage, but Rigg and Umbo were still talking and, more to the point, Umbo could still feel whatever part of Rigg he felt when he had a grip on his timeflow.

"Make sure you take the flyer with you," said Umbo.

"I definitely don't want to walk back, if that's what you're thinking," said Rigg. "By the way, I have a mouse on my shoulder."

"And I have a flea on my butt," said Umbo. "Have you locked onto the path you want?"

"Yes," said Rigg. "Do it."

Umbo threw Rigg back in time, and Rigg's own connection with the path put him exactly where he needed to be. Umbo could never have found that moment with such precision, but he recognized the distance in time when he felt it. Yes, that is *when* we were, and where.

Keeping his focus on Rigg during the return voyage was much harder, if only because they couldn't talk. The orbital phone only communicated with the ships and expendables that existed at the same time, not with a flyer moving over the prairie and woods a year ago.

But Umbo did not fail; he held on to Rigg. And while he could not trace paths, he knew when Rigg was back in place. It was a sense of rightness, of nearness. The flyer had completed its journey; now it was a fact that the flyer had landed nearby a year ago, and if Umbo brought Rigg back to the present, he would leave a path behind him, in the right place, at the right time.

The mouse, too, no doubt.

"I'm doing it now," said Umbo to Loaf and Olivenko. "I wish I knew where Param was."

"It's been long enough that she could be anywhere," said Loaf.

"With our luck, she'll be stubborn and angry enough to have perched in the center of where the flyer was when she got out of it," said Olivenko.

"Can you tell where Rigg will appear?" asked Loaf.

"He'll appear wherever he is in the time that's 'now' to him," said Umbo. "I know he's close, but I can't say where for sure."

"Just do it," said Loaf. "If something terrible happens, you can go back and warn yourself not to do whatever we did that went wrong."

"My whole stupid plan, probably," said Umbo. Then, with a sigh, he let go of the continuous pushing that had held Rigg in the past.

Nothing happened. No flyer appeared.

"Are you going to do it?" asked Loaf.

"It's done," said Umbo. "I brought Rigg back to now. I just don't know where he was when I did it." Umbo rose to his feet to scout the horizon. Then he remembered that if Rigg had returned to the present, and still had the flyer with him, the orbital phone should work again. He pulled out the knife and talked to it, feeling stupid the whole time. "Rigg?" he said. Several times.

And then the knife answered him. "What's so urgent?"

"You returned to our time," said Umbo, relieved.

"I decided not to come to an area where Param might have wandered," said Rigg. "I thought you'd figure that out."

"We did," said Umbo, "but what if I was wrong? What if I had stranded you somewhere else. Some*when* else?"

"You didn't. But I can only talk to you this way while I remain with the flyer. I was already a hundred meters away, walking toward you, when the flyer called me back. So let's hold the rest of our conversation till I get there."

It took twenty minutes for Rigg to join them. "How far did you think Param could have gotten?" said Loaf when Rigg returned.

Rigg looked annoyed. "She had five hours. If she slices time just barely enough to stay invisible, she can cover a lot of ground. And what if she got into those trees and stopped time-slicing? Then she could have walked at a normal pace and gotten anywhere."

"Can you see your own path?" asked Umbo. "The one you just made?"

"Yes," said Rigg. "We can do this now."

"And where *is* Param?" asked Olivenko.

"Over there," said Rigg, pointing toward the edge of the woods.

Olivenko looked, and when he did, Param reappeared. She turned away from them and made no move to join them, but she was visible again, and that was a good thing.

With the first pass, Loaf got a dozen mice to climb onto Rigg's clothing before Umbo sent him into the past. Umbo brought him back a few moments later, and the mice were no longer with him.

"I tested it," said Rigg. "I was in control of the Wall."

"Did you send them through?" asked Umbo.

"I was only there for a couple of minutes," said Rigg. "I wasn't going to strand them fifty feet into the Wall. It'll take a long time for mice to cover the distance, so I figured we'd move them all into the past and then open the Wall and let them all through."

With the next sending, a couple of hundred mice climbed up onto Rigg, or clumped up near him, all touching him in a continuous heap of rodentkind. A musine mound. A mass of musculinity.

Not that the scientific name *Mus musculus* still applied to these creatures, even if it was the correct term for their ancestors. More like *Mus sapiens* now. Or perhaps, recognizing their human kinship, *Homo musculus*.

Umbo collected his thoughts and focused on Rigg, preparing to send him.

"Wait," said Olivenko. "Don't go back to the exact place you went before."

Rigg got it at once, and Umbo understood only a moment later. If Rigg latched onto the same moment in time, while he was sitting in the same spot, he'd return to the past at the same moment and in the same place he had before. The two versions of Rigg would annihilate each other.

Rigg got up and moved a few meters away. "So the mice don't crash into each other, either," he explained.

Then the mouseheap remade itself, and Umbo gathered them all into his attention and began to try to push them back.

It was as if each one of them had a mass as great as Rigg. Like pushing a boat up a mountain. "I can't," said Umbo.

"Just send as many as you can," said Rigg. "Let's see how many that is."

Umbo gave a shove to the past. He could still see Rigg and the mice. But when the mice nearest Rigg scampered away from him, they vanished; Umbo had no hold on them. Other mice, however, were still in the present moment, and so as they moved away, they remained as visible as ever.

Umbo brought Rigg back, and they assessed how many they had sent. Only about fifty or sixty were gone, the mice told Loaf.

"That means it'll take about two hundred sendings," said Olivenko. "If you're going to do all ten thousand."

"We need to," said Loaf.

"Then we will," said Umbo.

"Can you do it?" asked Rigg. "You look tired already."

"I'll do all I can, and then I'll rest," said Umbo. "What does it matter if we spread the sending across several days, as long as they all arrive at the same time and place?"

"I told them to head for those trees," said Rigg. He turned to Loaf. "They do understand me when I talk, right?"

"They hear us just fine," said Loaf.

As the day wore on to evening, they did another dozen sendings, each time with more mice attached. They had moved a good way along the knoll. But by then Umbo really was exhausted, and it was getting dark.

"We'll continue in the morning," said Rigg.

"I can do another," said Umbo.

"These last two were smaller than the one before," said Rigg. "You're exhausted. We're done for the day."

Umbo was content to wait and rest.

Loaf had been cooking something over a fire he built. Umbo

was vaguely aware that Loaf had gone down to one of the Odinfold houses and apparently he got food, because he had corn roasting and a loaf of bread and a quarter of a cheese. "They eat pretty simply," said Loaf. "Not like what they fed us in the library."

"*That* was simple fare," said Olivenko.

"By the standards of Aressa Sessamo the library food was simple," said Loaf. "And by the standards of O. But for this region of Odinfold, it would be a banquet. This is the best they have here. And speaking as an old soldier, I think it's just fine."

As Umbo, Rigg, and Loaf ate, Olivenko took his supper over to Param. A few moments later, Umbo heard distant weeping. He looked over to the edge of the woods where, sure enough, Param was sobbing into Olivenko's shoulder.

She despises you, Umbo, he told himself. You'll never be anything but a peasant boy to her. And what do you care? You stopped being in love with her months ago.

But seeing her holding on to Olivenko that way stabbed Umbo with jealousy all the same.

In the morning, Param ate breakfast with them, and formally apologized for her "petulant actions" the day before. Just as formally, Rigg and Umbo apologized in return. "I don't know what we came back to prevent," said Rigg, "but I have a feeling I behaved very badly."

"Not in this version of history," said Param.

But Umbo noticed that she hardly looked at him. Was it shame for having pushed him off the flyer ramp? Or contempt because he was just a peasant boy?

For your information, *princess*, I can make you a pair of shoes out of grass and rose thorns. I have a skill; I'm a cobbler's son. Sort of.

It was the first time Umbo could recall ever being proud of something he acquired from his reputed father, the master cobbler Tegay. And it's not as if Tegay ever praised Umbo for his prentice work.

Breakfast done, they went back to pushing mice into the past. They were done well before noon.

"Eleven thousand, one hundred ninety-one mice," said Loaf.

"You're joking," said Umbo. "Why that number?"

"It's a holy number here, too," said Loaf.

"But they don't believe in holiness," said Umbo.

"No, *you* don't believe in it," said Loaf. "The mice are very devout. I don't think the number has any practical value. They just think of it as a sacred number and they expect their new colony will prosper if they start with that many settlers."

Thinking of mice as "settlers" jarred, but that's how it would always be, Umbo knew. Mice were hard to see as human, or of equal value. There were so many of them.

"What can they even *do*?" asked Umbo. "It's not like they can pull a plow."

"They don't have to farm," said Loaf. "They scavenge beautifully. They would never have developed civilization on their own, but because they inherited the human culture and knowledge of the Odinfolders, they could leap forward vastly. And they're designed to require less food than ordinary mice. So they can live as scavengers and still have leisure to create."

"Create what?" asked Umbo. "Can they wield a hammer?

Iron doesn't get any softer just because the blacksmith is very tiny. What can they actually make?"

"They seem content about their ability to establish a very high level of civilization in a very short time," said Loaf. "But now it's time for us to go."

Umbo turned to Param. "Are you coming with us?"

She turned away from him. Apparently she thought he was being sarcastic.

Olivenko thought so too. "Of course she is," said Olivenko.

"We need her," said Umbo, "but she has a choice. I wasn't being snotty, I was asking her intention instead of assuming things."

"I'm coming," she said. And then, after a momentary pause, "Thanks for asking."

They all held whatever bags and extra clothing they meant to take with them. It wasn't much.

And this time, Umbo didn't have to push. He and Rigg instead pulled together, shifting themselves and their friends all at once, leaving no anchor in the future they had just left.

The hill was teeming with mice, except in the spot where they arrived. Mice were so thick on the ground in every direction that it was easy to see the edge of the Wall, because mice were arrayed right up against the spot where the Wall's despair was first clearly noticeable.

"I'm letting the Wall down now," said Rigg.

The mice seemed to sense at once that it was gone, and they surged forward, down and across the little vale. It took hours for the mice all to go through the Wall. Umbo sat and watched the undulating sea of mice until they were gone. We are servants of the mice. We have opened a door for them. Does it even matter now whether *we* cross into Larfold?

It matters to Rigg and Param—their father died here. And to Olivenko, because Knosso was his mentor and his king. Maybe Loaf cares. But I'm just a tool of the mice, or the tool of the Sessamids, or Loaf's surrogate son.

No, I can't think that way anymore. These are my friends. It's my choice to go with them, to help them do the things that matter to them.

"Please come with us," said Rigg.

Umbo looked at him, startled. Did he know what Umbo was thinking?

"Of course I will," said Umbo.

"You're free to do whatever you want," said Rigg. "I couldn't have done this without you, so I'm glad you were with me. But now it's done. You never asked to be in the business of saving the world."

Umbo was moved. "You think it's a monopoly of the royal family?" The words could have sounded harsh, but Umbo said them with a grin.

"The Sessamids?" Rigg chuckled. "From what I know of family history, we don't save worlds, we take over what other people have built and slowly wreck it."

"Pretty much describes my old dad," said Umbo. "Except when he worked with shoes."

"We Sessamids make no shoes," said Rigg. "I want you with me, Umbo. I need your help. But if you choose not to come, I won't resent it. How many times do people have to die because they came with me?"

"So far death hasn't interfered with my life as much as you'd think," said Umbo. "I'm in."

"Let's go, then," said Rigg, and he held out a hand.

Umbo took it, bounded to his feet, and side by side they walked briskly toward the Wall, with Param, Loaf, and Olivenko following at a slower pace.

CHAPTER 19

Royal

"I've been trying to figure out why everyone was so angry with me," said Param as they walked through the Wall. Umbo and Rigg were far out of earshot ahead of them.

Loaf grunted.

"Any progress?" asked Olivenko. "Have you thought that pushing Umbo out the door might have been part of it? Not to make any suggestions."

"Don't you be sarcastic with me," said Param.

"I think he was being delicate and respectful," said Loaf. "If *I* had said that, it would have been sarcastic."

"I shouldn't have pushed him," said Param.

"We're making progress," said Loaf.

"Someone else should have done it," said Param. "I shouldn't be reduced to protecting the name of the royal family myself."

"The royal family that tried to kill us all back in Ramfold?" asked Loaf. "The royal family in which the queen tried to murder her own children while she bedded General Citizen?"

"Leadership comes naturally to some people. Look at Rigg and Umbo. Raised in the same village. But Rigg is a natural leader, and Umbo is . . ."

"A peasant boy," said Loaf. "I think that's what you called him, when you accused him of being a liar."

"I never accused him of—"

"I have perfect recall now," said Loaf. And when he quoted her own words back to her—"And we're supposed to take the word of a peasant boy?"—his voice sounded astonishingly similar to her own. All the intonations were exactly right.

"I didn't suggest that he was lying," said Param. "I merely said that it was unreasonable to expect someone like me or Rigg to take the word of a peasant boy as if it were indistinguishable from fact."

"So you studied the history of the wallfolds for nearly a year and you're still as ignorant as ever," said Loaf.

Instead of time-slicing to get away from Loaf, Param slowed down and let him move on ahead. But Olivenko stayed with her, walking at her slower pace.

Param could feel the hideous music of the Wall playing with the back of her mind, making her angry, sad, despairing, lonely, anguished; but not the way it was the first time she had experienced the Wall, not overwhelming, not terrifying. "Are you going to criticize me, too?"

"You were raised to rule," said Olivenko.

"Or so my mother said," Param replied. "I have no idea when her plan for me changed, but my education, such as it was, never changed. You don't announce to the cattle that you're going to slaughter them."

"You were raised with courtly manners," said Olivenko. "You heard people talking in elevated language, observing the courtesies."

"As Rigg does," said Param.

"But the expendable Ramex trained him to be able to do that."

"Exactly."

"So you and Rigg were *taught* to behave in a certain way. You were given skills. But how was Umbo raised?"

"As a peasant boy," said Param. "I didn't say it was his *fault*."

"He was the son of a cobbler in a small village. He attended the village school. In that school, he was taught the history of Stashiland. He was taught that the royal family were rapacious monsters, who came to Aressa as uncivilized barbarians from the northeast. They killed most of the ruling class of Stashiland, and raped the few women of that class that they allowed to live, after killing their children, so they could 'start fresh.'"

"I've read the history. I'm not proud of our origins. But that was many hundreds of years ago."

"Not so very many," said Olivenko. "And Umbo wasn't taught that history as a distant memory, to be ignored or glossed over. He was taught it as if it was a fair description of the way the Sessamids have always ruled in Stashiland."

"And that's a lie," said Param.

"So there was no murderousness when Aptica Sessamin

decreed that no male could inherit the Tent of Light and had all her male relatives executed like criminals, for the crime of being male? Including the male babies?"

"That was ugly," Param admitted. "But it was a long time ago."

"Your mother's grandmother," said Olivenko. "I'm not arguing with you, I'm reminding you of what Umbo was taught. The People's Schools taught children that everybody had the right to rule, when their turn came, and nobody was better by birth than anyone else."

"Obviously false."

"By birth," Olivenko repeated. "By lineage. Umbo was taught that just because your mother was powerful didn't mean you had any more right to that power than anyone else. He was taught that power had to be earned, and that if you showed merit, you could become anything."

"But that's not how the People's Republic worked at all," said Param with contempt. "I saw how those hypocrites pretended everything was so egalitarian as they promoted their relatives and friends and established a whole new class of nobles."

"I'm reminding you of what Umbo was taught in Fall Ford at the base of the Stashi Falls," said Olivenko. "So all of a sudden, his boyhood friend—a boy who was even lower in social standing than Umbo, remember, because he lived a wandering life as a trapper's son—his boyhood friend has a bag of jewels and starts talking like a lord. That came as a shock, you can imagine."

"Rigg was coming out of his disguise, coming into his heritage," said Param.

"Coming to prison as fast as the People's Republic could arrest him, is that what you mean?"

"It was our fate during that time," said Param.

"So Umbo does everything he can to get his friend out of imprisonment, and he does it just in time—"

"Rigg got us out of prison! Using his talent and mine together. He found the passages in the walls, and I got us through those walls into the passages, and—"

"You weren't free of danger until Umbo pushed you and Rigg back in time a few days—which is where you acquired *me*," said Olivenko.

"I was *not* saying that Umbo wasn't helpful and good," said Param.

"Only that his word was worthless, because he was born in a village to ordinary people."

"Not worthless, just uncorroborated."

"Remember, I'm trying to help you understand why Rigg got so angry with you. Umbo was his friend in that village, in a time of Rigg's life when other boys wouldn't have befriended him. Rigg was the stranger, the outsider, and everybody assumed he was a bastard. At least Umbo's parents were married."

"I know they're friends," said Param. "But Rigg's supposed to be my *brother*, and to take the side of—"

"When people were trying to kill you, he took your side, didn't he?"

"Nobody was trying to kill Umbo."

"And then I remember a time when you announced you weren't going to journey another step. You rebelled against Rigg."

"That didn't mean I wanted to follow Umbo!"

"And you didn't. You followed *me*."

"You're an educated man," said Param.

"Educated by the side of your father," said Olivenko. "But still born to a much lower class. Not a natural leader, right?"

"More of a leader than the others."

"Param, are you really this blind? I speak the language of court, in the accents of court, because I worked very hard to learn to talk that way. And so you followed me when you wouldn't listen to anybody else. But I was never the *leader* of that group. I was simply the one person who could get *you* to do anything."

"You led us!"

"They let me pretend to lead," said Olivenko, "because Loaf wasn't talking yet, and Umbo was taking care of Loaf. But the fact is, it was Umbo who did everything that kept us alive."

"You did it with him!"

"I did what he told me to do," said Olivenko. "Umbo understood that you were out of your element, that everything was strange for you. He also understood that you would only listen to me. So he made sure that I knew the right things to do, so that I'd be the one to say them, so that you'd listen."

"That's ridiculous!" said Param. "You make me sound like a helpless, spoiled infant!"

Olivenko shook his head. "I make you sound like someone who had lived inside the walls of a house, a prisoner, humiliated by any clown whom the People's Revolutionary Council allowed to come harass you. I make you sound like a young woman who was physically weak and who had a habit of vanishing whenever things became stressful. You were trying very hard *not* to disappear and retreat by reflex, only you got tired, physically exhausted for the first time in your life. Umbo and Rigg and Loaf and I had experienced that many times, and we knew how to go on anyway. You didn't. It's not an easy thing to learn, and you never had to learn it."

"You're on their side," said Param. She stopped walking at all.

"Have the courage to hear the truth from a friend."

"You're not a friend! You're a . . ."

"Jumped-up peasant boy who became a scholar and then a city guard. I'm not insulted by those facts—that's my life. Just as it's no shame to you that you were hopelessly unprepared to deal with rough living and endless walking. We are who we are. When changes come, we start with what we are right then, and then we work to try to become whoever we need to be."

The way he said it sounded soothing. Natural. But she was no fool. She knew he was patronizing her. *Handling* her, coping with her, getting around her, placating her, all those phrases for manipulation and control.

And yet she kept walking, and kept listening, because even though she wasn't in love with him anymore—she knew now that that had been a mere phase—she knew that he was a perceptive man, and he *had* been Father's friend, hadn't he?

"Param," said Olivenko, "we're not in Aressa Sessamo anymore. Out here, we're the people who pass between the Walls. We belong nowhere, we're citizens of nothing, and there are only two classes that matter: Time-shifter and non-time-shifter. Loaf and I are non-shifters. You and Rigg and Umbo are shifters. Not only that, Umbo was the first to be able to move into the past all by himself. Can you do that? Could Rigg, until we were in Vadeshfold? We all survived and escaped from Ramfold because of one person."

"Umbo," said Param. "I know that. But I saved him, too, you know."

"Yes, you were on the rock and when he finally let go of Rigg and me and Loaf, because he was about to die, you helped him disappear and dragged him off the rock. But even then, you couldn't safely land from that leap until he took you into the past. Right? Am I getting the story right?"

"Yes," said Param, and she got his point well enough. "It was unbelievably rude of me to forget how much I owed Umbo."

"No, you're not getting my point yet," said Olivenko. "Of course you were ungrateful and spiteful and nasty and mean, but that's what Umbo was taught to expect from royals, so that wouldn't have bothered him. In fact, it *didn't* bother him. You pushed him out of the flyer, but when he got up, he wasn't going to do anything to you. He probably wasn't even going to complain. It was Rigg who yelled at you. It was Rigg who, apparently, was going to push you out the door after him or some such thing, which Rigg and Umbo came back to prevent."

"Yes, and I'm still angry at Rigg for being so disloyal."

"Disloyal! No, Param. *I'm* the fool who still can't get over being loyal to you because you're a princess, next in line for the Tent of Light. But Rigg doesn't give a mouse's petoot about that, because he grew up like Umbo. Rigg wasn't being disloyal. He was being *loyal*. Because in our company, Umbo is the royalty. Don't you get that? Don't you see? In this tiny world where the only classes are shifters and non-shifters, Umbo is the first of the shifters. He's the one that everything depended on. He's the king."

"He is *not* the king," said Param. "We follow Rigg."

"That's right. Umbo is the king, but he doesn't rule, Rigg does, because Rigg has better training, and Rigg can see the paths, so Rigg can time-shift with more accuracy, and much farther, and Rigg has all that education that Umbo would have had if Ramex had chosen *him* instead of your brother. Umbo should be the highest among us, but he isn't. Rigg's in that place, partly because *you* treat him that way."

"Because he's a—he's one of—"

"He's royal," said Olivenko. "But that's not why any of the rest of us follow him. We follow him because he's smart and creative, because Ramex educated him to be ready for situations the rest of us aren't prepared for, and because he doesn't *want* to be boss and so his hand rests gentle on the reins."

"He doesn't want to lead us?" asked Param.

"It's something that he and I have in common. Whereas you and Umbo both think you should lead, but Umbo can't because nobody would follow him, and you can't because you're completely incompetent."

Param was so stung by those words that, by reflex, she began to time-slice, becoming invisible to him. Time-slicing made her slow down relative to him, though she was walking as quickly as before. For a moment she thought he hadn't noticed that she vanished, but no, he kept walking, kept walking; he had to know she wasn't by him; he wasn't going to stop and wait for her.

He isn't going to pamper me. He isn't going to let me control him by disappearing. He told me the truth, that's what he did, and if I can't take it, then too bad for me.

Param stopped time-slicing and called out to him. "Please wait for me," she said.

Olivenko stopped and turned around. "Oh, you're back," he said. "Well, good. That's good. I'm sorry I spoke so plainly. I hoped you'd have the courage to hear it, but I was afraid you might have too much arrogance to bear it."

"Both," said Param. "I have both."

"But here you are," said Olivenko. "I like you, Param. More to the point, I respect you. I'm the only one here who really understands anything about your life—and that's only from being close to your father, and hearing him talk about you. Watching him shed tears when he talked about how helpless he was to protect you. 'How am I even a man, when they can treat my little girl like that, and I do nothing.' And I said to him, 'What good will it do her if you're dead? Because that's what will happen if you try to stop them from treating her that way.' And he said, 'I would be a better father, dead because I stood between her and danger, than I am now, alive because I don't have the courage.'"

"He didn't have the power," said Param. "And look what he *did* die for!"

"He died to try to cross the Wall," said Olivenko. "And now we've done it. His dream, and we've fulfilled it."

"Turns out not to be so much a dream as a nightmare," said Param.

"Nightmare?" said Olivenko. "All those people—including

your mother the queen, and General Citizen the dictator of Ramfold—they're all *nothing* compared to us! We're the walkers-through-walls, the world-striders! The rest of them don't even *know* the world is about to be destroyed, but we're working to try to prevent it. We're the gods that the whole world will sing about one day."

"They'll get three notes into the song and the Destroyers will incinerate them," said Param.

"Well, we only get the song if we succeed."

"If the mice succeed, you mean," said Param.

"Whoever," said Olivenko. "We'll mention the mice, of course. We'll tell how the magical mice helped us save the world."

Param laughed at his joke. "Yes, that's what the People's Revolutionary Council taught us—whoever controls the history gets to be the hero!"

"Param, I honor your office as daughter of the Queen-in-the-Tent, I can't help that, it's my whole upbringing. And I like you because you're charming and when you're not feeling sorry for yourself you're even funny and happy and smart. But I respect you because you have had the hardest life of any of us, a life so lonely it breaks my heart to imagine it, and you lived it. Your mother was your whole world and she betrayed you—Rigg had only known her for a few months, he hardly knew her. But you thought you did."

"Oh, I knew her," said Param. "I wasn't as surprised as you seem to think."

"Not surprised, but still betrayed," said Olivenko.

"I'm glad you respect me," said Param. "And I'm glad you

took the time to talk to me. Because I do see your point. I spoke so harshly to Umbo, not because he deserved it, but because by putting him down as a peasant, I could cling to the only value I thought I had—my royal blood. But thanks to you, I now see how worthless that is."

"I wasn't saying that it—"

"'Worthless' was my word, not yours," said Param, putting her hand on his wrist so they both stopped walking. "But it's the right word. And I see your point. I am who I am. Even though my time-slicing is a pretty pathetic talent, since it makes me so vulnerable to anybody who knows how it works, and it makes me so *slow*, I'm a shifter. And I'm trying to learn how to be somewhat useful, and you respect me for my efforts, and I appreciate it. That's what I'm saying. Thank you."

"You're welcome, my lady," said Olivenko. Then he bowed over her hand like a courtier, and kissed it.

It was a gesture that had always been done by people who were only trying to suck up to Mother. But because Olivenko actually meant it for her, and because he was a good and wise man, and because she was, in fact, still desperately in love with him, Param was overwhelmed by it, and she burst into tears.

They walked the rest of the way through the Wall with his arm around her.

"Took you long enough," said Rigg when they finally reached him.

"So take us back in time so we don't waste a moment of this precious experience of Larfold," said Olivenko. "Though as far as I can see, it looks suspiciously similar to Odinfold. Complete with the mice."

"They're dispersing," said Rigg.

Umbo was striding down the slope toward them. Apparently he had had time to crest the rise and see what lay on the other side.

"Pristine wilderness as far as I can see," Umbo reported, when he was near enough for anyone but Loaf to hear him. "But you'll tell us if there are any human paths." Clearly Umbo was talking only to Rigg, though Param and Olivenko stood beside him.

"No paths," said Rigg. "Not even in the early days of the colony."

"They took to the sea right away," said Param. "And then they stopped talking to Larex, and we have no more of their history."

Umbo didn't exactly ignore her. He waited for her to finish talking, and he was listening. But he didn't look at her once. And when she was done, he said, "There's one thing we *should* be seeing, and we're not."

For a moment Param didn't know what he was talking about. But then he pulled out his jeweled knife, and she realized. "No expendable to greet us."

"There wasn't one in Odinfold, either," said Umbo. "But the way I see it, Larex has been without a job for eleven thousand years. He's too busy to come chat us up when we come into his wallfold?"

"The ways of expendables are inscrutable," said Rigg.

"Scrute them," said Umbo. "If you think it's a good idea, I'm going to call for the flyer. Do you want me to ask Larex to come with it?"

"Maybe later," said Rigg. "At some point we might want to see what the local mechanical man has to say for himself. At least his people aren't all dead, like Vadesh's."

"We assume," said Umbo.

"If we can still call them people," said Param.

Loaf spoke up. "Oh, my definition of 'people' is definitely broader than it used to be. The mice have decided to take my advice and *not* accompany us. We're weird-looking enough, what with this thing on my face and Olivenko being so butt-ugly by nature, without tipping off the locals about this smirky-smarty mouse invasion."

"In other words, they want time to get established before the Larfolders find out they're here," said Olivenko.

"They're already mating their little brains out," said Loaf. "They won't want to meet any Larfolders until their babies are having babies."

"Which should be in about an hour and a half," said Rigg.

"Gestation's a little longer than that," said Loaf.

"So?" asked Umbo, holding up the knife.

"Call for the flyer," said Rigg. "I'm trying to figure out how I used to get around. I vaguely remembered that I used my legs somehow."

"Yes, legs," said Umbo. "I try never to use mine."

Param chuckled. But the banter between the boys stung her. Olivenko was right. By blood, she was Rigg's sister. But by love and loyalty, Rigg's only sibling was Umbo. That was why Rigg had been so angry with her. He didn't want to have to choose between them. But if push came to shove, quite literally, he would choose Umbo. Had chosen him.

And he was right, thought Param. I haven't earned my place with them yet. Damsel in distress, even a talented disappearing damsel who's also your closest living kin, isn't automatically a dear and trusted friend. That will take time. And more strength and courage and self-control than I've shown up to now.

CHAPTER 20
Larfold

The flyer carried them over pristine landscape, but because Rigg saw with the eyes of a pathfinder, he was struck by how empty it was. Like Vadeshfold, only even more devoid of paths. Though Odinfold had billions of paths, they were all faded by the thousands of years that had passed, and in recent years the paths had been few, and clustered up against the Wall.

How different they all were from Ramfold, full of life, the webs of paths still weaving themselves afresh with every day's activity.

Odinfold was carpeted with ruins; Vadeshfold had its one empty city; but Larfold had nothing at all in this vast sweep of forested land, the hills and cliffs and mountains. Only the wispy trails of the colonists from eleven thousand years before, heading northward to the sea, and then nothing on land that was more than a few hundred meters from the shore.

Yet this land was similar in climate and terrain to the land the Sessamids had come from, the barbarian forests that had spawned invasions of the great valley of the Stashik River again and again through history. The land was the same, but untorn by slash-and-burn farming, unscarred by roads, ungraced by bridges and buildings.

It was not more beautiful than lands that human beings had shaped, thought Rigg. He remembered the ruins of the old arches that had once spanned the Stashi Falls, broken in ancient storms or earthquakes. He remembered the stairs cut into stone that led up in a breath-robbing highway to the crest of the falls; he remembered running up those stairs, and also staggering down them carrying bundles of pelts. Was the mountain somehow ruined because humans had cut away stone to make a stairway for themselves? Or was it made more beautiful as well as more useful?

What comes into being naturally is pleasing to the eye, yes, Rigg thought. There is a beauty to the wildness of it. But there was also beauty in the Great North Road that wound along beside the Stashik River, and beauty in the patchwork of farms, and in the rough raw buildings of Leaky's Landing, which was such a new place, and in the ancient buildings of O, so many of them built of stone barged down the river, as if humans had moved a mountain to make O. There was beauty in Aressa Sessamo, too, by nature a shifting swampland, but made by humans into a huge island of raised earth on which a city ablaze with life had been raised, a forest of wooden buildings where an empire was governed and people lived their lives of joy and misery, of boredom and excitement, leaving paths behind them in a tangle that to Rigg seemed the very tapestry of life.

The natural land is beautiful, and it is beautiful again when it reclaims the ruins of humans who are gone. But when humans are there, that is the beauty I love the most, because it's a web I'm part of, it's the fabric that my own life, my own path, is helping to create. What humans make is not less beautiful than what comes into being out of wildness alone.

"We're wild, too," said Rigg aloud, because he needed to hear the words, and so he had to say them.

Olivenko was the only one near enough to him in the flyer to look up at the sound of his voice.

"We're wild," said Rigg. "We humans. We shape nature, but our shapes are also natural. We shouldn't say that because humans shaped a place, it's therefore unnatural."

"Maybe we shouldn't say it," said Olivenko, "but I think that if you look at the meanings of the words, whatever humans do is unnatural."

"But that's the mistake, for us to think that humans aren't also a part of nature."

Olivenko looked out of the flyer at the ground they were passing over, the high thick cushion of leaves only beginning to turn color in preparation for winter. "Not a particularly prominent part of it *here,*" he said.

"No. We've never touched this place." Then he laughed with a little bitterness. "Except, of course, when the starships crashed so hard they blew rocks into the sky to thicken and brighten the Ring so that at night it reflects enough light to see by. And raised great circling cliffs like Upsheer, and killed almost all the natural life of Garden, and replaced it with the plants and animals of Earth. Except for that, which means that all of Garden is so vastly shaped by human hands that nothing we're seeing here is 'natural.'"

"Well, I can't argue with that," said Olivenko. "Except to say that when humans leave it alone, nature comes back and closes the gaps the way the sea fills in behind each passing fish. What we're seeing down there is natural now, even if it was once reshaped by human action."

"But now it'll be reshaped by mice," said Rigg.

"Humans masquerading as mice," said Olivenko. "But I don't think they'll be cutting down the trees."

"If they wanted to cut them down," said Rigg, "they'd find a way. That's what humans do."

"And if they wanted to build them up?"

"They'd plant them like an orchard."

"Or slaughter each other as they did in Vadeshfold," said Olivenko, "and let the trees come back and plant themselves."

"I really hate philosophy," murmured Loaf. "You talk and talk, and in the end, you don't know any more than you did."

"Maybe less," said Rigg, "because I thought I had an idea, and now Olivenko makes me wonder whether I did or not."

"One idea is as worthless as another," said Loaf. "Until you actually do something about it, and then it's the action, not the word, that matters."

"Who's philosophizing now?" asked Olivenko. "We take action because of the words we believe in, the stories that we think are true, or intend to make true."

"I don't think so," said Loaf. "I think we do what we do because we desire it. And then we make up stories about why the thing we did was right, and the thing that other people did was wrong."

"Or both," said Rigg. "It works both ways, all the time. We act because of our stories; we make up stories to explain or excuse the way we acted."

But the trees don't do that, or the squirrels, thought Rigg. They just do what they do. And they can't change what they do, because they don't have any of this philosophy.

"Our destination is the shore where humans are most often seen," said the flyer. "Far in the north."

"When we get closer," said Rigg, "skim the coast. I'll tell you then where to set this flyer down."

"What will you look for, to decide?" asked Olivenko.

"I don't know," said Rigg. "Wherever the paths are thickest and most recent, so we have the best chance of meeting people."

"Of getting killed in our sleep on the first night there," said Olivenko.

"We didn't come here to *avoid* the people," said Rigg.

"Can't save 'em if we can't see 'em," said Loaf.

Probably can't save them even if we do see them. "If it turns out I picked a bad spot, we can go back and pick another," said Rigg.

"But you can't appear to us here in this flyer," said Olivenko. "Right? Unless you took the flyer up to exactly the same path and matched the flight perfectly, because the path remains behind us in the air."

Rigg turned and saw their paths stretch back along the route they had just flown. "That's right."

"I wonder how far you have to go upward," said Olivenko, "until our paths stop being part of the sky of Garden, and remain inside a ship."

"Every starship when it crashed here had human beings aboard," said Rigg. "I should have looked for the paths, the incoming trajectories."

"You should have looked to see if their paths during the voyage stayed with the ship," said Umbo, who was finally joining in the conversation.

"I will the next time we're at a starship," said Rigg. "I should have done it before, but I had other things on my mind."

"That's right," said Umbo, "blame it on me for being so clumsy as to leave corpses lying around to distract you."

"You may not have killed them," said Rigg, "but you made them. Didn't your mother teach you to clean up your own messes?"

They had to traverse the whole of Larfold, from the south to the northern shore. The wallfold continued far out to sea—Rigg remembered that from the maps in the library, but most clearly from the huge map inside the Tower of O; despite the many other maps he'd seen, that one remained the true map to Rigg, the way he pictured the world. A globe with wallfolds delineated on its face, the Walls stretching out over land and sea alike.

"I wonder why they went underwater here," said Param. "Why not build boats and live on the shore, and sail where they wanted? Why go *into* the sea?"

"Better climate?" suggested Olivenko.

"I think it has to do with how they managed to handle the breathing problem," said Umbo.

"There wasn't a breathing problem until they went under the sea," said Param. Rigg hated the scorn in her voice, especially when she talked to Umbo.

But Umbo answered her scorn for scorn. "You don't start living underwater unless you already have a way of surviving there."

"They didn't suddenly start having babies with gills," said Param, "and then decide to go swimming."

"But they *did* start swimming fulltime within a few hundred years of the start of the colony," said Umbo. "Why would they do that unless they already had a way to breathe?"

Loaf said, "Why are you two arguing about it when we'll be there in a very little while, and then we can go into the past if we have to and see what we find out. See if they're even human anymore. From what Olivenko said about the death of the king, these are monsters that dragged Knosso out of a boat and drowned him. Maybe they've turned into sharks with hands."

When they reached the coast, Rigg had the flyer soar above the northern beaches, which is the general region where the Odinfolders' books said the Larfolders had established their one long-abandoned colony. Here along the coast there were many paths, and recent ones. But they all led out of the water and then back into it, like the tracks of turtles returning to shore to spawn. Rigg wondered if they would still count as human if the Larfolders had started laying eggs like turtles.

He tried to trace the paths out into the water. He could easily follow the paths when they ran just under the waves, but the deeper they were, the harder it was for Rigg to sense them. And they seemed to meander randomly. And why not? Underwater, the Larfolders could swim anywhere. There were no roads they had to stay on. Mostly they stayed away from the shore, out in deeper water, behind the breakers that gleamed in shifting white ribbons, and deep, where Rigg could barely sense them.

Returning to gaze at the paths that led onto land, Rigg tried to find some meaning, some pattern in the tracks. He failed. "When they come to shore," said Rigg, "it isn't for fresh water to drink."

"If they solved the breathing problem, the drinking problem couldn't have been too hard," said Param. She had saved a little scorn for Rigg, too.

"I bet the peeing problem was even easier," said Umbo.

"But cooked food," said Rigg. "That's the challenge. Human teeth need cooked food. We don't have the massive jaws and molars of chimps or australopithecines."

"How did they ever find a recipe for underwater bread?" said Umbo.

"I think they specialize in seaweed salad," said Rigg.

"What *do* they come ashore for?" asked Loaf, a little impatiently.

"We'll find out soon enough, once we land," said Rigg.

"They come to the beach for human sacrifice," said Param. "There's hardly a wallfold that hasn't invented it at one time or another."

"I wonder what it says about human beings that we keep inventing that particular excuse for murder," said Olivenko.

"It's an easy way to dispose of excess prisoners of war without offending a taboo against killing those who surrendered," said Param.

"Was that one of the theories you read?" asked Loaf.

"Yes," said Param, sounding quite prepared to take on any challenges.

"In my experience," said Loaf, "soldiers don't *have* a taboo against killing helpless prisoners. It's hard to get them not to."

Suddenly the paths below changed from individual forays onto land into a huge array of interlocking paths. Thousands and thousands of them, ranging from ten thousand years ago to the past few days. "Set down here," said Rigg to the flyer.

The flyer swerved to shore and gently settled to the ground about fifteen meters above the highwater line. "This is where they hold their annual beach party and sports tournament," said Rigg.

"Really?" asked Param, sounding skeptical.

"I have no idea," said Rigg. "But hundreds of them at a time come to shore here, and they've been doing it for a long, long time. From the beginning—their first colony was only a few kilometers farther inland."

"Maybe all those solitary shore visits you saw were women giving birth," said Param. "Maybe they have to come to land for that."

"Or men who got thrown out of the house by untrusting wives," said Umbo.

In answer, Rigg got out of the flyer and strode toward the water. There were no humans on the beach, but since he knew they often returned, he figured he'd meet them soon enough.

Rigg had never felt large quantities of sand beneath his feet before. It was hard to walk in sand; it kept sliding and he kept slipping.

Sure enough, in sand higher above the water, there *were* tracks—normal human footprints. "They don't have webbed feet," said Rigg.

"Or maybe they clip the webs between their toes, as we do with our toenails," said Param.

Loaf was looking at the tracks. "There might be toe-webs after all. That slight dusting of sand right . . . here."

Rigg saw what he was indicating, thin lines between the foremost toes on only a couple of the footprints. But Rigg had seen other such artifacts in the tracks of animals and men in the forests of Ramfold throughout his childhood. "Is that real, or just wind-blow?" asked Rigg.

"Could be either," said Loaf. "How long do we wait?"

"Well," said Rigg, "now that we've passed through the Wall, I don't see why we can't go back into the past to the most recent gathering of just a few of them. We'll go to them, since we can't signal them to come to us."

"We're using the Larfold flyer," said Umbo, "and yet the expendable hasn't come to us and the ship hasn't tried to talk to us beyond acknowledging the command to send the flyer."

"We're not looking for the expendable anyway," said Param. "I'm glad it's not here."

"The expendables are too powerful to ignore them," said Rigg. "Umbo's question is a good one, but Param's point is also good."

"We can't both be right," said Param.

"Yes you can," said Rigg, "and you are. We don't have to search for the expendable right now, but we also have to be sharply aware that whatever he's doing right now, it's not *nothing*, and might be dangerous to us."

"Very delicately done," said Olivenko.

"What a dance between your rival siblings," said Loaf.

"And how completely unhelpful for you to call attention to it," said Rigg.

"We're not at war and we're not rivals," said Param. "Or siblings."

"How can a peasant boy be a rival to a queen?" asked Umbo.

"What about my idea of going back in time to meet them?" asked Rigg.

"Why not go all the way back, and watch them go into the water?" asked Olivenko.

"If we could be sure we could watch undetected, I'd agree," said Rigg. "But why not meet them now?"

"I'd rather meet them back when they were human," said Olivenko.

"But are *we* even human?" asked Rigg. "And for all we know, they're as human as we are right now."

"We can't make any decisions until we know more," said Param, "and we can't know more until we make those decisions."

"Why not have one of us go back and look?" asked Umbo. "I send you back, and snap you home to us if something goes wrong?"

Rigg nodded, but it was the nodding of thought, not a decision. "That's good. Safer in some ways. But then I'm the one seeing them. And what if I change something back then that affects us now?"

"You don't want to face them alone," said Loaf.

"I don't know if I'll understand enough of what I'm seeing," said Rigg. "And I don't know how seriously they'll take me if I'm alone. I'm just a kid."

"Not so young as you used to be," said Olivenko. "And never *just* a kid even then."

"I'm an experienced old soldier," said Loaf. "Experienced enough to know that when somebody is cautious about his own ability to judge, it means he's much better prepared to judge a situation than people who don't doubt their ability to judge."

"I'd like to be able to quote you on that," said Param, "but I'm not sure I know what you said."

"I said Rigg isn't as young as he thinks, but he's also right. We should all go together."

"Back to a time when we have no control over the flyer?" said Umbo.

"Who's being cautious now?" asked Param.

"We didn't have control over the flyer until the very end of our time in Vadeshfold," said Rigg. "We can handle a few weeks without it now." Rigg rose to his feet and held out his hands. "A few weeks ago, there was a group of three people—and their paths look as human as anybody's, if that helps. They came ashore here, then walked up near the river. Maybe they were harvesting river mussels or something, but they could have done that from the water."

"They still walk," said Umbo. "That's something. They haven't turned into seals or dolphins or some other aquatic mammal."

"Otters," said Rigg.

"Sharks with hands," said Olivenko, and the reminder of Knosso's fate stilled the nervous merriment that Rigg and Umbo had started.

They joined hands.

"Any mice with us?" asked Olivenko.

"Three," said Loaf.

"Eight," said Rigg at the same moment.

"Stealthy little bastards," said Loaf.

"No secrets anyway," said Rigg. "They know they can't hide from me, and we have no need to conceal what we do from them."

"Do you have the path we're jumping to?" asked Umbo.

"I do," said Rigg. "Take us back."

"You can do it yourself," Umbo reminded him.

"I'm not sure I can take all of us at once," said Rigg. "And you're stronger and better practiced. I'll aim, you loose the bow."

So Umbo did.

There were three women near the river, their backs to the group of Ramfolders. Standing over them was an expendable. Larex.

"I guess this means that the expendable knows more about the Larfolders than the other expendables thought," murmured Umbo.

"Or they held back the knowledge from the mice," said Param.

"Or the mice held it back from us," said Olivenko.

The expendable looked at them and waved. The women turned around to look.

"I think he heard us," said Rigg.

"They do have good hearing," said Param.

Rigg strode forward, and the expendable came rapidly to meet him. The women stayed where they were.

Rigg tried to keep his attention on Larex, who looked so much like Father that Rigg couldn't help being glad to see him, and so much like Vadesh and Odinex that he couldn't help but mistrust him. Still, his eyes strayed to the women, who looked clothed and naked at the same time. They certainly had some kind of garment that concealed their womanly shape, but the garment was absolutely the color of skin, so that they seemed also to be nude.

Were they even women, or did he think that only because their hair was so long?

Was that really hair, or something else? It seemed not to hang quite right.

The women stood up, and as they did, their clothing seemed to change, to move, to become something else. They were definitely women, and naked, and the clothing wasn't clothing at all. It was another creature, one on each woman, which rode them like a mantle, and changed shape to fit on them in different ways. It draped when they were sitting, but now it furled like the sails on a ship, rising up out of the way across their shoulders, so they could fight or run if need be.

And their hair was hair, but it had looked wrong because it was growing as much out of the other creature as out of their heads. No, it was growing entirely from the creature. While it rode atop their heads, the hair seemed to be in the normal place. But now they were bald, and the hair had been furled up in the creature.

"Let me guess," said Larex. "You're the folks from Ramfold who crossed the Wall into Vadeshfold a few weeks ago. What brings you here? And what brings you *now*, for that matter, since as far as I know you're still in Vadeshfold, heading for Odinfold."

"We are," said Rigg. "We made it to Odinfold, learned many interesting things, and then came back to a time only a few weeks from now to come through the Wall into Larfold. And then we shifted in time to here, because I saw the paths of these women."

"Bet you didn't see mine," said Larex with a smile.

"You know that I can't," said Rigg. "There's not much about the Larfolders in the logs of the other ships."

"Because we know how the Odinfolders blab," said Larex.

"So you can conceal what you know from the shared logs?" asked Rigg.

"Of course," said Larex. "When there's a compelling reason to."

"And what would that reason be?"

"When you take control of all the ships and expendables, then I imagine I'll be forced to tell you," said Larex, still smiling.

"So why not tell me now?" asked Rigg.

"You're the man from the future," said Larex. "Why not tell me whether I ever tell you?"

This was a game with no point. Rigg's instinct to like him had been wrong; his instinct to mistrust him, absolutely right. "We're here to meet the Larfold people," said Rigg. "And it seemed practical to meet them first when they happened to be on shore."

"I saw where your eyes went," said Larex. "You're fascinated by their naked bodies."

"I'm fifteen years old, I think," said Rigg. "My eye goes to naked women. But I'm more interested in their living clothing."

"But don't you recognize it?" asked Larex. He looked pointedly at Loaf.

"They're wearing facemasks?" asked Rigg.

"A related species," said Larex. "Let's say that what lives upriver, in Vadeshfold, is the primitive version. What the first colonists found here in Larfold was a much more evolved cousin."

"So you helped Vadesh develop this?" asked Loaf.

"Not at all," said Larex. "I never told him anything about these symbiotes."

"Why not?" asked Umbo.

"He was having so much fun developing his own," said Larex.

"You're a renegade," said Rigg.

"Not at all," said Larex. "We all lie to Vadesh."

For the first time, it occurred to Rigg that this statement might itself be a lie. The one certain thing was that the expendables all lied to humans. It was far more doubtful that they actually lied to each other. Much more likely they lied to humans about lying to Vadesh.

But that was too complicated to sort out now. "Do you have any objection to our talking to these women?" asked Rigg.

"Would it matter if I did?" asked Larex.

Rigg made no reply. It was obvious that Larex stood between

the women and the Ramfolders, and that neither group was going to come any nearer to each other than they were, until the expendable made some gesture.

Larex smiled, then strolled off to the side, so he was no longer between them. Then he nodded his head, and waved the two groups together.

The Larfold women moved hesitantly toward them. They were staring as curiously at the Ramfolders as Rigg and his party were at them.

"Hi," said Umbo.

"Oh, what a diplomat," murmured Param.

"They've never been through the Wall," said Olivenko. "They don't understand this language."

"Until they speak," said Rigg, "we can't tell what their language *is*." He held out his hand in an open gesture, somewhere between begging for food and offering a handshake.

They took it the first way—or maybe offering food was how they shook hands. One of the women reached into a pocket in her living mantle and drew out—something. Something raw and shiny and moving. Rigg let her put it in his hand, but she did not let go.

She said something.

Rigg didn't understand at first. And then he did. She wanted him to close his hand. Because the thing was alive, and if he didn't, it would get away.

So he enclosed it in his fist, and only then did she slip her fingers out of his grip.

Then she gestured toward her own mouth, pantomiming dropping the creature into her mouth and swallowing.

"It's a hospitality ritual," murmured Param.

Or else a clever way to introduce their symbiotes' larval form into his body. But Rigg did not speak the thought aloud. Instead he smiled, lifted his fist over his open mouth, and dropped the creature in.

It skittered up his tongue as if trying to escape. For a tiny fraction of a second, Rigg thought of biting down hard on the thing in his mouth to keep it in place, to kill it. But then he thought of a cockroach or small frog exploding in his mouth, filling it with the flavor of guts and death and animal poo, and so instead Rigg simply swallowed the thing whole.

It wiggled all the way down.

At least it had no claws to catch at him, or jaws to bite the inside of his gullet.

The woman who had given him the bug nodded. "Can you talk?" she asked.

"A little," said Rigg. They'd have to say a lot more than this before the language of the Wall made him fluent.

"You are naked," she said, indicating his body.

By this Rigg understood her to mean that he had no symbiote. He looked at Loaf.

"He is half naked," said the woman. "He has an ugly on his face."

"That he does," said Rigg. "But it wasn't all that pretty before."

The woman seemed mildly perplexed. Clearly Rigg did not understand the context well enough yet to make a joke.

"We come from beyond the Wall," said Rigg.

The women looked at each other in astonishment, and then at Larex, who smiled and nodded, giving that slight bow of his head that Rigg had never seen Father do, but which Vadesh had done all the time.

"You came through hell to speak to us," said the woman, and the others echoed the sentence. To Rigg, it seemed that this was some kind of quotation. Maybe a bit of scripture or an adage or a ritual greeting.

"Hell stepped aside to let us pass," Rigg answered. Yes, they had sort of passed through hell, or parts of it, when they first crossed the Wall into Vadeshfold. But they had only heard faint echoes of hell when they came through the Wall to Larfold just now.

The woman came and enfolded him in an embrace that was anything but ritualized. She meant it with her whole body. And in a moment the other two women had embraced him as well.

"I told them you were coming," said Larex.

"How did *you* know?" asked Rigg.

"When the Odinfolders made you," said Larex, "the purpose was to make Wall crossers who would visit every wallfold. Eventually you'll get everywhere."

"That's not an answer," said Rigg.

"The knife is a communicator," said Larex. "I've been following your movements."

The women released him from their embrace—then stroked his body, his hair, his face.

"You live in the sea," said Rigg to the women.

"The sea," they answered, saying nothing but that word, several times, and meaning different things each time they said it. Rigg understood all the meanings: Home. Dark-and-dangerous. Eating place.

"Why did you come on shore?" asked Rigg.

"Why don't you come into the sea?" she asked in reply.

"I would die there," said Rigg. "But your body was made to walk on land."

"My body on land," she said. "And my mantle in the sea. Two friends made one by blood."

This last phrase seemed alien to Rigg, as if he were incapable of understanding some nuance that he had no mental preparation to receive. Clearly she was indicating the mantle when she spoke of friends made one, but Loaf didn't speak of his facemask as some kind of friend.

"Hard to believe it's a facemask," murmured Olivenko.

"Something like it," said Rigg. "I think we've answered the question of how they breathe." He said this in the language of Odinfold, which they had spoken so long in the library that it was the first that came to mind.

Loaf stepped forward. "Can you show us how this mantle lets you live in the water?"

"You don't know?" asked a woman.

Loaf shrugged.

"Then what is *that* for?" she asked, pointing to his face.

"Ugly. Ugly," murmured the other two women, as if they were captioning a picture of Loaf's facemask.

And it was true. Where Loaf's facemask made him misshapen, replacing his eyes with asymmetric imitations, their mantles seemed to blend seamlessly into their bodies. When they moved, it was as if the women's own skin moved. And maybe it *was* part of their skin now.

The woman who had fed a bug to Rigg passed her hand up the front of her body and closed her eyes. At once her mantle shifted, rising up her neck like someone pulling off a sweater. It covered her whole head, then suddenly sucked in and clung as if to a skeleton. New eyes—bigger ones—extruded from the sides of her head, like the eyes of a fish. And when she opened her mouth to speak, a membrane covered her mouth. It deadened her voice, though she could still speak through it.

"I can go in the water now," she said. "But I know that I am not myself a waterbreather. My friend breathes the water, and passes the result to me in my blood." She looked at Loaf. "He can't go in the water, not with that one. It's only an animal."

"And your mantle is not?"

"It is the companion of my heart," she said. "It is the sister of my soul."

"Air in the water," chanted another.

"Light in the darkness," murmured the third.

"So you all have these mantles?" asked Rigg.

"Without them we would die," said the leader.

"So why did you murder my father?" demanded Param.

So much for diplomacy, thought Rigg.

"Your father?" asked the woman who led them.

"Knosso, king of Stashiland," said Param.

"He crossed over far to the west of here," said Olivenko. "Then you dragged him out of his boat and drowned him."

The women backed away, puzzled by the accusation and by Param's vehemence in saying it.

"Do you mean the man who dances on water?"

To Rigg that seemed as apt a description of travel in a small boat as these people were likely to see it. "Yes," said Rigg.

"But he isn't dead," said one woman.

"Should we fetch him?" asked another.

"Yes," said Rigg. "In our wallfold, we thought him dead."

"Why should he be dead?" they asked. "Was he deserving of death?"

"No," said Olivenko, perhaps a bit too fervently. "So are you saying that this man-who-dances-on-water is still alive?"

"Of course," said the leading woman. "Shall we bring him now, or do you have more questions to ask us first?"

"Please bring him, yes," said Rigg.

"I thought you'd want to see him as soon as I saw you," said one of the other women.

"I know he'll want to see *you*," said the third.

"Let me send out a call for him," said the leader. Without further discussion, she ran to the nearest water—the river, in this case—and ducked her mantled head into it. She stayed a long time—at least it seemed long to Rigg, who instinctively held his breath as if his own head were also underwater.

Then she lifted her head out of the water, dropping a spray of water that caught the sunlight like stars.

She sat on the riverbank and laughed. "He's very happy," she called out. "He's coming now."

"Knosso," murmured Olivenko. "Is it really possible he didn't die?"

"They must have had a mantle waiting for him," said Loaf.

"Of course we did," said one of the remaining women. "Didn't the Landsman tell us he was going to float to us on the waves?"

"So when you dragged him under the water—"

"It was to keep his evil wife from killing him," said a woman.

"And he had so many questions saved up for us," said the other woman.

"I can't wait like this," said Param, sounding distressed. "I can't. I won't." And then she disappeared.

Of course, thought Rigg. By slicing time until she sees Father Knosso come out of the water, she will spend only moments waiting, while we might spend hours.

But it wasn't hours, it wasn't many minutes, until, out of the waves of the sea and the currents of the river, there arose a host of hundreds of mantle-wearing people, men and women, striding out of the water, their mantles receding from their faces, eyes appearing where they should be in human faces, mouths opening, smiling, calling greetings to the women, who called out in reply. Here, meet these people from overWall.

Then the Larfolders turned and parted and made a way for one man who strode laughing from the waves and fairly ran up the beach toward them. "Where's my Param?" he cried. "They said my daughter was here!"

Rigg knew that Param couldn't hear when she was slicing time, but she didn't have to. She must have recognized his face as soon as it emerged from under the receding mantle, and she became visible again, running across the sand to embrace her father.

He held her for a long time, stroking her in the gentle way the women had stroked Rigg after their embrace. "Param, Param," he murmured, and other words that Rigg could not hear at a distance. He did not want to interrupt their reunion, but this was Father Knosso, and he could not stop himself from walking tentatively nearer.

The man looked up from his daughter's hug, and then managed to step from the embrace without quite breaking it. Instead he gathered her into his forward movement as he strode to Rigg and then stopped only a couple of meters from him.

In Fall Ford, Rigg had rarely seen himself—only a few people owned mirrors, and since he didn't shave, there was no reason for him to consult the mirror in Nox's house. But once they arrived in O and later in Aressa Sessamo, Rigg had many opportunities to see his own face looking back at him from the glass; in Flacommo's house, there were so many mirrors that one could hardly escape from the sight of oneself.

So Rigg knew what he was seeing when he looked for the first time into his father's face. There were no images of him in Aressa Sessamo—a dead male from a female-centered royal line that was utterly discredited by the People's Revolution? It would be twice-over treason to treasure his visage.

Still, someone might have told Rigg how perfectly he resembled his dead father. Especially since he wasn't dead after all.

Umbo came up between them, looking back and forth. "No wonder my father hated the sight of me," said Umbo. "Never once, when he looked into my face, could he see his own face looking back at him like this."

"He said you would grow up to cross the Wall," said Knosso.

"He never told me you existed, or that I was your son," said Rigg.

"He wasn't supposed to. How could a child keep a secret like that? Better for you not to know until it was time."

"And is it time now, Father?" asked Rigg.

"Oh, and past time." Knosso opened up his arms and Rigg stepped into the embrace that Ramex, the Golden Man, had never given him, though Rigg had always called him father, and had loved him. But that love had been misplaced. This was the man, and Rigg was his son, and he belonged inside these arms the way these Larfolders belonged inside their mantles. I am a part of him. I was made from him. I am his. He is mine. And Rigg wept against his father's shoulder as his father's hands stroked and stroked him, and Knosso murmured again and again, "Rigg Sessamekesh, my son, my son."

CHAPTER 21
Companions

What surprised Rigg was how quickly it faded, the emotion he first felt in his father's embrace. It was pleasing, of course, that the man was so moved to see him. But while Rigg had longed for a father's affection, this was not the father from whom he had wanted it. The man he knew by that name had been unaffectionate and demanding, but he was also brilliantly intelligent, difficult but not impossible to please, and full of knowledge and wisdom about every aspect of the world. For months at a time, Rigg had had that father's undivided attention, had lived in constant dialogue with him.

Knosso had Rigg's face, but who was he, who had he ever been in Rigg's life? His presence here was the answer to some interesting questions from Rigg's time in Flacommo's house. There would be much to talk about. But for Rigg, that was all he could ever be. A resource, a person of interest. The lost opportunity of childhood was still out of reach. Rigg could go backward in time, but not in age. He was too old to need the sort of fatherhood that Knosso's arms were promising.

The embrace ended. Knosso held him at arm's length, to look at him again. It made Rigg feel uncomfortable, fearing just a little that the quick fading of Rigg's affection might be visible in his face.

"Here's your old apprentice Olivenko," said Rigg, turning to include the scholar-soldier in their conversation.

Olivenko came forward, but not with his usual bold stride. He was diffident, almost shy. "Sir," he said.

"Olivenko!" cried Knosso, shaking his hand, gripping his shoulder. "My companion in study, my fetcher of books and hearer of questions! What kind of scholar did you become?"

"No scholar at all," said Olivenko. "The library thought I had been too close to a certain runaway king."

"So I ruined your career after all," said Knosso, "just by being myself."

"I took a different path is all," said Olivenko. "The city guard didn't mind that I already knew my way around the library and could speak to members of the highest social classes. It made me useful as a sort of soldier."

"Then we have much to talk about, my friend—may I call you my friend, now that you're a man grown? I've found the answers to so many questions, and then so many more questions beyond those. And as you can see, I've found my way to a life under the sea, in a world far larger and lovelier than anything our poor folk of Ramfold ever made for themselves ashore."

Then Knosso turned—as kings must always turn, when surrounded by courtiers—to see who else had come to greet him on the beach.

"You must be Umbo," said Knosso. "Our landsman told me you were my son's true friend and fellow time-shifter."

Landsman, thought Rigg. The Larfolders' term for their expendable, apparently. Larex, the Odinfolders had called him.

Umbo tried an awkward bow, but Knosso laughed. "I'm no king here, my boy, and there's no bowing. What would a bow mean underwater? There we swim below the one we wish to honor, and turn our faces upward. But we have no kings in our sea. I had to explain the term to them, when I first arrived. It was strange, that I knew their language, which I had never heard before, and yet they did not know a word of mine."

"The Wall gives us languages, Father," said Param.

"So I guessed, my dear, although I could not fathom *how*," said Knosso. "And this one, this giant, is the innkeeper Loaf, a mighty soldier and protector. If I were a king, I'd make a lord of you for your service to my son and daughter along the way. As it is, I have to admire the ugliness of the Companion old Vadesh bred for you."

"You know Vadesh?" asked Rigg.

"*Of* him, I know *of* him," said Knosso. "But his only visit to Larfold came ten thousand years ago, and others must tell you of that. Meanwhile, I have to boast a little. Olivenko, my plan to cross the Wall by water turned out very well!"

"To us, it looked as if you had drowned," said Olivenko. "Murdered by some faceless water creatures."

"Faceless," said Knosso. He walked to the Larfolders clustered around the original group of three women and called out to them in their language—which Rigg understood quite easily now. "Show him what 'faceless' looks like!"

At once the mantles of all the Larfolders rose up from their backs around their heads, at first like collars, then cowls, and finally down over their faces like a prisoner's hood. But then, as if they had been sucked inward, the mantles clung tightly to the bones of their faces. There were no features then, except a slight protuberance over the nose and a hollowness where the eyes should be.

In a moment, though, a new pair of large round eyes sprouted on both sides of every head, at the temples, and where the ears had been, the slits of gills opened up. And at the mouth, a gaping toothy hole opened, the lips puckering and unpuckering like those of little fishes, rather than the gash of a shark's mouth.

"Those are the creatures that I saw," said Olivenko, almost laughing in relief. "Not monsters at all."

"Monsters indeed," murmured Param.

After only a moment of display, the eyes and gills and mouth dissolved into the skin again, the mantle unclung and rose back over the head and then slacked down the back.

Rigg was fascinated and horrified. What a perfect adaptation to the sea, yet how inhuman.

"The creature must have evolved to fit a very different creature, native to Garden," said Rigg, "and it was only making do with animals from Earth. The people who arrived to colonize were merely the next in line."

"They thought it was dangerous at first, I imagine," said Loaf.

"Let others tell it!" cried Knosso. "I know the story, but it belongs to those whose ancestors lived it, not to me. Mother Mock," he said, addressing the leader of the women they had first met, "you and the Aunts should tell the tale."

"And we will," said Mother Mock. "But with so many ashore, what will we eat? And these are freshwater drinkers, without their mantles—the river is hardly fit to drink here, with all the upland silt it carries, and saltwater backwash."

"I am Auntie Esh," said one of the other women, "and this is Auntie Wind. She's the talker, Auntie Wind, and she'll tell the tale."

"I will," said Wind, "to any who wish to hear it. Bend your bodies to the land, my fingerlings! For you'll be long ashore before this tale is told!"

Rigg sat down when he saw the Larfolders doing so; Knosso sat beside him on one side, and pulled Param down on the other side. She clung to her father, looking very young and vulnerable, and for the first time Rigg truly understood that she was, in fact, at least as young as he was. Not since their mother had tried to have her killed had she taken such a daughterly pose, and even then she had been trying to display toughness, independence, strength. Now, in the presence of her father, she had no toughness in her. It was as if all the fear and anxiety of the past year had been gathered up and now, by clinging to Knosso, she was finally able to let it slip away from her.

"We came as men and women to this shore," said Auntie Wind, "borne like dust through space until we settled as river silt into these waters. In those days we did not know our Companions-in-the-waves, except as jellyfish floating on the water. We thought they were from Earth, and dangerous because of their sting. But they had no sting, and were not from Earth. Instead they waited to cling to the noses of animals that came to the river to drink, and turn them into waterbeasts. The Companions would live on their blood, and give birth into their skin; they filled them with a love of the sea, so they would never stray from Grandmother Sea."

In their language, "grandmother" and "sea" began with the same sound; it was a lovely name.

"At first, when Companions clung to the faces of our ancestors, we panicked and tore them off, which damaged the humans deep inside, for Companions embed themselves deeply in an instant. For a long time, the humans were wary of the Companions, and tried to poison them or drive them away.

"Then came time for a great feast, of landbeasts and water-beasts, cooked over fires, and Vadesh came for the first time, visiting from his land to the south. The Landsman and Vadesh talked then face to face, for Vadesh wanted to show the people that the Companions were not perilous to us. 'It is too evolved into its niche for what I want,' said Vadesh, 'but here by the shore you have a need for it. Why not divide your people into two, those who take them as Companions and those who don't? That's what I have done,' he said to the Landsman.

"The Landsman said, 'I forbid no one; I have neither the will nor the power to do so. Neither will I command them, though, or force them. Let them wear the Companion if they wish, and see whether they wish to live the life it makes available to them."

From that day, there were only two who chose to wear the Companion, and it frightened the others and they shunned them. Lonely and frightened, they turned only to each other and the life under the water, where they soon mated. Do not return to land to spawn, the Companions said to them. Give birth in this place, where we can also give your children a Companion all his life.

"So the child was born, and all the humans discovered that even birth could happen underwater, and the child's lifelong Companion peeled away from its parent and gave him gills for his first breath there in the river's mouth. The child could swim from birth, and breathe in the water like a fish; but as he lengthened and aged, he was brought into the land of air and song and standing up, where he learned to walk, as we teach all our children to walk.

"But because of the Companions, they learn quickly, standing upright on the first attempt, walking within the hour, and letting speech pour from their mouths with perfect understanding. Underwater we speak into the drum of the flesh-over-the-mouth, and in the kiss of speech we understand each other. But here on land, one can speak to all at the same time, the way I speak to you today."

The audience murmured its ascent.

"After five years, another couple went into the water and took upon themselves Companions, and three years, and then one, and then another, and there were ten couples and their new children living under the sea.

"Then came the slimeworm, the disease that made the flesh rot on the body and slough away and leave only bone and agony and death. Who could live when the slimeworm crawled through his body? Only those who went beneath the waves—there the slimeworm died, and the Companion healed the flesh.

"All who were alive and could crawl or be carried came into the water, and the Companions took them all, and saved them from the slimeworm. So beautiful was the Companionable life that no longer did we call the slimeworm terrible, or think of its coming as a plague. Instead it was the slimeworm that pushed us into the water, and so the slimeworm was our friend. Only in wallfolds lacking in Companions was the slimeworm a disaster and a tragedy."

Rigg had never heard of such a plague, and yet she spoke as if it were something that had spread in more than one wallfold. Why would Auntie Wind believe such a thing, if the expendables didn't tell them about it? So did that mean that it was true—that it was a plague that could pass through the Wall? Or was it yet another lie of the expendables? Why was there no memory of it in Ramfold?

And then Rigg remembered the tales of the White Death and the Walking Death. They were more parable or allegory than true history, or so he had always thought. Could it be the same thing that Auntie Wind was speaking of? If so, then it must have come much earlier in history than Rigg had believed. He wondered if Param had run across these stories in every wallfold. But she was on the other side of Knosso, so Rigg could not ask quietly enough not to be overheard. He did not wish to interrupt the tale.

"In the water we lived for many generations, losing track of days in the trackless sea. We battled great sea monsters in those days, some brought from Earth and others native to this world, restored after the cataclysm. We tried and failed to swim through the Wall. We spread along the whole of our coast, and made our colonies far out in the sea and up the deep rivers. Always we returned to the land to speak and sing and dance from time to time.

"On one such time, the Landsman came to us and brought Vadesh to us yet again. Vadesh spoke of how many of the people of Vadeshfold had rejected the Companions he had made for them, even though the Companions also saved *them* from the slimeworm. The solitary people slew the men and women who accepted the Companions, and so the Companionable slew to defend themselves, until no humans of any kind were left alive in his land.

"'Come and wear this land-companion,' Vadesh invited us, but when we asked him, 'What does it do that our Companions cannot do?' his answer was full of things we did not care to do, and lacked the one thing most needed: The Companions he had made could not easily swim, and breathing underwater was quite impossible.

"'Then we will have none of them!' our motherfolk declared, and our fatherkin turned their backs on him and mantled themselves and plunged back under the waves, and Vadesh left us, sorrowing, while the Landsman laughed at him and said, 'I told you they were content with what they have, and will not trade it for something less.'

"'It is not less,' old Vadesh said, 'it is more.' But still he walked away, and in this wallfold he has not been seen or talked with since."

And that was the end of Auntie Wind's story.

"Is that all?" asked Rigg quietly. "It doesn't feel like much of a story."

"But it's not a story," said Knosso. "I assure you, when they make up stories here, they know how to make an ending, one that would leave you gasping or laughing, I can promise you! But this was simply an answer to your question. No one authored it, Auntie Wind just made it up as she went along."

"But it was poetry," said Param.

"So it was," said Knosso. "But that's the way of speech among the Larfolk. What is the point of coming up onto land, if the speech is not beautiful as well as clear and loud and spoken to many at once? This is their library, their orchestra, and their dance. Watch now, and listen, as they sing it back to her and dance the story to make it true."

To Rigg's surprise, the gathered Larfolders really did sing what she had said to them, word for word the same, only now with many beautiful melodic lines. And when they were done with that, they sang it again, only this time without the words. Yet such was the power of the music that when Rigg heard each tune, he knew the words that went along with it. And with the singing, in many harmonies, the people also danced, and in their movements the slimeworm made their skin slough off, and the mothers birthed their young, and the men explored and fought the mighty beasts of the deep, and Vadeshex came as a comic supplicant, carrying pantomimed facemasks as if they were made of especially noxious dung. Loaf laughed the loudest at this.

When the buffoonish Vadeshex left, the people swam their dance and cheered the tale, its teller, and the singers and dancers.

"Now that song is part of their lives for at least this generation," said Knosso. "And if they forget it, some later Auntie Wind will echo it in other words, and it will be sung to other tunes. Nothing is lost. This is their library, the poetry of their life on land."

"No wonder you love this place," said Olivenko. "If only you could have sent a message to us."

"But I did," said Knosso. "I told the Landsman to tell the Gardener to tell you I was safe. I wouldn't be coming back, of course, since I had left only in time to save my life, and those who wanted me dead would make short work of me if I returned."

"Who wanted you dead?" asked Olivenko.

"My wife," said Knosso. "Hagia told me herself that she had no choice but to have me killed, so that if my researches didn't take me out of the wallfold, then someone's knife or a bit of poison would do the job before too long. I thought it was kind of her to warn me."

"Kind!" cried Param. "She tried to kill me, too!"

"That was wrong of her," said Knosso.

"That's all? Wrong of her?"

"Kings- and queens-in-the-tent have been killing their mates and children for a good many generations, and parents and siblings, too. That's what royalty's about among the Sessamids. Didn't they teach you history?"

"They didn't teach me anything," said Param.

"We got the People's History," said Rigg.

"We always thought that it was lies, made up by the People's Revolutionary Council to discredit the royal family," said Umbo.

"It would be hard to invent stories of worse atrocities than those the royal family inflicted on each other," said Knosso. "But no matter. She failed to kill you, and here you are, and I am happier than I ever thought I'd be."

"So you left your daughter to save your own life," said Rigg, "knowing that her life was also in danger."

"I was rarely allowed to see my daughter," said Knosso, "and I had no reason to think that Hagia would harm her heir. Killing children is common but not universal among the royals, or there'd be no royals left. Usually it's done upon remarriage, so that only the children of the new mate will be left alive to inherit. I had no way of knowing that your mother would remarry after I left. But it makes sense to me now. I well knew Haddamander Citizen, an ambitious man. I thought that when your mother died, it would likely be at his hand; it never occurred to me that they would mate, until the Landsman told it to me as a bit of gossip from my old life."

"He couldn't have protected her if he had stayed," said Olivenko. "He couldn't have protected himself."

"I knew that," said Param. To Rigg she added, "But it's sweet of you to be outraged on my behalf."

I don't like the way these people think, thought Rigg. When I saved Param, I didn't understand that she was as utterly arrogant and self-obsessed as Mother; and now I find that Knosso is the same. A nice man, a good scholar, but unable to see past his own needs and desires. Now, though, I understand Param's behavior since we left Aressa Sessamo. She's a child of her family.

"Thank you for giving me to the Gardener, sir," said Rigg, "to raise me outside of court."

"It was the only way to keep a pathfinder like you alive," said Knosso. "In the royal house, as soon as word of your gift seeped out, those who believed in the female line would have had you killed, for fear you'd use your powers to displace the queens from the Tent of Light and take it back for the male line."

"You knew I was a pathfinder?" asked Rigg.

"You were tracing the paths as soon as you could crawl."

"But how would you know?" asked Rigg.

"Because I'm a pathfinder too, of course," said Knosso. "But nothing like you are, according to the Landsman. He says you can see paths a hundred years old."

"Ten thousand years," said Umbo. "And older."

Knosso beamed. "I knew you would be something, my son!"

"What paths do you see, sir?" asked Rigg.

"I can barely make out paths ten years gone. And those are blurred and hard to trace. Easier to track yesterday's path, or last month's. But it did mean none could sneak up on me—don't you find it convenient to be able to sense paths behind you as easily as those in front?" Knosso squeezed Rigg's shoulder. "I've been out of the water a long time now, and Mother Monk and the Aunties even longer. We also spread our gills to show you, and now the gills are dry. So we'll return to the water for the night, I think. Will you stay here on land, so we can talk tomorrow?"

"Of course," said Param.

"We have so many questions," said Olivenko.

"I never thought I'd meet a king," said Umbo.

"Well, technically you have," said Knosso, indicating Rigg. "Though I'm not dead, I think I can be considered to have abdicated my right to the Tent of Light. So Rigg is king, if you believe in kings. And if you don't, then Param's next in line to be the queen. Or neither of them is anything, if you're republican."

"More to the point," said Loaf, "we're not in Ramfold, so we really don't care anymore, and won't care in the future, either, unless we decide to go back to Ramfold."

"A born republican," said Knosso, "but I remember meeting you as a soldier in my army, I believe."

"Yes," said Loaf. "We met once at a victory celebration, sir, but why would you remember me?"

"Left to myself, I wouldn't have," said Knosso. "But my Companion brings all my memories to life, and the moment I saw you, the mantle saw behind your facemask and knew you, and replayed for me the memory of when we met."

Loaf bowed his head. "I am republican," he said, "but that doesn't mean I bear any enmity against the royal house."

"I'm glad to hear it," said Knosso. "And now good-night. Sleep peacefully in the sharp hard air of land; I'll be rocked to sleep in cool darkness for another night."

The Larfolders were on their feet, walking into sea and river, their mantles rising, covering them, their gills emerging as they sank or splashed or launched themselves into the water. And soon the Ramfolders were alone on the shore, and filled with wonder, all of them.

All of them but Rigg, who was filled with something else. There had been a plague at the very beginning of human life on Garden that forced the Larfolders into the water. And the expendables had told each other far more than the Odinfolders had known, or admitted they knew. Had the mice known all this?

Rigg looked around and saw that there had been no mice here listening today. Good. For the moment I know something that they don't know. Or at least, I know something that they knew but didn't want to share with me. Either way, I'm ahead of them by just a little. For I know now what the mice intend to do, and I know that I must stop them, and I cannot do the thing from here, from Larfold, and I cannot do the things that I must do with anyone beside me. I will have to act alone, and quickly, before it can be known or guessed by anyone what I must do.

"May I borrow the knife from you, Umbo?" Rigg asked.

"Of course," said Umbo, drawing it out and handing it to him.

"Thank you," said Rigg. "I'll try to return it as soon as possible after this moment."

Rigg started walking back to the flyer.

"Where are you going?" asked Umbo, falling into step beside him.

"To Vadeshfold," said Rigg.

"That liar? That snake? What for?"

"I need to ask him something," said Rigg.

"And what might *that* be?" Umbo asked.

"I need to ask him for a facemask," said Rigg. "And I need to know when Ram Odin died, and which wallfold he was in when he did."

"You're going back," said Umbo. "You're going to talk to him."

"No," said Rigg. "That might undo the whole world. It might undo ourselves."

"Nothing we do undoes ourselves," said Umbo. "We've had that discussion too many times. Or at least Loaf and I have."

"I'm going forward," said Rigg.

"You can't do that," said Umbo. "Only Param moves forward in time."

"Not true," said Rigg. "All of us move forward, at the rate of one minute per minute."

"Well, yes, that way. What do you mean? That you're going to just . . . pass the time away from us? Take me with you! I can keep you company."

"The thing I'm going to do, Umbo, I wouldn't ask you to do, and you wouldn't do it if I did."

"I'll do whatever you think is right. Don't you believe me, Rigg? I'm over being jealous of you. I really am. I'm your friend, and loyal to you to the end."

"I'll come back to you and give this knife to you when my job is done, if I succeed in it."

"What job?"

But they were at the flyer now, and Rigg solemnly shook Umbo's hand, a thing which he couldn't remember ever having done before. "You're the most powerful shifter in the world," Rigg said to him. "Learn all you can from Knosso—he's wise and clever, and he's a pathfinder, too. So if you need to go into the past the way a pathfinder can help you do, he'll help you."

"He looks like you, Rigg, but he's not you. I don't know him."

"Get to know him, then. And please don't be angry with

Param. She's what she was raised to be, and she's trying to get over it."

"I'm not angry," said Umbo. "I just don't like her."

"I know," said Rigg. "And that's a shame, considering that you're still in love with her, and it doesn't make sense for either of you to marry anybody but each other."

And with those words, Rigg left a flabbergasted Umbo behind him as he jogged up the ramp into the flyer and gave the command to take him to the Vadesh Wall.

CHAPTER 22
Warning

When Umbo walked back to the others, they were full of questions. They had seen the flyer take off, and when Umbo explained that Rigg was gone, Param was hurt, Olivenko baffled, and Loaf enraged.

"The fool!" he cried. "He thinks he wants one of these? What for? To put himself in Vadesh's hands again—Vadesh is the champion of all the liars, and that's saying something, since I don't think one word in ten that I've heard in my life was true! And none since we left Ramfold, not one thing that anyone has told us."

But it was done, and they didn't blame Umbo for it.

"Arrogant little twit," Loaf grumbled. "Rigg I mean, not you, Umbo. Arrogant foolish stupid brave little—he's going to take this whole thing on himself, I'm sure of it."

"I think he's backed out of it," said Param. "I think he's frightened."

"Well, he's not," said Umbo.

"I think he doesn't want to face the Visitors," said Param. "They'll be here in only two years, and he's making sure he's not with us."

"Why talk him down, when you're glad he's gone?"

"I am not!"

"You want your father all to yourself. You hated it when he was so happy to see Rigg—I was watching you," said Umbo.

"Stop it," said Olivenko. "We don't know what Rigg is doing and we don't know what his motive is but we know that we can trust him to do right, because he's had so many chances to do wrong and he's never taken them. But it's up to us to act as if whatever he's doing *won't* work, so it's all entirely up to us to try to stop the Visitors from reaching whatever decision they reach that leads to the destruction of this world. Don't you think?"

"Father will tell us what to do," said Param.

"He won't tell *me* what to do," said Umbo. "Though I'll listen to suggestions."

"You're just jealous because I *have* a father," said Param.

"I've had a father," said Umbo, "and I'm not impressed."

"When the two of you become capable of rational thought," said Loaf, "consider this: The Larfolders have their own way of remembering things, and they know a few facts that somehow missed the all-knowing Odinfolders. I'm for laying out all that we know for them to hear, and getting their counsel."

"*All* we know?" asked Umbo. "Even about the mice?"

"Yes," said Olivenko.

"No!" cried Param.

"We don't know anything about the mice," said Loaf, "except what they've told us themselves, and they're liars."

"We know that there are thousands of them here," said Umbo, "and that we brought them, and in the day since we arrived they've probably already had a thousand babies."

"Mice aren't *that* quick," said Loaf.

"Really? How many of them were pregnant?" asked Umbo. "How many were about to pop?"

"Probably half of them," said Olivenko. "The real question is, will telling the Larfolders make them trust us more, or less?"

"They'll stop talking to us," said Param. "They'll cut us off from Father. Or hurt him because he's one of us."

"He has a mantle like theirs," said Loaf. "He's not one of us."

"He's more a part of me than you are," said Param.

"Whatever you say," said Loaf, turning away from her impatiently.

Umbo wanted to answer Param: *You're* not part of *us* and never have been. But he knew that Loaf's silence was the wiser course, and added nothing to it. He knew he shouldn't have said as much as he already had.

"I think we need to tell them everything," said Olivenko. "Or we're as deceptive as the mice."

"They're actually *good* at deception," said Param.

"We resent how little we can trust others," said Olivenko, "so let's be the kind of people that others can believe. They may not approve of what we do, but they can believe what we say."

"If we tell the Larfolders about the mice, then we're betraying *their* trust," said Param.

"The mice already don't trust us," said Loaf, "and we never promised them we wouldn't tell."

Umbo realized that there was no point in arguing any further. When it involved a secret, one person's decision to tell would always defeat any number of other people's decision not to.

The real problem was figuring out what the mice intended to do. Umbo didn't really know what the mice *could* do, without full-sized humans creating the real technology. He had never figured out the problem of how their tiny hands could do any serious work. They could never work with hot metals, for instance—a man with a heavy glove and apron could get close enough to a fire for him to lift iron out of it with tongs. But a short-armed mouse trying to lift a teeny-tiny bit of molten metal with teeny-tiny tongs would still have to stand so close to the fire that its entire body would be instantly cooked.

So how could they *make* anything comparable to what humans made? What could their technology be in Larfold, where Odinfolders hadn't already created an infrastructure of tools and machinery?

The mice manipulated genes—they admitted to having done that, when they claimed to have created Knosso and Umbo. Well, actually, it was the Odinfolders who had claimed those feats, but then it became clear that really accurate displacement was done only by the mice.

So the Odinfolders had worked metal and built mighty cities; the mice worked with time and with genes, and made new species.

Then Umbo reached the only sensible conclusion. The

mice must use time-and-space displacement for everything that humans used tools for. They never had to stand close to a fire; they could shift masses far too heavy for them to move by hand.

So if the mice made it all the way to Earth undetected, what if their time displacement didn't work? There was no reason to believe that any of this planet-rooted time-shifting could function away from Garden. If it didn't, what was their fallback plan? To reproduce at an insane rate, eat all the food on Earth, and starve the human race to death? Not likely—mice were too easy to kill.

Perhaps they could genetically manipulate the humans of Earth. But in what way? Any genetic change they made would take many long human generations to take effect. It couldn't stop the destruction of Garden a year after the Visitors left.

And now that he was here in Larfold, Umbo couldn't go to the library in Odinfold and try to learn more about what the mice could do. He couldn't even ask Mouse-Breeder, which he'd like to do, even though he knew Mouse-Breeder would probably lie to him. Or the mice were lying to Mouse-Breeder so any answer he gave would be wrong.

The mice could move items from one place to another, and from one time to another. If that power continued to work on Earth, they would have a wide range of possibilities. They had killed Param by inserting a slab of metal into her body. But could they have simply *removed* a vital organ from her?

What were the rules governing their powers? How many mice did it take to handle a single displacement? Did the items they shifted in time and space have to be already detached or detachable from all other items? Or could they move a section of a pillar out of place and collapse a roof? And how large an object could they move? A building? A starship?

Could they move the Visitors' starship into space very near the Sun and let it roast?

No, that couldn't be it—if the Visitors did not return to Earth, it would only signal the humans of Earth that Garden posed some kind of threat.

All Umbo's questions went around and around in his head.

Until, in the middle of the night, he got the answer.

He woke up Param.

"What do you want?" she demanded. "I was asleep!"

"I know," said Umbo. "But how can you sleep, when I have the answer?"

"What answer?"

"The answer to the problem that we don't know enough to decide what to do about anything. We don't even know enough to know what questions to ask."

"For this you woke me?" asked Param. "Go away."

"I woke you because you're the solution."

"You have no problems, I assure you, to which I am a possible solution."

"We need to go into the future and meet the Visitors and see what happens with them and then come back here and figure out what to do about them."

Param closed her eyes, but at least she was thinking about it. "So you want me to slice time to get us into the future faster."

"And then when we've seen enough, I bring us right back here. Tonight. Nobody even knows we went."

"But I've never sliced time that far," said Param. "It would take weeks."

"You've never *wanted* to slice time to that degree," said Umbo, "because you didn't want to miss whole days and weeks and months. But if you really pushed it . . ."

"Maybe," said Param.

"And we still get a quick view of what's happening. Day and night, seasons changing."

"So we'd know when two years had passed," said Param.

"We're the ones with these time-shifting abilities," said Umbo. "Let's use them."

"Without Rigg."

"Rigg's doing whatever he thinks is right. Why should we do anything less than that?"

Param sat up and rubbed her eyes with the heels of her hands. "I don't actually hate you, you know," she said.

"That's good to hear," said Umbo. "Because you had me fooled."

"I don't *like* you," said Param. "But I don't hate you, either. The others keep lecturing me because I don't treat you right."

"You treated me right when you took us off the rock in Ramfold," said Umbo. "And when you got us through the Wall. In the crisis, you come through."

"And so do you."

"So let's try it. If it's more than you can do, or want to do, you can just stop and I'll bring us back here."

"*Can* you bring us back with any kind of precision?" asked Param. "I thought you needed Rigg's pathfinding in order to hook up with an exact time."

"If I overshoot in coming back, then you can slice us back up to tonight. *You're* precise even if I'm not."

Param got up. Loaf stirred. Olivenko didn't move.

Param rummaged in her bag and took out her heavy coat.

Umbo looked at her like she was crazy.

"What if it's winter when we stop?" asked Param.

Umbo got his heavy coat out of his bag, too.

They took each other's hands, facing each other.

"I think you two are reckless fools," said Loaf, who was apparently awake after all.

"But we can't stop them," said Olivenko, who was awake as well.

"Thanks," said Umbo. "We'll be back in a minute."

Param began slicing time.

Umbo had been through this before, as they leapt from the rock. It didn't feel like they were moving forward through time at a different pace. Instead, it looked as if the rest of the world were speeding up. Only this time, Umbo didn't see people or animals move quickly by. He didn't see them at all. Just glimpses of a person here, a person there. Days flitted by in a blur of suns passing overhead, flickering with stars that appeared in a momentary darkness and then were gone.

Snow on the ground, gone, back, gone, deeper, melted, back again, gone again. And then spring, a profusion of green; a summer just long enough to feel the heat, and then it was cool and the leaves were gone and the grass was brown and there was snow again. Spring. Summer. And Param slowed down the world around them and gradually they came to a stop.

It was night. There was no one on the beach, no one farther inland either, as far as they could tell.

Rigg could always tell where other people were, or whether they were there at all, thought Umbo. I wish that he were here.

But then the wish passed from him. He didn't want to be dependent on Rigg right now. He and Param could do this thing alone.

"I don't think we want to be seen," said Umbo. "I think we want to watch from hiding."

"Then let's turn invisible," said Param with a smirk. "It's my best trick anyway." She took his hand again, and walked with him toward a stand of trees and bushes, as the night raced by around them.

Even when they came to a stop amid the trees, and the sun rose swiftly, Param kept on slicing time. But now the world was moving slowly enough that they could see the blur of scurrying mice. Mice everywhere among the trees and grass.

Mice going into and out of holes in the ground.

Of course they don't build buildings. They dig holes. They don't have to shore up tunnels so they don't cave in; mice can move through such tiny passages that they hold themselves up without any additional support. These fields could now be a city of a hundred million mice, and no one above the surface would know it.

Rigg would know, because of the paths. But could even he sort through the movements of all these tiny mammals?

The great hole in Umbo's plan was now obvious. They could move into the future, but *where* in the future did they want to be? Where would the Visitors come, when they came to Larfold?

If they came to Larfold. There was a thought. What if the Visitors saw no trace of human habitation in Larfold, and so didn't bother to come there?

What if the mice had insisted on invading Larfold precisely because they knew the Visitors would not come, and perhaps the Destroyers would not destroy the wallfold because they thought no humans lived there? After all, the account of the destruction of "all" of Garden in the Future Books might not be accurate.

Or maybe this was where the mice were trying to construct underground shelters where they could live for decades without coming to the surface. Maybe they meant to wait until Garden was habitable again, and only then emerge and inherit the world.

Why did we always assume the mice were trying to attack Earth? All they had to do was hide deep enough to escape notice.

How much about the mice was in the ships' logs? Would the Destroyers be looking for them? They couldn't have been on any previous visit, because the mice had only existed for the first time on this go-round.

The Visitors will come to Larfold, thought Umbo. They'll be thorough. The ships' logs will tell them that there was a colony here and that somehow it went underwater. So they'll come here looking for the site of the colony.

And that's where we are, or nearly so.

Umbo raised a hand in a stopping gesture, and Param slowed them down. The mice resumed a normal pace—which was still pretty frantic. Almost instantly, there were mice on their clothing, up on their shoulders.

"You know who we are," said Umbo softly. "We're about

to go into the future. If you want to see your families again, get off."

The mice understood and scampered down their clothing and got about a meter away before they turned and sat watching Umbo and Param.

"Why did you make us stop?" asked Param.

"We want to be about three hundred meters that way."

"How do you know?"

"Because that's where the colony was, so that's where the Visitors will come."

Almost at once, the mice took off in the direction Umbo had indicated. "It's nice to be regarded as an authority by somebody," he said.

"Since the mice already know where we're going, can we just walk there in realtime?"

"Sure," said Umbo. "Though if there are any Larfolders on shore, they'll see us. Not to mention the Visitors themselves, who might be watching from space right now."

Param sighed. "I've spent plenty of time slicing time already. A little more won't kill me."

Though of course if the mice decided to try their little stunt with metal again, it *might* kill her. "Never mind," said Umbo. "I prefer to walk in realtime myself." He let go of her hand and started to walk out into the open.

She hesitated a moment, then followed him.

"I wonder," said Umbo, "what would happen if I peed while time-slicing. I mean, as soon as the piss leaves my body, it's not part of me. So does it keep moving in sliced time, or does it immediately become part of realtime? So I'd pee, and it's like it would move really fast and hit the ground almost before I peed it."

"I can't believe you're making me listen to something so disgusting," said Param.

"Come on, you can't tell me you never thought of it. I bet you tried it."

"It was better when we were slicing time," said Param. "We couldn't talk then."

"So if you don't like what I think of to say, you say something."

For a minute or two she remained silent. Then she spoke. "Thank you for not making me slice time when the mice knew where I'd be."

"I think if they wanted us dead, they'd find a way, but sure, I could see why you didn't want to do it. And I didn't want you to run the risk either."

"So thanks," she said.

Umbo wanted to laugh. It was such a simple thing, saying thanks, but for her it was hard. Probably not hard to say thanks—just hard to say it to *him*.

"We're going to have to slice time eventually, though," said Param. "We didn't pack a lunch."

Something perverse in him made Umbo return to the previous subject. "Farting, too," said Umbo. "Bet it completely fades before we can smell it, if you fart while slicing time. And no, I absolutely won't believe it if you tell me you never did *that* while slicing time."

"I never—"

"I have sisters," said Umbo. "Girls fart and snore and belch and pee and all the really gross offenses. They just pretend they don't, and expect everybody else to go along with the lie."

Umbo expected Param to say something cutting. Or move away from him in disgust. Or disappear.

Instead she farted.

"Oh, you couldn't wait till we time-sliced," said Umbo.

"I don't know what you're talking about," she said.

"I'm sure it was a collective fart from all the mice around us."

"The mice broke wind?" she said. "How advanced of them. They have evolved to the level of boys. Still, that leaves a long way to go."

Umbo smiled. Only a little. Maybe she wouldn't notice. Wasn't it amazing that she could say rude things one moment and it felt like hatred, and then say equally rude things the next moment, and it sounded like an offer of friendship.

They reached the boundary of the colony, as far as he remembered from the map in the flyer's display. But he had a good memory for where things were, a good eye for landmarks. It was here.

"Tired?" asked Umbo.

"You woke me out of a sound sleep two years ago and I've been walking continuously since," said Param. "How could I be tired?"

"Can you slice time in your sleep?"

Param hesitated. "Sometimes I wondered if I disappeared in my sleep. If it was such a reflex that I slept all night but only got a couple of hours' sleep."

"Tired all the time?"

"I wanted to go back to bed the moment I woke up."

"Sounds like my mother," said Umbo.

Param was about to say something, then thought better of it.

Something insulting about Umbo's mother. And then a decision that this might be out of bounds.

Good call, Param.

"The mice know we're here. So we could probably both sleep at once. But I'll keep watch if it makes you feel safer."

They were in the shadow of the woods now, and Umbo piled up this year's leaves to make a large sleeping area without much work. Param lowered herself gracefully onto the leaves. Umbo sat up with his back leaning against a tree.

After a little while, Param moved herself closer to him. She held out one hand.

Umbo looked at the hand.

"Hold my hand," she said. "In case I slice time in my sleep."

Umbo took her hand.

It felt good.

In a few moments, she was snoring. She didn't slice time. The mice left them alone. So instead of waking her to take her turn, Umbo eventually lay down beside her, still holding her hand, and caught some sleep as well. When he woke up, she was awake. But still holding his hand.

"Did I fart much?" asked Umbo.

"It's been so long since you bathed, it's hard to tell," said Param.

"That was good," said Umbo. "You're getting good at this."

"At insulting you? That's not even a sport, Umbo," she said. "It's so easy."

But because she called him by name, it didn't sting. In fact, it made him feel kind of good.

Awake now, they took care of their morning ablutions, taking turns going down to the river, which was near enough to have been of use to the colony when it was new. Unlike the facemasks in Vadeshfold, the mantles in Larfold were larger and easy to avoid in the water.

Rested and a bit cleaner and emptier, Umbo mentioned that they should have thought of food, and Param said that she hardly thought of anything else, and then she sliced time again, days, weeks, until . . .

There was a flyer setting itself down a few hundred meters away.

Param and Umbo moved swiftly toward it. Of course, because they were in sliced time, the people around them moved even quicker.

They watched as the Visitors set up all kinds of equipment whose purpose Umbo couldn't guess at. And very soon, mantled Larfolders began showing up to talk with the Visitors.

The Visitors looked like regular people. There were sharp differences between them—some with skin so light you might call it white, others so black it was blue. Far more variety than the rather uniform brown of the wallfolds they had visited so far.

Umbo decided this meant that on Earth, races that originated in one geographical area tended to marry within their tribe, while on Garden, everybody had intermarried so much within each wallfold that, because the colonies had been identical at startup, they all evolved into the same intermediate brown.

We won't learn anything if we don't talk to them, thought Umbo. That meant coming out of sliced time and taking things at a normal—and visible—pace.

Then there was a flurry of motion near the Visitors' flyer, and Umbo realized what it was. Mice were scurrying up a bit of cable dangling from the ramp leading up to the flyer's door.

Not all scurrying, though. Some of them moved downright sluggishly.

Why so slow?

Pregnant, he thought. More babies.

No. They wouldn't want their babies to be born en route. It would be hard enough to conceal adults; younglings would be impossible to hide.

So why else might some mice be more sluggish than others in climbing the rope?

And then Umbo realized: They were sick.

Why would they send sick mice as their agents?

Because the sickness was the purpose of their stowing away.

The mice had created a disease of which they were themselves the vector. They would go to Earth and pass the disease to humans.

A crowd of Larfolders assembled. Umbo signaled a stop and Param slowed the movements of the people around them to a speed approaching normal.

One of the Visitors, a woman, was talking, and after a very short time, Umbo understood the language. She would speak a sentence, and then a Larfolder would translate for her. How does the interpreter know the Visitors' language, he wondered. Then Umbo remembered that the Larfolders had held on to the ancient language with some stubbornness. And because they could ordinarily speak only on shore, they spoke more rarely, and so their language would evolve less. Maybe it was still very similar to whatever the Earth people spoke.

"I know what the mice are doing," whispered Umbo.

"Sneaking on board the ship?

"With a disease," said Umbo.

"I wonder which disease."

"I don't want to find out by catching it," said Umbo.

"Poisoning them," said Param. "The mice are going to murder the entire population of Earth."

"Have you got her language?" asked Umbo.

"Yes," said Param.

"You go to them invisible, then appear and warn them," said Umbo. "I'll take you back in time with me the moment you show me a fist."

"What message?" asked Param.

Umbo thought for a moment. "A warning. Something about how the mice are smart and very dangerous and they can't let a single one reach Earth."

Param nodded and disappeared.

Umbo kept his eyes on the Visitors; he could not afford to be looking away at the moment Param appeared. They'd only have a few second before the mice would react. Perhaps by killing her again.

Param appeared. The Visitor who had been speaking stopped

and inclined her head to look at Param, then said something to her.

Param held up her hand in a gesture of silence. Wait. And then she was blurting out something and suddenly her fist was extended. It was the signal. Umbo took hold of her and dragged both of them backward in time.

Param dropped in a heap to the ground. The flyer was gone, so her position on the ramp had become a point in midair.

But she was unhurt, and in this particular timeframe there wasn't a soul here. Not even the mice.

"I think I may have brought us back a little earlier than I wanted," said Umbo.

"Or later," said Param. "I don't know if it will matter."

They walked back toward the camp in realtime.

Whatever doubts he might have had, Umbo found as they approached that it was the very night when they had left. There was Loaf, and there was Olivenko, exactly as they had been; and there were Umbo and Param, asleep.

"No," whispered Umbo when Param seemed about to speak. "Say nothing if you can help it, not till our earlier selves are gone. We don't want to let them see us. It complicates things sometimes."

"I was going to say," said Param softly, "that you got us here within half an hour of the time we left."

"In the wrong direction," said Umbo.

"Before is better than after," said Param.

They waited in sliced time then, wordless until the sleeping version of themselves woke up, packed quickly, and set out, disappearing moments after they started walking.

Was that the same way it had been earlier? Or did Umbo remember that Param started splitting time *before* they walked away from camp. Was it possible that they had inadvertently changed something in the past? Might they have therefore bifurcated themselves, so that a complete duplicate set of themselves would be wandering around, thinking they were the real Umbo and Param?

Maybe they were.

Param and Umbo walked back into camp.

"What did you learn?" asked Loaf.

Umbo had forgotten that Loaf and Olivenko had been awake when they left. "The Visitors came but I didn't have much chance to hear them."

"We saw mice getting in their flyer," said Param. "They moved sluggishly. As if they were sick."

"We thought, what if the mice developed a disease to carry back to Earth?" said Umbo. "Something the humans of Earth can't defend against."

"So instead of learning the answer to your 'what if,' so you could decide whether to intervene," said Loaf, "you intervened."

When he put it that way, it didn't seem like such a good idea.

"Did you *know* that any mice were sick?" asked Loaf.

"They looked sick," said Param defiantly.

Umbo was grateful that she was backing him up on this; she could so easily have laid all the blame on him. In fact, he suspected that the blame *was* his. But then, to blame him would imply that she had been taking orders from him. Her pride could never let her do that.

"What did your intervention consist of?" asked Olivenko.

"I told them that the mice on their ship were smart and deadly," said Param, "and they needed to kill every last one of them so they'd return to Earth with none aboard."

"And the mice didn't stop you," said Loaf.

"I'm not sure any of them saw that she was there," said Umbo. "Param delivered her message so quickly."

"So you're going to get away with having a whole bunch of half-human mice slaughtered," said Loaf. "What a relief."

"What if having the mice reach Earth was the only way to save Garden?" asked Olivenko.

"Then next time around," said Umbo, "we'll let them go."

"What next time?" asked Loaf. "Maybe next time, the mice won't alter Knosso's genes, or give you your real father. What if they completely undo *us* so that next time we won't interfere in their plans?"

"You forget," said Umbo. "They can't go back in time."

"They can write letters," said Loaf, "and send them back, and read them, and act on them."

"On your information-gathering mission, did you learn *anything* to guide us on how to prevent the Visitors from hating and fearing us?" asked Olivenko.

"We were too busy trying to save the lives of all the humans on Earth," said Param.

"I thought saving the lives of all the humans on Garden was a slightly higher priority," said Olivenko.

"Isn't it enough to have learned what the mice were doing?" asked Umbo.

Olivenko shook his head. "You saw mice getting on the Visitors' flyer, and you *assumed* that they were doing what you already thought they were doing. You *assumed* that your previous guesses were right. But you had no evidence."

"Are you a lawyer now?" asked Param.

"I try not to be part of indiscriminate murder," said Olivenko. "Which is pretty much what you just did. *Will* do."

"Maybe warning the Visitors will prove to them that they shouldn't get us all killed," said Umbo. "Maybe we just saved Garden *and* Earth."

"Think!" said Loaf. "We know they destroyed Garden nine times—before the half-human mice were ever created. So how can warning them about the mice *stop* them from doing something they repeatedly did before there were ever any mice at all?"

Why hadn't Umbo thought of all this himself? Why had he just . . . acted? For that matter, why hadn't Param thought of all these objections even if for no other reason than to undercut Umbo? Why, this time of all possible times, did Param actually *cooperate* with him?

Umbo saw the way Loaf looked at him, then glanced languidly at Param, then back at Umbo, and he knew what Loaf was really saying. You were showing off, Umbo. You were impressing the girl. You weren't thinking with your head.

"So maybe we blew it and maybe we didn't," said Umbo. "Or maybe we saved the world. Let's see how things turn out."

"If the mice don't kill us all as soon as they find out what you've done," said Loaf.

"For all we know, the future mice are putting poison in our food right now," said Olivenko.

"Then we'll die," said Umbo. "But you don't *know* we were wrong any more than *we* know we were right. So back off!"

"What *we* don't know hasn't killed anybody," said Loaf.

"Or saved anybody," said Umbo. "Or accomplished anything at all."

"There are so many mice," said Param. "Who'll even notice they're gone?"

"There are so many humans," said Loaf savagely. "So many peasants. So many of our enemy. So many of the poor. So many ugly people, so many stupid people, so many people who aren't as good as me. Who'll miss a few dozen or hundred or million, if my actions happen to kill them?"

Param reeled at the accusation. She looked about to cry.

She disappeared.

"Now look what you've done," said Umbo.

"You foolish boy," said Loaf. "You're more upset over my hurting Param's feelings than you are about the murders you just committed without any evidence that you were accomplishing *anything*."

Umbo knew that Loaf was right. Excruciatingly, humiliatingly right. And it was Loaf, of all people, whose high opinion Umbo wanted. Needed to deserve.

In his anguish, Umbo cried out, "I'm just a kid!"

His words hung in the air. Nobody said anything.

Param returned to view. "I'm not running away from this," she said.

"Well, it's nice to see that *somebody's* growing up," said Loaf.

Param glanced at Umbo, saw the tears on his face. "We did what we thought was right," she said. "And it was a smart plan. And Umbo thought of it, and I agreed with it, and we did it. And he loves you as much as I love my father. So why can't you show him a little understanding. Isn't that what fathers are supposed to do?"

"I didn't ask to be his father," said Loaf.

"Yes you did," said Param. "When you came along with him and Rigg, that's what you were doing."

"If your father were here and knew what you did, he'd be telling you off, too," said Loaf.

"No he wouldn't," said Olivenko.

"Why, because he's so much better than me?" said Loaf angrily.

"No," said Olivenko. "Because he's a weak and selfish man, and he wouldn't care."

Param looked as if Olivenko had slapped her. "I thought you loved him!"

"I love him," said Olivenko. "But I also know him better than you. Strengths *and* weaknesses. He left you to your mother. He cared about nothing but his own researches. He still lives that way. You can't expect anything from him, because he won't come through. If you don't understand that about him, he'll break your heart. But Loaf, here. He'll stand by Umbo through everything. Even when Umbo's wrong, and needs to hear just how wrong he is. *That's* a father. If I ever have children, that's the father I want to be."

"Then I hope you never have children!" Param snapped.

But all Umbo could think was: Loaf loves me. He cares what I do. And he threw himself into Loaf's arms and wept. "I'm so sorry," he said. "I'm sorry, I'm sorry."

"Tell it to the mice," murmured Loaf. But his arms went around Umbo and held him close.

CHAPTER 23

Murder

To kill a man isn't something you decide lightly, Rigg knew. But he also understood that there were times when you had no choice.

Rigg had discussed it with Loaf long ago, during the time they spent in O, waiting for a banker named Cooper to convert a jewel into money they could spend. Rigg and Umbo had only begun learning how to use their talents together. Alone, Umbo could only go back a little way and appear to someone, like a ghost, and give them a brief message. Alone, Rigg could only see the paths that people made as they went through the world.

Together, though, they could actually change things. Rigg could fix on a particular path; then Umbo could send him to that time, and bring him back. Rigg was in the past time, but Umbo, who was still in the present, could also see him; he was in both times at once.

That was how Rigg got the knife—he stole it from an utter stranger, someone whose path he fixed on. "I could have taken his knife and killed him with it," Rigg had said to Loaf.

"Why would you even think of that? From stealing to assassination in one quick step." Loaf looked contemptuous.

"You were a soldier," said Rigg. "You killed people."

"Yes," said Loaf. "It was war. They were trying to kill me, I was trying to kill them. I didn't always succeed in killing them, but so far they've always failed at killing *me.*"

"So I guess you don't think it would be fair for me to go where I know an enemy soldier was, and then go back in time and kill him when he had no way of knowing I'd be there."

"Fair?" asked Loaf. "There's no 'fair' about killing in war. If you can kill the other man, without any danger to yourself, then you do it."

"But you just said it was wrong for me to—"

"Enemy," said Loaf. "War. He knows he's at war, he knows he has enemies, and suddenly out of nowhere an enemy kills him. That's war. If you know how to kill the enemy without putting your own troops in danger, then you do it. You save the lives of your own, and take the lives of the enemy."

"I would never just kill a stranger on the street," said Rigg.

"But that's what you said. You robbed him, and then you talked about how easy it was to kill him."

"I said it would be easy," said Rigg, "not that I would have killed him."

"You're wrong, though," said Loaf. "It might be safe, it might be impossible for him to stop you. But if it's ever easy for you to kill a man, then something has already died inside *you.*"

"So you can kill a man in a war," said Rigg. "Any other time? What if someone was attacking Leaky?"

"Leaky would kill him without any help from me," said Loaf. "Don't argue, I know the point you're making. You and Umbo, you can do this thing with time. So you know a man is going to kill somebody because he *did* it. There's the person, dead. So you go back in time, and just before he kills the other guy, suddenly you appear and slit his throat."

"That's all right, isn't it?" asked Rigg.

"You're so eager to kill? You want to find out what the rules are, so you can do it?"

"I'm just asking a simple question," said Rigg. "But if you're afraid to give me an honest answer . . ."

"I gave you one. You're too eager to kill. Go back farther. Before he ever reaches out to kill. Trip him on the way in. See if that stops him."

"Trip him? He's a murderer!"

"Do you know why he kills the other guy?"

"I'm making this up, how would I know why?"

"Was it a plan? Was someone else making him? Does he think this man wronged him terribly? What if he finds out later that the guy didn't do it. He's so grateful then that he tripped on the way into the roadhouse or the bank or wherever it was. Now both men are alive, and you didn't kill anybody."

"So you think all the murders in the world are done because of mistakes?" asked Rigg.

"I'm saying that not everybody who kills is a murderer. Sometimes killers are idiots. Sometimes they're just boys. Sometimes they're idiot boys."

"Stop bringing me into this," Umbo had said from the other room, where he was reading something. Rigg didn't remember what. He just remembered that Loaf finally came around to saying, Yes, this power you have, it can be used to kill, and there might come a time when you have no other choice.

This was that time.

Rigg didn't leap to that conclusion. It came on him gradually. It began with all the lies. The Odinfolders were sure they had all the information from the chat among the expendables and the ships' computers, and yet some of the information they had was false, and things were missing. The clincher was the fact that the Odinfolders and the mice had said that there was nothing from Larex about the Larfolders—but instead, Larex met with them all the time and was aware of what they were doing every step of the way.

"We all lie to Vadesh." What did that even *mean*? Why Vadesh in particular? Yes, he had lost all of his humans, but now it turned out that Vadesh had actually left his own wallfold to visit Larfold.

What would it mean if he were told the truth—why would they bother lying to him?

So who was really lying? Had the Odinfolders lied to Rigg? Or did they tell what they believed was the truth, and the mice lied to the Odinfolders about what they had learned from their interception of expendable communications?

Who ordered the killing of Param in the library in Odinfold? Was it the mice, acting for their own self-interest, and they blamed it on the Odinfolders? Or did the Odinfolders order it? And if so, why? Who was served by it? Was it to try to kill Param, or to try to get Rigg and Umbo and the others to do exactly what they did—go on to Larfold and take ten thousand mice with them?

Who was in control of all this? Whose plan was being served? What if all the living creatures—human or part-human—were being lied to by the expendables and the ships' computers?

Which led to yet another round of questions. What if the expendables had gone rogue? The ships' computers hinted at the possibility; certainly Rigg had gotten different results from giving orders to the ship from the orders he gave to Vadesh.

Yet Vadesh had claimed that he had to obey the owner of the jewels, right from the start. The ships assured him that he was absolutely in control of everything. And yet they were all doing things that had nothing to do with anything he ordered, and sometimes that completely contradicted what they had told him they had done or were going to do or even *could* do.

How can machines lie? Were they lying when they said they had to obey him? If so, how did they get programmed to be able to tell that lie? In other words, who had ordered them to be capable of disobeying orders?

Ram Odin had ordered the killing of all the other Ram Odins so that the computers and expendables would not be forced to deal with contradictory orders. Yet one of the Ram Odins *had* lived, and the computers and expendables all knew it, because there existed both Ramfold and Odinfold, named for the founder of the colony.

The kind of lying that was going on—what if it wasn't lying at all? What if everything that every single expendable and computer ever said to Rigg was true. No, not true, but *honest*—that is, they were conveying exactly the information they had been ordered to give him.

When they told him he was in command of everything, it was true. But what if shortly afterward it stopped being true, and they were ordered not to tell him that?

Or they were ordered to tell him that he was in control when in fact he was not, so they were lying, but not by their own choice.

Who could possibly give such orders? Rigg was in possession of the jewels, the ships' logs, and by all rights he should be in command.

But only if the previous commander was gone. Dead.

What if the previous commander was unavailable, so Rigg took command; but then the previous commander *became* available, and so Rigg was not in command anymore. Or he was in command, but in a subordinate way, the way Umbo was in command in Odinfold because he had the copies of the ships' logs that were on the knife—but he still served under Rigg and could not countermand an order of Rigg's.

What if Rigg was also subordinate to another human commander, and the expendables had been ordered not to tell him?

Then it all made sense. All the lying by machines stopped being lies and started being a systematic plan of deception by a commander who didn't want his existence to be known.

This is the way Father had taught Rigg to think. If things don't make sense, then question your assumptions. When your assumptions all seem to be wrong, then think of ways that they might be right after all. Find new possibilities.

Here was the possibility that nobody ever talked about, yet it seemed obvious once it occurred to Rigg.

Ram Odin was still alive.

Eleven thousand years later, still alive?

Every starship had that room where sleeping colonists were revived and awakened from stasis. That's where Vadesh had brought Rigg and Loaf, pretending it was the control room, but really intending to slap a facemask on one of them. Rigg had always assumed he meant to do it to him, not Loaf at all. But now he wondered: Vadesh had put the facemask on one of the two men in their group who had no power over time.

That was when Rigg realized that if he had the enhancements to his senses that Loaf had received, he might be able to use his power far more effectively. Wouldn't the facemask also enhance his ability to see paths, the way it had enhanced Loaf's sight and hearing and smell, his quickness, his memory, his mental acuity?

There in Vadesh's revival chamber, Rigg had all the answers in front of him if he had only known the right questions. This was a room that was still in use. Not for the facemask—Vadesh didn't have to bring him there to put the facemask on someone, he could have done that in any room in the starship.

So why did Vadesh choose that room? Because then Rigg would know what it was. What it was for. That it existed.

Vadesh was trying to tell him the truth even though he had been forbidden to tell it. Someone is still being kept in stasis. Someone who gets revived from time to time, then goes back to sleep. Someone who has slept his way through eleven thousand years of human history on Garden, only waking up for a few days here and there to give orders, to make tweaks in human history.

Ram Odin. Only he was not in Ramfold, where he had founded a colony and left his seed behind. He was in Vadeshfold, where Vadesh had tried to create a symbiosis of humans and native organisms.

"We all lie to Vadesh"—that was their code, their desperate attempt to signal Rigg, against all of Ram Odin's orders, that there was something in Vadesh's starship that they all were trying to resist as best they could.

This was the conclusion Rigg had reached when he heard the story of the mantles of the Larfolders, the tale of how they went under the sea. The contradictions had become too great, the web of lies too complicated. So he thought and thought until he made the leap that brought him to this conclusion: Ram Odin is alive, and Ram Odin is manipulating everything.

Then he made one more leap: It is not the Visitors who trigger the destruction of Garden. It is Ram Odin.

In the Future Books, the dying Odinfolders spoke of Destroyers from Earth, but did they know this was true, or had they been told this by the ships' computers, by the expendables? Here was the key point: the Destroyers worked through the orbiters—the satellites from the original nineteen starships that circled Garden in stationary orbits.

The satellites obeyed their programming by threatening to destroy any wallfold that developed dangerous weapons. But those dangerous weapons were actually thwarted by the expendables, who forestalled any experimentation along those lines. What weapons were considered too dangerous to allow?

Any weapons that could threaten the starships' control of this planet.

There were terrible slaughters in the wallfolds. The humans of Vadeshfold had made themselves extinct. There was apparently some kind of terrible plague that affected all the wallfolds early on. Many horrible wars and massacres and famines and genocides had happened, but it never triggered any reaction from the orbiters.

But then the Visitors come and a year later the Destroyers activate the orbiters to destroy every single wallfold.

Nine times the Odinfolders had tried various ways to placate these vengeful, terrible gods, remaking themselves, unbuilding their society, leaving everything, even their own bodies, in ruins; devolving all their powers and knowledge upon sentient mice; even contemplating the slaughter of the human race on Earth in order to prevent the destruction of Garden.

What if it wasn't the humans from Earth who did this?

What if it was Ram Odin?

The Visitors came. They got complete access to all the ships' logs. Then they went away.

What if they studied those logs and realized what had happened. The whole system was under the control of the man whose *first act* upon discovering the accidental nineteen-copy, eleven-thousand-year time-shift event was to order the murder of all other copies of himself, and then the destruction of almost all life on Garden to make room for his colonies. The man who used Garden as a means of creating people with his own strange time-shifting powers, only enhanced, clarified.

Now this same Ram Odin saw the people of Earth returning. Maybe they even got near enough to send an order to the ships' computers, *taking command away from Ram Odin*.

Only Ram Odin had already programmed in an automatic response to this move. The result of any order that took command away from Ram Odin was the immediate destruction of all life on Garden.

If Ram could not rule, he would destroy.

The humans from Earth had tried to *save* Garden from its secret god, and the god had wrecked all rather than let his own power be curtailed.

Now it all made sense. No matter how many times the Odinfolders tried to make a better impression on the Visitors, nothing would ever work because the Visitors had always gotten a good impression and had never turned against the people of Garden.

All the lies were part of Ram Odin's mad or evil plan to keep control over Garden while creating a race of time-shifters who were subservient to him without ever knowing it was him whom they served.

Speculation—all guesswork. Rigg knew this.

He also knew that with mice listening in on everything said among Rigg's little company of five, and no doubt relaying the information to expendables or computers that passed it along to Odin, he couldn't discuss his conclusions with anybody.

But there *was* a way that he could figure it all out. He could go to the starship where Ram Odin lived—in Vadeshfold. He could look for the path of Ram Odin. He could see how often he had been revived.

More to the point, Rigg could enhance himself the way Loaf was enhanced. It was possible that Ram Odin would forbid it—he might already have forbidden it, which would explain why Loaf got the mask, and not Rigg. It was also possible that Rigg would not have the strength of will that had allowed Loaf to overmaster the powerful forces that the facemask used to try to control its symbiote.

Either way, the world would not be any worse off than it was before. Rigg blocked from access to a facemask, or driven mad by a facemask, or even dead—how would that change the world for the worse?

But if he could get those enhancements, he could find out the truth, and if his suppositions turned out to be right, he could set the world free from this godlike monster who was set to destroy it in only a few years' time, in order to prevent being called to account by the humans from Earth, who had the power to override his control of the computers and expendables.

Only when Rigg actually *had* those enhancements would he know how it would affect his time-shifting. Everything depended on his being able to get to Ram Odin at a time when there was no way an expendable could save him. No way that Ram Odin could command the mice to send some kind of object into the past that would prevent the assassination.

Or Rigg might find out that he was wrong, that Ram Odin was not alive, that the expendables were simply capable of lying, that the situation really was as chaotic and unknowable as it seemed. Maybe this brilliant guess of his was just wishful thinking. Maybe there was no theory that could unify and explain everything.

So Rigg tried to keep himself calm during his flight to the Wall. But then, he didn't really need to conceal his trepidation, his excitement. After all, whatever changes in his behavior and vital signs the flyer's sensors picked up could be completely explained by Rigg's stated decision to go get a facemask. Who wouldn't be tense, flustered, fearful, excited?

The flyer landed and Rigg got out.

Waiting on the other side of the Wall was Vadesh, looking so much like Father.

Rigg's first thought was to wave him over. Don't pretend you can't go through the Wall, because I know you can.

But no, better to just go along with the way the expendables pretended the world worked.

Rigg walked into the Wall and felt the frisson of distant dread and anguish, the rekindling of language. In both the jewels and the knife, the ships' logs would be updating. Rigg kept his attention focused on Vadesh.

"I was right, wasn't I?" Vadesh said when Rigg was close enough.

"No," said Rigg. "You weren't *right.* You let all your people die. You're a failure. But I don't want to be a failure like you. When the Visitors come, I need to have the enhancements that Loaf has, so I'm better able to assess them and figure out how to prevent the destruction of Garden."

It was a long speech. It sounded rehearsed, even though Rigg had not known what he was going to say. How would Vadesh interpret it? Or, more to the point, how would Ram Odin, listening, interpret it?

Am I defending myself when nobody has challenged me? Probably. But will the expendable conclude from this that I'm deceiving him? Probably not. Humans always defend themselves when they think they might be wrong. And anyone about to receive a facemask who doesn't wonder if his decision is wrong must be an idiot.

"In other words, I was right," said Vadesh. "But it's perfectly understandable that you don't want to admit it. Ego plays such a strong role in the self-deceptions of human beings."

"With a facemask, will my self-deception be even more effective?" asked Rigg.

"Oh yes," said Vadesh. "But so will your ability to see right through your own self-deceptions."

Even now, knowing what he knew, suspecting what he suspected, Rigg couldn't help feeling a closeness to Vadesh, especially when he talked in conundrums and paradoxes the way Father always did.

He also felt as much loathing for Vadesh as ever.

Any human who is guided by his emotions is a fool, thought Rigg. Because we can feel absurdly opposite things at the same time.

"Did you bring a facemask to me?" asked Rigg.

"No," said Vadesh. "You don't want to take on the struggle for dominance here, where there is so much outside stimulation to distract you. You'd be swallowed up."

"You found that out by seeing people go mad?"

"Of course," said Vadesh. "There's such a steep price for failure."

"But you never pay it," said Rigg.

"I'm a machine," said Vadesh. "And the Pinocchio story is absurd. Machines don't want to be real boys. Real boys are so corruptible, so easily distracted, deceived, killed."

"And no one deceives *you*?"

"Many think they do," said Vadesh. "And I pretend that they've succeeded."

"So you're the deceiver."

"We're all deceivers, Rigg Sessamekesh," said Vadesh. "I'm just better at it."

"So is there any point in my asking you whether you have prepared a facemask for me that will be too powerful for me to master?"

"No, there's no point in your asking, and no, I have prepared nothing different to what I prepared for Loaf."

"So you did prepare it for Loaf."

"I prepared it for whoever chose to accept it," said Vadesh.

"Loaf took it to save me."

"He chose to be a hero. Who was I to refuse to allow him to play the role?"

"But you weren't going to force it on me?" said Rigg. He found that hard to believe.

"I don't force anyone to do anything," said Vadesh. "I explain and let them decide for themselves."

"You didn't explain anything to Loaf," said Rigg.

"He didn't give me time."

Rigg searched back in his memory. Did Loaf really cause the facemask to leap onto his body, or did Vadesh flip it up into place? Human memory was so unreliable. As soon as Rigg tried to imagine either scenario, each seemed equally real and equally false.

"Did you bring a flyer, or were you going to carry me to the starship?" asked Rigg.

"Do you want a flyer? You merely asked me to meet you."

Rigg shook his head. "Bring the flyer and take me there. Or don't, and I'll walk. I enjoy solitude and I know my way around a forest."

Of course the flyer was close by—expendables could move faster than humans, but not fast enough to get to the Wall without using a flyer, not in the amount of time Rigg had given Vadesh to comply with his orders.

"Why did you decide on my poor primitive facemask instead of those wonderful Companions of the Larfolders?" asked Vadesh.

Rigg did not answer.

"Are you going to leave me in suspense?" asked Vadesh.

Rigg wanted to retort, Why would a machine feel suspense? But instead he did not answer at all. Why should he pretend that the normal human courtesies applied in a conversation between a man and a machine? Especially when the man was the one who supposedly commanded all the ships and expendables.

Man! Rigg inwardly grimaced at his own vanity. How I strut. I'm not a man, I'm a boy, trying to do a man's job.

Or commit a monstrous crime.

One or the other.

The flight was without incident. They landed, not at the city, where they would need to take the high-speed tram through the mountain, but at a structure inside the crater made by the ancient impact when the starship collided with Garden. Then there was an elevator ride down to the starship far below.

But they crossed the same bridge from the wall of the stone chamber to the outside door in the starship's side. All the starships dwelt inside an identical wound in the stone of the world, because all those wounds had been shaped by the forcefield that protected the starship and its passengers from all the effects of collision and sudden changes in inertia.

Rigg followed Vadesh carefully, trying to be aware of any new hazards, trying to notice all kinds of things he had overlooked before.

But the main thing Rigg searched for was the path of Ram Odin.

It was surprisingly easy to find, now that he knew it might exist. It was the oldest path in the starship. It was also the newest. It led again and again from the control room to the stasis chambers and then to the revival room and then back to the control room.

But in the past eleven thousand years, Ram Odin had not left the starship. Not since he crossed through the Wall from Ramfold.

Interesting. The Ram Odin that had been on the Vadeshfold copy of the starship had been killed by his expendable. And yet his path was here in the ship. A path markedly older than the already ancient passage of Ram Odin from Ramfold into Vadeshfold.

For a moment, Rigg wondered if that meant that the Ram Odin of this starship had not been killed; maybe all of them had lived, the way the Ram Odin of Odinfold had lived.

But no. That most ancient path moved throughout the ship, and then abruptly ended in the control room a few decades before another version of Ram Odin came through the Wall.

Thus Rigg learned the answer to a question that had bothered both him and Umbo ever since they learned about the starships. Paths were tied to the gravity of planets, and moved through space with the world where the paths were laid down. But when people were in space, their paths stayed with the ship transporting them. Unlike boat passengers on the Stashik River, whose paths stayed in the same position relative to the river, and not with the boats, the path of Ram Odin during the starship's voyage stayed with the starship, even after the ship impacted with the planet's surface.

I can see it all, thought Rigg. When the time comes, I can watch Vadeshex murder the Ram Odin of this starship.

But no. Being there as an observer would be hard to conceal from the expendable, who would then know there were such things as time-shifting humans from the future. It might cause the expendable—all the expendables—to behave differently. It might utterly change the course of history.

It couldn't erase Rigg, of course—he and Umbo had settled that long ago. The agents of time change could not be undone by the shifts they themselves caused. They called it the "conservation of causality," like the conservation of matter and energy. As causers, they had to remain in existence, even if the future they came from was otherwise erased.

But I'm not the only one whose existence I need to protect.

Rigg followed Vadesh to the revival chamber. "I need to do it here in case you have an adverse physical reaction," Vadesh explained. "Loaf was robust and needed no life support. You might need to be sustained during your struggle for control."

"When will you know if I've failed?"

"I'll know," said Vadesh.

"Tell me the symptoms that will lead you to that conclusion," said Rigg.

Vadesh said nothing.

"I think I gave you a command."

"I don't have an answer," said Vadesh. "I don't know the symptoms that would lead to that conclusion, because you're only the second person to receive one of this particular genotype of facemask, and the first one did not fail."

"You've seen failure with early genotypes."

"They were so different that they *could* not be the same."

Rigg didn't believe him. But should he show that, or would it lead Ram Odin—who was no doubt giving orders to Vadesh from his current location in the control room—to suspect that he knew too much?

"What concerns me," said Rigg, "is that you might conclude that I had failed when I don't think I've failed."

"Here's a simple test," said Vadesh. "If you think, from my actions, that I have concluded that the facemask is in complete control, all you have to do to avoid my actions is to jump into the past and out of my reach."

"Here's a simpler test," said Rigg. "I order you not to take any action at all concerning me and the facemask for three years, and even then you have to tell me what you're planning to do."

"In three years," said Vadesh, "the Destroyers will be here."

"That's why I chose that number," said Rigg.

Vadesh paused a moment, then said, "I will obey your command."

"How nice of you. Did you have any choice?"

"I don't have to obey a command that cannot take effect until after your death. But my programming does not permit me to regard facemask domination as death. Rather it is temporary disablement, so I will follow those rules instead of the death rules."

"How nice of you," said Rigg.

"You asked," said Vadesh.

Rigg sat on the edge of the revival table. "Get me my facemask now," said Rigg. "I assume you already have one picked out?"

"I have several dozen facemasks. I have no criteria for choosing one over another."

"'Several dozen,'" echoed Rigg. "You know an exact number. Say it."

"One hundred and seventy," said Vadesh.

"You have quite a supply of them. Expecting that many visitors?"

"It was to avoid that false conclusion that I used the term 'several dozen,'" said Vadesh. "The large number is because that's how many happened to survive and remain viable in stasis."

"So you keep the facemasks in stasis," said Rigg. "Like the voyagers in flight."

"Someone's been researching the starship," said Vadesh.

"Yes, Umbo. And then he talked about what he learned."

"Stasis and revival work almost identically for humans and facemasks, which is not a surprise, since these facemasks have been genetically designed for compatibility with humans."

"Please get my facemask," said Rigg. "Now."

Vadesh left the room at once, and returned within the minute. "This one is as healthy as any other."

"Then let's . . ."

Rigg didn't get to say "do it," because the facemask flew out of the basin containing it. Did Vadesh fling it, or did the facemask somehow propel itself? Or had Rigg, without realizing it, bowed his head over the basin to look inside? He had only a split second to contemplate this question, and then there was agony and panic as his face was covered, his breath choked off, and tendrils inserted themselves with brutal irresistibility into his nostrils, his mouth, his ears and, most painful and frightening of all, his eyes.

This is irrevocable, he thought. My eyes are gone.

Then the tendrils reached through otic and optic nerves into his brain and the struggle began.

It was not like a tug of war. Not like a wrestling match. It was more like being lost in a maze. He could sense that his body was feeling things. Doing things. Yet he could not find his body, could not find the way to control his body.

It was as if the maze were constantly being changed so that

nothing was in the same place twice, and barriers popped up where there had been no barriers before.

Pains came and went. His body needed to urinate. Then it did. It got up and walked, but not at Rigg's command. It acted for its own reasons.

No, not its own reasons. The facemask's reasons.

A rush of rejection swept over him; the feeling of hostility Rigg had seen in the faces of the people of Fall Ford when they gathered outside Nox's house, intending to kill him in punishment for the death of Umbo's little brother, whom Rigg had tried so hard to save. It was as if the facemask knew such a memory was there, and now used it to overwhelm Rigg with feelings and memories from his own past.

Rigg decided that this sudden emotional rush came because the facemask recognized that Rigg had somehow attempted to assert control over his own body. When it got up and moved at the facemask's command, there had been no resistance from Rigg. But Rigg's *thought* that his body was moving at the facemask's command must have felt, to the facemask, like resistance.

My thoughts are my weapons in this war. What did Loaf say? Something about its being pointless to try to give orders to his own body, at first anyway. So the resistance is in my thoughts. In making my brain hold the thoughts I put there, and not letting them be swept away in the feelings and desires the facemask forces on me.

Easy enough to think this thought; hard to hold on to it when every desire of his body cried out for his attention.

It was like the Wall. Only instead of anguish and despair,

what threatened to overwhelm him was thirst and hunger and lust, the urges of elimination, the inchoate yearnings of an adolescent boy.

In the end of this silent war, it turned out that the vulnerability of the facemask came from the sheer sameness of its weaponry. Once Rigg was swept by all the desires of his body, over and over, he began simply to get used to them, and through it all his mind remained his own, and it held the thoughts he reached for.

He opened his eyes.

He knew that what was opening were not his eyes at all, but the new eyes created by the facemask. But it was his nerves that controlled them, his brain that received and interpreted the signals from those eyes.

Whatever the facemask was, it was now part of himself.

Did that mean the facemask had failed?

No, it meant that the facemask was broken to his will, like a horse to its rider; it was still itself, and its needs would still be met. It would be alive. It would reproduce and continue, which was the goal of every kind of life. The native fauna of Garden was alive in this facemask, and had become a part of Rigg. It was Rigg's servant, yes, but Rigg would now see the world through its eyes, and its needs and desires would form a part of his decision-making. It would not die until he died; he would never remove it; it had found a home embedded in his flesh.

But I am still Rigg Sessamekesh.

No. Not Sessamekesh. Simply Rigg. Rigg the pathfinder. Rigg the man of Garden. Rigg the keeper of the ships' logs.

His eyes were open. He saw the entire room at once. He

wondered how long he had been trapped in the struggle for control and without even trying to calculate, he knew: seventy hours and thirty-two minutes. In that time he had drunk water that Vadesh had brought, but it had been the facemask that made his body drink. Now he looked at Vadesh, who stood nearby, and said, "I'll have more water now."

"I'd suggest cleaning yourself as well," said Vadesh.

"All in due time," said Rigg.

"Welcome back."

"Thank you."

But already Rigg was testing something else: He was finding out what the facemask had done with the paths.

Immediately his mind was flooded with information. He almost lost himself in it, for the onslaught was as great as anything the facemask had thrown at him before.

He saw every nearby path, but not as a path. He saw each path as a person. He knew their faces, he knew where they had come from. Without conscious effort, he knew the whole path of each life, from beginning to end.

There is no way my mind can hold so much information about each of these people. Yet when he looked for it, there it was.

There was Ram Odin, again and again, path after path. Going into stasis, coming out. Into stasis, out again. Sitting in the control room making decisions, giving orders. As he was doing now.

And there was Ram Odin, eleven thousand, two hundred two years ago—how clear the time was now, without thought or calculation or uncertainty.

And Rigg knew another number: His age. With all his skipping around in time, he should have been confused, for he had repeated several stretches of time because of going back, to live them over again. This was the year in which Rigg had turned fourteen, but he had lived through nearly a year in Odinfold before going back again, so he was sixteen now, regardless of what the calendar year might be.

But there were other tests he needed to perform. For instance, while Rigg could connect to any path in the past and go to it, he could not rebound into the future without Umbo anchoring him there.

Did he still have that limitation?

It was simple enough to test it. He slid a half-meter to the right, and then jumped a minute back in time.

Then he shifted forward. It was a sensation he had felt many times, when Umbo pulled him back, but now he could make it happen as an act of will.

When he went back in time, he could see himself sitting beside him; when he jumped forward again, that self was gone, because he returned to the exact moment when he had jumped back in time. He could go back, then rebound himself.

Another test yet to perform. Could he move forward the way Param did, slicing time and skipping over bits of it? He had felt that sensation, too, when he held her hand and she sliced her way into the future at a speed much faster than the natural world.

Now, because he had the facemask's enhancements to his brain, his body, he could slice his way forward. Slowly at first, the time differential very slight. But then more rapidly.

Vadesh came into the room, holding a carafe of water. He did not see Rigg.

Rigg waited until Vadesh went outside to see where he had gone, before he stopped slicing time. He did not want Vadesh to know that he could duplicate Param's ability. Let him think that Rigg had shifted backward and then returned, and that's why he was gone. Let Vadesh think that Rigg had only an enhanced version of abilities that he had possessed already.

Rigg went to the door and found Vadesh walking in the corridor. "There you are," Rigg said. "I'm so thirsty."

Vadesh hurried with the carafe. He said nothing about Rigg's absence. And if Rigg had really been gone into the past, and then returned, he wouldn't know that Vadesh had come into the room in his absence. So he simply drank the offered water.

There was one more ability to look for, and this was one that he had never directly experienced: The ability of the Odinfolder mice to move an object in both space and time. He had no idea how it would feel to do it. He had never even seen it done, though he had seen its effects—the metal cylinder in Param's exploded throat; the knife that he took from the sheath at the waist of a passerby.

Rigg did not make the conscious decision to use Vadesh as the object he would attempt to transport. He simply felt the will to move something and Vadesh was near at hand, Vadesh was the thing that Rigg was looking at, and so Vadesh moved. Only a finger's width, but he moved without passing through the intervening space. One moment he was a meter and fourteen centimeters away, and in the very same moment he shifted to a meter and fifteen centimeters away, plus a quarter of a centimeter to the right.

It had been so smooth that Vadesh didn't even change his stride, and if he noticed the difference in his location he gave no sign of it.

He must have thought through what giving a facemask to me *might* mean, and so he's looking for signs of what I can do now, and how I've changed.

"Well, Vadesh," said Rigg, "don't you think it's time I met Ram Odin?"

Vadesh turned to him. "Of course," he said. "I assume you already know the way?"

"I've seen him walk the route a hundred times," said Rigg.

"Should I come with you?"

If I say no, will Ram Odin suspect something of my intention? "Whatever Ram Odin tells you to do," said Rigg, "is what you'll do, and nothing I say can change it."

"He leaves it up to you, as the keeper of the logs," said Vadesh.

"Then come with me," said Rigg, "and let's meet the master of this ship, and of all the ships."

Rigg led the way, reveling in the total awareness that the facemask delivered to him. He could sense all the paths he was passing through, experiencing them as people; yet their presence didn't interfere at all with his ordinary light-based vision, which now had extraordinary clarity. He could see each fleck of dust in the air, the whole surface of the walls and floor and ceiling, and yet none of them distracted him from his purpose. It was as if he was now joined with an autistic mind, hyper-aware of detail, and a normal human mind with its ability to focus on one thing and let all other things fade to unnoticeability. He was aware of all things and focused on one thing at the same time.

And why not? He was two minds at once, an alien beast and a human, both functioning at peak effectiveness.

Ram Odin was an old man. Rigg saw every crease in the skin of his face, every wattle of his neck, the sparseness of hair, the droop of eyelids. There was a pallor to him. He was a man who needed to be outdoors, and had not been.

"I have a proposition for you," said Ram Odin. "Now that you've joined with the most interesting native creature of this world."

"I was just about to say the same thing to you," said Rigg. "After greeting you as the founder of our world."

"All the colonists were founders," said Ram.

Rigg walked around the control consoles; Ram swiveled in his floating seat to stay facing him.

"But you were the one," said Rigg. "The one who shaped the world while they were all asleep."

"Come here and stand with me," said Ram. "I want you to see my view of things, from this console. I want you to see the world through the orbiters' eyes. If they can be said to have eyes."

Rigg could sense tension in the man. Old and weary as he was, he was on edge right now.

He is afraid of me, thought Rigg. He made me, and yet he's afraid of what I'll do.

Rigg did as Ram requested, and came between two console stations to stand beside Ram Odin's chair.

"Here," said Ram, pointing at a three-dimensional display, a view from space of the ring of cliffs, the forests, the crater that marked where the starship had entered the crust of the planet in this wallfold. "I think of you as something like a son—you don't mind if I think of you that way, do you? I've longed to show this view to a son of mine. Look how we can zoom in closer to see."

As he spoke, he made the image larger, as if they were plunging downward in a flyer.

Rigg knew that this move was designed to draw his full attention to the display, and it worked. He was, as a human, fully engaged in the bright moving object that attracted him.

But as a facemask, he was also completely aware of the knife in Ram Odin's hand, the hand that was darting forward to plunge it into Rigg's kidney.

Rigg, by himself, could never have dodged the blow.

But Rigg-with-a-facemask easily slid to one side, whirled, caught the hand, and twisted it, forcing the knife free.

The knife dropped, but Rigg, quicker than thought, had his hand under it. He had planned to use the jeweled knife that he and Umbo had obtained on that first deliberate trip into the past. But since Ram Odin had so thoughtfully provided a different weapon, it would be ungrateful of Rigg to refuse it.

In the very moment he caught Ram Odin's knife, Rigg shifted half an hour back in time, to a moment when Ram was focused on the display in a different console, one that put his back to Rigg. That was precisely why Rigg had chosen that moment in Ram Odin's path.

Ram Odin had not equipped himself with a facemask. He was not aware of Rigg's silent appearance directly behind him.

You have not yet tried to kill me, Ram Odin, but you will, and so I kill you first.

He flashed his hand forward. Because of the speed and accuracy of the thrust—for the facemask had not yet had the time to build up Rigg's physical strength enough to make a difference—the knife easily passed between the ribs of Ram Odin's back and pierced his heart. A little flicking motion and both ventricles of Ram Odin's heart were split open. The blood of his arteries ceased to pulse. He slumped over and, without time even to utter a sound, he died.

Rigg dropped Ram Odin's weapon, then took the jeweled knife from his belt and held it in the field where the ship's computer could recognize it.

"Is there any other living soul who can take the command of these ships and computers from me?" Rigg asked.

"No," said the ship's computer.

"Is there anyone in stasis who can take command away from me?"

"No," said the ship's computer.

"Is there anyone in the universe who can take it?"

"No," said the ship's computer.

But this could not possibly be true. Then Rigg realized what he had actually asked, and phrased the question in another way. "Is there any person or *machine* that can take control of the ships against my will?"

"Yes," said the ship's computer. "Upon synchronizing with any starship authorized by the admiralty, I must surrender complete control to that computer."

That was the thing that Ram Odin must have feared. But Rigg did not fear it. And so Rigg would not have to destroy the world to prevent it.

Only when he had this information did Rigg Pathfinder put out his hand to touch the shoulder of the man that he had killed.

Ram Odin fell forward onto the console.

Rigg could sense, as clearly as by sight, the eleven-thousand-year-old path in which a different copy of Ram Odin also slumped forward in this very chair, onto this very console, his neck broken by the expendable that stood behind him.

"Kill or be killed," murmured Rigg.

How many animals had he killed when he found them still struggling in his traps? A number immediately came to his mind but he ignored it. Sometimes accuracy at facemask levels was simply not appropriate. Rigg had killed again and again. He knew the feel of life giving way to non-life. He knew the slackness of the empty body.

But this time, this time, it was a man. It was this man. It was Ram Odin. And, his hand still resting on the dead man's back, Rigg wept.

CHAPTER 24

Destroyers

Having once used Param's time-slicing ability to skip ahead into the future, Umbo and Param saw no reason to wait three years to see whether they had made the right choice in warning the Visitors about the stowaway mice. Umbo suggested it, but Param agreed at once and she proposed it to the others.

"We can't go back into Odinfold—for all we know, the mice are planning some kind of vengeance. And even if they're not, there's nowhere here in Larfold for us to live while we wait three years."

"We were spoiled by our life in Odinfold," said Loaf. "More luxury than during our time as wealthy hotel patrons in O."

"And a better library," said Umbo.

"Did we find King Knosso here, alive, only to leave him behind?" asked Olivenko.

"Why not invite him to come into the future with us?" suggested Umbo. "If it turns out the Destroyers arrive on schedule, we'll be returning to the past in order to try something else to block them. We can take Knosso with us."

"What about Rigg?" asked Loaf. "He won't know where we've gone. And he can't skip into the future without Param."

"If Rigg wants to join us," said Umbo, "he can come to this spot and find our paths and shift into this moment."

"If he doesn't come to us before we begin our journey forward," said Param, "then it means that he chose not to."

"And that's all you have for Rigg?" asked Loaf.

"He's the one who left *us*," said Olivenko.

"We don't know if he'll even be himself after he has the facemask," said Param.

"If Vadesh doesn't kill him," said Olivenko. "He chose to walk into danger."

Loaf sat looking at the sand in front of him.

"Loaf," said Umbo, "don't forget who and what we are. If Rigg doesn't join us at the end of the world, then no matter which way it goes with the Destroyers, we can always go back and find him."

"And stop him from getting himself destroyed by *this*?" asked Loaf, gesturing toward his own face.

"Why do you assume that it destroys him?" asked Umbo.

"Because I know how close it came to destroying *me*."

"And you think that Rigg is weaker?" asked Param.

"Rigg is a child," said Loaf.

Umbo laughed. "And so is Param, and so am I."

"You're not going up against a facemask," said Loaf stubbornly.

"We're going up against Destroyers," said Umbo.

"We're going to see if they come," said Loaf, "and then run away if they do."

"Rigg is stronger than you think," said Umbo.

"Stronger than I am?" asked Loaf.

"Strong enough," said Umbo. "It wasn't physical stamina that prevailed over the facemask, was it?"

"No," said Loaf. "It was strength of will."

"And you think Rigg lacks that?" asked Umbo.

"He's always been so eager to please," said Loaf.

"He's eager to do right," said Umbo. "That's not the same thing at all."

Knosso came to them when the sun was high enough to warm the beach to a tolerable temperature. When they proposed the jaunt into the future, he agreed at once. "I thought my passage through the Wall was the only adventure of my life. Now you've brought another to me here at the end of the world."

"Did you already know it was the end?" asked Umbo.

"Oh yes," said Knosso. "The Landsman told us—told the people of the sea. Many generations ago. From what you've said of the Odinfolders, he told us as soon as the Book of the Future appeared in Odinfold."

"So Larfold was informed," said Olivenko, "but not the people of Ramfold."

"In Ramfold," said Param, "they made *us*. And who would have believed such a prophecy, anyway? Here they know what their expendable is. In Ramfold, he's a legend. A myth. A miracle man."

"Worldwalker," said Umbo.

"The Golden Man," said Olivenko.

"The Undying One," said Loaf.

"The Gardener," said Param. "And even Rigg, who called him Father—what would he have done with the information, if Ramex had told him? It would have deformed the history of Ramfold. Whereas Larfold—does it really have a history?"

"Didn't you hear Auntie Wind's account?" asked Knosso.

"They have tales and memories," said Param. "But nothing changes. Life under the sea is—"

"Is filled with infinite variety," said Knosso.

"But no *events*," said Param.

"You don't even have weather down there," said Umbo. "Or seasons."

"Well, that's not quite true," said Knosso, "but it's close enough. I'm happy there. But no, we have no wars, apart from the constant struggle against the great predators of the open sea, which forces us to remain a single tribe, united to defend against them. After eleven thousand years, the monsters have learned to avoid our shore. But the Larfolders have been wise enough never to hunt the great killers of the sea to extinction. They could have done it—the barrier of the Wall keeps the sharks and orcas trapped inside, where they could never have escaped from our harpoons, if we had wanted to kill them all."

"So you keep your nemesis alive," said Param.

Umbo noticed that Knosso had switched from "they" to "we." He's no longer a man of Ramfold. He might be glad of our adventure, of a chance to slice time with us, but he's happy with the

Larfold life. This is the world he wants to save. He dreams of no triumphant return to Ramfold.

And if *we* ever went to Ramfold, it might be triumphant for Param and Rigg, as royals; they might be able to rally an army to defeat General Citizen and Hagia Sessamin and take their place in the Tent of Light. But there'd be no place for me.

Then, because he had thought of Rigg and Param as King- or Queen-in-the-Tent, it occurred to Umbo that, Ramfold history being what it was, Rigg and Param might easily become rivals there, and fight a bitter civil war between those who wanted a king and those who still believed that Aptica Sessamin had been right to kill the men of the royal line, allowing only queens to rule in the Tent of Light. And there would be others who wanted to restore the People's Republic, and probably the loyal followers of General Citizen would make yet another faction, and it would be a thrilling history, and they would all be desperately unhappy and lead exciting, terrible, tragic lives.

Who was to say that Knosso hadn't made the better choice?

Not that any of it mattered. For Umbo didn't really think that anything they did would make a difference. Nine times already the Destroyers had come. The only difference this time would be that instead of sending letters or books into the past, they would return themselves, as eyewitnesses. Though with the Destroyers remaining out in space until all life on Garden was extinct, it would be hard to say just what they might witness from a beach in Larfold.

"There's nothing to wait for," said Loaf. "We might as well go right now. No need to pack a picnic for the trip. We'll go forward far enough to see what happens, and then come back."

"Even if the Destroyers don't come?" asked Umbo. "How long will we wait to know that things have changed?"

"We can decide once we get there," said Param.

So they joined hands and Param took them into the future, slicing time in great swaths, leaping forward faster than she had before. Not two times around the seasons, but three, slowing only when they got near the expected time of year, and stopping when they could see a great gathering of Larfolders on the beach.

Larex was there. And Vadesh.

"I didn't want to watch for this alone," said Vadesh.

But, as always, Umbo thought that there was more to his presence there than Vadesh was willing to say.

How could Vadesh seem furtive and Larex open and honest? They had the same face, the same voice. They were machines. They were no different in any way from Rigg's father, Ramex. Or from Odinex, for that matter. Yet when Umbo confided these thoughts to Loaf, the man with facemask perceptions agreed with him. "There are microdifferences," he said. "Your eye has picked them out, and your ear, even though without a mask of your own, you can't bring those details into the forefront of your consciousness. In eleven thousand years, even identical, self-repairing machines acquire differences in experience, in wear, in habits. Vadesh has an aversion to solitude. He's always been so eager for human company, far more than the others."

"Maybe they're all eager for it," said Umbo, "but only Vadesh has been deprived of it long enough for the loneliness to show."

"Or it's a deliberate attempt to deceive us into thinking there's a difference among them," said Loaf. "But even *that* would be a real difference, so it amounts to the same thing."

The people of the sea all gathered around Knosso and celebrated his return—to them, he had disappeared three years ago, and though the Landsman had informed them that Knosso was time-slicing with the Ramfolders, they had missed him and been sad that he had left without bidding them good-bye.

"But I'm coming back, if the Destroyers come," said Knosso. "I mean to come back anyway." Then, confused, he turned to the Ramfold party and said, "Should I *already* have come back? Shouldn't they already know what happened because I came back and told them?"

"If you go back," said Umbo patiently, "then you change the causal chain, and this meeting will never happen—not this way—because they will have lived a different life these past three years, a life with you in it, a life in which you were gone barely a day."

"I'm that important to them, that my presence or absence changes *everything*?" asked Knosso.

"We're all that important," said Umbo. "But it doesn't change everything. People who are married now will probably be married next time through, and were probably married on the previous pass. There's really only the one pass."

"What about babies?" asked Knosso.

"Most of the babies will still be born," said Umbo. "But they won't be quite the same. The mix of genes from their parents will be different on each passage through conception. Perhaps conception will happen on a different day. Or a different sperm will win through."

"Do we have to discuss this so . . . candidly?" asked Param.

"We're candid about all such things in Larfold," said Knosso. "But I've learned what I needed to. We can drop the subject for a while." Then he thought of something else. "But will we remember this conversation, once we go back?"

"Our memories will stay with us," said Umbo. "Whatever happened to us before we went back in time remains in the causal chain—in *our* causal chain. It isn't time, it's causation that can't be lost. Any cause that still has effects in the time-shifters, we keep in memory. It happened, even if the results that had no effect on us are gone and we can never recover that changed version of the future."

"You must be geniuses to keep this all in mind," said Knosso, and then he went back to join the Larfolders who were eager to talk to him.

"There was a time," said Olivenko, "when he wouldn't have been able to leave the matter alone until he understood it perfectly."

"We get older," said Loaf. "The exuberance of youth is replaced by a knowledge that learning things doesn't ever bring any clarity."

"So you stop learning?"

"You keep learning," said Loaf, "you just have a lot less hope in the results. A lot less faith that what you learn today will still seem true tomorrow."

"I'll never be that old," said Umbo.

"I never was that young," said Loaf. "But I enjoy watching you lambs cavort upon the lea."

The hours passed, and then the expendables told them that the exact moment recorded in all the Future Books from Odinfold was nearly upon them.

The time-shifting group gathered together and linked their hands, so Umbo could take them all back into the past before any damage could be done to them by whatever weapon the Destroyers used. "The writers of the Future Books had time to write," said Olivenko. "We have no reason to think that it will be too quick for us to respond."

"And if it is," said Param, "then we'll be dead and won't complain about some minor error in our planning."

Only a minute before the appointed moment, and Rigg appeared. It was Loaf, of course, who noticed him, and for a moment he let go of Umbo's hand, breaking the chain that linked them.

"Rigg!" he called. "You made it through!"

"You came!" cried Umbo.

Rigg looked terrible, his facemask new and not yet blended to him the way that Loaf's had gradually done. His eyes were not yet properly placed in the facemask, so they were askew and disturbing to look at. If Umbo had not seen how Loaf's mask and the Companions of the Larfolders eventually adapted and came to seem natural, he would have grieved for Rigg. He grieved a little anyway, because his friend had once been handsome, in his way, and now he would be forever freakish in the eyes of anyone in Ramfold. There would be no returning to become King-in-the-Tent for Rigg. That was a civil war that would never happen, after all. No one would follow him.

Not that Rigg would ever want to be the king. Umbo understood now that Rigg did not want to be the boss of anything. That he only wanted what was best for everyone, and when he insisted on something, it wasn't because he had to get his way, it was because he wanted things to turn out right.

Like now, as he bossed everyone about, telling them to get back into their group and link hands again, then inserted himself at the end of the line, holding Olivenko's hand on the other side from Knosso, who also held Param, who held to Umbo's hand, who held to Loaf.

"Why aren't the others joining us?" asked Rigg. "We could all go back, if the Destroyers come."

"And have two copies of us to live another few years to see this day arrive again?" asked Mother Mock, who had been standing near Knosso, talking with him, when Rigg arrived.

"It's time," said Vadesh and Larex, both at once, the same voice double-speaking, perfect twins again.

They waited.

"It's past time," said Larex, this time speaking alone, "and there are no sightings of the Destroyers by any of the orbiters."

"But there wouldn't be," said Rigg. "Because the Destroyers never came from Earth."

Letting go of hands, the others demanded to know what he meant.

"It wasn't the people of Earth. The Visitors had nothing to do with it," Rigg explained. "Ram Odin wasn't dead. He stayed alive in stasis on Vadesh's starship, waking up now and then to meddle in the world and override my orders to the ships. He was terrified when the Visitors came, because they took control of everything away from him. So before they could come again, to bring new colonists, or to trade with us, or whatever they really intended to do, Ram Odin ordered the destruction of the world. The orbiters slaughtered everyone at his command."

"So what changed his mind?" asked Umbo.

"The knife he tried to kill me with," said Rigg. "The facemask helped me take it from his hand, and then I went back in time and killed him. In preemptive self-defense."

"You fool," said Vadesh. "Well, at least I understand why you did it. And I believe your claim that he tried to kill you—that's no surprise. He was afraid of what you'd become with a facemask—that's why he made me put it on Loaf or Olivenko, and not on you or Umbo or Param."

Rigg seemed genuinely surprised. "Then why did you put it on me after all?"

Vadesh smiled. "He changed his mind. And then he changed it back again."

"He's lying," murmured Loaf.

"I can't lie to the keeper of the logs," said Vadesh. "Please remember that you can't whisper softly enough for me not to hear you. And now I'd suggest that you join your little hands again, because the only thing that has changed this time around is that the Destroyers are arriving three and a half minutes late."

"No!" cried Rigg, letting go and striding to the expendable. "I killed him! That's the end of it!"

"You wasted a murder, my dear boy," said Vadesh. "Poor Ram. All these years alive, and then assassinated by a child who jumped to false conclusions."

"I knew he was alive!" cried Rigg. "I was right about everything."

"Everything except what causes the destruction of the world. Join hands with the others, Rigg, or die with the rest of us—I don't care which you choose."

Umbo chose for him, wrapping his arms around Rigg without letting go of Param or Loaf. And then, as fire came out of the sky, Umbo pulled them all with him into the past.

CHAPTER 25
New Paths

Rigg knew at once what he had to do. The others had their opinions, there on the beach in Larfold, freshly returned from the destruction of the world, an event that once again was three years away.

For an hour, Rigg listened miserably as the others justified his killing of Ram Odin, marveled that Ram Odin had been alive at all, or agreed with Rigg that the murder had to be undone.

Finally Rigg said, "I'm going to do what I have to do. Again. It's time for you to discuss what you're going to do about your warning to the Visitors about the mice."

Umbo looked stricken. "But it made no difference."

"Exactly," said Rigg. "While leaving them unwarned might save the world."

"And wipe out the human race on Earth," cried Param.

As if she really cared about another planetful of people.

Well, maybe she did, thought Rigg. Maybe she was learning some empathy for faceless ordinary unmet people. Most people never did, so she would be ahead of the game.

But it seemed to him that she was really still trying to justify the warning.

"We all made the same mistake," said Rigg. "We leapt to conclusions and acted on them. Our conclusions weren't stupid. They were partly right, but they were also partly wrong, and now we need to find out more of the truth so we can make better choices next time around."

"Some choices can't be unmade," said Umbo. "You'll have that facemask no matter what."

And I'll know that I'm a murderer, a killer who stabs his victim in the back, that won't change either, thought Rigg. He said nothing of this thought aloud, however, or there'd be a new round of insistence that he was acting in self-defense, that even though the Ram Odin he killed hadn't yet attempted to kill him, the Rigg who killed him *had* been attacked with intent to kill by the half-hour-later version of the man.

Enough of that. Enough of talk. Or rather, enough of old talk, and time for something new.

"The trouble with undoing the warning," said Umbo, "is that I don't want to lose some of the things I've learned since we gave it."

Rigg's first impulse was to say, You won't lose anything. But then he realized the dilemma Umbo faced. He could not go back to a time *after* the warning and counteract its effects. He would have to go back before it, and prevent himself and Param from interfering with the mice getting on the Visitors' flyer. All he'd really need is to give a warning, and his and Param's earlier selves would not transport Param to give her message to the Visitors.

But then that *would* erase the future version of themselves, wouldn't it? How many warnings had they given themselves, changing their own behavior so they never became the people who had given the warnings in the first place? And Umbo's unspoken fear was that his new relationship with Param would be transformed.

Knowing Param, Rigg agreed completely. If Param, ready to be the agent who gave the warning to the Visitors, suddenly had Umbo tell her, No, my future self came back and warned me not to do it—it would frustrate her, disgust her. They would not come back to the beach as friends.

"Don't do anything yet," said Rigg. "You don't really know if you were wrong. We don't know why the Destroyers come; we only know that it has nothing to do with the man I killed. It still might be right to stop the mice. And even if it isn't, there has to be another way to handle it. I don't want you and Param to undo your lives like that."

Umbo looked at him with such unconcealed gratitude and relief that Rigg was embarrassed. Who am I to be the judge and decision-maker?

But he knew what Father would say—what Loaf would say, for that matter, if Rigg laid out the case before either one of them. You didn't decide a thing for Umbo. You merely confirmed him in the decision he already wanted to make. Your responsibility in the matter is very close to zero. Think no more about it.

Rigg had other things to think about. And yet there was nothing to think about at all. He had to go back and stop himself from killing Ram Odin, even though he knew the unavoidable result. He would have to live with that. When he and Umbo started fiddling with time, they hadn't known the rules and weren't responsible for the consequences. But they had learned the rules, or had learned a lot of them, anyway, and now Rigg understood well that not everything could be undone, or rather that undoing had consequences too, which you had to live with.

This time there was plenty of time for Rigg to say good-bye to the others. He explained to them what the facemask had done for him. How he could do what both Umbo and Param could do. "But don't think this means that you should get facemasks of your own," said Rigg. "We don't yet know what Leaky will say when Loaf goes home."

"Home," said Loaf. "Like this?"

"Yes," said Rigg. "You *must* go home. If this had come on you as the result of some horrible skin disease, she would stay with you. Let her choose for herself, Loaf. You know it's what Leaky would insist on."

Loaf grumbled and looked away. He had no argument—he knew that Rigg was right. Loaf was good at giving out wise-and-tough advice, but not so happy to receive it.

"Umbo will go with you," said Rigg, "so that if things don't work out right, he can help you try it again and again until it's fine. And I think you should go back to a time soon after you left her the last time."

"That's before you opened up the Wall," said Umbo.

In reply, Rigg handed him the jeweled knife. "Use the Larfold flyer to get to the Ramfold Wall, and then call the Ramfold flyer to take you back to Leaky's Landing. It won't be safe for you to go over land. Even if General Citizen isn't looking for you, Loaf's too pretty now to wander around in Stashiland without attracting a lot of attention."

They agreed, even Umbo, without a hint of resentment. For once, they simply recognized that Rigg wasn't giving orders, he was just stating the obvious.

No one asked, and Param didn't volunteer, to say what she would do. If she went with them, she could take them back into the future. But if she stayed with her father in Larfold, she'd have no way of escaping back into the past next time the Destroyers came.

Whatever happened would happen. Umbo would make his way back to Param, or Param would decide to go with Umbo and Loaf. Olivenko would make his own decisions, too, and for all Rigg knew, Knosso and Olivenko would get Umbo to push them to some era far in the past, where they could live out their lives without any further complications or sudden ending of the world.

The group was breaking up. Maybe it would come back together. Maybe there would be some reconfiguration that would have Rigg in it. Rigg didn't know.

What he knew was this: He could not live on with the knowledge that he had killed the wrong man. Loaf had said it long ago. It's good to prevent a murder, but killing isn't the only way. Rigg could stop Ram Odin from stabbing him in the back without going back and stabbing Ram Odin first. He had been so sure that Ram Odin was a monster that he never had the chance to find out if he was a man, or at least discover how he justified his lies and manipulations to himself.

Rigg got Umbo to call the flyer for him, and with a brief good-bye and a wave, he took off once again for the Wall. But now, without the knife, when he crossed the Wall he was on foot.

And that was how he wanted it. He went back in time a thousand years and traveled through the pristine wilderness of Vadeshfold. If Vadesh knew that he was there, so be it. Vadesh was a complicated machine, and knew far more than he ever told. But he had been right about the facemasks, and the people who extincted the human race in Vadeshfold had been mistaken, though their mistake was understandable. This symbiosis between mask and man was a good thing. Not for everyone; maybe only for a handful of people who were content to sacrifice their own eyes and ears to have these better, uglier ones put in their place. And maybe someday Rigg would get used to this terrible new face and not be frightened or saddened by his own reflection.

Today, though, each day, each hour of walking through the forest, trapping an animal now and then when need arose, but mostly living lightly, working off the little bit of adiposity that life in Odinfold had given him, Rigg was as happy as he had ever been since Father "died." Yes, he was alone, but he needed to be alone; until now, he had not really understood how painful and heavy it was to have the needs of others always in his heart and on his mind.

I have only my own need now—to unmake my crime and see if that will clean my soul.

Near the starship, Rigg sliced his way in great leaps forward into the future, to the time only a week after he had killed Ram Odin. Now he made himself obvious, walking into the empty ruins of the city, inviting Vadesh to come for him.

Vadesh did not pretend to be happy to see him. This was a Vadesh who knew of the murder but did not know of the end of it all, with the Destroyers once again burning Garden's life away. This Vadesh only knew that Rigg had gone away, leaving Vadesh to dispose of Ram Odin's corpse.

"What business do we have now?" Vadesh asked him.

"I was right about many things, but wrong about Ram Odin," said Rigg.

"I told you that, and you refused to undo it."

"I'm here to undo it now, and then you'll never remember that I did it, because I won't have done it."

Vadesh gave a little bent smile—the smile that Father used when Rigg got an answer half right, or said something smart-alecky. "You passed through the Wall, Rigg. The ship's log will remember that version of history. And *you'll* remember, won't you."

"That's right, Vadesh. I'll remember. Thanks for making sure I know how unredeemable I am."

Vadesh took him down and once again they rode the high-speed tram through the tunnel to the starship; once again they crossed the bridge. Vadesh went with Rigg into the control room, where Ram Odin's blood still stained the console.

"You didn't clean it up?" asked Rigg.

"I wasn't expecting company," said Vadesh.

"I'll clean it now, by making sure this blood was never spilled," said Rigg.

Rigg looked at the paths, his own and Ram Odin's, to make sure he was positioned in the right place before he went back in time to fix this thing. But first, he turned to Vadesh. "You could save a lot of trouble, you know, by simply telling me the truth."

"I've never told you anything but the truth."

"Tell me the things you haven't told me, that I need to know."

"How can I predict the things you need to know?"

"The truth, that's what I need."

"Truth!" said Vadesh derisively.

"Yes, there's such a thing!" said Rigg. "Things as they are, things as they were, things as they will be."

"You of all people should know that there's no such truth," said Vadesh. "Just the way things were and are and will be . . . for now. Till some shifter comes along and changes it."

"This world will be destroyed."

"Yes," said Vadesh, "and if I knew why, or how to prevent it, I would tell you, because ever since we learned of it, I have done nothing but try to prevent it. Why do you think that facemask exists? Did you think I kept breeding those even after all my humans killed each other? No, I had nothing to do, I put myself in standby mode and did nothing at all until the message came about the Future Books, and the ship's computer woke me. *Then* I woke Ram Odin, and we decided I should make a facemask that could do the things it does."

"And what are those things?" asked Rigg.

"Don't you know by your experience with it?"

"I know what it does for me because I ask it to. But what can it do that I don't know enough to ask?"

"I've never been a human. I've never worn the mask. You know infinitely more about it than I ever will. Tell me what you learn—I'd love to know."

Rigg realized that he would never get a full answer from Vadesh. But one thing was certain: Vadesh knew things that he had never told, and Vadesh lied despite his protests that he was programmed not to lie.

Without so much as a good-bye—for why bid farewell to a being who would cease to exist the moment you changed the past, and so would never remember what you said?—Rigg pushed into the past, into the moment when Ram Odin, half an hour before attempting to kill Rigg, sat at the console and the earlier version of Rigg appeared behind him, knife-in-hand, ready to kill.

Rigg stood in plain view of both of them. Ram Odin looked up, startled.

"Stop," Rigg said. "Both of you. Neither one of you can afford to die today, or to kill, either."

Ram Odin heard "both of you" and saw Rigg look at something behind him. Ram turned then and saw the other Rigg, the knife-armed Rigg, the Rigg who had not yet killed in preemptive self-defense.

Ram Odin recoiled from knife-wielding Rigg, leapt to his feet—but then he stopped. It was still half an hour before he would attempt to murder Rigg; Ram Odin was not yet armed. Ram Odin also knew how pointless it would be to try to fight a time-shifter with facemask reflexes.

"Two of you?" Ram Odin asked.

"In half an hour, when you tried to kill me, I—and he—took the knife from your hand—you recognize it, don't you?—and came back half an hour later to kill you," said Rigg. "And I succeeded. I just left a future with the blood of Ram Odin all over the control room."

"Then why are you here?" demanded Rigg-with-the-knife.

"Because I was wrong," said Rigg. "Ram Odin is not the Destroyer. It really is ships from Earth. I killed the wrong man."

"It doesn't matter," said Rigg-with-the-knife. "He tried to kill me."

"And you tried to kill him, and I did kill him, and none of it did any good," said Rigg. "I have no idea what will happen now, but I will not let either of you commit a murder here today, and you both know I can stop you if I want."

"Why not?" said Rigg-with-the-knife—the version of Rigg who had not yet killed a man, and now never would. "He's a murderer. He'll only try again if I don't kill him now."

"Now he knows he can't sneak up behind you, or take you in your sleep, because the facemask never sleeps, and because your reflexes are too quick."

"This makes no sense," said Ram Odin. "How can both of you be alive?"

"You already saw two extra Umbos get created on Odinex's ship," said Rigg. Then it dawned on him. "You gave him the order to kill the extras."

"How can there be two of you?" said Ram. "Or three?"

"You're so quick to resort to killing to get rid of copies," said Rigg, letting his contempt for Ram Odin show.

"I'm not the one who gave those orders," said Ram Odin. "I'm the one who hid."

"And he's not the one who killed you," said Rigg, gesturing at Rigg-with-the-knife. "I am. But until this moment, until I appeared in this room and stopped him, he and I were the same person. Or rather, I used to be him. Only now I'm the one who felt the knife slip in between your ribs, and he's the one who only planned to do it. One person all my life—our life—and now two people, one with blood on his hands, and one without. Doesn't this sound like your own life story, Ram Odin?"

Ram slumped, looked away. "You really thought that I was the Destroyer? That I would give the order to wipe out all the wallfolds?"

"It seemed plausible at the time," said Rigg. "Now that I know it isn't true, it sounds ridiculous. But after all the things you've done, I had no way of knowing which terrible things you were capable of, and which you were not."

"I made this world!" said Ram Odin. "How could you imagine I would ever kill it?"

"You killed a world before," said Rigg. "You crashed nineteen ships and wiped out almost all the life of Garden."

"But that was the plan I came with. Those were my orders. The machines would have done it even if I'd been in stasis," said Ram Odin.

It was a thought that would never have occurred to Rigg. "The program was originally to wipe out the life of Garden?"

"We didn't even know if there *would* be life, when the voyage set out," said Ram. "But we were desperate to make a world where we could establish the human race. If this were truly a world within the zone of life, then this ship—*these* ships by then, but I started out with only one—would have to reshape everything as quickly as possible, so other ships could follow after me."

"And the Destroyers—what are they?"

"Do you think I haven't asked myself that a thousand times?" said Ram Odin. "Garden is fully terraformed. The proteins growing here are mostly edible by humans, and the world is still empty enough to make a place for any colonists who might want to come. They could settle colonists from a thousand ships in Vadeshfold alone and still be uncrowded. Why do they decide to kill everything? Civilizations with a longer history than humans know about on Earth. I meant to persuade them not to colonize here after all, to find some other world, but I couldn't prevent them if they decided not to listen to me, to come anyway."

"So you did communicate with them? You told the Visitors not to come back?"

"I don't know what I did—what I will do," said Ram Odin. "I only know what I meant to do. The Future Books don't talk about me or what I do or don't do—did or didn't do. I'm flying blind here, just like you."

There was a sound as Rigg-with-the-knife set down Ram Odin's would-be murder weapon on a flat surface and drew the jeweled knife that carried the ships' logs. The knife that now existed twice as well—the copy Umbo had, and this one. "There are two of us *forever*," said the earlier, younger Rigg. The one who had been prevented from killing Ram Odin. "And we're not the same person any more."

"I'm the one who spawned you," said Rigg, "by preventing you from killing Ram Odin. So I get to keep the name 'Rigg.' You pick another."

"No, *you* pick one."

"I called it first," said Rigg, drawing upon the memory of childhood games and childhood quarrels.

The younger Rigg smiled. "I know," he said. "I'll call myself Kyokay. Because however you might brag about your murderings, Ram Odin wasn't the first to die under my hand."

"I didn't kill Kyokay," said Rigg.

"I failed to save him. But now I have a facemask," said the younger Rigg. "Now I think I can."

"And undo everything that's happened up to now?" asked Rigg.

"No, you fool. Did you ever realize quite how stupid you are?"

"The more you talk, the clearer it becomes," said Rigg.

"I'll save him after the fact. I'll take him into the future. I'll restore him to his brother *now*. But no, I won't take his name—he'll be alive, he'll be using it. I'll take the surname Noxon, after Nox."

Rigg knew her, of course—the woman he once thought was his mother, the woman Father had entrusted with the original set of jewels.

"I'll call you whatever you want, and you'll do whatever you think you must," said Rigg. "I divided us, but I don't own you. Just remember that if we prevented every preventable death, they'd eventually die anyway, and what would we have accomplished? Kyokay was a reckless child who would have got himself killed eventually the way he killed himself by accident that day. It's not our responsibility."

"It's *all* my responsibility," said Rigg Noxon. "And you know that as well as anyone."

"What have I created here?" said Ram Odin, looking back and forth between them.

"You've created nothing," said Rigg. "We are who we are, and you didn't make us, even if we have some seed of you and at some point along the way you intervened in our making."

"Whatever we are," said Noxon, "we're what we made ourselves, by our own choices, by what we did with the opportunities that came along. Just like you. We're not machines."

"But I am," said Vadesh, who was standing in the door. He looked at each of them in turn, and laughed. "Two for the price of one. You really need to be more careful what you do, Rigg A and Rigg B. Or you'll run out of souls to populate these bodies that you accidentally make."

"Shut up, Vadesh," said Ram Odin.

Vadesh fell silent.

The machines obey Ram Odin. But they also obey me, thought Rigg.

And then, because both Riggs were, in fact, Rigg, they proved that in this case, at least, they still thought alike, for both of them drew out the bag of jewels. Two complete sets now, besides the jeweled knife that Noxon was holding, the one Rigg had given back to Umbo on the beach in Larfold.

"See?" said Vadesh. "See how you clutter up the world?"

ABOUT THE AUTHOR

Born in Richland, Washington, in 1951, Orson Scott Card grew up in California, Arizona, and Utah. He lived in Brazil for two years as an unpaid missionary for the Mormon Church and received degrees from Brigham Young University and the University of Utah. The author of numerous books in several genres, Card is best known for *Ender's Game* and his online magazine, *Orson Scott Card's InterGalactic Medicine Show* (www.oscIGMS.com). He teaches writing and literature at Southern Virginia University and lives with his family in Greensboro, North Carolina.